Also By Dorothy Clarke Wilson

Hilary. The Brave World of Hilary Pole

Lady Washington

Lone Woman Doctor (formerly: Lone Woman: The Story of
    Elizabeth Blackwell, The First Woman Doctor)

Moses, The Prince of Egypt (formerly: Prince of Egypt)

Palace of Healing (formerly: Palace of Healing: The Story of Dr.
    Clara Swain, The First Woman Missionary Doctor)

Queen Dolley (formerly: Queen Dolley: The Life and Times of
    Dolley Madison)

The Awakening of Jesus (formerly: The Gifts)

The Brothers, James and Jesus (formerly: The Brother)

Wheel Chair Doctor (formerly: Take My Hands: The Remarkable
    Story of Dr Mary Verghese)

Woman of Mercy (formerly: Stranger and Traveler: The Story of
    Dorothea Dix, American Reformer)

Jezebel

Wicked Woman of the Bible

Dorothy Clarke Wilson

This book is a publication of StoryWorkz, L.P.
http://www.StoryWorkz.com
Email: publisher@StoryWorkz.com

Dorothy Clarke Wilson's Website
http://www.DorothyClarkeWilson.com

UNITED STATES OF AMERICA
First StoryWorkz, L.P. Edition 2012
Copyright 1955, 1983 by Dorothy Clarke Wilson

Library of Congress Cataloging - in - Publication Data is available
ISBN: 978 -1-938659-16-4

PART ONE—TYRE

1

The image was small, no longer than the distance between his extended thumb and forefinger, but with every breath he drew Ahab was conscious of it lying within the pocket of his girdle. And, though of cool clay, it burned through the several thicknesses of leather and homespun into his very flesh.

Satisfying himself that Obadiah, lying by his side, was asleep, he drew the object cautiously from its hiding place and, in spite of the darkness, flushed again hotly as his fingers encountered its exaggerated curves of hips and breasts. Just so he had flushed last evening when the bold young officer in his father's army had enticed him into the cheerful group gathered about a campfire and without warning thrust the object into his hands.

"You—you know my father doesn't allow such things in camp," he had protested helplessly. "You know—"

"Sure, we know." Beneath the young officer's good-natured amusement had lurked veiled insolence. "We're good soldiers of Yahweh, and when we went into battle we took an oath to abstain from women and all uncleanness. But, my dear son of Omri, a mere lump of clay—!"

"It's—not just—" To his further shame the words had choked in his throat and, though he was a man full grown, of sixteen years, had foundered on a boyish treble.

"A lump of clay? Sure, we know that too. It's an image of the goddess Ashtart, bless her. I bought it at the last spring festival."

Words had rushed from his lips then, glib, scathing, such as his grandfather Joseph might have spoken.

"Such things are an abomination to our God Yahweh. They belong to the Canaanites who possessed this land before our fathers conquered it, and we Israelites should have nothing to do with them."

Someone had laughed then and spat into the fire. "Who says so?"

"My—my father Omri, general of the army and—and *king of Israel.*"

Again the fire had sizzled. "He's not king yet, and won't be unless he conquers Tibni. Four years already, and, by Anath, what has he done to his rival? Lifted him up, yes, but not on a spear point. On a hill so easy to defend, Tibni can pick off ten men for every one he loses. We'll be sitting here in these rank-smelling goat's-hair tents until they rot!"

"Unless we go to join Tibni," one of the sprawled shapes had drawled softly, reaching with the shaft of his spear to stir the fire.

There had been a startled hush, bursting into words with the leaping sparks.

"Why not? We wouldn't be the first!"

"There are women, they say, in Tibni's camp. His soldiers take no vows."

"By Anath, I'll wager Tibni at least has sons who can fight, who don't turn pale at the sight of their first severed head!"

"Or crimson at the touch of their first clay loins and breasts!"

Remembering, Ahab lay staring into the dark and trembling. So the soldiers in his father's army thought him a coward. Well—perhaps he was. Certainly he had been one last night. He should have flung the image into the fire then and there, yet here he lay, the blood pounding in strange hot tides through his veins, his fingers stroking it gently and shaping themselves to its contours.

In spite of the summer heat and the sweat dewing his forehead, he shivered and wished that he and Obadiah had not chosen to sleep on their cloaks outside the tent. Here the night gave no protection. The stars bombarded his vision with the sharpness of sword thrusts, and the very silence smote his ears with a thundering impact.

Suddenly he sat upright and, drawing his arm backward in a wide arc, sent the image hurtling into the darkness. He heard its brief soft whine, then, far down the hill beyond the outer limits of the camp, the sharp challenge of a sentry. Good! He was free from it now. Drawing a long breath, he let the pure upland air cleanse him through and through. The earth, its blurred outlines of hills washed in starlight, became almost unbearably beautiful. Just so, when his father became truly king, would Israel become cleansed, the lewd cults of fertility replaced by the stern, pure worship of Yahweh. And Mishpat—that code of justice which his ancestors had brought with them long ago from the desert—would be enforced throughout the land.

But not unless Tibni was conquered. And the rival aspirant to the throne was growing stronger every day. At first Ahab's father had possessed the advantage, for, while Tibni had rallied to his side the supporters of the revolutionist Zimri, including half the chariot force, Omri, the counter revolutionist, had been commander-in-chief of the army, and his troops had been loyal. Now, tired of the four years' struggle and lured by the wealthy Tibni's promises, many had deserted. The rest were openly grumbling. Omri, a peasant's son, had no wealth with which to bribe. Unless he won through sheer military strategy, and quickly, he would not win at all.

Ahab clamped the long V of his first and second fingers over the sharp peak of black hair jutting into his high forehead, thrust back the two waving locks which persisted in falling over his temples, and concentrated his far-sighted gaze on the looming shadow which was Tibni's mountain stronghold, circled at eye level by a close-strung necklace of watch fires. Above them, he knew, were the tents of the rival camp, Tibni's bright crimson pavilion standing out among its satellites of black goat's hair like a peacock feather in a crow's tail.

"What!" It had taunted day after day, month after month. "The great Omri, favorite of the country yokels, anointed king by that crackpot Elijah who calls himself the Man of Yahweh, is powerless to tear down a mere scrap of silk?"

Omri must win. For *Yahweh and Israel.* Noiselessly Ahab gritted the words through his teeth. Some way must be found either to entice Tibni from his rocky stronghold or to get a spearhead of troops past his tight line of defense. Chariots were useless in scaling the steep slope. Attack by wedge formation was impossible up that sheer ascent. Every night sally was trumpeted by a sentry before its participants had clambered even to the first of the rocky terraces. The one easy ascent, a narrow ridge on the south, was defended by Tibni's entire chariot force, not only resistant to all offenses but protecting an inexhaustible line of supply between Tibni's camp and the neighboring walled towns, all of which were the wealthy courtier's allies.

"If only there were some way," mused Ahab, his gaze furiously scoring the dark bulk of hill, "some way to go, not up, but through…"

His eyes burned and his throat turned dry. So intense was his sudden thirst that he actually visioned the cool stream of water trickling from the rocks at the foot of Tibni's hill, heard its deep gurgling as it gushed through a rocky cavern just before emerging. The night he had taken part in one of the sallies, lying full length in a rock cleft almost up to the line of the watch fires, with arrows whining about his head, he had heard the same sound.

His narrowed eyes suddenly widened. Noiselessly he left his cloak, entered his tent, and, fumbling in the dark, fastened on his heavy leather shin guards and kneepads, attached his quiver of arrows to his girdle, and slung his lightest bow over his shoulder. Groping for the small clay lamp on the stand, he made sure by dipping his finger that it was filled with oil, then, cupping it carefully, returned to Obadiah's side. Stooping, he shook his comrade's shoulder. The stocky figure barely stirred.

"Rachel," it mumbled. "My—little love—"

Ahab smiled grimly, then seized the shoulder more firmly.

"Obadiah! Wake up! And don't make a sound, do you hear?"

He felt the huge muscles tense, saw the whites of eyes flicker in the starlight. "What—who—Ahab—"

"Sst! Not a sound. We're going to the spring to get a drink of water."

2

The sentry's glance was mocking behind his circumspect salute. "Is the son of the general sure he doesn't need an escort to the spring?"

Ahab leaned over the watch fire to light his lamp. "Very sure," he returned curtly.

Obadiah, half asleep yet ready, as usual, to follow him without question, stumbled after him down the hill. But when they had reached the spring grotto and Ahab, now indifferent to thirst, had divulged his plan, there was no sleep left in the suddenly incredulous eyes. Glittering in the light of the small flame, they stared at Ahab out of square features turned as gray as the walls of the tiny rock cavern where they stood.

"You—you mean we—"

"You're not going with me," Ahab hastened to assure him. Queer! For a moment he had forgotten his comrade's congenital antipathy to small dark places.

"Of course I am. I go wherever—"

"No!" Ahab talked fast and furiously to hide his own misgivings. "If there's a passage at all, it's a small one. You'd have less chance of getting through. Besides, you can help more by staying here. I'll pound on the rock with the hilt of my shortsword if anything goes wrong. Remember—our old signals?" He swallowed hard and lowered the lamp, for in spite of Obadiah's superior size and stockiness their eyes were on a level. "Anyway, there's no real danger—couldn't be—that is, not likely."

But once he had succeeded in convincing Obadiah and had crawled through the small opening in the back of the grotto, he was so smitten with terror that he almost turned back. Then, when the thin flame of his lamp revealed a narrow, tortuous passage with no end in sight, he began crawling up its shallow incline with a panic-stricken urgency, knees floundering on loose scales of limestone, free hand grasping at any hold indiscriminately. But when his bow, catching on a jutting shelf of rock, drew him up short and almost jarred the tiny lamp from his hand, he stopped, trembling, knowing that unless caution and reason replaced the urgency, he was defeated before he had even begun.

Carefully then, he examined the fragile clay saucer to see that no drops of precious oil had been spilled, and after that he treated it with both tenderness and respect, steadying his hand before each forward thrust of his body, testing each fissure or prong of rock before trusting it to maintain his balance.

He thought seriously of discarding the bow. Unlike the stout leather kneepads and shin guards, without which progress along the tunnel floor, strewn with sharp bits of marl and shingle, would have been sheer torture, it was at present only a liability. But he could not bring himself to part with it, for he was more expert with it than with a shortsword. True, he did not anticipate any use for it. His object was only to discover some means of penetrating enemy territory, certainly not to divulge any such discovery to Tibni's men.

Strange no one had thought before of the possibility of such a passage! Streams always wore beds in soft limestone and, if they happened to drop underground, often hollowed out long tunnels. He had delved into more than one such on Gilboa—but never alone. One or more of the sons of Naboth had been always at his heels— yes, and their ugly little tomboy sister Rachel. She had been a game playmate, he admitted grudgingly, but—*little love* indeed!

He might have been crawling through the slimy belly of a snake. Sometimes his knees dragged through the stream itself, its ice-cold waters numbing his flesh. In other places the stream had worn a deep furrow, leaving on either side a rock shelf along which he could move fairly comfortably on hands and knees, even lift his shoulders half erect. Once he was forced to crawl the length of his body through an opening so small he had to divest himself of bow, arrows, and shortsword and push them on ahead of him; then, in spite of his wiry leanness, his muscular shoulders became wedged in the narrow aperture. When finally he wrenched himself free, he lay trembling with pain and exhaustion, hot sweat mingling with the chilling water.

He lost all sense of time and distance. Only by the steady upward ascent of his course did he judge that he must be far up the slope of Tibni's hill. Had he reached the circle of watch fires? Were the sentries even now cocking their heads at the sound of movement in the rocks below? Were there fissures into which they could probe their spears? Only by the occasional windy flickering of the lamp flame could he tell when the bewildering route through tunnels, small chambers, and up sheer ladderlike ascents brought him close to the surface.

"All well," he signaled once to Obadiah by the tapping code they had worked out years ago; and again, "Climbing," and "Still climbing." But now he dared make no unnecessary sound. The sliding shingle and jags of crumbling limestone he was constantly displacing were loud enough. Impossible that even Tibni in his crimson tent on the top of the hill could not hear him!

Then it happened. To hoist himself upward from a tiny chamber through a high narrow opening, he placed his lamp on a shelf of rock; sound, it proved, but slippery. Suspended by both hands in the air, with horror he watched the lamp sliding, leaped to catch it, but too late. The chamber was plunged into darkness. The crash of his own falling body reechoed in his ears with thunderous impact. When finally he cautiously groped his way upward, he discovered that he had given his ankle a sharp twist in his fall.

What followed was a nightmare. With stubborn desperation he felt his way, inch by inch, following the course of the stream with his hands until he found that his fingers were fast losing all feeling, then sensing its direction by groping motions with his uninjured foot. Once a bat brushed against his face and for a few horrifying instants tangled in his hair. Another time he was sure his half-numbed limbs felt the slithering scales of a snake.

For Yahweh and Israel! Again and again his stiff lips shaped the old battle cry, until its rhythm blended with his breathing, with the motions of his hunched body, with the spasms of pain shooting through his ankle. And for Omri, the anointed one, the son of Joseph—yes, and for his son Ahab, that after this day no one—least of all himself—might think him a coward!

The caverns were growing larger now. One was so big he could stand fully upright and touch its sides by extending both arms to their finger tips. There were occasional chinks of light, too, in the ceiling, so he knew that not only was he near the surface but the night was past. He moved more cautiously.

Suddenly it was over. Bright sunlight smote his eyes. He climbed up out of the stream bed into a bowl-shaped hollow open to the sky and rimmed with untidy masses of rock. Through a thin fissure he caught the glint of bright green foliage. Eagerly, but with intense caution, he moved toward it...drew a sharp, deep breath...Was he dreaming, or had his journey through the darkness led him backward through time to the beginnings of things? He had emerged from Chaos into the dawn of Creation, when a fragment of sky had been tossed down into a hollow and brushed with silver, when the young earth had brought forth grass and plants and trees, all after their own kind, and Yahweh had called it good. Even while he watched, an invisible Hand flung a newly finished bird into the air, where it hung poised on scarlet wings, then plunged into the pool in a tremulous burst of silver. A coney crept warily from beneath a bush and froze in tense alertness, small ears thrust high and dainty nose aquiver.

Then Yahweh said, Let us make man in our image, after our likeness; and let him have dominion over all the earth...So Yahweh created man in his own image...

The words, heard sung so many times by wandering bards, pulsed with a sudden tumult through all his veins. For there, rising out of the pool, was Man himself, newly created in all his splendid vigor and beauty. His flesh, glistening wet in the sunlight, was like a newly polished bowl...no, like gold as in the ancient song...

> "His arms are rounded gold,
>   set with jewels.
> His body is ivory work,
>   encrusted with sapphires.
> His legs are alabaster columns..."

Ahab's throat burned. The ecstasy of beauty seemed almost more than he could bear. Then the figure in the pool turned, laughed

13

loudly, and tossed a lewd jest at some companion hidden in the bushes. Ahab saw his face, handsome, arrogant, its bold strength slightly coarsened by rich living and dissipation, and knew that he was looking at his father's rival, Tibni, standing naked, taking his morning bath in a pool close by his tent. Luckily his sudden plunge beneath the water drowned Ahab's smothered exclamation.

With steady fingers Ahab swung the bow from his shoulder, selected an arrow—one of the sharpest, bronze-tipped—from his quiver, and fitted its shaft to the string. Then, bracing his feet firmly between the rocks, he drew the bowstring taut, aiming at the spot where Tibni was likely to emerge. His every nerve and muscle sang with a wild triumph. Call him a coward now, would they? Thank heaven he was a good shot, as good as any archer in his father's army! He needed all his skill. Tibni must fall with no more than a whisper of sound, without even an instant to cry out; otherwise Ahab himself might not escape alive.

Tibni rose, still laughing, shook himself like a wet animal, showering drops of sapphire, then flung up his head to toss back his hair.

Now, thought Ahab grimly.

Again he braced himself, drew the string taut, and aimed...not at the heart—that would give him time to cry out—but at the throat, the round, full throat...then waited for the resonant whine of the bowstring, the faint singing of the arrow. They did not come. His muscles remained frozen, his gaze riveted on the golden column from which the bubbling laughter issued.

So Yahweh created man in his own image...

With horror he watched Tibni give his wet body a final shake, climb from the pool, stride into the bushes. Only after the last widening, gold-rimmed circle had washed against the rock rim of the pool did he lower his arms, return the arrow to its quiver, sling the bow back over his shoulder. Then, with grim lips and tortured eyes he made his way noiselessly back through the bowl-shaped grotto, let himself down through the narrow opening into the darkness.

CHAPTER 2

1

Ahab was a hero. The soldiers of Omri were wild in their acclaim. For had not their general's son boldly burrowed through the earth to discover how the enemy might be conquered? Whereupon had not three of Omri's cleverest archers set forth by way of the caves that very night, lain in ambush beside a mountain pool until daylight, and slain Tibni when he came to bathe a little after dawn?

King Omri, his title no longer in dispute, rode to Tirzah, the capital city, in his chariot, but his son, lifted forcibly to an improvised litter made of plaited reeds strung across two poles of cypress, was borne high on the shoulders of a group of loudly cheering captains, one of them the young officer who just two nights before had called him a coward.

To Ahab their adulation was as bitter as wine poured from the bottom of a cask. Fine champion of Yahweh he had turned out to be! And yet—had it not been for Yahweh's sake that his hand had been stayed on the arrow? It had seemed suddenly unthinkable to slay a being fashioned in God's very image!

The road to Tirzah was lined with rejoicing throngs—peasants, most of them, from the little walled towns along the way. They spread their cloaks of heavy striped homespun before Omri's chariot, shouted until their throats were hoarse.

"Hail, Omri, son of Joseph, servant of Yahweh!"

"Protector of the poor!"

There were *nabis* there too, members of those prophet bands that roamed about the country, showing their zeal for Yahweh by shouting and dancing to music and inducing a state of religious ecstasy.

Suddenly Ahab gripped the two poles of cypress and leaned forward. Micaiah, the son of Imlah, royal tax collector for the district of Esdraelon, with the shaven head and branded forehead, the coarse goat's-hair garb of the *nabi?* Impossible! The prophets were poor men, and Micaiah was a nobleman's son. It had been as much his fine clothes as his unmuscular physique which had made the Jezreel boys hector and bully him when he had first come to the town with his father. Yet there was no mistaking that undersized torso and spindly limbs, that too large head with its monstrous dark eyes.

"We might have killed him," thought Ahab guiltily, recalling the brutal games of merchant and robber in which Micaiah had been victim, the occasions he had played Goliath or Sisera in cruelly realistic revivals of patriotic drama.

But the boy had proved his mettle. The stout young rustics of Jezreel had come grudgingly to regard the frail little city dweller with respect, and during his frequent visits to Jezreel he had become one of them. He had been present, Ahab remembered, on that memorable night when Omri had returned suddenly from Gibbethon with news that Zimri had killed King Elah and that his soldiers were importuning him to lead a counterrevolution. So vivid was the memory that Ahab was suddenly reliving that night with all its tense excitement, crouching beside Micaiah on the housetop, staring over the parapet at the scene in the courtyard below—the two soldiers guarding the door, bronze spears and helmets flashing in the torchlight... Omri's spare figure pacing... Grandfather Joseph sitting on his mat. He could even remember words...

"It will take a strong man to hold the throne of Israel. I'm not afraid for myself, but—if I thought Ahab would be hunted like the sons of Baasha—!"

"Baasha and his sons were enemies of Yahweh. They deserved to die."

"I'm sure of the support of the army, at least all but Zimri's chariots." Omri had continued his slow, even pacing. "In any other nation that would be enough, but in Israel a king must have the people behind him, and that means—the *nabis*. If I could be sure—"

And suddenly there had been another figure in the courtyard. Blinking, Ahab had seized Micaiah's frail fingers with such a fierce grip that he had felt their knuckles crack. Together they had stared at the towering figure dressed only in loincloth and sheepskin, long hair and beard bleached as yellow as the whorls of curling wool. By contrast the deeply sunburned features and protruding limbs had looked almost as black as the hide of a mountain goat. Just to look at him had been to smell the raw aromas of wild broom and nomad campfires.

"You are Omri, the son of Joseph?"

"Yes, my father. I bid you welcome in the name of Yahweh."

"It is in Yahweh's name I come."

16

Scarcely daring to breathe, the two youths had watched the towering stranger remove a vial of oil from his girdle and pour its contents on Omri's head.

"As Yahweh lives and as I am Elijah, his servant, I anoint you, Omri, the son of Joseph, defender of the faith given to our fathers, to be king over Israel."

Ahab leaned forward on his makeshift litter. "Micaiah!" he cried loudly.

The slender figure breasted the crowd to his side.

"Ahab!" The eyes beneath the livid prophet's brand were ablaze with excitement. "Peace to you, beloved prince!"

"And to you," returned Ahab somewhat dryly, "beloved— pauper. Though I would as soon have expected to see myself in the one role as you in the other."

A small purple vein in the center of the white scar swelled and throbbed. "It's here, Ahab, the day he told about when Yahweh's champion should be king!"

"Yes," agreed Ahab. His gaze narrowed on the blazing eyes, the pulsing forehead. Ecstasy induced by wild dancing and crashing music or by an intoxicating potion? No. Micaiah's excitement was kindled solely by fire from within. There had been the same rapt intensity in his vision when he had sat in his fine embroidered coat and listened to Joseph's fiery sagas of the pilgrim fathers.

"Why did you do it?" he demanded bluntly. "Shave your head and change your rich man's garb for *nabis'* sackcloth?"

The answer came promptly, sparked by a gleam which was half humor, half challenge. "For the same reason, I hope, that you are changing your poor man's homespun for prince's scarlet. To better discover the will of Yahweh and do it."

"What—" But before he could even voice his question, the crowd swept forward and bore Micaiah away on its crest.

The triumphal procession was drawing near to Tirzah. Already the ranks of soldiers and peasants were swelled with officials and courtiers in long double robes with gold-embroidered borders. *The same, no doubt,* thought Ahab grimly, *who had rushed to pledge allegiance to the bloody Zimri after the murder of Elah.* What a shock to their complacency when they should discover that Omri, unlike his predecessors, was a strict defender of the ancient law of Mishpat, which proclaimed every Israelite of equal importance in the sight of Yahweh, poor peasants as well as rich city baals!

The frenzy of the *nabis* mounted to fever pitch. Some, incited by the accelerating music, had reached the stage of prophesying. One, casting off all garments, threw himself in the path of Ahab's bearers, halting their progress so sharply that the makeshift litter folded and Ahab was flung awkwardly on his back, bereft of both helmet and dignity.

"My lord prince! Brave conqueror of Tibni! For this carelessness may our tongues taste dust instead of bread!"

It was the bold young captain's powerful arms which restored him to balance, and, though both act and speech were circumspect, Ahab read the old familiar contempt in the twist of heavy lips, the insolent eyes.

Hero, are you? they appraised silently. *Then how happen you didn't kill Tibni yourself? You had bow and arrow and knew where and when he could be found, so you must have seen him. Coward! A man grown but still wet behind the ears. Scared even to let on you'd touch the loins and breasts of a lump of clay!*

Ahab strove vainly to regain dignity with balance, while shame washed over him in hot waves. Lifting his fingers to brush back the two unruly locks, he was acutely conscious of their long-boned slenderness. Fortunately the impassioned speech of the *nabi* seemed to require all his attention.

"Hear this word, sons of Israel! Blessed is the name of Yahweh, the destroyer, who has anointed Omri his servant to be king. Blessed are you, son of Omri, who have delivered the enemy of Yahweh to the avenger. So will your hand search out all your enemies and make them as a blazing oven. And Yahweh himself in his wrath will swallow them!"

Ahab's lips clamped suddenly together. The hands which had fumbled for his helmet grasped its bronze casing and deposited it on his forehead with an almost savage gesture. There was no need of inquiring from Micaiah what was the will of Yahweh. Were not all the *nabis* Yahweh's spokesmen?

It was questioning, not cowardice, which had stayed his hand on the mountain. Now he need question no longer. Yahweh the creator, tenderly shaping earth and sunlight into indestructible beauty? No. Yahweh the destroyer, sweeping from his path all obstructions, even those of his own creation, to his immediate purpose. Very well. Now that he knew what was expected of him, Ahab would not again be accused of cowardice. He looked straight into the young officer's eyes.

"Be thankful it is only dust your tongue tastes. Were your offense against the king's son insolence instead of carelessness, you might be tasting blood instead."

The young captain blinked, and for an instant his mouth gaped. Then hastily he bent his powerful shoulder to the cypress poles.

2

On the night following Omri's coronation Obadiah talked again in his sleep.

"Rachel! Little dove! My pure white wind flower..."

Ahab, wakeful from excitement and the unaccustomed softness of his couch, smiled grimly but with a certain tolerance. Lucky the palace had stout doors and his newly appointed steward was expected to sleep inside, not outside, of his chamber! If one of the guards ever heard him dribbling such inanities——! But when Ahab at last slept, it was to dream of lying in the sun in a cup-shaped hollow on Gilboa...of sinking bare feet in the bubbling crimson of a wine vat...of running in the wind after a spindly figure with burdocks in its tangled hair...

"You want to go to Jezreel?" Omri's spare features remained, as usual, tight with restraint, but his deep-set eyes sharpened into pinpoints. "Why?"

Ahab flushed, not sure that his father would approve his real reasons even if he could put them into words.

"It—is nearly time for the Festival of Ingathering," he replied lamely.

Omri visibly relaxed. He felt almost as great relief as when the fierce pain he frequently experienced ceased suddenly to twist its blade beneath his ribs. So it was not to run sniveling and tattling to his grandfather that the boy had conceived this sudden notion. He was actuated by the normal instincts of a normal youth lured by prospect of a holiday. Judging by his guilty flush, there might even be some country wench with whom he visioned creeping off behind a hedge. Well and good. There were certain routine matters which might well claim the new king's attention during his son's absence, including necessary elimination of personnel at which the boy with his rigid training might rebel. What he had to do must be done competently and quickly, before that final intense orgasm of pain which would forever bring surcease. How long would he be given to accomplish his purpose? Seven days, like Zimri? Seven months? Seven years? He must be as prepared for one as another. And no one must guess—least of all Ahab—that it was his secondary, not his primary, purpose to render Yahweh, the God of his ancestors, supreme in Israel.

"By all means go," the king told his son with a surprising mellowness. "Take Obadiah with you and don't hurry back. You were a boy when you left Jezreel. Now you are a man. See that you conduct yourself accordingly."

3

"Change your clothes." Grandfather Joseph gave the new princely accouterments a contemptuous glance. "Then help Haran and me clean out this mess."

For an outraged moment Ahab stood on the lip of the stone wine press and stared down at the lean, half-naked figure delving into the year's accumulation of debris.

"Well, what's the matter? Too fine a prince to get your hands dirty?"

Ahab grinned. Then with swift, vigorous gestures he pulled off his new crimson-dyed coat, embroidered girdle, and fringed *undergarment,* all carefully adjusted that morning by his new keeper-of-the-wardrobe, even his linen tunic, tossed them in a pile, and, stripped to his loincloth, jumped down into the deep stone hollow. Haran the gardener, seamed face wrinkling delightedly beneath his habitually disarranged turban, tossed him a short-handled wooden hoe.

"The two fig trees we planted are bearing!" he chattered happily.

"Fat and purple as King Solomon in all his fancy robes. Wait till you taste them!"

The luxurious weeks in Tirzah might have been a dream. Life in Jezreel during autumn festival was as it had always been—the building of the leafy shelter with Haran on top of the watchtower, the brimming vats and savor of grapes on his lips, the riotous songs of the vintage, even the familiar bickering between Grandfather Joseph and Abner, Naboth's father, over the ownership of the small strip of vineyard within the latter's boundary stones. Nothing was changed...and then everything.

"What's the matter?" Wearied from the vigorous round of dancing on the first day's festivities, Ahab joined Obadiah on a stone terrace. "What are you doing here alone, with your mouth wide open and your eyes staring like a silly owl's!" Then Ahab's own gaze followed that of his friend, and his mouth dropped open. "Obadiah, look! Let my eyes be blinded if it isn't—But it can't be—"

"Rachel," the other replied simply. "Haven't you noticed her before?"

"But—she was just a child and rather an ugly one—"

"Not to me."

"And when we played with the sons of Naboth she was always getting in our way."

"Not in mine."

"That's right." Ahab made the admission grudgingly. "You were always insisting on her tagging along, sympathizing when she barked her skinny shins." His voice was whetted to sudden sharpness. "You're in love with the girl, Obadiah!"

Confused, dismayed by the unfamiliar surge of emotion, he turned from the slender graceful figure dancing the *meholah* to Obadiah's guilty but rapt features. Then, almost roughly, he pushed his friend down off the terrace. "Get yourself into the dance, then, you stupid oaf!" Their way with each other had always been one of affectionate reviling. "It won't be the first time a man of Israel pursued the maid of his choice at an autumn festival. Remember the Benjaminites! You may not be allowed to kidnap your bride these days, but you can steal a kiss or two behind the hedges—and maybe more."

"No!" Steadying himself, Obadiah clung stubbornly to the neat wall of stones, his square features turning the color of oven-baked bricks. "I'd as soon think of—of entering the holy place of Yahweh behind the curtain! And you know how awkward I am. You go. Dance with her for me."

Obeying, by no means unwillingly, Ahab stilled his uneasy conscience by glib reassurances. Surely his concern as he pursued the swaying figure through the intricate steps of the meholah was wholly for Obadiah! It was only to further his friend's cause, keep her from bolder admirers, that he sought her as partner, timed his step to hers, responded to her slightest motion until it seemed that their hearts must beat in unison. Even that dusk, late in the festive week, when in their merry whirlings they unraveled themselves farther and farther from the gaily woven pattern and he had drawn her into the narrow space between two hedges, his friend's name was the first word on his lips. "Obadiah—"

"Yes, Ahab?" Her eyes, soot-black and set wide apart, regarded him with a cool steadiness. They had never been evasive eyes, and more than once, caught in some boyish prank, he had found them disconcerting. "What about Obadiah?"

"He—he wants you to know—" But Obadiah seemed suddenly even farther away than the faint jangling of tambourines and sistrums. "You—you're beautiful, Rachel. I—never dreamed you could grow up as lovely as this."

"Is that what Obadiah asked you to tell me?"

"No!" He threw loyalty to the winds. "It's I, Ahab, speaking, not Obadiah."

Her laugh was low and musical but teasing. "I was an ugly little spindleshanks, wasn't I? Almost any improvement would seem like beauty by contrast."

"Don't tease. You—you've always been beautiful to me. I know that now."

"That isn't true, and you know it." Her candid gaze shattered his thin shell of pretense. "To Obadiah, perhaps, yes. But not to you."

"Then—you know about Obadiah—that he—?"

"Of course. A woman always knows."

"Then you must know how I feel about you too." His obligation at least partially discharged, Ahab gave release to his new flooding emotion. "Even if I never thought you beautiful in the old days, I think so now. You—you're like the country maiden the bards sing about—your lips like a scarlet thread, your cheeks like slices of pomegranate, and your hair—" He reached out eager fingers. "If I were to slip back that scarf and unbind those pleats—"

"No." The simple negative checked both gesture and flow of words. "It is not seemly for a maid of Israel to unbind her hair. You thought I was ugly, and now you have suddenly decided that I am beautiful. Let's leave it at that."

"But—you don't understand—"

"Yes, I do. Remember, I've known you a long time, and the fact that your father has become king isn't likely to have changed you."

Her features blurred before his hurt and angry gaze. "Just—what do you mean?"

Her grave eyes continued to regard him steadily. "You've always been rather a slave to beauty, you know, Ahab. Remember the day you sat spellbound before a field of anemones, refusing to let us pick even one of them? And—the next day you were chasing a gorgeous butterfly and trampling them under your feet."

Her features swung again into focus, and he noted with a strange relief that they were not the perfection he had first thought them. The mouth was too large, the nose brief and upward tilting, the cheekbones far too prominent. And beside the full-bosomed ruddiness of most of Jezreel's maidens her small-boned body looked chastely immature, her olive skin bloodless and coolly transparent.

"I was mistaken," he told her simply, sensing somehow that words, a well as emotions, must be stripped to the bare bones to meet the challenge of that clear gaze. "You're not beautiful. At least, not the way I've always thought of beauty. You're just—Rachel, my beloved."

"Don't!" Her cry, quivering behind closed eyes and uplifted hands, was that of a wild, wounded thing. "Don't say such things unless you mean them!"

"But I do." With the withdrawal of her gaze his tone became gayer, more confident. "I've been wanting to say them ever since I saw you on the first day of the feast, with your lips stained purple and your head scarf awry and your funny little nose uptilted as if to catch the sunlight."

She laughed shakily. "You—were always teasing me about my nose."

"I'm not teasing you now. I'm telling you how much I love you—and everything about you. Don't you believe me?"

"I—want to believe—"

"I would have told you before if I hadn't thought you and Obadiah—"

"Oh, no!" Half laughter, half tears. "Obadiah is kind and good, but—"

"Then—you've felt it too?" The tumult in his veins swelled to a rushing flood. "For you this week also it has been just you and I?"

"Yes—oh, my beloved, yes. And not just this week. Always."

"Rachel—my own, my love—"

But when he reached toward her, hungrily, she pushed him away with an anguished little cry. "No, no! You can't—How could I have forgotten!"

"Forgotten what, my darling?"

"That—that you're a prince—and I'm only a peasant."

"And what more am I?"

She retreated still farther until her bare arms were thrust deep into the thorns of the hedge. "But—your father is king!"

"Listen, my sweet!" So intense was his emotion that his hands seized her shoulders with an almost savage grip. "My father is going to be king, yes, but not like other kings, who take to themselves the power of gods and make themselves fat on the flesh and blood of their people. Don't you know what sort of king the son of Joseph will be?"

Her clear gaze reflected nothing of pain, either from his viselike fingers or from the thorns pressing into her flesh. "No. Tell me, Ahab."

"He's going to be the servant of Yahweh, of course. That's why Elijah anointed him, that Israel might at last have a leader who was a true champion of the people. Every man, no matter how poor, will have equal rights with every other. And you and I—"

"Yes?" Her voice was scarcely more than a breath. "You and I?"

Still gripping her shoulders, he drew her toward him out of the thorns. "You and I have the same dreams for our people. We've been suckled at the same hard breast, bred by the same stern disciplines. Could a nobleman's daughter or princess help me fulfill these dreams? I'm going to be king some day—and you'll be my queen. We'll fulfill our dreams for Israel together."

At her sudden glad, eager yielding, his fingers relaxed their tense grip, and he drew her gently into his arms, urgency turning instantly to contrition as he saw the ugly scratches. "My darling, I've hurt you! The thorns—"

"It's nothing. It doesn't matter."

"But it does." Tenderly with his fingers, his lips, he caressed the soft bruised flesh, fondled it with remorse against his cheek, as once, long ago, he had done to trampled flower petals. "My sweet, my beloved, I promise, by all that's holy, I'll never hurt you again!"

"I—I tell you it doesn't matter, Ahab!" Her voice held a frightened urgency. "If you love me, nothing else matters. Don't promise me anything, just—just make me believe it—"

Her lips, when he finally found them, were soft and eager and tremulous, the ecstasy of their touch flowing through his being like wine...no aged and heady vintage such as he had furtively sipped

24

from the silver flasks of the young courtiers in Tirzah, nor yet one of those hot spiced mixtures which set the blood on fire—rather the new wine, sweet and fresh and cool, as it overflowed the wine presses into the clean stone vats.

4

"My lord Ethbaal, King of Tyre, son of Melkart, he who sits in the seat of the gods and in the midst of the seas, begs his brother Omri, son of Yahweh and king of Israel, to accept these gifts of gold and silver vessels. And as tokens of affection and admiration for his son, Prince Ahab.

In astonishment Ahab stared at the rich gifts emerging from the huge sacks and crates borne on the heads of the Phoenician slaves. Not until the envoys of Ethbaal, humility tacitly belied by the arrogance of supercilious eyes and upthrust pointed beards, had backed ceremoniously from the audience chamber, did he give vent to his amazed curiosity.

"But—why should the king of Tyre be sending all these gifts to *me?*"

Omri watched his son silently, saw him move as if magnet-drawn to the array of treasures, curve his hands to the contours of a green goblet...and his eyes darkened with satisfaction.

"Ethbaal sent also an invitation that you visit his court during the coming spring festival."

"But why?" Ahab continued to gaze at the fragile bubble of green glass, which, even here in the dim chamber, caught the sunlight, held it quivering in iridescent flame. "And why all these gifts to me instead of to you, the king?"

Omri's thin lips tightened to a white line. The fingers of his right hand, resting on the short handle of his scepter, clenched into such a tight knot that the knuckles paled. Unfortunate that the pain should come just at this moment when he needed all his faculties—but it could not be helped. If perchance he was not to be given seven years, or months, or days, to fulfill his purpose, then he must accomplish it in seven minutes.

"It is hardly surprising," he said without emotion, "that a man should wish to send presents to his future son-in-law."

Apparently Ahab was still so enrapt by the green bubble that even these startling words did not at once penetrate. "I—I don't understand—"

Judging by the sharpness of the pain, there was no time for equivocation. "King Ethbaal and I have been exchanging letters relative to your marriage with his daughter, the Princess Jezebel."

There! He had struck fire this time. The boy's eyes were blazing like hot coals, and his hands, still holding the goblet, trembled.

"I—marry the daughter of Ethbaal! You must be mad!"

"Wise, my son, not mad." To keep his voice steady Omri spoke through gritted teeth. "Surely even you, an uncouth rustic, must see the advantages of a close alliance with Phoenicia. A market for our grain and oil—"

No use to proceed, for Ahab was merely staring, one hand rubbing his cheek, as if he had received a physical blow. "You— called me an *uncouth rustic*—!"

"And so we are, both of us. You're as awkward in the role of prince as am I in that of king. But we will learn, my son, we will learn."

"If it means being like other kings, I don't want to learn," retorted Ahab hotly. "Nor do you. It's because they knew you would be different that the people and the *nabis* supported you."

"I shall be different. And so will you. The names of Omri and Ahab will be remembered when those of Jeroboam and Baasha have been buried in dust."

Ahab came close to the dais, his fingers gripping the fragile stem of the goblet so hard they seemed in danger of snapping it in two.

"But how?" he demanded sharply. "As champions of the poor? As defenders of Yahweh?"

"Yes," returned Omri evenly, the mere motion of his lips resulting in sheer agony. "For Israel is poor, an object of contempt, a laughing-stock. I—and you—shall make her rich. And how could any king defend his God more ably than by raising him to a position of honor and power among the nations?"

"But"—the goblet in his hand tipped uncertainly—"Elijah—he anointed you—"

"Exactly. And Elijah is the champion of Yahweh. Surely his action signified our God's approval."

Omri watched his son narrowly, half relieved, half regretful that the fire seemed to be smoldering out so quickly. The boy was confused, bewildered.

"I—I thought it was understood that I was to marry Rachel."

"And so you shall. This marriage with the daughter of Ethbaal need be no more than a political alliance. Once it is consummated, you may take to wife any one you choose. There is plenty of precedent in Israel. Look at Solomon."

"Solomon!" The fire sprang again to white-hot heat. "You're asking me to be like Solomon, the tyrant, whose yoke our fathers struck off in our war of independence, who took to wife daughters of foreign gods and set up their temples in Jerusalem? No! You can't make me!"

"That's right. I can't make you." In spite of the agony the motion caused, the king leaned forward in his chair. It was worth the longer battle, the more crafty campaign, just to know the boy had the backbone! "If you refuse to marry the daughter of Ethbaal—"

"I do refuse. Ethbaal is a tyrant and a murderer, and his god Melkart is just like him. They say he even demands human sacrifice and drinks the blood of children. I want nothing to do with them— no, nor with their gifts!"

Ahab flung the goblet from him. It struck the stone wall with a tinkle of shivering glass. He uttered a gasp of dismay.

"I trust, however," said Omri calmly, "you will be willing to take the trip to Tyre. If we scorn Ethbaal's offer of a bride, the least we can do is accord him the courtesy of a friendly visit. And while you're there you might pick up a few trinkets—some ivories, for instance, and perhaps"—he shot the stricken face a keen glance—"another emerald goblet." Ahab stared down at the fragments of splintered sunlight.

"Yes," he said, "I will go to Tyre."

CHAPTER 3

1

Hungrily, with the fierce ardor of a lover's embrace, the flames leaped to possess the bound figure. A face sprang into focus, eyes wide and staring, lips twisted into a half smile, half grimace. Then the streaming locks of hair and beard blazed into voracious tongues. Face, figure, even the huge pyre of oil-drenched cedar logs were fused into a solid pillar of flame.

Seated on the marble balcony above the temple courtyard, Ahab stared with such intensity that his eyes felt like live coals. In spite of the cold beads frosting his goblet of wine, the fingers clutching it were hot and dry. Was the horror he had glimpsed briefly in those eyes the illusion of a clever artist's brush? Some said it was a wooden effigy of their god Melkart which the Phoenicians burned each spring, others that the figure they placed bound on the pyre was human flesh and blood. He could not be sure.

"I fear my brother Ahab is uncomfortably warm from the heat of the pyre. Here! Another goblet of this spiced wine chilled by the snows of Lebanon, and a slave to set the fresh currents from the sea in motion!"

"My brother, Prince Baalazor, is most kind," murmured Ahab politely.

Without turning his eyes he could picture every feature of the youth lolling beside him—full cheeks and sensual lips, stubborn jutting of chin emphasized rather than subdued by its fringe of sparse golden beard, flaring nostrils, and, the one indication of alertness, those restive, watchful eyes, full of mocking glints. He knew that beneath the thin veneer of impeccable courtesy Baalazor was laughing at him.

He should not have come to Tyre. From the moment of his arrival he had felt awkward and ridiculous. The wagonloads of rich gifts which had looked so splendid streaming through the gates of Tirzah had shrunk to beggarliness before the towering citadel of Tyre, and, in spite of King Ethbaal's kind reception, Ahab had watched with mounting chagrin and mortification the depositing of the huge jars of oil and wine, the bales of dressed skins and wools and balsam, on the marble floors of the luxurious audience chamber. And now again in the eyes of the sophisticated prince he was making a fool of himself, turning pale and trembling at the mere suspicion that a man was being burned to death.

Wrenching his gaze from the pillar of flame, he attempted to hide both shock and distaste beneath a mask of polite curiosity.

The long ritual of mourning was approaching its climax. Faster and faster wove the circle of white-robed priests, their limping dance quickening to convulsive frenzy. There was a flashing of bronze knives and the hot spurting of blood as one devotee after another laid bare his veins in arms and breasts and cheeks. The crowd of worshipers swarming the courtyard rocked and swayed in an ecstasy of grief. Melkart, their Lord, was dead, and with him had died all flowering and fruitfulness. What good the planting of seed, whether in furrows of soil or in a woman's loins? What good eating, drinking, living, dying? In their agony they beat their breasts, tore their hair, rent their garments, uttered cries of anguish so old that their meanings had long since been forgotten.

"My lord, the lord of destiny, lives no more.
The shepherd, the lord Baal, lives no more.
My lord, the shepherd of the folds, lives no more.
The consort of the queen of heaven lives no more.
The lord of the folds lives no more…"

The rhythm pounded against Ahab's senses, sent waves of coldness coursing through him. Instinctively seeking warmth, his eyes turned again to the pyre and discovered that the thing upon it had burned almost to embers. He shivered.

"Is my brother, Prince Ahab, indisposed? Perhaps our Lebanon wine is too strong for his tender palate. Or—could he be so stirred with emotion—?"

"No!" denied Ahab curtly, then shivered again.

"Ah, but it is emotion. I beg you, let not the son of Yahweh be concerned. The death of Melkart happens every year, and only once so far has our Lord failed to return from the dead."

"Once?" Startled, Ahab stumbled into the trap.

"To be sure. This once." The mocking eyes danced with laughter. "But let my brother contain his fears and grief but a little longer. They will soon be ended."

As swiftly as the obscuring of the sun by a dark cloud, the mood of the crowd changed. Lamenting ceased. Necks craned, fingers pointed. The doors of the temple were flung open, and a procession emerged, headed by a figure magnificently robed in purple, a high jeweled crown lending some height and dignity to its squat rotundity. The dark cloud moved closer, and Ahab saw that it was not a cloud at all but a huge flock of quail making its spring migration northward. Moving lazily on a southwest wind, heavy bodies so low-flying that the whirring wings fanned the column of smoke into a hundred whorls and spirals, the dark mass plunged the court into shadow, then swept on over the housetops.

As the sun flashed again into view, jubilant cries burst from the crowd.

"Our Lord! He has returned from the dead!"

"Melkart has regained his youth, he has lost his old age in the fire!"

"Melkart, king of the city! He lives again!"

Even Baalazor's languid figure straightened. "Holy river Adonis! A flock of Melkart's own sacred quail flying over the city at the exact moment when the old graybeard was scheduled to come to life! Do you know what that means?" In his excitement the young prince became garrulous. "Never again will my father's right to the throne be questioned—nor mine. Fifteen years it has been since he became king by a—er—slightly unusual turn of events." He shot a bold sly glance at Ahab. "But I hardly need to go into details, for the son of Omri!"

Ahab flushed angrily. Was the son of Ethbaal daring to compare his father's treacherous disposition of his predecessor with Omri's heroic patriotism in slaying the murderous impostor Zimri?

"My father is safe now," exulted Baalazor. "Melkart himself has given his sign of approval—and what a sign! If he liked, my father could order the head of the High Priest himself delivered to him on a silver platter."

Ahab's brow suddenly furrowed. He leaned forward so that his hands rested beside Baalazor's on the carved railing. "Is it not your god," he inquired, "who has returned from the dead?"

"Of course. Melkart, King of the City."

"But—the people all seem to be singing the hymns of praise to the king."

Baalazor turned his head deliberately. "That's right. Why not?"

Conscious of the full, mocking gaze, Ahab floundered. "But—I don't understand. Your father is—is a king, not a god."

"Who says so?"

"Why, I—"

"Exactly. You. But you are an Israelite, my dear prince, not a Phoenician. It is what the people of Tyre believe that is important—to the king of Tyre. Listen, my dear son of Omri, and you will have your answer."

Ahab listened. The burden of the enraptured chant was unmistakable.

> "Praises to the lord, our king,
> To him who sits in the seat of the gods,
> In the heart of the seas;
> To him who is the seal of perfection,
> Full of wisdom and complete in beauty.
> In Eden he dwelt..."

He turned back toward the mocking eyes. "It—is not so in Israel," he said slowly.

"No?" Baalazor yawned and reached for another honey cake. "What a pity! Divinity is sometimes so—convenient. I'm afraid, then, I don't envy you your future kingship, my dear son of Omri."

2

Lolling against the cushions, the young prince of Tyre studied the features of his guest with an intentness belied by lazily moving jaws and drooping eyelids. A handsome fellow, Prince Ahab, he had to admit grudgingly, even though he actually smelled of the rank olives with which his oil-ridden little country was dripping. But that was easily remedied. A delicate tincture of cassia and aloes, with a dash of attar of roses... And with a profile like that, clean as the strokes of a stylus on a fresh clay tablet, a man could afford to smell like an oil press.

How old would he be—sixteen, seventeen? With these hard-muscled uplanders it was difficult to tell. His square chin and sunburned cheeks had barely begun to sprout a decent crop of down, and his skin had that freshly scrubbed ruddiness of an innocent child's. *Innocent*—that was the word. Sitting there straight as a spear shaft and with his eyes fairly popping, trying to make out whether it was a man down there going up in flames or a wooden dummy! Ha! Innocent. Chuckling, Baalazor almost choked on a swallow of the heady Lebanese wine. He would wager a cargo of the best spices from India that the little prince had never lain with a woman. But that too—he chuckled again—was easily remedied.

So this was the man Ethbaal had accepted as husband for his only marriageable daughter. Cheap enough price for the oil and wheat and wine which the rich but land-poor Phoenicians so desperately needed! Did Prince Ahab know about the exchange of letters which had already sealed the bargain? Baalazor himself had stumbled on the knowledge only by accident. One thing was certain: the leading lady had not yet been apprised of her role in the prospective comedy.

Baalazor's mind toyed lazily with the idea. A tiger yoked with an ox? No—hardly a fair analogy. A tiger was too elemental and predictable a creature. But take a leopard, sleek and velvet-pawed and golden... And the ox, too, was an inept symbol. Ahab was more like a headstrong young bullock. That was it. A leopard yoked with a bullock! It would be something to see.

3

Melkart was alive again. Bewildered by the sudden change, Ahab watched the courtyard blossom into a garden. Bright streamers fluttered from walls and parapets. The white-robed priests were magically replaced by dancing children, unclothed save for spring garlands. White doves darted over the heads of the crowd, and little slave girls were everywhere, shrilly crying their wares.

"Buy an image of Ashtart!" "Cheap!" "Only two copper rings!"

Baalazor signaled to a slave, and instantly one of the little girls was at his side with a full tray of the little figurines. Lazily the prince selected two and presented one to Ahab. "A mere lump of earth," he shrugged disdainfully, "but it gives the general idea. Remind me to give you a silver one later."

The little image was warm and smooth. Disconcerted by his swift upsurge of emotion, Ahab thrust the hated object into the folds of his coat, just above his girdle. This time there was no escape. He could not fling it from him. He must sit with Baalazor's amused gaze probing his every expression and gesture and with every breath he drew feel the hard, pointed breasts pressing into his flesh.

Leaning back among the cushions, Baalazor withdrew his attention from the courtyard, finding it far more diverting to see the pageant unfold through Ahab's innocent eyes, to gauge the emotional temperature of the crowd by the heightened flush or tightening of muscles in his lean brown cheeks. That would be the *kedeshoth* now, the holy women, emerging from the temple to dance about the altar. Even without the rattling of sistrums he would have sensed their arrival by the wave of color flooding Ahab's face. He couched carefully groomed fingers to his guest's arm.

"Look them over well," he suggested lazily. "You'll notice that each one wears a different colored dress, if you can dignify it by such a term. Just make a note of any one that takes your fancy, and later we'll pay a visit—"

"No!"

So replete with finality was the simple negative that the prince drew back, startled. "Why not?" he countered with curiosity.

"I am a servant of Yahweh," replied Ahab stiffly,

"And does not your Yahweh have *kedeshoth* and *kedeshim* in his temples?"

Ahab hesitated. "In some of the cities, yes. But—I—my father—That is, we have been busy late years with the wars," he finished lamely.

The amusement returned to Baalazor's eyes. So the princeling was a peasant as well as an uncouth uplander. His soft body shook gently with merriment.

Ahab's eyes burned. One scene succeeded another with bewildering swiftness, fertility the subject and motif of every act. Vines planted in baskets of earth were pruned and dressed and tied, sprouting seeds poured into outstretched hands; animals brought together in the heat of desire; mock battles fought between husbandmen and Moth, the black-robed god of death. Snakes twined on poles were hoisted above the heads of the crowd, who tried to reach and fondle them, while on one small altar of live coals a little kid, swiftly killed and dressed, was seethed in its mother's milk.

Around the great altar the dancing of the holy men and women became more and more abandoned. Impeding garments were discarded; gestures and postures became increasingly seductive. Girls bared their heads to the priests' flint knives and let their long hair fall

33

as offerings to Ashtart. Seizing other knives, young men sacrificed their virility at a single stroke, then, naked bodies pouring libations of crimson, joined the ecstatic *kedeshim* about the altar. Ahab felt suddenly a little faint. His eyes cast swiftly about for some steadying area on which to fix their vision. *It was at this moment that he saw her.*

"Who—" The word caught in his throat, so he wet his lips and tried again. "Who is that—are those—those persons standing just outside the temple door?"

Baalazor hoisted himself reluctantly, then sat up straight. "Ah—those. By the holy Ashtart, they are something to look at, aren't they!" But it was at Ahab's face that his own sharp glance was directed, not at the little group of white-clad maidens. The idea which had suddenly occurred to him was so amusing that he almost laughed aloud. "Ah, yes." He sighed eloquently. "Almost it makes a man wish he were a *stranger*, like yourself."

"A—stranger? I don't understand."

"That's right. I forget that you are ignorant of our customs. Those maidens are the fairest virgins of Tyre. Before they become wives, they must first be consecrated to the god. Tonight they will offer themselves for hire to a stranger, some unknown visitor from outside the city. The price of their hire they will give to Ashtart."

Ahab could not trust himself to speak. He tried to simulate indifference, to center his attention on another segment of the drama, but inevitably his eyes returned to the figure of the girl in the group near the temple entrance. Was it her hair which made her stand out from the others, like the ruddiness of a pomegranate in a bower of sober green leaves? Never in his life had he seen such hair—the color of dark wild honey or of a tawny lion's skin!

"Will she—will they be offering their hair to Ashtart?"

"No." Not until Baalazor spoke was Ahab aware that he had spoken aloud. "Not those. Maidens have a choice when they come to womanhood. They are permitted to offer either their hair or their virginity. Naturally the latter is the offering of greater value. These are they who have chosen to make the supreme dedication."

It was not just her hair. Had her head been shorn, Ahab's gaze would still have been drawn to her like a moth to a flame. Perhaps it was the way she moved, not with feverish abandon as did most of the group, but with a fluent rhythm as charged with leashed energy as a flowing mountain stream. Once, coming up into the hill country from the Jordan Valley, he had seen a young mountain lion moving with that same superb grace along a high ledge of rock, and, though his companions had fled in terror, he had stopped and gazed fearlessly, spellbound by the sheer poetry of its motion.

Baalazor cleared his throat delicately. "If there should be one of these maids whom a stranger like yourself should especially—er—fancy, I think that certain—er—matters could be arranged. The keeper of the temple chambers is a friend of mine. And not often do we have a royal 'stranger' in our midst."

Ahab felt as if he were sinking in a thick golden flood. "I—I am a servant—"

"Of Yahweh. Yes, of course. Were you a servant of Melkart, then you would not be a 'stranger.' Don't decide now. Just tell me this." The prince stifled a tiny yawn behind gently tapping fingers. "Suppose you were to choose among those fair flowers of our city, which one would it be? My brother is such a connoisseur of fine woods and ivories, it would be interesting to observe his taste in—women."

The thick lids drooped over the mocking eyes, shielding their bright wariness. Behind the tapping fingers the full lips hung poised, ready at an instant's notice to assume either a more prodigious yawn or a sly smile, depending on Ahab's answer.

"The—the one in the center," said Ahab hoarsely. "The one with the hair that—that is different. I—don't know how to describe it."

Baalazor's soft body sank back languorously against the cushions, but his eyes shone even brighter, and the tapping fingers did not hide a yawn.

"Don't try," said the young prince of Tyre dryly. "Others have attempted it and failed. In fact, I am of the opinion that in more ways than one this particular flower of our virginity defies description. And I ought to know. You see," he added lightly, "she is my sister, the Princess Jezebel."

CHAPTER 4

1

She awoke that morning with a start, afraid that it was too late. Throwing aside the linen sheet, she sprang from her bed and ran lightly across the carpeted floor to the lattice. Then she drew a long breath of relief. It was not too late. Mount Hermon still wore only a pale yellow halo. Quickly she drew the curtain separating the balcony from her chamber and, dropping to her knees, folded slender ankles and tucked them comfortably beneath small hard thighs.

The balcony was a little wooden cage projecting from the palace wall high above the city. Every morning since a day in her early childhood the girl had risen before dawn and sat here quietly, waiting for the Moment which had become both torment and release for her tempestuous spirit. But this should be the last time. Once this long anticipated but dreaded day was over, she would be free.

"Jezebel, priestess of Melkart." She whispered. "Jezebel—" The word grated harshly against her tongue.

"Why is my name Jezebel?" she had asked on that day years before. *"Unhusbanded.* What does it mean, Meribaal?" Already confidently aware of her beauty, she had laughed teasingly. "Did they think I would grow up so ugly they could not find me a husband?"

Meribaal, the priest who was her guardian and teacher, had not laughed. Nor had he answered her question—then. However, later on that very day he had taken her hand and led her... But she need not remember that now. Time enough when the bands of brightness above Hermon began to be tinged with crimson.

The sea was an unfathomable color, as if the warehouses lining the water's edge had emptied their precious stores during the night and spilled it dark with Tyrian purple. In the tremulous half-light the island city seemed to float nebulously on its surface, as, so the legend said, it had done once long ago.

But there was no time for musing. The Moment was close. Swiftly her eyes darted from one to the other of the carved openings, noting not only the crystal clearness of the air above the white terraced roofs but the reason for it—no smoke was issuing from the furnaces of the dye houses along the waterfront.

No need for that, she thought, frowning. Suppose it was a festal day, did that mean that every laborer in the city must take a holiday? And all those ships in the southern harbor! Certainly those two nearest the eastern quay had yesterday morning been loaded and ready to go! She clenched her hands so tightly that the nails bit into her palms. Oh, if she and not Baalazor were destined to inherit the kingdom! Or—yes, if she and not her father were ruler now of the Phoenicians! Did the ships of Tyre travel by hundreds to every part of the world from India to Spain? She would not rest until they traveled by thousands. Were the anchors of the mighty ships of Tarshish made of silver? She would have them made of gold! Many things she had learned, sitting here each morning and looking out over the city, things which Ethbaal and Baalazor, still lying in their soft beds, would never know. But she could not make use of her knowledge. She was too young, and—she was a woman.

So furious were her thoughts that she did not notice the shifting of colors from yellow to orange and from orange to crimson. Now suddenly the white brows of Hermon were rimmed with blood, and the bands of light haloing its head throbbed and glowed like rays from a blazing furnace. Drawing a deep breath, the girl fixed her gaze steadily toward the flaming vista. The Moment had come.

2

Now she must relive that day when Meribaal had taken her by the hand and led her out of the palace chamber where she had had her morning lessons, through the long corridors and courts, out through the massive gate of the citadel. Only it was not the past. As always, when she relived those hours, it was the present.

"Where are we going, Meribaal? To the bazaar? May I buy anything I wish?"

"You will see, my child. You will see."

They climbed into a boat, not one of the sumptuous royal barges, but a small clumsy thing rowed by two men standing in the center and smelling of fish and garlic. The side was so low that she could peer over and look down through the clear water, blue as liquid turquoise, and watch the fronds of waving green seaweed clinging to the sandy bottom. Behind them the island city became smaller and smaller, its white terraces rising like carved ivory.

"I shall be angry if you don't tell me, Meribaal. I shall order your tongue to be seared with a red-hot iron!"

"You will see, my child. You will see."

Out of the boat and along the shore...then a seemingly endless road where the sun was hot and her short legs became tired and she began to cry. But, though she stamped her foot and screamed a dozen threats, the priest moved steadily on. Leaving the road, they began climbing into the hills by a maze of narrow paths, now beside a rushing stream, now through the cool darkness of overhanging trees.

"Mm! I like that smell of almond and lemon blossoms, Meribaal. Let's make ourselves a couch out of leaves and moss and rest awhile and then play."

But they did not make a couch. They did not rest or play. They went on, up and up, where there were no more trees, only piles of rock, and then suddenly a bare place, with a huge pillar of stone and what looked like the dead trunk of a tree, and behind them the low entrance of a cave.

"No, no! It's dark in there. I don't want to go in. If you make me go, I—I'll have your tongue cut out, Meribaal!"

"Hush! We are entering a holy place. There is no turning back now."

Sharp blackness, followed by glaring light and such a stinging in her eyes that she had to close them tightly and rub them hard with her fists. When she finally made them stay open, she saw that the red glare came from a fire burning in a hole dug deep in the floor of the cave and that, towering over the fire, head reaching clear to the ceiling, stood a bronze figure with outstretched arms.

"Our Lord Melkart," whispered Meribaal. "Stay very still and watch."

Fiercely she willed her streaming eyes to stay open. A priest took shape first, his white robe wraithlike in wreaths of smoke, then other figures in darker dress. She heard the shuffling of feet, a stifled moan, the thin wail of a child.

She watched. A figure detached itself from the dim forms, entered the glowing circle, placed some object in the hands of the priest who, lifting it high, laid it on the outstretched arms of the bronze Melkart. She saw, plainly outlined by the red glare, a tiny waving arm and hand, an upthrust foot.

"It's a baby," she whispered wonderingly. "A little, little baby!"

"Hush! If you cry out, our Lord will be angry."

She did not cry out. She could not. Though she opened her mouth wide and every muscle in her throat seemed swelled to bursting, not a sound came. Fascinated, she watched the bronze arms slowly lower, the curved fingers straighten, then tilt downward, the tiny wailing form slip gently from them into the blazing pit. There was a smothered outcry from somewhere in the shadows, stifled as abruptly as the thin wailing. Then another figure emerged, placed another small bundle in the hands of the priest. He lifted it toward the outstretched arms.

Again she opened her lips, and this time sound came, a choked, convulsive sobbing which was barely audible but which racked her whole body. She was no longer in the cave but outside in the warm sunlight, breathing in great gulps of fresh air which made her choke still more convulsively. Meribaal patted her gently on the back. "Come. It is over now. We will go down again."

Retracing her steps through the maze of paths, she tried to think of some way to punish Meribaal, but her imagination, usually lively enough in this respect, was for the moment deadened. Besides, she was all at once a little afraid of him. There was an unyielding hardness within him which imparted itself even to the muscles of his hand. Giving him a sidewise, upward glance, she saw that his thin lips had become hard also, as if carved from ivory, that his slanting, slightly nearsighted eyes had changed from warm earth-brown to the black of ebony.

"Why did they—do what they did up there in the cave?" she inquired with a respect amounting almost to timidity. "Why did the mothers bring their babies—?"

"Because," replied Meribaal slowly, "they had made a vow. They had promised the Lord Melkart that if he would give them something they wanted, they would give the best of all gifts to him. When a man makes a promise"—his fingers stiffened, sending a spasm of pain through her arm—"he must keep it."

"I—I don't like it here. I don't like you any more, Meribaal."

Wrenching herself free, she ran blindly down the path, but soon lost it and, when he found her, was struggling frantically to make her way out of a thicket of thorn bushes. Gently extricating her, he carried her on his shoulders until they came to a little stream, where he washed the ugly scratches on her arms and face and rubbed them with oil from the small cruse fastened to his girdle. Then, still gently, he set her on a fallen log and stood looking down at her.

"It's no use, my child," he said gravely but with the utmost tenderness. "It will do no good to stamp your foot or cry or threaten. And you cannot run away. Listen well, for I have something to tell you. *You are one of those who should have been placed in the hands of the priest and lifted to the arms of Melkart.*"

She listened well, and, even though a child, she understood. Her father, Ethbaal, had been a priest of Ashtart. He had made a sacred vow that if he could become king he would give his child, soon to be born, as a living sacrifice to the Lord Melkart. He had not kept his vow. The child, a girl of unusual beauty, had been allowed to live. Ethbaal was easy-going, lenient, and the Lord Melkart apparently in good humor. Probably, the king had reasoned, he would take as much pleasure in a living sacrifice as in a dead one. The priest Meribaal would see that she was brought up properly, made a fit consort or priestess or whatever the god might want of her. And, as long as Melkart continued to bless the reign of his divine counterpart on earth with prosperity, broken vow or not, Ethbaal was not going to worry.

"So," the priest concluded gently but inexorably, "you know now why your name is Jezebel—*Unhusbanded*. Henceforth you must belong, not to yourself, nor to any man, but to the Baal alone. From this day forward you will have no other lord than Melkart. You understand, my child? You will remember?"

She had understood. She had remembered. Each day, when the Moment came, she had remembered. Now, opening her eyes wide, she fixed her gaze steadily on the blazing pit...watched the rising sun fashion itself a body from molten metal, gather into its brazen arms all the infant beauty of a new day...watched until her streaming eyes dissolved into shooting sparks, each one a quivering core of pain. Then she rose blindly and groped her way back to the couch.

3

"By Anath and her blessed snakes, look at her lying there with the sun shining right in her eyes, so that the tears are running down her cheeks, and she not knowing it! Come, lamb."

Keeping her smarting eyes tight shut, Jezebel made a pretense of yawning and stretching. Jael, her nurse, had come early this morning, had almost surprised her,

"No, no, my stupid little cockroach, no going back to sleep this morning. Here, I'll lift you myself." The harsh voice sank to a croon. "Lovely, soft golden shoulders, like the petals of an almond blossom. Dainty little feet."

Giving her eyes one final rub, the girl opened them wide, then gasped.

"Jael! What have you done to your hair!"

The nurse lifted stubby fingers to the ebony corkscrew curls protruding from each temple like overripe bananas. "It's the latest style from Egypt." The beady eyes in the flat, lumpish face were both hopeful and appealing. "It's—becoming, don't you think?"

Jezebel was seized with a fit of coughing. When it was over, she patted the pudgy hand. "It's beautiful," she said gently.

The flat cheeks flushed with pleasure, even while the hand administered a vigorous and not too playful slap. "Enough dallying," the harsh voice adjured brusquely. "Off that couch and into the bath, my lazy little snail."

Tanath, the pretty maidservant who awaited her mistress in the marble-tiled bath, gasped audibly at the sound of percussion, then, ostrichlike, crouched terrified among the silver bathing vessels, closed her eyes, and clamped both hands over her ears.

"Well! A fine posture for a lady in waiting! Have you gone to sleep?"

"No, no, my lady—I—I just thought—"

"When you're in attendance, you should know better than to think. And how do I know that, while your eyes were closed, you didn't let another prowler—"

"Oh, no, I swear— My eyes were closed such a little moment! And that other time— Have I not assured my lady many times that I had nothing to do with it?"

"Too many and too glibly. And don't think I haven't seen the way you look at Eshmun and whisper with him when you think I'm not looking. But don't worry. I'm not going to punish you for it—*yet*"

"The beloved of the gods is always wise and kind."

Carefully Tanath tested the water in the tall silver pitcher. Finding it too cold, she began pouring hot water from an earthen jar. Her hands no longer trembled. For an instant they clutched the steaming vessel with a fierce purposive energy, tensed as if to fling its scalding contents over the golden figure standing relaxed in the shallow pit of marble tile. Then she set the jar down, tested the water again, and, lifting the pitcher high, began pouring gently...

When Jezebel returned to her chamber, incense was burning in the little limestone shrine of Ashtart, shaped like a tiny house with doors and windows, and Eshmun, the eunuch, was arranging breakfast on a silver tray. Going directly to the shrine, she stood sniffing the fragrance and watching the smoke curl from the open mouths of the four cherubim carved at each corner. With reluctance her fingers moved toward the naked Ashtart leaning from an upper window, rested lightly on the prominent breasts, then traced the sinuous outlines of the two serpents coiling upward to plunge their heads between the goddess' thighs. It was Meribaal who had given her the little shrine.

Ashtart, my child, is the great earth-mother from whom all life springs. The day will come when you yourself must become Ashtart.

The day *had* come. She drew back her hand as abruptly as if the coiled shape had struck at her with its fangs, and, turning from the shrine with swift distaste, encountered the steady gaze of Eshmun.

"The morning repast of the most beautiful of all princesses awaits her pleasure. Does the mistress of men's destinies desire further service from her—slave?"

The tone was as circumspect as the words. Strange, therefore, that both should seem to convey a subtle insult! The dark eyes, too, bereft of those infuriating twinkles which they had held on the memorable day she had first seen him, were but burnt embers. Why, then, should she feel seared with two hot coals?

"No, Eshmun. Nothing. You may go."

The eunuch left the chamber so unobtrusively that his feet seemed barely to touch the thick carpet. Jael, comb in hand, looked after him have to call him, that frightens me. I—I can't help feeling it may uneasily. "There's something about that—that man, I suppose you still have to call him, that frightens me. I can't help feeling it may have been a mistake—"

Jezebel frowned. "What would you have had me do? Let him go free to boast—"

"No, no! Melkart forbid!"

Jezebel shook her head with such vehemence that the knot of bright hair fell in a bronze cascade. "Crime enough his merely entering the royal apartments without permission, but to make a wager with the other servants that—that he could look upon the princess in her bath, and then to hide—" She choked.

"I know." Jael's fingers on the restless head were as soothing as her voice.

The girl turned with such abruptness that the comb spun from the nurse's hands. "And then you blame me for giving him the most logical punishment possible! Did he scheme to enter the royal apartments, to observe the women of the harem in their most intimate surroundings? Then give him the opportunity, not once, but continually, by making him a fit member of such surroundings—a eunuch!"

Jael stooped awkwardly to retrieve the comb. "I know. But—I'd feel easier in mind if it were his head he had lost."

Jezebel laughed softly. "He couldn't have been named better, could he? Eshmun—patron god of all *kedeshim* and himself a eunuch! And he does make a handsome chamberlain. With such a name and face it would have been a pity to behead him."

"A pity, maybe, but safer. By Ashtart, I'm almost glad you're going—" Drawing a sharp breath, Jael clapped her hand over her mouth. "No, no, Melkart strike me dead, what am I saying! A day of sorrow this is, to be taking my lamb from the safe fold where her Jael can watch over her."

"Nonsense," interposed Jezebel irritably. "You're going to the temple with me."

"Yes, but what for?" The nurse sniffed. "To anoint your sweet golden flesh for some outlandish foreigner!"

The girl's lips compressed, possibly to hide their trembling. "Hurry, Jael."

Tearfully the nurse finished her combing of the long shining hair and slipped the plain white linen garment over the golden shoulders. "It's a bridal dress of crimson I should be putting on you, not this dull habit of a priestess. Why can't my lamb be like the other maidens newly come to womanhood, who, after they do their duty by the god, return home to get themselves husbands?"

The girl's fingers shook on the delicate ivory lotus stem which formed the handle of her bronze mirror. "I—can't tell you that, Jael."

4

Melkart was alive again, and Tyre had gone mad with joy. The rich rubbed shoulders with the poor; the master embraced his slave. The smoke-blackened stoker from the dye house stood next in line to his soft-skinned and perfumed employer as each waited his turn for admission to the dark stalls of the *kedeshoth* or *kedeshim*, bare foot and soft leather sandal alike tapping the rhythms of the seductive song floating out to their ears.

> "We are women, each the wife of the god, and his slaves.
> He shall cleanse our lips, shall lift us up.
> Our lips are sweet, sweet like the pomegranate.
> With us are kissing and conception."

Melkart was alive, and Ashtart, the wife-mother, was smiling again. Once more her arms were outstretched with desire, her limbs unloosed. No more weeping, no more hunger, no more fears. Earth would yield her increase; both beasts and men would be fruitful and multiply. But Ashtart was capricious. She needed much persuading and cajoling. And the day was short, the night still shorter.

Make haste, then, while she may still be beguiled, weave swiftly and skillfully those patterns which she must be constrained to follow. Let corn be moistened and made to sprout. Let the vine be primed and the palm tree be sprinkled with pollen. Yes, and let lips seek lips and pulses quicken with desire. Let every maid be Ashtart and every man her reawakened Baal!

Before the lofty entrance of the temple the two pillars of Melkart, one of gold, the other of emerald glass, set both mood and tempo. All day the former flashed and glittered, speeding the feet and firing the emotions like a white-hot branding iron. But with night come, it stood cold and lusterless, its fires burned out. Quietly now the great green monolith came into its own. Illuminated from within by a perpetually burning lamp, it throbbed and rippled in the darkness, setting a more languorous pulse beat. Yet its subtle essence was not quietness. It flowed and pulsated through the passion-ridden city in restless currents, creeping into the now languid bloodstream and turning it to new, more devious channels, driving men into deeper darkness to commit strange sodomies and perversions.

"It *is* like the wind," thought Jezebel in surprise.

She was glad she had thought of climbing up on the marble couch in her temple chamber and looking out through the narrow slit cut high in the wall. It was better than walking back and forth from wall to wall of the tiny cubicle which was like a prison ceil. Why could she not be like the other maidens, whispering and tittering in the stone corridor outside, indulging in excited speculations? Out there in the court, dancing, she had been freer than they, a true Ashtart, her whole being alive and tremulous with the miracle of her lord's awakening. Would his face cloud with anger if he found her like this, cold and cowering, when he should come to her tonight in the form of a stranger?

She strained her eyes, peering beyond the two pillars into the opening between them, but she could see nothing. In there somewhere, beyond the inner court, was the dark cave which was the god's true dwelling. Sometime, after this night was over, she would become High Priestess of Baal. Her father had promised it. Then, she felt sure, she would be truly free. But not yet. First there was this night to be lived through. Restlessly her eyes returned to the luminous pillar, and she gazed at it steadily until it became a blue-green wave of the sea, sweeping her along on its crest above waving fronds of seaweed... No—not a wave, for she was riding high in the air, and the green fronds were the tops of palm trees. She had been right in the first place. It was like—

"What is like the wind?"

Unconscious of having spoken aloud, she supposed the question, like the thought, must have come from within herself.

"The pillar," she replied dreamily. "The green pillar is like the wind."

"Why?"

"Because—" Odd, she thought, to be speaking out loud to oneself! "Because, if you could see wind, it would certainly be green—cool green and rippling with movement and all lighted up inside."

"Yes," returned the voice, a little nearer this time. "And if you could hear the pillar, it would probably have a rushing sound, and a faint rustling, like wind in the tops of date palms."

"It would," she responded delightedly. "And, anyway, it should be like the wind. Remember the story Meribaal used to tell of the creation? 'After the giants came the two brothers, Shamenrum and

Usoos. Shamenrum invented huts of reeds, rushes, and papyrus. He was a home-loving man. But Usoos was a hunter. He—' "

The girl turned suddenly, her dreamy recital ending with shattering abruptness. She was not riding the wind above the treetops. She was standing on the marble couch in the little temple cubicle, talking to—a stranger.

"I'm sorry. I—didn't mean to startle you. I—I just—" There was an awkward pause.

For a few seconds the girl stood tense and motionless, as if carved out of the cold stone of the wall. Then slowly her tightened muscles relaxed. This person, whoever he might be, was young like herself, and both awkward and embarrassed. Dropping to the couch, she tucked slender ankles under her thighs and regarded the newcomer with lively curiosity.

"I suppose you are—the stranger."

"I—hope you'll forgive me for startling you. I knocked on the door, but—there was no answer."

Now that her ears had become aware, she detected a sharp terse quality in his voice which was quite unlike the slurring Tyrian speech.

"Who are you?" she demanded abruptly. "And where do you come from?"

"It is better," he replied with dignity, "if I do not tell you that."

She looked more critically at the figure, enveloped in a long cloak of nondescript linen, with an attached hood which almost covered the face. With only the flickering light from one small oil lamp set in a wall niche, she could distinguish none of the features. She made a gesture of annoyance.

"Throw back your hood."

"No." The refusal was courteous but firm.

She stirred uneasily. "You mean I—I'm not even going to see your face?"

"It is better for me to remain—a stranger."

"But—" She found it a new experience having her commands ignored. As he moved forward, her muscles tensed again, but when instead of approaching her he turned hesitantly toward the other end of the marble couch and seated himself, almost with an air of apology, she relaxed, her lips curling in an amused smile.

"You didn't finish the story," he reminded her.

Her face lighted. "Why—it was you who said that about the pillar, wasn't it? I—I thought—" She stopped in confusion.

"I know," he said. "I've often felt that way, too, uncertain whether I really heard words or thought them. Tell me the rest of the story. There were two brothers—what was it you called them?"

"Shamenrum and Usoos."

"And Shamenrum was a home-loving man, and Usoos was a hunter. What then?"

"There was a violent storm," continued Jezebel obediently, "which caused the trees to rub against each other until they caught fire and all the forests were consumed. But Usoos had taken a tree and broken off its boughs and made a boat, so he could ride on the sea. And he came to an island, this island, and dedicated two pillars, one to the fire and the other to the wind."

"I see." She was conscious of his eyes, deep within the hood, regarding her steadily. "The gold one is the fire pillar, and the green one is the wind pillar. My people also have a story about the two brothers, one of them a home-loving man and the other a hunter."

Her eyes sparkled. "And were their names Shamenrum and Usoos?"

"No. Jacob and Esau."

"Tell it to me," she commanded imperiously.

"No." Again his voice held that firm but quiet dignity. "Sometime I may tell it to you—but not now."

For the second time he had refused to obey her command. Opening her lips for a furious rebuke, she closed them again abruptly. For tonight she was not a princess. For all this stranger knew, she was no better than her low-born whispering and tittering companions. To him she was only a woman.

He leaned toward her, his hand a dark outline against the white marble of the couch, and, as if it were her flesh he had touched, something within her leaped to startled awareness. It was a lean, long-boned, sensitive hand, and on one of its fingers gleamed a heavy seal ring of black obsidian. She stared at it, her eyes struggling hopelessly with its intricate pattern. To see better, she swayed toward it a little, bending her head so that two wings of bronze hair slipped forward, hiding her face. Now, with eyes shielded, she could look more intently... But the hand was no longer there. First with annoyance, then with that same startled awareness, she felt the long fingers threading the strands of her hair.

"I—couldn't believe it was really that color when I saw it this morning." The deep voice was muted now, its sharpness reduced to a vibrant earnestness. "I thought it must be the sunlight which made it so—like dark honey or—or a piece of polished red sandalwood. I couldn't see your face—I was too far away—and I could hardly bear the waiting, wondering if it was as beautiful as I imagined it must be."

In spite of her confused emotions her keen mind was busy. He had seen her that morning, close enough to note the color of her hair, yet too far removed to see her features clearly. He must have been standing, then, above the crowd. On one of the balconies? But those were reserved for Tyrian noblemen and their guests. On one of the lower terraces? Yes, a foreigner could gain access there, even a very humble one, and if he happened to be exceedingly straight and tall...

"How did you know you were going to see me again?" she asked suddenly.

"I—I didn't, of course." She could sense his confusion. "I only—hoped— And I—that is, a friend of mine—bribed the keeper of the temple chambers—"

She laughed aloud, a spontaneous laugh filled with childish merriment. Then, disengaging the long fingers, she drew his hand gently but firmly into the narrow area of vision bounded by the two bronze wings of hair. So sudden and overwhelming was her emotion that she drew a swift breath and closed her eyes.

But not before she had noticed the pattern of the small rotating seal of polished black obsidian—a tiny, exquisitely carved figure with the head of a bull and the body of a lion, its two wings spread wide.

CHAPTER 5

1

"You see that hill?" Omri's habitual restraint mellowed into an animation approaching enthusiasm. "No capital in the world will compare with it."

"Except Tyre," demurred Ahab silently.

"See that sheer drop on the west? A good four hundred feet! And steep slopes both north and south. It would resist siege, not for weeks or months, but years!"

Grateful for his father's suggestion that he take the place of the royal charioteer on the morning's drive from Megiddo, Ahab had found momentary release in the swift journey through the winding valley from Ibleam, a half-dozen mounted *gibborim* clearing the road of caravans and peasants. But now as his gaze scored the stony hills, already brown and blistered by the summer's drought, the frustration which had been simmering since his return from Tyre seethed to the boiling point. Prince though he was, what did he have to offer a daughter of Ethbaal? He could almost hear the scoffing quips which the Tyrian courtiers were bandying this minute behind the backs of Omri's envoys.

"Prince Ahab? Never heard of him."

"You don't mean that bungling rustic!"

And the princess herself—would she feel more—or less—contempt for his suit if she knew him for the "stranger"? Had it been his too eager imagination which had fancied a response to the fever of excitement within himself, a fever which leaped again now, causing his flesh to burn and his palms, clenched about the reins, to go clammy with sweat. What had she thought of him? He could not even remember her expression as he had risen to leave, only his own words. *My people also have a definition of a "stranger." My grandfather taught it to me, when he made me promise never to take part in the fertility rites observed by our neighbors. A stranger, he said, is a sojourner in our midst, one to be treated with respect and permitted to serve his own gods as he sees fit. As such a stranger I come to you tonight—and leave you—after the custom of my people.*

"The owner of the hill," continued Omri calmly, "is a big *adon* of Shechem named Shamer. If he is willing to—to sell"—he cast a wary glance toward his son—"we can start building operations at once. I have already negotiated with Ethbaal to provide us with designers and artisans from Tyre, as did his ancestor Hiram for Solomon. The new city must be worthy of an Israel which will take a position of leadership among the nations. It must be as magnificent as Tyre."

As they swept the skyline of the magnificent hill thrusting itself straight up from the valley's wide basin, Ahab's moody eyes brightened. She had imagination. He himself had kindled it. Surely he could make her see a vision of this also.

"You say we can begin immediately? But how? Israel is poor."

"No poorer today than eighty years ago. And Solomon did it."

"Solomon!" Again Ahab's fingers strained taut. "Yes, with taxes and forced labor. But—you're going to free our people, not enslave."

"Look at it, son." In the dry, clipped words there was nothing to show that the success or failure of a man's life-purpose was at stake. "In the citadel you and I can build on that hill we will be sitting astride the great highways of the world. The wealth of Egypt and Arabia, yes, and of Tyre, will flow past us, into our laps. Poverty? With the world's riches ours for the taking? Forced labor? With slaves from our conquest of Moab and the desert tribes to build for Israel and her God a stronghold worthy of their leadership among the nations? Do you call that slavery for our people?"

Omri had finished. He could only offer his son a kingdom as glorious as Solomon's. He could not make him take it. The choice Ahab was about to make was more momentous than the mere selecting of a capital. It was between two ways of life. For the purchase of the hill of Shamer would be a violation of the ancient law of Mishpat, which decreed that land inherited by an Israelite from his fathers was his sacred heritage, inalienable. Eyes inscrutable beneath heavy, jutting brows, Omri watched the clean-cut profile raised toward the majestic eminence which might or might not become the foundation of a kingdom—and waited.

"But—" Even the horses stood motionless, heads upreared as if listening. "Suppose," Ahab continued finally, "Shamer will not sell? What then?"

Except for a slight shifting of weight from rear to forward foot, Omri's spare body gave no indication of the relief which charged it suddenly with fresh vigor. "That," he said, "we go to Shechem this very morning to discover."

2

Shamer was well named, decided Ahab grimly. He looked like a watchtower. If this man chose to stand on his rights, he would be as unshakable as the limestone core of the hill which bore his name. Yet had not his father called him a big *adon?*—landowner? Surely a man who had extended his holdings through the seizure of land for debt could not retain the old prejudice against land selling.

Prejudice! The word shocked him into startled awareness. Could he have forgotten in so short a time all his grandfather's patient teaching of the years?

Land, my son, is the free gift of the Eternal to his children. It is not a commodity to be bought and sold, so that one may have too much to eat while another goes hungry...'No land is to be sold in perpetuity said the Eternal, "for the land is mine, and you are only guests of mine, passing wayfarers."

"Shamer is expecting us," muttered Omri shrewdly. "Either the agents I sent to make inquiries are less discreet or he is more clever than I thought."

The wealthy landlord had established himself on a richly carpeted platform close to the center of the market place. Assisted by a small army of slaves, his steward, and a harassed scribe, he was making an accounting of his fresh assets accruing from the barley harvest, and the waiting lines of harvesters, all bringing varying amounts of grain for inspection and division, were obviously his tenants, once owners of the little holdings they were now cultivating on shares. Each accounting was a lengthy and noisy process, accompanied by shrill pleading and bitter incrimination.

"Three parts to our one! Have mercy! Our children will starve!"

"May Yahweh burn the bones of your fathers!"

"May you have nothing but the ground for a bed and the sky for a covering!"

Shamer neither prostrated himself nor interrupted his routine of business, merely made room for the king on the carpet beside him. As Omri quietly took his place, Ahab ground his teeth. In Tyre such insolence would be impossible. Ethbaal would have lifted one chubby, beringed finger, the *gibborim* would have dashed forward and Shamer would have bitten the dust. But Ethbaal, Ahab knew, would not have come here in the first place. If the king of Tyre wanted a piece of land, he would not sit down in a market place and bargain for it. Again he would have only to lift his finger...

Ahab stopped short, appalled by the implication of his thoughts. It was to escape from them as much as from the sight of his father's humiliation that he turned abruptly and, fists clenched beneath the long sleeves of his coat, went scuffing aimlessly in the direction of the nearest booths.

Instantly, to his dismay, he was plunged back into his boyhood, for the market place of Shechem was but a replica of the one in Jezreel, even to the inevitable band of *nabis* strumming their harps and rattling their cymbals. Deliberately he turned in the other direction, for in his present mood he wanted no sight nor sound of prophets. They reminded him too much of Grandfather Joseph.

"Cloth for a new coat or *simlah?* See, stranger!"

The sight of a bolt of striped cloth, red and brown and white, aroused such a vivid memory of the purchase of his first long coat that, reaching out to touch it, his very fingers tingled. *Feel, Grandfather! Just feel how soft! And so fine!*

"You call that fine linen?" Scornfully he tossed the length of coarse homespun into the vendor's lap. "Have you ever seen the stuffs the Sidonians weave?"

In the sweets bazaar some half-naked urchins—he and Obadiah and the sons of Naboth?—were scrambling in the wake of a fruit vendor tossing overripe figs from his basket, and a scrap of a child with spindly legs, like Rachel...

Muttering a sharp exclamation, he dashed out into the lane and snatched the tiny darting figure almost from beneath the wheels of a lumbering oxcart, then, after gently pushing back the tangled hair and wiping away the tears with an end of his coat sleeve, set her down abruptly.

"Little fool! Watch where you're going. You might have been killed!"

He walked unseeing now, more loath to be reminded of Rachel than of Jezebel. Time enough to think of her later, when this fever in his veins should have somewhat abated, when every attempt to summon a vision of tranquil features and midnight hair did not materialize, as now, in a blinding composite of ivory and copper and red-bronze. It was part of his bitter but exquisite torture that he could not recall how *she* looked. He remembered that her features were like carved ivory and her eyes full of copper glints, yet he could not picture them. And had her hair—?

"Yahweh will deliver you from your oppressors. When Israel was oppressed in Egypt, did he not raise up Moses? When the burdens laid upon us by Solomon..."

Too late Ahab discovered that he had proceeded to the exact area he had wished to avoid, the very center of the group surrounding the band of *nabis*, and, to his further dismay, that it was his friend Micaiah speaking. About to slip back through the crowd, he suddenly changed his mind. Why should he wish to avoid the prophets? Had they not helped to put Omri on the throne? Were not both working for the same purpose, the exaltation of Yahweh?

"But what hope is there for us if we have no land?"

"With four parts of barley there was not enough to divide among our children. How then shall we keep them alive with only one part?"

It seemed natural to be among a group of peasants bemoaning their lot. Except that these complaints issued from strange faces, he might have been back in his grandfather's courtyard. But the faces were not all strange. The man with the deeply hollowed cheeks and burning eyes—yes, and a half dozen others—had been among those bringing grain to Shamer.

"If Yahweh has the power, why does he not return to us our lands?"

"Yes, *if* he has the power! Was it not the baals of the land who caused it to bear fruit when our Yahweh was still but a guardian of flocks and herds in the desert? Perhaps if we had served them more and him less..."

"Shame, men of Israel!" Micaiah's voice rang out clearly. "Yahweh has delivered us before from those who would oppress us, and he will do so again. Your deliverer is already among you—*your king!*"

Someone laughed harshly. The crowd began to mutter and scoff.

Was the prophet joking? Had he forgotten Baasha, who had spent his quarter century conscripting them for losing wars? And Elah, the sot whom Zimri had ambushed at one of his carousals? Why should they expect more from this Omri, who had murdered Zimri after only seven days?

Ahab's hands clenched. Slander the king, would they, within a stone's throw of his person? Such a thing, he sensed helplessly, could never have happened in Tyre! Within an instant the scoffers would have felt spears pricking their backs,

"Why?" Micaiah's ringing voice took up the challenge. "Because both King Omri and his son have been reared to revere only Yahweh, to fulfill his purpose of justice and freedom for all his people. Is it not so, grandson of Joseph?"

The abruptly pointing finger, while taking Ahab unaware, was like a signal trumpet note, releasing his hot tension. He flung back his head. "Yes," he replied clearly. "It is so, Micaiah, son of Imlah."

3

The bargain had not been consummated. Omri looked harassed, Shamer obdurate. Sweat was streaming into the furrows of the high brow beneath the king's conical cap, but the round face beneath the landlord's silk turban remained serene.

"He refuses to sell," muttered Omri in a swift aside, then resumed his shouting bombardment. "A talent and a half of silver, heavy weight!"

Ahab was startled. It seemed an enormous sum, over three thousand silver shekels!

Shamer shook his head, as unimpressed as if the talent had been only a mina. "The king does not comprehend," he said regretfully. "The hill is my patrimony."

Ahab stared at the *adon* in amazement. Did the man expect them to believe that land admittedly being worked on shares by its previous owners had been in his family for generations? He opened his lips for a hot rejoinder, but at the warning touch of Omri's fingers closed them. His father was right. In refusing to sell, Shamer was acting fully within his rights as a man of Israel.

"A talent and forty minas," offered Omri, a note of desperation in his voice.

The turban continued its regretful wagging.

"Fifty!"

"My king drives a sword into these vitals, but—no."

Ahab felt the hand, still gripping his arm, tremble. Panic seized him. The new city *must* be built on that hill. Only if it was really begun, the first circlet of the diadem in place on that lofty brow, could he hold his head proudly when—*if*—he brought his bride from Tyre to Tirzah.

"Two talents!" Omri's voice held the calmness of finality.

It was Ahab now who trembled. His throat was dry. Sweat matted the thick hair under the cord of his headdress. His eyes, clinging to the face beneath the silk turban, noted the calculating flicker beneath the half-closed lids.

"If it were a question of price, but—no. Let it never be said of Shamer that he accounted wealth above honor. The hill of Shamer it is, and the hill of Shamer it shall remain, if Yahweh wills, forever."

The refusal was as baffling as it was disappointing. Omri could have sworn the stage was set for the completion of the bargain. The scribe was present, equipped with rolls of papyrus, both red and black ink, and brushes. And could it be merely accident that the venerable silversmith squatted on a mat close to the platform bore no implements of his trade except his bag of weights and scales? Regretful, but not a man to stoop to cajolery or threat, he resigned himself to defeat.

"Wait!" murmured Ahab, and whispered in his father's ear.

Omri's gaze narrowed. He rose abruptly to his feet.

"An Israelite has spoken," he declared without emotion. "So be it. The hill of Shamer it shall be known to the few souls living in the shadow of Mount Gerizim. A pity when, as the *City* of Shamer, it might have been known to all the world!"

Without a word the *adon* leaned forward, removed the sandal from his right foot, and handed it to Omri in token that the bargain had been completed.

4

"How did you know that Shamer's weakness was simply his vanity?"

"Oh," replied Ahab vaguely, "something about the way he spoke his name, I suppose—the hill of Shamer—as if we were talking about the Holy Mountain."

He was holding the reins again, driving his father's chariot down the long ramp into the sunset, the road to Tirzah flaunting a ribbon of tantalizing whiteness before plunging into the shadow of Mount Ebal. His mood of exhilaration demanded fast and intense motion. The city would be built. He would become king. Israel would be great, greater even than Tyre, and her Yahweh stronger than Melkart. He, Ahab, would bring it to pass, as surely and swiftly as he would speed across the valley and into the shadow of Ebal. Nothing should stop him.

But something did. At the foot of the ramp a man, shouting and leaping, appeared suddenly in his path, causing the startled horses to veer, and, to avoid plowing into the carts and donkeys and pedestrians crowded to one side by the *gibborim,* he pulled up sharply.

"Steady!" warned Omri evenly. "Let the *gibborim* handle him."

But before the rear detachment had overtaken the chariot, it was surrounded by men, all shouting, some pressing so close that, had the horses sprung forward, they would surely have been crushed. Presently the shouts became intelligible.

"Hail, Omri! Deliverer sent by Yahweh!"

"Friend of the poor, restorer of bread to the hungry!"

Omri waved his hand with a good humor not unmixed with grimness. "We'll have to bear with them," he muttered. "We'll be needing such adulation from the peasants soon enough. Wave at them, but keep your whip handy. We're under complete control of the situation. The *gibborim* are just behind, awaiting my signal."

Ahab curbed his impatience. The man with the hollowed cheeks and burning eyes was in the forefront, clinging to the leather rims of the chariot wheels. Following his father's example, Ahab waved with friendly tolerance. After Micaiah's declaration it was natural that these peasants should wish to express their affection for their king. Then suddenly his grip on the reins tightened.

"When shall we get back our land?" a voice shouted. "Why does the king return to Tirzah before completing his task of deliverance? Give it to us now!"

"Face your horses back toward Shechem!"

"Nay, we'll face them for you!"

The horses upreared and pitched, plunging dangerously as eager hands grasped at braided manes and plumes and harnesses. Ahab was hurled to his knees as the light chariot was lifted bodily from the ground.

"What are the fools saying?" demanded Omri sharply. "Can you make any sense of their gibberings?"

"Yes," said Ahab, his face bleak with dismay. "They—they think you bought the hill of Shamer in order to restore to them the land which was their rightful heritage." Hastily he recounted the details of the episode in the market place.

"I—see." Omri's lips were grim. "The *gibborim* already have the crowd dispersed. The road is clear now. Turn the chariot about and go ahead."

"But—" The reins remained stubbornly taut.

"Yes, my son?"

The red glow of the sunset blinded Ahab's eyes. Turning to the one side, he met his father's demanding, penetrating gaze; to the other, the burning visage of the peasant with the hollowed cheeks, who had escaped the vigilance of the *gibborim* and, hands clinging like claws to the railing, climbed up on the wheel spokes.

"But—we are the sons of Joseph!"

"I am the king of Israel," returned Omri tersely. "And you are my son. Or—are you? Perhaps it will be well for you to decide here and now whether you are the son of Omri or the grandson of Joseph."

"You—you mean—"

"I'm giving you your choice. The hill of Shamer is yours. I bought it for you and for the kingdom I hope to build for you. Turn back if you choose. Parcel it out among a handful of griping peasants who had neither the cunning nor the enterprise to keep it when they had it. Let it become a sheep range and a field of lentils, a straggling orchard and a barley patch—all symbols of a declining people and their backward deity. Or go forward and help me make it the foundation of a great city, worthy of a greater and yet greater Yahweh."

Ahab struggled to marshal his confused senses. It was unfair of his father to force him to this choice. Omri was king, not he. Turning from the level, penetrating gaze, he met the peasant's burning eyes, red-rimmed from the strong winds and fine dust of the barley winnowings. The man had climbed up on the hub now, his face thrust close to Ahab's, and as he opened his lips to plead further, the words were preceded by unpleasant whiffs of leeks and rotting teeth.

"Our land! Give us back our land, son of Joseph! For Yahweh's sake!"

The sunset was fading swiftly now, soft golds and amethysts instead of blazing saffrons and crimsons. The clouds lay massed above the hills, tier upon tier, like the walls and turrets of a city carved from yellowed ivory—no, not like a city...like the features of a woman wearing a crown of gold and a robe of purple, and trailing long tawny tresses across the rounding bosom of the hills.

He pulled sharply on the reins and swung the horses, then without an instant's hesitation uncoiled his lash. He was halfway to Ebal before he remembered the peasant who had been standing on the hub of the chariot wheel.

CHAPTER 6

1

The end of her long weeks of waiting had come at last. She slipped her finger beneath the curling edge of papyrus, unrolled it with crisp abruptness.

"Ethbaal, son of Melkart, king of the Sidonians, he who sits in the seat of the gods, summons his daughter the Princess Jezebel to meet him in his private council chamber at the hour when the golden pillar falls into shadow."

The golden pillar... Swiftly the girl crossed the room to the adjoining balcony. There it stood, bright metal sheath reflecting every scintillating ray of the morning sun. Not for hours yet would it have fallen into shadow!

In the three months since the spring festival this temple chamber to which she had been assigned had become a prison. She had expected a short period of probation, perhaps of rigid discipline, before her promotion to the office of priestess, but not this interminable silence and exile. It was on Meribaal, her teacher, that she poured the full flood of her bitter frustration.

"It's Abd-ashtart, the high priest," she had stormed only yesterday. "He's afraid that when I become chief priestess, I will take away some of his power, discover some of his secrets. I wouldn't trust him not to have his eyes on a loftier seat than the priesthood of Melkart!"

"It is possible," Meribaal had replied gently. "Priests have been known to conspire against their kings, yes, even against their— brothers."

Jezebel had whirled angrily, then, meeting the gaze of the fearless, candid eyes, her own had fallen. Uncertainty akin to panic had rendered her speechless. Phelles, heretofore only a name, a shadow, had become suddenly a man, flesh and blood, her own uncle. Her father, a priest like Abd-ashtart, had killed him. How? Where? Creeping up on him in the dark? Near the altar? In one of these very temple chambers?

"You are wondering why you have not been made a priestess. And you are blaming others when you yourself may be at fault. Is it not so?"

"I! How dare you—" The uncertainty, the panic, had been consumed in a swift flame of anger, to be followed by bewilderment. "What—I don't see—"

"Tell me this." The priest's voice had lost its gentleness. "Since the night of the spring festival has your spirit known no desire save to find fulfillment in the being of our Lord Melkart?"

Now, as yesterday, the girl lifted her hands to hide burning cheeks. Still painfully aware of the priest's pitiless gaze, she turned with sudden swiftness and found herself looking into the inscrutable eyes of the eunuch Eshmun.

"Stupid ox! You know better than to come into my presence unannounced."

As the eunuch bowed low, Jezebel found herself staring with fascination at the huge tightening knots of forearm muscles, oddly incongruous beneath the filmy sleeves of the flowing feminine robe.

"May the queen of women requite her slave for his blunder. He will return to the corridor and wait until some attendant happens by to properly announce his presence. There is doubtless no urgency about the news he brings."

"Wait!" Bowing with elaborate humility, he had almost reached the door when her sharp voice recalled him. "It is my pleasure to overlook your misbehavior."

The burnt embers which were his inscrutable eyes reappeared.

"The most beautiful of earth's princesses is as generous as she is—predictable."

Jezebel frowned. But she was in no mood for sparring. "You— say you have brought news?" Dropping languidly into a chair, she attempted to conceal both excitement and suspense beneath a studied carelessness.

Bowing again, Eshmun proceeded with maddening deliberation. "As the mistress may remember, she commissioned her servant to locate the source of a certain jewel and, if possible, discover the identity of its owner. An unusual jewel it was, a seal ring of black—"

"Yes, yes, you needn't describe it." It was all she could do to keep her hands anchored to the smooth cedar arms of the chair. "Just tell me—"

"The command of the most beautiful of princesses is the law by which her servant lives and moves. For more than two moons he has had no other thought, no other desire than to fulfill her commission."

"Then you have found it?" Her blood was pounding so she could scarcely breathe.

He lifted a deprecating hand, its palm (considering the feminine tasks with which it was generally occupied) curiously calloused. "Let the mistress be patient. First I visited all the skilled jewelers in the city of Tyre. For I said to myself—"

"No matter what you said." Merciful Ashtart, one would think he was deliberately trying to be infuriating! "What did you find?"

"Nothing," replied Eshmun imperturbably.

"Oh!" Before she knew that it had been uttered, the exclamation was there between them, sharp and quivering, alive with revealing hurt and disappointment.

"Then I traveled to Sarepta and Sidon and Berytus and even to Gebal and inquired of all the jewelers there. A bull, yes. A lion, yes. But none had ever heard of a winged animal with the head of a bull and the body of a lion."

"So—you discovered nothing?"

"Then I journeyed to Damascus, and here also I searched. I made inquiries among jewelers and artisans and merchants. And I found—"

If he paused a breath longer, she would surely scream. "Yes? You found—?"

"This, my mistress."

"What!"

It was a stout bar of ebony, a handle, perhaps, for a dagger or shortsword, carved with exquisite sphinxes, in its center a beautifully executed winged animal, half bull, half lion. Had she not been so disappointed, she would have exclaimed in delight. Lifting her eyes, she met Eshmun's intent gaze, its burnt embers amazingly kindled into flame. With unreasoning rage she clutched the object hard in both hands, trying with all her strength to break it but finding it as resistant as stone or iron.

"Stupid—ox! It was a seal I sent you to find, not a carved bauble."

Fascinated, she watched the well-groomed hands, calloused palms hidden within tensed fingers, move toward her, and for an instant terror locked her throat. Fear changed to incredulity as she saw the huge knots of muscles tighten, the calloused palms close about the bar, heard the explosive snap, then the dull clatter as the two fragments were tossed negligently to the stone floor.

"You—are strong, Eshmun."

The eunuch's eyes were again but cold embers. "An ox needs to be strong, especially a stupid one," he replied evenly. "It is one of his few—assets."

Jezebel drew a long breath. "And—that is all you have to report?"

"That is all, mistress of men's destinies. It would seem that the owner of the jewel must indeed be a—stranger."

Jezebel rose abruptly. For a moment she could not trust herself to speak. Then, bronze head held high, she moved blindly toward the balcony. "You may go now."

"Of course, if the mistress desires, I can go into the hill country, among the barbarians, and make inquiries there."

"No, Eshmun." This time she managed just the right nuance of lightness and indifference. "It's such a small matter, I'm tired of discussing it."

She knew he had gone when she no longer felt his eyes upon her. Slipping to her knees, she buried her head in her folded arms, and for a long time her slender body shook with tearless sobs. When she again lifted her face, she raised her eyes to the golden pillar, gazing at it so steadily that its radiance seemed to pierce her eyeballs, explode through all her being in sharp tongues of flame.

Had Meribaal been right? Was the Lord Melkart angry with her because at the hour of testing she had proved herself to be less priestess than woman? If so, then now he must be satisfied. Her infidelity was over. Henceforth she would know no other loyalty, no other desire, save toward the god to whom her life had long ago been vowed.

Returning from the balcony, she picked up the two fragments of ebony. The break was clean and sharp, straight through the exquisite carving of the winged bull-lion. She felt an unreasoning anger with Eshmun, less for breaking it than for leaving her in uncertainty. Why had he brought it? Was it offering or taunt—symbol of devotion or of hatred? It was infuriating that she might never know.

2

"The eyes are not right. A little more kohl on the upper lashes and a bit deeper shade of turquoise on the right lower lid." With the critical discernment of the true artist Jael contemplated her handiwork. "Ah, Ashtart be praised, it is good!"

Jezebel lifted the oval of polished bronze by its lotus-stem handle. The face that looked back at her revealed nothing of the fury of emotion it concealed. Eyes large and wide-spaced, lips full and gently curved, the two lines tapering from high cheekbones to small but determined chin as clean-molded as if shaped by a sculptor's chisel—it might have been carved from fine, deeply yellowed ivory. The hair arrangement, as always, was Jael's masterpiece—innumerable bronze coils above the forehead, each shape a perfect replica of the rosettes of twisted gold wire and lapis lazuli set in the high coronet. She looked more like a queen dressed for coronation than an expectant priestess.

"Jael! You—" Lips opened in sharp rebuke, she closed them. She had always wanted to be a queen. Why not play the part for once? After today she would never again have the opportunity—unless...She drew a quick breath, fingers tightening so that the fine veins of the lotus-stem handle scored their imprint in her palm. Meeting the gaze of the reflected eyes, sharply aware and calculating, she hastily averted her own.

"You—have really outdone yourself, Jael. Now go. I must be alone."

Glad for these few moments in her own palace apartment where she had returned to make ready for the interview, and relishing the soft luxury of the gold-embroidered purple gown after the coarse simplicity of temple garments, she crossed the room to the balcony and drew the curtains. The narrow streets were black with an endless procession of slaves, bullock carts, little donkeys, all burdened with treasures from far places. Her bright eyes took swift inventory of chests and bales, cartloads of logs and lumber, bulging packs, cages filled with exotic animals.

"Gold and silver and sandalwood." Her small foot tapped out the rhythm. "Rubies and emeralds and ivory and apes and peacocks."

But the caravans did not keep pace with the rhythm of her foot. *Faster*, she willed them, faster! Where were the captains of the slave gangs with their lashes? Traitorous coddlers of both men and beasts!

Oh, by the rushing tide of Adonis, if she were down there they would do no dallying! If she were a man—a foreman or captain! *If she were queen...*

The monstrous thought came again, and this time there was no mirror to frighten her with its revelation of sharp, calculating awareness. Deliberately she faced it. Distasteful, yes, but not the monster she had first thought it. The line between hero and traitor, valiant and cowardly, was so finely drawn! Success or failure made all the difference. Her father had been successful, and—her lip curled— he was not a strong man. His method had been no doubt crude, for he would have had the imagination to conceive no better—a creeping in the dark, a clumsy thrust...There would be easier ways. Not in her father's lifetime. She felt for him genuine affection. But for Baalazor...

She shivered. The sun was no longer sifting its warmth and brightness through the lattice. And the golden pillar must also have fallen into shadow.

3

At sight of the crowded audience chamber she felt swift dismay. Then her slender figure straightened. So she was to be made priestess, perhaps high priestess, of Melkart with all the officials of the court to witness. She drew a deep breath of relief. The long years with their agony of guilt were over.

Ethbaal shifted his great bulk sufficiently to extend his scepter and incline his head. He nodded toward two attendants. "Bring the Princess Jezebel, the beloved of Ashtart, to the seat beside me."

Jezebel frowned. The term "Beloved of Ashtart" belonged especially to those who had fulfilled their duty to the goddess and were soon to become brides. But there was no time now for vexation. Devoutly thankful that she had dressed worthily of the occasion, she stepped on the thick crimson carpet and, queenly coifed head held high, mounted the steps with a royal dignity.

The king leaned toward her slightly, expending a minimum of energy. "You're looking well, my dear. It agrees with you, it seems, to be beloved of Ashtart." He chuckled noisily. "Or should we give more credit to the 'stranger'?"

Jezebel's small sharp teeth bit hard into her lower lip. She sensed the amused raising of eyebrows, the twitching of lips. And Baalazor, lolling in a great chair just below the dais, was openly gloating. She could feel his mocking eyes drawing her gaze, willing her to look at him.

Instead she fixed her eyes on Meribaal, sitting in a distant corner, drawing reassurance from his steady, kindly gaze. Her angrily tapping foot came to rest. She reached out and patted her father's arm.

"If my appearance finds favor in my father's sight," she said clearly, "let him take it as a sign that I am ready to fulfill his wish, whatever it may be."

"Ah! Baal be praised! That is good news indeed. Knowing your—er—let us say decisiveness of temperament, my dear, I had— But my anxiety is all past." The monarch dissolved into the comfortable embrace of his chair. "Then why are we waiting? The scribe has the documents. Let us get on with the business."

With difficulty she concealed her surprise. Surely she had made it plain that she was willing to make amends for his broken vow. Was he simulating relief for the sake of his courtiers? There was the high priest Abd-ashtart, a wary watchfulness masking the narrow face beneath the gold tiara. He would not be pleased with the pronouncement that the king's daughter would be made chief priestess. Her half-brother, too, was still gloating. He looked as if he were rolling a juicy morsel beneath his tongue. He had always been jealous of her, perhaps because he recognized in her dynamic energy the sole threat to his accession to the throne. Did he think she would be less dangerous as high priestess of Melkart?

The king's scribe rose importantly, clearing his mean little throat, unrolling the scroll with its conspicuous emblem of a palm tree and two writhing serpents. Jezebel darted a glance of triumph at the watchful Abd-ashtart. Had he also seen the royal seal, marking the document as the king's final and irrevocable decree, which no amount of threatening or cajolery could alter?

"His majesty Ethbaal, king of the Sidonians, son of Melkart and beloved of all the gods, he who sits in the seat of the gods and in the midst of the seas ..."

Jezebel's palms closed rigidly over the hard little ivory lions' heads which completed the slender arms of her chair. Would the long pious preamble never end? It was like the slow, impressive removal of layer upon layer of elaborate garments, only to find a few bare bones beneath. For it was with concise but unmistakable clarity that Ethbaal announced to his courtiers and all others concerned the betrothal of his daughter, the Princess Jezebel, to Prince Ahab, son of King Omri of Israel.

She sat like a stone. The whisper of the papyrus rolled by the scribe's deft fingers sounded like the cracking of a drumhead, and the smile on Abd-ashtart's thin lips was a disembodied monstrosity. When she finally lifted her hands from the chair arms, there was imprinted deep within the flesh of each palm the outline of a lion's head.

But when the courtiers had gone and there were only Ethbaal and Baalazor and herself in the chamber, she turned to raging fire.

Father, did Ethbaal call himself? King? Human counterpart of Melkart? No! Say rather traitor, deceiver, murderer of his own flesh and blood! Twice now he had broken his promise to the god. And if he must play such treachery, why, by the snakes and doves of Ashtart, had he not chosen a fit husband for her? Must he go into the hills among the barbarians? Oh, better, far better if he had kept his first vow and sent her into the fire! Jezebel—unhusbanded, indeed! The promise of her name would at least be kept, for who would call it husbanded to be mated to an ass or ox? But she wouldn't do it! She would die first, she swore it. By every god who had ever cursed mankind—!

It was Baalazor who checked the volcanic flow, merely by gesturing languidly toward the inert mound of flesh and purple. Ethbaal was asleep.

"Save your energy," advised the young prince bluntly. "You'll need it all for your crusading job as queen of Israel."

"But—" The word emerged like a puff of steam from an almost quiescent crater.

"You know there's nothing you can do. It's a royal edict."

"But—*why?*"

Baalazor turned his eyes away. To gloat over a Jezebel with head held high and proud neck unbending, even one pacing the floor like a caged tiger—that was one thing. But it was quite another to fling scorn at this vulnerable creature, standing very still and looking like a frightened child. Even the droll bit of mischief perpetrated on the night of the festival had for the moment lost its ironic luster.

"It's simple," he said. "This fellow Omri has a grain pit and wine jug big enough to feed and drown all Tyre. We have golden plates and goblets, pretty and in excellent taste beside his earthen ones, but not much good empty."

"But—" The desperate little puff was a mere wraith.

"And another thing." Baalazor was subjecting himself to an unprecedented expenditure of exertion. "This Omri is no ordinary fellow. Already his big leather sandals are astride more land than encircles all our Sidonian cities. And don't forget that our own Hiram didn't consider an alliance with these barbarians a thing to be despised."

He shot the still figure a sidelong glance. Good! The lost, hopeless look was gone from her eyes. Already they were beginning to narrow with speculation. "And think of all the cities that need building in that raw country. And all the thick necks just waiting to be adorned with imported gems and Tyrian purple!"

"But—" This time the puff was accompanied by a spurt of flame. "He had no right! It's the second time he has broken his promise. What good to fill our bellies with wheat and have oil to swim in if we make Melkart angry?"

"Angry? A strange way for him to show it—filling our coffers with treasure, sending a flock of his own quail over the king's head!" Baalazor cast another sidelong glance. Now for the final well-aimed missile! "Who knows? You might be of less value to Melkart as his priestess than as queen of Israel."

The arrow had hit its mark. "What—do you mean?"

He shrugged. "It must be the desire of the god, mustn't it? You don't think our father would take such a step without consulting the oracle?"

"I—hadn't thought of that."

"Perhaps," he shrugged again, "the Lord Baal is weary of his narrow confines within an island. Perhaps—he wishes to extend his domain."

Baalazor sank back into his chair with a sigh of relief. The head was high again, the proud little neck as unbending as the stem of a gold goblet. He could turn the full barrage of his mocking eyes upon her, laugh silently until his heavy body shook with merriment over the delicious irony of the joke he had played.

"And if it's any consolation," he could not resist adding blandly, "Prince Ahab isn't such an ugly specimen. I met him once. Uncouth, of course. But—not bad. Not bad at all, for an outlandish foreigner, a—stranger."

4

Meribaal responded to her newly kindled zeal like stone to the flame of a candle.

"So—you believe that you can again break a promise to the god and still purchase his favor. I was a fool to trust your father's word. Better if I had left you in the holy place that day when I took you to the mountain. It would have been easy then to redeem the broken promise. The brazen arms were strong—"

"You wouldn't have dared," Jezebel interposed quickly, "any more than you would dare now to defy the will of the king. Is he not the embodiment of the god? When he speaks, is it not the voice of Melkart giving utterance?"

So obvious was the answer that she was startled by the sudden bitter skepticism in his eyes. Yet his reply was circumspect enough.

"So it is written. So it has been spoken by the kings of Tyre from the beginning: 'I am a god, I sit in the seat of the gods, in the heart of the seas.' "

Hastily Jezebel pressed her advantage. On her lips the arguments of Baalazor sounded even more persuasive, perhaps because she wanted so passionately to believe them herself. Oh, in the name of Ashtart, what was the matter with Meribaal that he could not see! She as queen in Israel and he as high priest of Melkart—what could they not do together! Did the god have a temple in Tyre which surmounted the city like a hilltop? In Israel he should have one towering like a mountain! Did he have two hundred priests and as many prophets? In this barbaric hill country he should have four, five hundred, all devoted to his service! And as for the broken promise, was it not one life only which had been denied him? He should have hundreds of lives. By Ashtart and her holy doves, she swore it! She would do better than her father, who had promised him but an unborn daughter. She would promise...

The words died suddenly on her lips as she found herself staring into the eyes of Meribaal, coldly stern as on the day she had gone with him into the mountain, their pupils dilated as by some inner darkness into polished ovals of ebony.

"Your first-born son?" he demanded tersely.

She tried to draw away her gaze, but the eyes held hers. There was no escape. "Yes," she replied faintly. "My—first-born son."

"It is a vow? You promise it?"

"I—promise—"

"By Ashtart and all her holy doves, you swear it?"

"By Ashtart and all her holy doves—" She made one desperate effort then, like a wild thing trying to withdraw itself from the spellbinding of a snake, but it was no use. "Yes, yes, of course I do. Why should I refuse anything to the Lord Melkart? By Ashtart and all her holy doves, I—I swear it!"

CHAPTER 7

1

By the Feast of Ingathering plans for the citadel on Shamer's hill had been determined; by the coming of the winter rains its rectangular site had been marked out. And by springtime the rock had been partly quarried along the exterior lines of the proposed fortress, leaving a solid core of limestone with a perpendicular scarp, a majestic crown of dazzling whiteness visible from the Great Sea to Shechem.

All of Ahab's doubts about his coming marriage had been banished. Yahweh through his oracle had given approval. Messengers sent to far cities for worthy bridal gifts had returned with what seemed to his uncritical judgment rare treasures. Even the palace at Tirzah, clay brick walls freshly tinted with red ocher and earth floors topped with thick layers of stamped limestone chips, presented a creditable appearance. Impatience was the only flaw in his happiness until the day Obadiah...

He was lying half naked on a linen sheet submitting to the ministrations of his new Egyptian masseur and hairdresser, who had once served a son of the Pharaoh.

"Such arms—hard like the trunks of palms! My master should have felt the softness of the son of Sheshonk. Not a bone in his whole body! If my master will relax, let his flesh flow through the fingers of his slave like water..."

Ahab ground his right shoulder and thigh into the cushions and attempted to reduce his left to the desired fluidity. What a price to pay for conformance to the norms of royalty! But if it would make him more acceptable to the sister of the soft-fleshed and sweet-smelling Baalazor, he supposed it was worth it.

"I thought my lord should know. This letter has come to me from Jezreel."

Ahab turned so suddenly that he upset the vial of perfumed oil. Remembering how he and Obadiah had both laughed behind the tails of their turbans at the oiled and perfumed fops who had occasionally strayed into Jezreel, he scanned the square, stonelike features with suspicion, noting with relief that the peculiar luster in the gray eyes was born of excitement, perturbation possibly, but not ridicule.

"A letter?" Propped on his elbow, Ahab puzzled out the markings on the wooden tablet. Suddenly he sat bolt upright. "Leave us," he ordered the Egyptian curtly.

"But—the oil is spilled, the finest imported oil it was, flavored with myrrh and cinnamon—and I have anointed only half... Yes, yes, my lord, I am going."

Ahab shivered. He reached for his tunic and, though his left shoulder and arm were still glistening with unrubbed oil, pulled it on over his head.

"How long have you known about this—this proposal?"

"As I live and breathe, not until today. Believe me, my lord—"

"I believe you." Ahab reached for his coat, slipped his arms through the openings, lapped the folds of the skirt, and tied his long embroidered girdle—all without the slightest awareness. It was Obadiah who, seeing the oil trickle like beads of sweat from the glossy curls, wiped it away with an end of his headdress.

"I—I can't understand it."

"Nor can I, my master."

"I thought of course she understood. She must know this contemplated marriage of mine is just a—a formality for the sake of the kingdom."

"Is it, my lord?"

Ahab flushed. He felt hot now instead of cold. "Of course it is. You should know, of all people. And for heaven's sake stop calling me your 'lord' or 'master'!"

"Yes, son of my lord the king."

Raising his eyes in panic, Ahab discovered himself looking into the face of a stranger. The features were Obadiah's, rocklike, dependable. But the eyes...

"What—what will you reply to your father?"

"I—haven't decided yet. It is a thing that must be carefully considered."

Ahab's panic grew. An Obadiah who from boyhood had followed his every dictum, walked in his very sandal prints—now thinking of making a decision for himself? "Then wait," he pleaded. "Promise me you'll do nothing until we talk of this again."

"I promise," said Obadiah gravely.

Alone, Ahab read again, unbelievingly, the markings neatly inscribed on the clay surface of the tablet, stating that Joab of Jezreel greeted his son Obadiah in the name of Yahweh, prayed for him the best of health and many sons, and desired to announce that he had been approached by an intermediary in the name of Naboth, who desired that a marriage be arranged between Obadiah and his daughter Rachel.

2

Omri had not approved of the trip to Jezreel.

"This is the month when the District of Issachar will impress its first labor levy," he had explained caustically, "and make its annual contribution to the court expenses. I would avoid it like a lion with a litter of cubs."

Now, after less than an hour in his home town, Ahab agreed. He was glad that, before going down into the fields to find his grandfather, he had changed his clothes and put aside princely trappings. Passing unrecognized through the streets, out the gate, down the hillside by one of the winding paths separating tiny plots and orchards and vineyard hedges, he was conscious of sullen looks and mutterings:

"...thought we had a king to keep us from being slaves, not make us."

"...wonder what Joseph thinks of his son Omri now!"

"One hundred bushels of grain a day! Twenty oxen!"

"A new city for the king to live in? What's the matter with Tirzah?"

Ahab seethed with uneasy anger. His grandfather, at least, had always been a good patriot. Surely he would approve of the strengthening of the kingdom and the exaltation of Yahweh. True, he tended to be stubborn about some things, like that bit of land, no bigger than a dozen paces each way, about which he was always arguing with Abner, Naboth's father. It was a part of his patrimony, he maintained with vigorous and, since Abner was deaf, loud eloquence. Any fool could see, the way it jutted into Joseph's property, like a wedge cut in a barley cake—!

Ahab's step quickened now at the sight of the familiar gesticulating figures, beards bobbing excitedly. Slipping behind the hedge, he worked his way quietly toward the two men and, smiling to himself, listened for the first shrill indications of the historic argument. Suddenly he froze.

"Better," the voice of Joseph, harsh with bitterness, came clearly to his ears, "to see one's son a goatherd than a king who betrays the teachings of his fathers!"

"Easy, neighbor." It was Abner's voice now, high-pitched and gusty, with an occasional whistle, like wind through a crevice, where his teeth were missing. "Your Omri hasn't been king long. Don't judge him too quickly."

"How long shall I wait? Until we're all marched away to grovel in the earth and quarry stone for his new cities? We might as well be back in Egypt making bricks!"

"Not all. Only one man from each household. You can send your gardener Haran."

"Send my gardener to dig rocks when the barley is ripe?"

"Then go out by the gate and hire somebody."

"No! Yahweh forbid that the house of Joseph let strangers pay its debts!"

"Then—what will you do?" The words exploded with a gusty whistle. "You don't mean—you wouldn't dare defy—"

"When the day comes, you will see what I shall do."

"Aie, aie! Have you seen the size of those *gibborim*—the length of their spears? But I forget. The king is your son. You have nothing to fear."

"It's Yahweh's displeasure I fear, not that of my son. If I still have a son."

"At least you have your grandson Ahab."

"Heaven forbid that I should be reminded! To think that the seed of my loins should take to wife a heathen—"

"Easy, neighbor, I meant no harm. I was only trying to say—"

"I know. The boy is probably being forced into this marriage against his will. I'd stake my right eye he has no part in this enslavement of free men of Israel. But—I'd *give* my right eye if he were marrying Rachel."

Abner cleared his throat. "I'll confess I would have preferred Ahab to Obadiah."

"Obadiah!"

"You didn't know? Naboth has already approached Joab. It was at Rachel's own request. No hard feelings, I hope. We've always been good neighbors."

"No—hard feelings." Joseph's reply was barely audible. "Good—neighbors—"

"These foolish arguments—they've meant nothing."

"No—nothing."

"You know you have no more claim to this vineyard than the Queen of Sheba."

"I—Why, you lying, thieving—! Any fool could see that the landmarks..."

Ahab crept back behind the hedge, up the path toward the town gate. His lips were twisted in a grim smile, but there was no laughter in his eyes.

3

At least Haran was glad to see him. Before an hour had passed, he appeared at the door of the housetop chamber, earth-stained hands cupped tenderly.

"See! A surprise for the little master! A perfect dove's dung blossom."

Ahab took the flower, white petals opened wide into a six-pointed star. He and Obadiah had searched all one hot noon to find just such a perfect bloom for Rachel, who had said it was her favorite flower. It was Obadiah who had found it and taken it to her, and she had cried over it.

"So beautiful," she had mourned, "to have such an ugly name."

"Haran!" Ahab's voice was suddenly urgent. "I want you to do something for me."

Though the gardener was gone only minutes, they seemed as many hours,

"You found her? You gave it to her? You told her who had sent it?"

"Yes, yes. I did just as my little master told me."

"And what did she say?"

The gentle eyes clouded. "I—I'm not sure I remember the exact words—"

"Try, try, Haran!"

"She said—'Tell him,' she said, 'it—it's better to leave some flowers in the earth they were born in, for they bloom only—only in the bright sunlight.' "

"But she took it?" demanded Ahab.

"Yes, little master. She took it."

"Good! Then listen again, Haran..."

But this time the gardener was not so prompt in executing his commission. As time passed, Ahab's nerves grew taut almost to breaking. With the town in its present mood he had no wish to venture into the streets, and in the house the disapproving silence of his grandfather surrounded him like a thundercloud. Only once did they exchange significant words.

"So, Ahab, you have come home."

"Yes, Grandfather. It—has been a long time."

"Long enough for the hopes of a people to be born—and die."

"I know. You don't approve of what my father is doing. I'll confess I wouldn't have once. But—you'll have to admit, Grandfather, that times are changing."

"As Yahweh lives, they certainly are. Or should I say—as Yahweh dies?"

"That's unfair! Does one die by becoming richer and more powerful?"

"It has been known to happen. Take Zimri."

"But—" As so often in his boyhood, Ahab felt helpless, not knowing whether the gleams in the two deep crevices beneath the jutting brows sprang from grimness or from laughter. "Yahweh isn't a human being. He doesn't change."

"Good! I'm glad you realize that. I had begun to wonder."

It had been laughter, Ahab decided in relief, noting the slight shaking of the fleshless body. "It's all for Yahweh's sake, can't you see?" he burst out eagerly. "It's for him we're going to build these cities—"

"And impoverish his people?"

So it had not been laughter. There was only grimness in the deep-set eyes, yet the bony frame was still agitated by that silent tremolo. With sudden dismay Ahab noted also the transparency of the flesh overspreading the jutting cheekbones. His grandfather, the epitome of strength, was getting old and frail!

"I tell you it's for Yahweh! Who but a stubborn bigot would resent having to pay a few taxes—yes, and give a few weeks of labor—to build him cities that will contain greater temples, a kingdom of greater cities—all for his glory?"

Aghast at his temerity, Ahab stared at his grandfather, expecting at the least a thunderous rebuke for his defiance of ancestral authority. But the fleshless body only shook more violently, this time unmistakably with laughter—bitter laughter.

"I've waited years to see you develop enough backbone to stand up and fight for your convictions. And now, when you do, it's myself you're fighting and for other convictions than the ones I tried to give you."

"But I'm not—they're not—"

"I know. That's the worst irony of all—that you don't know the difference."

"I delivered your message, little master. As she was going to work in the fields with the other young women, I came up behind her and said what you told me.

> " ' Awake, O north wind,' I said,
>   'and come, O south wind!
> Blow upon my garden,
>   let its fragrance be wafted abroad,
> Let my beloved come to his garden—' "

"Were not those the words you told me to speak, little master?"

"Yes, yes, those were the words. But this evening, did you—"

"By my hair and beard, yes. I did just what the little master told me. I hid behind a hedge close to the old stone watchtower. But—she did not come."

It was their old signal, the refrain from the popular wedding song which any man of Israel passing on the road or working in the fields might be singing. It was their old place of meeting, the ruined watchtower, overgrown with a tangle of vines, belonging to a town ne'er-do-well who found banditry more profitable than husbandry. Impossible that she had not understood! Yet each night when Haran brought his report, it was the same story. She disregarded all his messages.

It was his last day in Jezreel. Tomorrow he must return to Tirzah in order to start at dawn on the following day for Tyre. Grimly Ahab's feet kept pace with the interminable mounting and descending of the sun. The housetop, wedged tightly against the town wall, its parapets overlooking nothing but the courtyard and a narrow street, enclosed him like a prison. Oh, he had been a fool! Waiting on the whim of a peasant girl, accepting the humiliation of her refusal to see him, even, when he might have issued a royal command summoning her into his presence!

"Come, little master! I did again what you said, caused it to be whispered that the king's son had returned to Tirzah. And this time she did not return home with the other women. She went straight to the old watchtower."

4

He picked his way noiselessly up the moss-cushioned steps. Strange, how just the sight of her stilled all his impatience! Perhaps it was the way she sat on the low wall of crumbling stone, utterly passive yet vibrantly alive, as if the very act of relaxation were the expression of abundant energy. Hot and tired after her day's work of pruning vines and believing herself alone, she had pushed back her headdress and unbound her long hair. The last red-gold rays, drifting through a tangle of leaves, turned its smooth blackness to Tyrian purple.

"Dark stream the tresses of your hair,
    like goats a-down the slopes of Gilead..."

Before he knew it he was softly singing the words of the old love song. She sprang from the wall, both hands flying to her unbound hair and confusion suffusing her features—but not before her eyes, nakedly luminous with the joy of seeing him again, had given away her secret.

"I—I thought you had gone—"

He was across the intervening space, and she was in his arms, the fragrance of clean winds and sun-drenched earth in his nostrils, her lips cool and sweet beneath his. Pushing back the curling tendrils, his fingers probed beneath the silken blanket, marveling briefly at the fine delicacy of skull bones and the arch of slender neck, then buried themselves with a half-tender, half-savage gesture in the tumbling cascade.

"Ahab! Please—you're hurting me—"

Instantly contrite, he released his tense grasp. "I'm sorry. It was only that when I saw your hair like that, it—turned me a little mad. It's—so long since—"

"It's all right. I understand."

Did she? Could she possibly sense the unuttered words which throbbed behind his lame excuse? *When I saw your hair like that, it reminded me of a night in Tyre, and it turned me a little mad. I wondered if yours also would be like fire to the touch. It's so long since I sat beside her and stretched out my fingers...*

"It has been a long time," said the daughter of Naboth gravely, "so long that I too acted impulsively, without thinking. But—I am thinking now."

She had slipped out of his arms and, seated again on the crumbling wall, was smoothing back her tumbled hair, pleating it with strong sure fingers.

"Rachel—" As he reached toward her, her quiet dignity was like a wall.

"No. Don't touch me again, please. I must bind up my hair."

"Why? I like it so. It is like goats flowing in black ripples down a mountain."

"You know why," she replied evenly. "It is not fitting for a good woman to unbind her hair before any man except her husband."

Ahab flushed. "But I'm going to be your husband," he cried out almost angrily.

"Are you?" The strong fingers continued their pleating. "In Israel, I hope, it is still impossible for even a king's son to impress a bride against her will."

Ahab's jaw stiffened. Then he saw the quick downward motion of her head to hide the trembling of her lips, and his anger was submerged in a flood of tenderness.

"You think this marriage to the Tyrian princess changes things for us." He plunged earnestly into his carefully prepared speech. "But it doesn't. Princes have to enter into such alliances. Think of David, and of Solomon."

"Yes," she replied, her eyes again level with his. "I am thinking of them. What are you trying to tell me, Ahab?"

"Why, that—that you also will be my wife, and—and the only one who really counts. I promise it. This princess of Tyre means nothing—"

"Doesn't she?"

Ahab flushed again, his eyes dropping before her level gaze. "B—but—" He stammered, confused, "You can't permit your father to arrange this marriage with Obadiah. You—you don't love him!"

"I shall be a good wife to him," replied Rachel earnestly.

"You know very well it was you, not he I was thinking about."

"Then feel no concern, either, for me. Perhaps contentment is as great a gift to ask from life as ecstasy—especially if thereby you can give another both ecstasy and contentment."

She had pleated her hair smoothly, concealing it to the last velvet strand beneath her virgin's veil, and somehow, with the same smooth deliberation of motion, had slipped along the crumbling wall and rendered herself as remote from his reach. In the falling dusk her features were a pale blur, her dark dress, except for its crimson embroidery at neck and bodice, indistinguishable from the wavering shadows. But with the passivity the cool serenity also had fled.

"Wed your Tyrian princess," she said, her eyes ablaze, "whether to satisfy your own desire or to further your father's policy. Yes, and build your new city, rear it out of the bones and sinews of free men, fill its warehouses from the meager grain pits of little towns like Jezreel. But never tell me again that you're doing any of these things for the good of Israel or for the glory of Yahweh."

Ahab started after her in sudden panic. "Rachel! Wait!"

The steps were crumbling and plunged in shadow, and he had to feel his way down. There was not even a rustle of leaves to tell which way she had fled. By the time he had blundered his way out of the old vineyard, he was forced to acknowledge that she had gone—both from their trysting place and from his life.

As he groped along the path, he thrust his hand into a drooping tangle of feathery aspen and stopped short, frozen with a sense of aching loss. Her flowing black hair had been as soft and quiveringly alive. But the touch of it had soothed rather than inflamed. Unlike that other, it had given no promise of fiery ecstasy. Why then should the consciousness that he might never again know its touch be attended by a sense of such irreparable loss?

5

Ahab sprang wide awake out of a troubled sleep, ears tautly attuned to an unusual noise. It came again, sharp, metallic—once, twice, three times, followed by unintelligible shouting. Seizing his coat, he fumbled into the armholes and rushed from his chamber to the parapet, bare feet plunging through the bundles of flax which had been laid to dry on the housetop.

It was still very early, not yet sunrise, yet the narrow street below was dense with people. They bore an odd resemblance to ranks of soldiers, except that they were shuffling, not marching, and they were certainly not soldiers. Even the poorly equipped armies of Israel wore helmets, not leather-bound headcloths, and their uniforms were scarcely the homespun loincloths and rough jerkins of peasants.

Then Ahab saw the *gibborim* and understood. This was the labor levy being impressed this month, one man from each family in Jezreel. But—surely Omri had not intended these men of Israel to be bound in cordons, herded like sheep.

"Get along there, dogs, no dallying!"

"No back talk, and unknot those fists, or I'll do it for you with a spear!"

The three metallic poundings came again, followed by the hollow rapping of a spearhead on a doorpost. "Open, in the name of King Omri of Israel!"

Ahab watched, anger mounting, while Jered, son of Joseph's neighbor Arnoz, emerged from the adjoining courtyard, was seized roughly and tied with a rope to the end of a cordon. As the procession started forward, Jered, always slow and bungling, dropped his knotted bundle and, reaching to retrieve it, stumbled. Instantly there was the swift motion of a spear shaft, followed by a howl of anguish and the blur of an object hurtling over the courtyard wall.

"Get along, clumsy lout. If you can't hang on to your baggage, you'd better not take it. Anyway, you'll need nothing but a loincloth where you're going."

Ahab's hands clenched. Strike his boyhood friend Jered, would they, these barbaric hired mercenaries? Not with the king's son standing by! He opened his lips, then remembered just in time that to the *gibborim* he would seem no prince, merely another of these stubborn Jezreelites. Except for the testimony of his fellow townsmen he could give no proof of his identity, and the king's police force would spare no time for introductions. He gave vent to his anger by pounding his knuckles on the stones of the parapet.

"Open in the name of King Omri of Israel!"

Ahab's hand unknotted, froze on the stones. The three brazen strokes throbbed like drumbeats against his temples. Until this moment it had not occurred to him that the next summons would be from the house of Joseph. Whom would his grandfather send? Haran? But Haran had promised to come to his housetop chamber and waken him soon after sunrise. Some hireling? *No! Yahweh forbid that the house of Joseph let strangers pay its debts!...You will see what I shall do.*

Cold sweat stood on Ahab's forehead. The spearhead pounded again on the shield, drummed against the doorpost with a violence which dislodged bits of the loosened mortar about the stones of the parapet. The captain, a burly Philistine, raised his black-bearded face, and Ahab dodged swiftly back.

"You, there on the housetop, I saw you! Throw stones at the king's men, would you? Open this door, or, by Dagon, I'll pound it into splinters! I'll—"

Ahab heard the doorpost grating, then Joseph's voice speaking calmly. "Peace, son of a foreign god—and an impatient one, it would seem. No need of your knocking the house down upon your heads. I heard you the first time you knocked."

"Then why in Dagon's name didn't you come?"

"As you see, I am an old man and move slowly. I came as quickly as I could."

"Well—it wasn't quick enough, but—we'll let it pass."

Ahab felt weak with relief. Joseph was not going to defy the royal order.

"The son of Dagon has business with the house of Joseph?"

"Stupid peasant! You know very well I have business, and what it is. Deliver your son or slave or hireling to the king's labor levy and be quick about it."

"Very well, I am ready."

"*You!* B-but—the king wants able-bodied men, not babes and graybeards."

"Does the edict say so?"

"N-no. It just says one laborer from each family."

"Very well then. Here I am. It's you now who are dallying."

"And you who are acting the stubborn fool. This isn't any work for old men or weaklings. These men are going to be building cities, lifting blocks of limestone!"

"And also, it seems, wearing the shackles of slaves. Must I put them on myself as well as wear them? Or must I prove to a Philistine a second time that human strength is not always measured by the girth and muscles of a Goliath?"

"Why, you—! All right, dog, you'll get the shackles—tight."

Ahab was conscious of no voluntary motion. One moment he was looking down in horror, the next he was in the street clawing with animal fury at the hairy hands which were knotting the braided strands of hemp about Joseph's waist.

"Take your hands off my grandfather, you uncircumcised heathen!"

He was lifted bodily from the ground by a huge arm clamped over his chest. His teeth tangled with the long hairs on the Philistine's giant wrist.

"Ho! Another fool asking for trouble? The men of this house must have tigers' seed in their loins. And who do you think you are to defy the strong men of the king?"

Ahab spat furiously and managed to eject the wrist, but the arm remained solidly clamped. "Let—me go," he gasped, "and I'll—tell you—who I am." Writhing and kicking, he managed to twist himself free. "I'm the son of King Omri of Israel, and this man you have the audacity to bind as a slave is my grandfather."

"So?" The Philistine hooted. "And I'm the king of Gath. Here's my royal seal, five finger marks." He planted a stinging blow on the young prince's cheek.

"And here's mine," returned Ahab, thrusting out his right hand. "See it? The personal seal of Prince Ahab of Israel."

The Philistine gasped. "I—I don't believe it!"

As he leaned forward to examine the ring, Ahab observed with relish that the flesh above the black thicket of beard had turned a pasty hue. The blur of figures lining the narrow street was resolving itself into familiar faces, and he was sure that one of them belonged to Rachel.

"You'll believe it soon enough after I've returned to Tirzah and told the king what you've done to his father."

The *gibbor* turned to Joseph. "Is this the truth? By Dagon, I'll have your blood if you're making sport of me! Are you the father of King Omri?"

"I'd own no man my son," replied Joseph clearly, "who puts a yoke of bondage on the free sons of Yahweh."

"Ha, that's telling us!" The Philistine lifted a hairy paw and gave Ahab a shove which sent him crashing against the wall. "So you *were* making sport of me!"

"Ask any of these people," gasped Ahab. "They'll tell you—"

But, looking around at their faces, stony and closed as the windowless walls from which they had issued, he knew they would do no such thing. The men of Jezreel would take their cue from Joseph, because they were born of the same unyielding stuff, suckled at the same defiant breast.

"Have it your own way," he told the Philistine bitterly. "You'll find out who I am as soon as I get back to Tirzah. If you march my grandfather away in this conscription, you'll regret it to your dying day—which won't give you long for penitence."

The captain threw up his hairy hands. "By Dagon and his fishtail, I don't want to take him!" He turned again to Joseph. "For the last time, graybeard, this is no job for weaklings. Go in the house and bring out a servant."

"No," replied Joseph grimly.

"Then send to the gate and get a hireling. I'll take even a blind beggar."

"No."

"If the grandson of Joseph is displeased," spoke a high-pitched voice, preceded by a gusty whistle, "he knows what he can do. Let him go himself."

The Philistine clapped his spearhead against his shield. "By Dagon, that's it! What do you say, graybeard? Will you send this hot lion's cub in your place?"

"Yes," replied Joseph instantly. "If my grandson is willing to go, I shall be glad to send him."

Now it was Ahab's turn to sweat. Though the watchman had just blown his ram's horn proclaiming sunrise, already the narrow street seemed turned into an oven. Go with the conscription and postpone his trip to Tyre? It might be days, weeks, before he could get a message to his father, and tomorrow his wedding procession was due to leave. The daughter of Ethbaal was not one to be kept waiting.

Beneath Joseph's probing gaze Ahab could feel himself flushing scarlet. Vaguely he was conscious of another pair of eyes fixed on him with a grave intensity, yet when his gaze swept the faces he could not find them.

"Well—make up your mind! Is the old man going or are you? Whichever it is, I'm warning you, you'll start the journey with a good flogging. One stroke of the lash for every minute of the king's time you've wasted!"

Ahab felt his thigh tingle at the bold pressure of a spear point. Let his grandfather's frail body be bent, perhaps broken, beneath the knotted leather thongs of this heathen? No, by Yahweh! He flung up his head, opened his lips to call on heaven as witness, then slowly closed them as his eyes tangled in a fleece of cloud turned red-gold by the newly risen sun.

"I—I can't go with you. I—have to make a trip to Tyre."

"All right. The old man goes." The captain nodded curtly to his underling. "Give him ten strokes, no more. I'd rather have a weakling than a corpse. Better yet, by Dagon, give them to this bold young 'prince'!"

Ahab found his voice. "I—I tell you I *am* the king's son!" he cried furiously. "Wait till I get back to Tirzah. Before the sun sets I'll have my grandfather released and this rope you've dared to bind him with circling your own neck! I'll—"

But before the ten strokes had been delivered, Ahab was blessing the Philistine, not cursing him. At least he had been permitted to spare his grandfather this final ignominy. Even while he quivered beneath each blow and gritted his teeth to keep from crying out, he derived bitter pleasure from each pulsing wave of pain.

The two pairs of eyes were still upon him, he could swear it, the one grimly penetrating, the other grave and steady and more than a little pitying. But when the waves of pain had washed away and he could look about him, the procession had passed on around the corner and the street was empty.

CHAPTER 8

1

Two nights out of Tyre, and still the wedding caravan was crawling along the narrow belt of shoreline bounded by sea and mountains! Ahab's nostrils were surfeited with the cloying sweetness of lush fruit groves. The unfamiliar pounding of the waves entered his blood, set his pulses beating like hammer strokes. When he closed his eyes, it was to see the long snakelike coil undulating with exasperating slowness along the blinding white strip of sand.

Scarcely had he settled himself on his sheet than he was up again, throwing a dark coat over his tunic. "I'm going out," he said to Obadiah, who shared his tent. "Along the beach, I guess. No guard! And don't send one after me."

It was better once he had reached the beach. There were adversaries to be faced—the salt wind pushing like a muscular hand, the clinging sand. Soon he was breathing hard, his lungs hurt, and the muscles of his legs were throbbing. He was glad he had stopped for neither headdress nor sandals. Some deep urgency reveled in the harshness beneath his feet, the fingers of spray combing his hair.

Presently it seemed less imperative that the journey be ended as swiftly as possible. Suppose he were back in Tirzah. The day of his marriage, already set by auspicious omens, would be no closer—nor his grandfather's self-imposed term of labor in the quarries! Ahab had kept his word to the Philistine. The day of his return to Tirzah a royal messenger had been dispatched to intercept the labor levy and before Ahab's departure had brought back Joseph's answer.

"You say my son *orders* me to go back home? Then tell him, by the hair and beards of all our common ancestors, *no!* If the king demands labor of the house of Joseph, then by the house of Joseph the obligation will be fulfilled."

And Omri had been as stubborn as his father. "Very well. He's within his rights. A son in Israel, even though he be a king, has no right to coerce his parents. If he persists in playing the fool, I can't stop him."

Angry, tormented by guilt, Ahab had set off for Tyre. Unfair that this expedition which had promised to be a march of triumph should be completely spoiled! Now he would be unable to show his bride the white crown on the hill of Shamer, for, knowing that his grandfather, frail back bent to a crushing burden, might be watching him ride by in princely splendor, he would find the sight of it unbearable. The caravan must go by way of En-gannim instead of Megiddo. His bare feet plowed in frustrated fury through the clinging sand.

When he saw the Phoenician tents mushrooming against the starlight, he knew why he had come. Leaving the beach, he moved swiftly through the fringe of laden oxcarts and tethered animals, careful to avoid the little groups squatted about the embers of the cooking fires. There! That was her tent in the center of the circle. He himself had insisted that it be crimson, the bridal color, and made of silk, though the royal encampment of Israel knew nothing better than goat's hair. Seeing it now, outspread like the petals of a huge rose and softly illuminated from within, he was not sorry. One did not put an ivory inlay in a slab of olive wood.

Suddenly his cheeks flamed hot. His pulses raced. The thin silk might create a bower of beauty but hardly of privacy. How could he have dreamed, watching her in the dance or sitting by her side in the temple chamber, that the rhythmic grace animating the shapeless priestess' robe was cast in a mold of such supple yet palm-straight slenderness, that the smooth-flowing limbs were so exquisitely slim, the small breasts so gently rounded? All these months he had been dreaming only of her hair and its vibrant magic, her eyes with their copper glints, and the cameo-pure line of her profile. Now...The roseate haze suffused him, turned to fire.

He felt himself lifted in powerful arms, borne away so swiftly that the breath was forced from his lungs. Attempting to struggle, he found both arms clamped to his sides with a viselike grip.

"So," a voice hissed, "spying on the princess, are you? No matter whether you're a Tyrian or a dog of a barbarian, this will teach you!"

Set down abruptly within a circle of flaring torchlight, he was brought face to face with his captor, a big handsome young Phoenician who, in spite of Ahab's superior height, overtopped him by half a head. Breath partially retrieved, he eyed the huge knotted muscles and blazing eyes with both fury and respect.

"Fool! You are making a mistake—"

"So you *are* a barbarian! I can tell by your accent. Lucky for you! Were you a Phoenician and meant harm to the princess, I would kill you."

Harm to the princess! Ahab saw red. What right had this hulk of a foreigner to pose as the heroic defender of *his bride?* It was he who should be demanding what the Phoenician was doing in the vicinity of her tent. Focusing his gaze on the bold line of square, outjutting chin, he was about to strike at it in a fury of jealous rage when, suddenly noting the smooth-shaven flesh and feminine garb, he unclenched his fingers and laughed aloud.

"Why do you laugh?"

Ahab sobered instantly, for the eunuch's eyes had become two blazing pits. "If I laughed," he said hastily, "it was at the stupidity of my—my master the prince. Thinking he must send an emissary to assure himself of the well-being of his bride, when she has one like you to guard her! I shall return immediately—"

"Not yet." There was grim triumph in the eunuch's voice.

Again Ahab felt the vises clamp about his arms, lift him effortlessly. With unbelieving horror he saw the rose bubble float toward him, heard the swift exchange between his captor's suddenly emotionless voice and a harsh treble which sank to a croon the moment its owner returned to the silken shelter.

"It's that Eshmun. Says he's caught a barbarian prowling around your tent. Wants to know what to do with him. As if he of all people shouldn't know what to do with spies!"

Ahab waited, trembling, for the sound of her voice.

"A barbarian, Jael? What fun! I'm not sure I've ever seen one, close to. Give me that long cloak. No—don't bother to bind up my hair—"

Slipping from the eunuch's grasp, he dropped to his knees, grateful that he wore no distinguishing marks—no seal ring, no banded headdress. The light had been dim in the temple chamber, and the hood would have shielded his features. If he was careful to keep his head bent and did not speak—

"Where did you find him, Eshmun?"

"Just outside, my lady, not a dozen paces from your tent."

"So? And what were you doing there, barbarian?"

Ahab's inability to speak was no feint. He had dreamed too long of this moment—the nearness of her, the sudden fragrance of cassia and aloes drifting from her unbound hair. He could not have uttered a sound had he tried.

"What's the matter with him, Eshmun? Has the barbarian no tongue? What a pity! Its removal would have made such a fitting punishment!"

"He was using one a little while ago," replied the eunuch grimly. "Said his master sent him to assure himself of his bride's well-being."

"Indeed? How thoughtful of his master! And what message will you take back, barbarian—provided you discover some means of communication? Will you tell him that his bride is ugly, so that you couldn't bear to lift your face to look at her?"

Ahab uttered animal sounds which, he hoped, might be interpreted as negatives, and ventured a swift upward glance through the tumbling cascades of his hair.

"Ah! He has eyes, if no voice. I saw them. Hold the lamp down, Jael. Let me see if these barbarians are men or animals."

"They are *men*, mistress." In Ahab's ears the eunuch's voice grated with a peculiar harshness. "Subject to the same follies and to the same punishments as Phoenicians. And—*and I caught him spying.*"

A sudden coldness traveled down Ahab's spine. For the first time it occurred to him that he might be in a dangerous as well as an embarrassing predicament, a long distance from his own men, and without the slightest means of proving his identity.

"Oh?" The princess' light laugh fell on his coldness like a warm caressing hand. "And is that such a crime, Eshmun—to spy?"

"Does the beloved of Ashtart mean that the barbarian is to go unpunished? "

Ahab shivered again. There was a quality in the eunuch's voice which suggested a sword blade swathed in velvet.

"Yes, Eshmun. That is exactly what I mean."

"Did my lady understand that—the man was spying upon her privacy?"

"Perfectly, Eshmun. It is my pleasure to pardon his effrontery. Is there any reason why I should not do so?"

"None, mistress of men's destinies."

Ahab stopped shivering. The sword blade was gone, sheathed so completely that he decided he must have imagined it. The eunuch's voice was all velvet.

"Then you may go, barbarian."

He ran swiftly, blindly, stumbling among fire embers and baggage trappings and tent pins, for he was taking no chances with the uncertain temper of the eunuch. He had sensed strange dark currents surging beneath the placid acquiescent surface, and the fellow's strength was uncanny. Only when his feet sank in the cool clear sand of the beach did he stop running.

There was less of urgency in his motions now. He was unpleasantly conscious of rough sand and drenching wind, and he picked his way gingerly, head bent and shoulders hunched. Even though the night was moonless, it was easy to avoid the scatterings of shells and rock chips sown through the white sand, for the stars were as stinging sharp as the spray.

When his eyes caught a winking of pale green, he stooped, picked the object from the drift of shells and pebbles where the waves had flung it, and held it in the palm of his hand. Slender it was, finger-long and shaped like a tiny cylinder—or like a pillar, pale green and luminous, rippling with motion as if lighted from within...the color of wind.

As he placed it carefully in a fold of his girdle, a figure loomed out of the darkness, slow-moving and square, familiar even in these strange environs.

"Obadiah?" he called softly.

The friend of his childhood fell into heavy step beside him. "I thought you should know. A messenger came to your tent from—from hers."

"From the princess?" To cover the sharp eagerness of his question, Ahab tried to make his voice sound coolly casual. "She—desires something more, perhaps? She is displeased with some small detail?" Ahab tried to adjust his pace to the measured steps of Obadiah.

"I would hardly call it a *small* detail."

Ahab ground his feet deep into the sand. Deliberately he counted ten steps before exploding. "In heaven's name, what does she want? By the gates of Tirzah, if a starving man waited on you for his food, he would die of hunger!"

Obadiah carefully measured five more steps before replying. "The princess of Tyre demands," he said, "that the banner of her god, Baal Melkart, be placed at the head of the procession beside that of Yahweh."

"I—I see." Ahab pushed back a curling tendril, and it felt wet and cold to his touch. He winced as his right foot encountered the razor sharpness of a murex shell. Float the emblem of another people's god beside that of the Lord of Israel? He was as shocked by the suggestion as Obadiah. *You shall have no other gods before me.* In his ears the pounding of the waves echoed the thunders of Sinai, that sacred mountain deep in the southern wilderness where his people had kept their first and most holy tryst with Yahweh. "What—did you tell him?"

"That I would deliver the message of his mistress to the prince of Israel."

Again Ahab pushed back a damp tendril, and this time he felt beads of sweat mingled with the wind-driven spray. The first request she had made of him, and he must refuse it! But—she *demands,* Obadiah had said. An ultimatum? It was still not too late for her train to turn about and go back to Tyre. The signed agreement had promised her the right to worship her own god as she saw fit. If she construed the right to include the privilege...Well, why not? It was her wedding procession as well as his.

A face reared itself out of the sands, haggard, gray with the dust of the quarries, silently accusing. What! Make even further denial of the stern code his grandfather had taught him? Yahweh forbid! It was bad enough now remembering how he had failed him. And yet—was it his fault if the old man stubbornly defied the king's order?

You shall have no other gods before me. Before...But the banner of Melkart need not fly before that of Yahweh. She had asked only that it be borne *beside...*

Deliberately he plunged his feet into the white patch of sand, blurring the accusing features into shadow.

2

It was an insult. All her satisfaction in seeing Melkart's gold and purple emblem breasting the sunlight beside Yahweh's crimson bull was shattered like a bubble of blown glass. To be immured like a desert nomad in an odorous sheathing of goat's hair! And why? The excuse had been flimsy enough.

"The prince desires that his bride receive the full protection of his Yahweh. As she approaches his domain she should be sheltered after the custom of his people."

She had almost flown into a rage and ordered her servants to bundle her belongings back into the carts...would have if the proximity of thick-piled rugs and inlaid bedstead to the ugly black-hued fabric had not seemed so incongruous that instead she had broken into peals of laughter.

She was sitting in her tent languidly submitting to Jael's ministrations when the thing happened which dispelled all languor.

"Lovely soft skin," crooned the nurse. "A wonder it isn't rubbed raw as a dressed fowl after riding all day in those coarse rags the barbarian furnished for his bride. But they're better than those ugly white things—" The soothing voice jumped an octave. "Who's there in the doorway, and what are you doing? Spying?"

The shadow bulked larger. "May the brightest of earth's suns shine kindly upon her devoted slave. I was bidden to bring this—this token to her tent."

Jael looked suspiciously from the eunuch's inscrutable face to the object in his hand. "It looks like a common goatskin bag, and a dirty one at that."

"So was the fellow who gave it to me, insisting that it be presented immediately to the bride of the prince, the son of his sovereign."

Jael took the bag gingerly. "Merciful Ashtart, What's in it! Rocks?"

"Were I able to tell its contents," returned Eshmun imperturbably, "I would not be my mistress' devoted slave. I was asked to deliver, not examine it."

"Well, now that you've delivered it, why don't you go?"

The eunuch bowed. "Does the leaf fall from the tree unless the branch consents?"

"You may go, Eshmun," Jezebel ordered him listlessly.

When she saw the imprint on the flattened lump of wax, a swift warmth awoke every fiber of her being to tingling awareness. Then there was a rushing in her ears, a pounding...She broke the seal. "Where did Eshmun say it came from?"

"One of the prince's men, a dirty fellow. Why, it—it's nothing but shards, broken bits of an old earthen pot with things written on them!"

As the girl drew out the pieces one after the other and silently studied their scrawled markings, the nurse watched in an agony of mounting frustration.

"It—seems to be a story," murmured Jezebel more to herself than to Jael.

"A—story?" The bright beads of eyes were gleaming.

"It's about two brothers. Their names were Jacob and Esau..."

Jezebel lay in the goat's-hair tent and tossed. *The stranger was a member of the prince's wedding party.* She had found him!...No, she had not found him. Except that he was a man of Israel, she knew no more about him than before, and—could she be sure even that he was a man of Israel? There were undoubtedly men of other races and nations in the prince's entourage—slaves...But would a slave wear a seal ring of obsidian? Possibly. Men of noble birth were taken into slavery for debt, or as prisoners of war.

Why had he sent the bag of shards? *Sometime I may tell you the story...*Was it simply a reminder of the few moments of fragile beauty which they had held between them, like the vessel of pottery, now broken to bits, on which some hand had scrawled an old folk tale of his people? Or had he some ulterior motive—perhaps blackmail? Was the winged bull to become a symbol of unrest and terror, following, tantalizing, threatening?

Eyes wide and sleepless, she watched the star-spangled triangle which was the opening of her tent turn from black to purple to pale amethyst What should she do when the new day came? Summon Eshmun, order him to find the man who had given him the bag and bring him to her? But Eshmun knew too much already. He might have noticed the mark of the seal and recognized it. Find some excuse to order her litter through the vanguard of the caravan, scan every face and figure? Impossible. A bride, even a princess, did not do such a thing. It was forbidden to look on the face of one's groom until the final feast night, or evil would befall. And besides, how would she know him if she did see him? She had seen almost nothing of his features. Unless she could see him walk—hear him speak...

"Come, come, wake up, you lazy little snail! Every tent but ours is dismantled. At this rate it will be a year before your wedding day."

Jezebel rubbed her eyes. "I—must have slept—"

"A dirty little urchin brought this to the tent. One of the men, he said, told him to bring it. Though what you would want with a lump of green glass—!"

Jezebel's eyes flew open. She took the object from Jael's fingers—a bit of emerald glass shaped like a tiny cylinder and polished smooth as satin. Lying in her palm, it shone with a soft lambency as if lighted from within. Cool and flowing, it seemed, and rippling with motion.

"It is," she whispered. "It's the same color. It's the color of wind."

Turning it over, she noticed a bit of foreign substance clinging to one end—a small lump of wax bearing the imprint of a winged figure with the head of a bull and the body of a lion. And the impression made upon it was still soft and yielding to her touch.

3

The strip of green paradise widened that day into the broad plain of Accho, sending the hills scuttling into the distance like frightened antelopes.

Jezebel settled back among the cushions of her litter, glad that she had been given one last day of reprieve. The hills, grim abode of the strange god into whose domain she was journeying, had for the moment receded. They belonged to tomorrow. Yesterday also had been disturbing, its ecstasy of discovery so mingled with foreboding that the touch of her fingers against the bit of green glass tucked deep in her girdle stirred her pulses less with rapture than with panic. But she could do nothing about it now, could not even strain her eyes toward the forward end of the caravan in a vain attempt to distinguish a tall figure who might or might not be wearing a seal ring of obsidian. So uncurving was the road that nothing before or behind was visible. The hills were still far away. Better to enjoy these hours of reprieve while they lasted, for the time would soon come...

It came sooner than she expected, for she had forgotten Carmel. A sudden sidestep of the bearers to avoid a sandy gully, and there it was between the curtains of her litter, crouched against the sky like a couchant beast, head thrust forward and upraised, paws plunged deep into the sea. The reprieve was over.

They camped that night almost in the shadow of the huge headland, so far from the sea that there was no sound of waves pounding on yellow sands. She found sleep impossible. The mountain's bulk seemed to press down upon her, crushing her spirit so that she could scarcely breathe. She had left the abode of Melkart and come into the abode of Yahweh.

Lying in the darkness, she tried to picture him. She had felt fear of Melkart, stood quaking and speechless beneath his brazen arms, but it had been fear of the familiar, the tangible. Here there was nothing to fear, only silence, vacancy. Slipping from her bed, she groped her way across the thick carpet until her bare feet touched the hardness of reed matting, her outstretched hands encountered the warm roughness of camel's hair. One more step, and she felt the cool night air against her face.

There! She could breathe again. And the mysterious entity had become tangible, for there were the outlines of the headland, etched black against a purple sky. There was life upon it. Here and there she could see pinpoints of moving light. Where were they going? To some high place of the god Yahweh, to greet the rising of the sun with strange orgies, as once on this very headland her own ancestors...?

It was then that the idea came to her.

At her first glimpse of the tall figure awaiting her outside the tent, she drew a startled breath. While he bent low, her eyes flew to his hands, and she breathed normally again. No ring. And the fingers were short and stubby. She frowned with annoyance. Was she to display such weakness every time a tall, straight figure...?

The man lifted his face, disclosing square-cut features, so sharply defined that they might have been carved out of rock. The eyes also possessed a peculiar stonelike quality. Deep gray in color and unusually lustrous, they gave the appearance of being shaped from bits of hard flint.

The prince his master, he said, with a directness noticeably lacking in humility, was pleased to comply with her request that the caravan be halted long enough for her priests to render homage to their god at his ancient shrine on Carmel. He himself, Obadiah, the prince's steward, would himself give the order. And a detail of soldiers would be assigned to carry out her wishes. Surely she must admit—the bits of flint suddenly struck sparks—that neither he nor the prince could do more, as true servants of their own Yahweh.

Jezebel's lips tightened. Her head lifted arrogantly. "I shall need no soldiers," she replied curtly. "And as for the loyalty of your master and his servants to his god Yahweh, is that not a matter for the prince himself to define?"

Their glances interlocked in unmistakable antagonism. Then the prince's emissary bowed again, his manner still pointedly lacking in humility. Jezebel stood and watched him go, lips still tightly compressed but with more of thoughtfulness than anger in her eyes. She knew that she had made her first enemy in Israel.

4

According to her plan they pitched camp early and started up the mountain in the late afternoon, taking equipment for remaining at the place of sacrifice overnight. So steep was the trail that the last part of the journey had to be made on foot, yet even this discomfort failed to dull the sharp edge of Jezebel's triumph. What an entrance she would make into this land of Yahweh! Fitting omen of the conquest which her coming to Israel portended—greeting the very first dawn with the smoke of sacrifice to Baal!

It was the sight of a wandering shepherd halfway up the mountain which caused her to turn to Meribaal in sudden dismay. "The animal for the sacrifice! Did you remember—"

Meribaal had not remembered. His tired face turned pale with consternation. He would go back. Perhaps in the village at the foot of the mountain—

"No!" Jezebel issued a swift command, and the ragged shepherd with his handful of sheep was dragged into their midst "There! Take your choice. Surely you can find something which will be acceptable."

The priest made his choice—a young ewe, fat-tailed and heavy with wool, the best of the sorry and meager flock. The shepherd was stubborn. He had raised the sheep from a lamb and was saving it for breeding. It was his prize, his darling... But the attendants knew how to handle him.

"Dolt! Son of a dirty swine! On your knees—or, better yet, your belly!"

"It's the bride of your prince speaking, understand? If she asked for your whole flock, you should consider yourself favored. Here, take these silver rings, driveling imbecile, and lucky you are to get them instead of a spear point!"

They found the ancient altar, a heap of strewn stones in the midst of a dense thicket. So well did Meribaal remember the spot, which he had visited once in his youth, that he went straight to it, passing another neatly piled heap of stones on the way. At sight of the two altars so close together, Jezebel's eyes flashed. Soon, she promised herself grimly, the condition would be reversed. It would be Yahweh's altar...

The pillar of smoke caught the first rays of the sun, was shot through and through with bold shafts of light. And instantly, as if kindled from the same blazing torch, the wood piled on the altar of stones leaped into flame. A hoarse cry of triumph burst from the throats of the dozen white-robed priests. In spite of their deathly weariness they drove their aching muscles to an even more prodigal display of energy. The limping dance quickened its tempo, whipped into a whirling frenzy. Knives flashed, their glittering edges licked by tongues of spurting crimson. The smell of raw blood and scorching flesh was heavy on the air.

Jezebel surveyed the scene with satisfaction. To be sure, the fire was scanty, the priests few, the sacrifice a scrawny sheep instead of a fat bullock. But for the moment it was sufficient. From the encampment at the foot of the mountain the shouts would be clearly heard, the pillar of smoke and flame plainly visible. She had been afraid of this hill country and of its strange god. Yet here she was on almost her first dawn in Israel, not imprisoned by hills but looking down upon them, smiling contemptuously over the dead altar of Yahweh, while the smoking pillar of Melkart flung its challenge to the far horizons.

Surfeited with feasting, drunk with both wine and weariness, they were descending the mountain to the encampment when Jezebel felt her litter jolted to a rude stop, then abruptly lowered and deposited at such an uneven angle that she was flung off balance. Furiously she pulled at the curtains.

"Clumsy dolts! What is the meaning of this! You deserve—"

But one look at the bearers' faces, mouths agape, eyes fixed, bulging, on the path ahead, was proof that she was wasting her breath. Impatiently she tugged at the fastening, slid back the sliding door, and set both feet firmly on the ground. Then her own mouth fell open.

"Wh-where did he c-come from!" stuttered one of the bearers. "By Ashtart, he wasn't there—and—and then he—was—"

With a terrified cry the servant fled, clawing his way up the rocky path, empty now, for the litters following had not yet come into view. Catching the contagion of his panic, the other bearers followed him.

"Cowards!" Jezebel vouchsafed them only a contemptuous glance, then continued to stare at the strange figure perhaps a dozen steps away, blocking the path.

The man, if man he was instead of animal, was of towering proportions yet so lean of flesh that each jutting bone was as sharply delineated as a bare mountain crag. He wore a rough sheepskin wrapped around his body and fastened with a leather girdle. His head, bare like his arms, limbs, and feet, was covered with a growth of hair as thick and curly as a lion's mane and bleached almost as tawny. It fell over his shoulders in long ragged locks, cascaded from cheeks and chin in a streaming torrent descending below his waist and half hiding the sheepskin. Out of this thicket, the only features visible, emerged two jutting cheekbones, a high forehead, and two brilliant eyes. Not, Jezebel decided in swift relief, the eyes of an animal—nor of a madman.

He's like a mountain, she thought with less fear than admiration, with its crags blown bare.

They stood silently, measuring each other. It was Jezebel finally who broke the silence. "Who are you," she demanded impatiently, "and what do you want?"

"I am Elijah—a servant of Yahweh, the God of Israel."

"And I," the girl drew herself up to her full height, "am Jezebel."

"I know who you are." So swift and bitter was the denunciation that, like an unexpected gust of cold wind, it took away her breath. Her eyes clung to the bony, leveled finger. "You're a sinner against the God-given right of a son of Yahweh. You have taken away the ewe which he cherished, which was his prize, his darling. And as Yahweh lives, before whom I stand, you shall suffer the consequences of this act. He who breaks the laws of Yahweh must himself be broken."

It was over. The cold gust had passed. She blinked her eyes, to shake off the spell of the bony, leveled finger, and when she opened them he was gone.

The bearers were back again, their courage remarkably restored.

"The accursed barbarian! We can't let him escape with this!"

"If it is the will of the queen of heaven that we should go after him—"

"*No!*" Her eyes blazed at them. "Say nothing about it, do you hear? Forget it. But I shall not forget. Be sure you will be well rewarded for your—devotion."

She returned to the litter, was lifted, carefully but with hands which trembled, to their shoulders, went swaying down the uneven path. So swiftly had it all happened that the bearers of the following litter, hidden on the ridge above, had not noticed. Perhaps it had not really happened. Perhaps the strange figure had been what he had at first appeared—an apparition.

But his words had been real. So was the hot tide of anger which kept sweeping, wave upon wave, through her body. And the amazement. That most of all. For the strange creature had denounced her, not for performing sacrifice upon a rival altar or for worshiping another god in his deity's domain, not that at all...*but for requisitioning the sheep of a dirty peasant!*

CHAPTER 9

1

On the final day of his wedding feast Ahab rose early to sacrifice to Yahweh.

"The son of my lord the king is distressed?" asked Obadiah with concern as they returned to the palace side by side in the chariot.

"Distressed!" Ahab's tone was truculent. "What makes you think so?"

"Because of the touch of my master's hand on the reins."

Instantly Ahab relaxed his tense grip, and the horses subsided to an even pacing. It was the reminder of the hill of Shamer, he thought bitterly, which had caused his sudden tension. His dismay on discovering, after his return from Tyre, that his grandfather still refused to comply with the king's order releasing him from duty in the labor levy had hardened into dull resentment. It was unfair for this day of his marriage to be marred by a sense of guilt! Seeing the sun leap now from the edge of the parapets, he should be exulting in its ardor, not fretting because in another hour it would be turning the limestone quarries on the hill of Shamer into a scorching oven.

"May my lord have reason to bless this day as devoutly as does his servant!"

Ahab gave his chief groomsman a sharp glance. The usually impassive features were suffused with excitement. "What has happened?" he inquired abruptly.

Obadiah's cheek flushed. The square fingers grasping the chariot rail were trembling. "A letter has come from my father Joab," he blurted out eagerly. "The *mohar* [bride price] has been agreed upon. As soon as you can spare me I am to return to Jezreel to sign my betrothal contract."

"Rachel?" Ahab's lips mouthed the girl's name stiffly.

"Of course—Rachel." Obadiah's repetition of the name was hushed, his approach to it devout. "When I knew she was my master's choice, I rejoiced because it meant that in serving him I might be serving her also. I never dreamed of—" The flush mounted to the square forehead. "I would as soon have thought of—"

"Of becoming a *kedesh* in a Canaanite temple," Ahab finished for him bluntly. In spite of the sun's warmth his fingers felt cold on the twin strips of leather.

> "My king has made him a sedan
>   of wood from Lebanon,
>   silver the feet of it,
>   golden the back of it,
>   purple the seat of it,
>   inlaid with ebony."

He felt no coldness now. Though it was evening and the sun's warmth had fled, the canopy over his head was a suffocating tent, his voluminous wedding garments and twining garlands a stifling net. A far cry, he reflected bitterly, this litter in which he was being borne to fetch his bride, from the palanquin of Solomon made famous by the wedding song. Of cheap cypress, not of cedar, its trappings brass, not gold and silver! He could imagine the amusement and contempt his bride was feeling toward these evidences of Israel's backwardness. Had she been amused also by his bag of shards and little fragment of green glass? If not, she could at least have given some sign that she remembered their meeting in the temple chamber!

The joking ceased. They must have reached the house of the courtier where his bride and her maidens were lodged. Presently, mingled with the loud voices of his male attendants and the playful clashing of their swords, he heard the tinkle of anklets, the jangling of castanets and cymbals, the lilt of female trebles. Good! The women of Israel were joining the Phoenician handmaidens in accompanying his bride to the palace. Yes, and singing her charms as lustily as if she were a peasant wench mounted on a threshing sledge!

> "Ah, you are fair, my dear, so fair,
>   with dovelike eyes
>   behind your veil!
>   Dark stream the tresses of your hair
>   like goats a-down the slopes of Gilead..."

Ahab felt a swift unreasoning anger. That was Rachel's song. Hers was the hair like black goats streaming down a mountain, like flowing purple. What right had these women of Israel...? Then, smiling with grim irony, he berated himself for his stupidity. Fool! If he had reason for resentment, it was for his bride, not Rachel, because the words did not do justice to her charms. He could give them words. He had only to summon a vision of her and, swift as the throbbing of his pulses, they were tumbling from his lips.

> "Ah, you are fair, my love, so fair,
>   bronze eyes agleam
>   behind your veil!
> Bright stream the tresses of your hair
>   like molten fire..."

2

She should feel, Jezebel supposed, some stirring of curiosity toward this man sitting under the canopy on the platform beside her, profile obscured by garlands and festoons, figure shapelessly enshrouded in wedding garments. But once she had satisfied herself that the *stranger* was not among the guests occupying the seats of honor, her interest had subsided into an indifference approaching lethargy.

How did she know he was not there? She could not have told, except that she had let her eyes linger on each one, noting the set of his shoulders, the shape of his hands curved about a slice of fruit or a bowl of wine, then waited for some instinctive response within herself which had not come. Of course he might be among those in the lower seats, and the crowds massed under the balconies were but blurs through her veil, but at least he was not one of the prince's courtiers. The discovery aroused little emotion, either of relief or of disappointment. The wedding feast, it seemed, had been dragging on interminably, turning even apprehension as insipid as the warm wine in her goblet, as tasteless as the morsels she occasionally lifted beneath her veil and slipped between her lips.

The impact of harsh voices was like a dull beating of drums. Though these Israelites spoke a crude dialect of her own tongue, their accent was atrocious, and in her present mood of contemptuous indifference she caught only a few snatches of the customary ribald wedding banter.

"What's the matter, bridegroom? No more wine?"

"...saving his lips, maybe, for a softer, sweeter vessel!"

"If the groom gets the maid, what do the groomsmen get? Her maidens?"

But as she awakened to harsher undertones, her ears sharpened. At first there was only a faint grumbling mingled with the ribaldry, all too far removed from the king's vicinity to attract his attention. Yet even when the complaints became clearly audible, Omri gave them no notice. Glancing at his tightly knit features, eyes scarcely visible beneath heavy brows, lips an unsmiling stroke, Jezebel made a gesture of impatience. Impossible that he could be cognizant of this overt criticism and sit calm and unmoved, lean fingers carelessly crumbling a bit of bread! If it were Ethbaal, he would be swelling with choler, have every guard in the room flashing his sword.

She glanced covertly at Prince Ahab. Though she could see nothing of his features except a firm line of chin, she knew that the figure beneath the voluminous garments was tensed with awareness. She sensed rather than saw that the hands hidden by the long embroidered sleeves were gripping the arms of his chair—sensed too a certain irresolution, a slowness of decision which she hoped, for the sake of her mission in Israel, might indicate not strength but weakness. Easier to mold soft clay than melt and shape hard metal!

The grumblings became louder. Full sentences leaped to her ears.

"Why not a woman of Israel? Cannot our women bear sons?"

"Is this the end of foreign wives or the beginning? Remember Solomon—"

"Why should not a prince's bride also sit with her groom upon the threshing sledge? Why should she not prove her prowess in the sword dance?"

"The sword dance is for robust brides, not weaklings."

Jezebel's small hands clenched into fists. She shot another outraged glance at Omri. What were kings made of in this disgusting country? Acacia stumps instead of cedars? Why didn't he either silence the traitorous tongues or pluck them out by the roots? Then slowly her hands unclenched, turned upward, the fingers uncurling like soft petals. The angry flashing in her eyes dissolved into tiny sparks.

Rising suddenly, she descended the steps of the platform and, proud head held high, turned toward the complaining courtiers.

"The women of Tyre are not weaklings," she proclaimed loudly. "A dance is it you demand of your brides? One which calls for strength? Then judge if a daughter of Tyre cannot dance as well as a woman of Israel!"

Amid a silence heavy enough to be cleaved by the thick blades hanging from the groomsmen's belts, she moved swiftly to the open space lined on three sides by the banquet tables, on the other by the wedding platform. What was it, this dance which the bride of Israel was accustomed to perform to show her strength and prowess? She did not know, could only try to guess, drawing on all her instincts, all the skills acquired in long years of tutelage as a devotee of Melkart. This also was in the service of the god, not this time for his pleasure, but for the sake of his honor, perhaps even to determine the measure of his future greatness.

She moved slowly at first, accustoming herself to the feeling of the rough stone floor, the impeding folds of the bridal veil, the burden of heavy necklaces and bracelets and anklets...then faster...faster. When the welcome sound of tambourines and sistrums broke the silence, she could have wept with relief. Without the music, it had been like sinking every step in waves of water. Now she was the waves themselves, advancing, receding, mounting up on flashing wings into the sunlight, whirling, foaming, flinging white spray high into the air.

Then suddenly the waves could not rush and glide and circle where they would, for there was a wall closing in on either side. She watched them warily through the gauze of her veil—the two long lines of groomsmen whose weapons she had seen flashing in the torchlight of the procession. So they were giving her a chance to dance according to their own custom, beneath the glittering canopy of their crossed swords! Did it matter what steps she took? She did not know. She knew only that it was to be a test of her strength and endurance. Very well. She was equal to it. Had she not been disciplined to dance without respite from the hour the golden pillar was first gilded with sunlight until it fell into shadow?

So—she could no longer be the waves moving on the sea's smooth surface. Then she would be a stream gliding between its banks through a pleasant valley, the sun's rays arching above. A mountain stream she would be, leaping, gushing, tumbling over rocks, eddying, swirling... No, not a stream—a torrent, swelled to fierceness by the rains, rushing, foaming, overflowing its banks, cruel, ruthless, formidable, plunging with a fierce fury to lose itself in the sea.

On and on she danced, with undiminished vigor, through the long glittering path and back again, in and out among the lines of groomsmen, whirling, leaping, and circling...she moved endlessly. The groomsmen let their swords waver. One after the other lowered his weapon, ruefully nursing exhausted arms. The rattle of tambourines and sistrums grew fainter, ceased. Lamps burned low and were refilled.

Her feet burned like fire. Her limbs and arms felt heavy as stone, and the weight of the jewels throbbed through her every fiber, so that it was the rhythm of pain now which set the pace for motion. The silence had long since been broken. Hands were clapping, arms waving, voices shouting approval, bursting into song.

> "Maid of Shulem, turn, ah turn,
>   turn, ah turn, that we may see you!"
> "And what would you see in the maid of Shulem?"
> "We would see her in the sword dance!"

She had won. She held the courtiers of Israel in her soft palm. Yet she could not come to rest. She was still waiting.

"Stop!"

Above all the clamor and singing she heard it and knew it for the voice which she must obey. Gratefully she turned toward it, saw that it had come from the wedding platform and that her husband, Prince Ahab, was descending the steps.

"Enough!" he ordered his groomsmen sharply. "Are you not yet satisfied? Do you want to kill her? Put your swords back in their sheaths."

She tried to move toward him, but she could not. Perhaps it was her utter weariness which, now that the fierce compulsion of rhythm had died, seemed to lock fast every muscle. Or perhaps it was just the sight of the tall straight figure moving toward her, looking so strange and yet so familiar, the bold lines of his features half hidden beneath garlands and festoons. Just so, face shadowed by the hooded cloak, he had come toward her in the temple chamber.

She would have fallen if he had not reached out his hand. As it was, she found herself sinking to her knees before him, head bent low over their clasped hands. But that did not matter. It was exactly where she wanted to be, not just at this moment, in weariness, but always, in triumph, in exultation, yes, even in submission. Oh, what a blind fool she had been not to know who he was, when he had tried so hard to tell her!

As his hand clasped hers firmly, lifting her to her feet, she felt something hard and sharp pressing into the flesh of her palm. The pain of it was exquisite, so mingled with the ecstasy of awareness that she wished it might never end. Even after he had led her back across the room and, seating her again beside him, had released her hand, she held her palm tight shut beneath her veil.

When she finally opened it and looked down, she was not surprised to see imprinted in its soft flesh the faint outlines of a tiny figure with the head of a bull and the body of a lion, its two wings spread wide.

3

"Of all places for a bride to be brought on her wedding night!" Jael exclaimed. "A tent of black goat's hair set on a housetop! Oh, I know why they do it. I've had it all explained to me in the kitchens. It's to remind them of the years their ancestors lived in tents before they had the sense to build cities. Well, as for me, I wouldn't want to be reminded. By Anath and her blessed snakes—"

"It's all right," said Jezebel with quiet firmness. "You may go now, Jael."

The shrill scolding ceased abruptly. Jael cast a sharply curious glance at the veiled figure, then without another word pushed aside the curtain of the tent and joined the waiting women outside. Jezebel caught a brief glimpse of a white stone parapet, a triangle of velvet sky sown thickly with stars. Then the curtain fell back into place and she was alone.

A bride, she knew, should be seated on her couch, head bent demurely, when her husband came to lift her wedding veil. But she did not want to be seated. She wanted to be standing like this when he came, straight and proud as one of her own Lebanon cedars, knowing that her pride was the most precious offering she had to give him. She was no longer conscious of weariness. The dance in the banquet hall seemed as long ago as Tyre—as childhood. Knowing that he was coming, she could have stood so, quietly waiting, forever.

The women outside the tent were restless. She could hear them whispering and giggling, moving excitedly to the parapet to see if the groom and his party were coming. Some of them began humming one of the wedding songs.

> "Wear me as a seal close to your heart,
>   wear me like a ring upon your hand;
>   for love is strong as death itself..."

The singing ended abruptly in shouts of excitement. There were sounds of many shuffling sandals, of flutes and drums and breaking pottery, of male voices raised in hilarious merriment and banter.

"Look! He faints already. He can hardly climb the steps."

"One of us had better go first. The shock of lifting the veil may be too great."

"There's the tent. Show him the entrance, somebody—"

"So be it. Go in unto her. Take her according to the law of Moses."

The curtain opened, closed. His hand was on her veil, lifting it... No, no, not like this, not standing straight and proud like a cedar! Down on her knees with head bent, face hidden, pride bent before him like the stem of a flower! She felt his fingers touching the chaplet of myrtle leaves, resting on her hair.

"It's just as I dreamed it was—only I still couldn't believe it."

He lifted her gently to her feet and, placing his fingers beneath her chin, raised her face, turning it toward the lamplight.

With swift eagerness she devoured his features, eyes critical in spite of their hunger of emotion. Bold, strongly cut, with a shade too much of leanness. Eyes like his father's, keen and darkly probing, overset with heavy, projecting brows. Lips like his, too, but fuller and more mobile. Square chin. Her glance turned briefly calculating. Not easy to sway once he made up his mind. Metal, not clay. A pity if to serve her purpose he must be broken, plunged into fire...Hair jet black and curling.

"Why—it was you who came that night to my tent!"

"Yes. I—had to come. I wanted to be near you."

Jezebel caught her breath. Suppose she had not yielded to that perverse impulse to torture Eshmun! Suppose she had ordered the interloper punished—

"Did you get the little piece of emerald glass I sent?"

"Yes—oh, yes! I have it right here—"

"Was it the right color—like the pillar? The color of wind?"

"Just the right color. But I—" No, she wouldn't tell him. There was no need of his knowing that she had been so stupid.

"What's the matter?" someone called loudly from outside the tent. "What takes the prince so long? We're still waiting to hear how he likes his bride!"

"Perhaps he's trembling so hard," another shouted jovially, "that his fingers can't lift the veil."

Jezebel gave Ahab a little push. "Say something," she whispered. "They will think you—you aren't pleased with me."

He uttered a loud cry in which were mingled in just the right proportions astonishment, delight, and gratitude. Striding to the tent's entrance, he flung aside the curtain. "It is well," he shouted in a voice which must have penetrated to every corner of the palace. "My bride pleases me."

For a brief moment Jezebel saw the stars glittering above Ahab's shoulder. Then the curtain fell. In another moment his arms were about her, and the stars were there once more, quivering, bursting, shivering into dagger points. He was not the stranger, she the goddess Ashtart. He was her husband, and she was just herself, the woman, Jezebel. No, no, not Jezebel—*unhusbanded!* Never again, please Melkart—

With a sudden terrified sense of urgency she lifted her lips to his, pressed herself more deeply within the hard encircling arms. "My lord—"

From this day forward you will have no other lord but Melkart. You understand, my child? You will remember?

It wasn't real, there wasn't any other voice—only his, whispering words of endearment, only her own heart answering soundlessly. *Take me, wear me as a seal, wear me like a ring.* A hard black bruising ring... No, no, that was not what she meant! What was she saying, thinking?

"My lord," she whispered again with a hint of panic in her voice. "My—"

No other lord—no other...

4

When Ahab rose from his couch and, leaving his bride sleeping, slipped out of the tent, dawn was breaking over Tirzah. A few stars still glimmered weakly, like clinging particles at the bottom of a wine bowl long since drained dry. In the courtyard below servants, working by the light of a single fast-wasting lamp, were clearing up the litter of the feast. The scraping of their short brooms and the dull clink of broken pottery were the only sounds which broke the silence.

No—there was another sound, the whisper of bare feet on the stairs leading to the housetop.

"Master?" The stocky figure of one of Omri's aides emerged from the shadows. "My lord the king sent this letter."

Ahab took the flat parcel and dismissed the bearer. As his fingertips traced the design on the broken seal of the leather envelope, he felt swift relief and exultation. Thanks be to Yahweh! The superintendent at the hill of Shamer had written to say that Joseph had complied with the king's command to stop working in the quarries. That must be the message, or Omri would not have taken the pains to send it to him this early. Now this night of fulfillment would be complete.

He had to know. Back in the tent the flame in the shallow saucer was still flickering, but he did not go to it at once. Unable to pass the couch where she was lying, one arm flung carelessly across the cushion where his own head had rested, he stopped and gazed hungrily, then, careful not to wake her, gently lifted a wing of the flowing bronze and let it fall in a cascade over the budding golden breasts. Then he turned toward the lamp, slipped the wooden tablet from its envelope.

The seductively perfumed air became suddenly cloying and unbearable. Rushing from the tent, he cast toward the cushioned couch a look of keen distaste, almost of loathing. To think that while he had been lying there...

Joseph had indeed complied with the king's command to stop working in the quarries. He was at this very moment being returned to Jezreel. On a bier. Crushed to death by one of the foundation stones on which Omri meant to build his kingdom.

PART TWO—SAMARIA

1

Omri had been given seven years, and he had made the most of them. The great hill which he had bought for his new capital towered in arrogant majesty, the city cresting its brow as proudly as the crown which adorned the head of its new young monarch—and, Ahab sometimes had to admit, with greater stability. He was admitting it now to his chief steward Obadiah at their customary morning conference.

"But—" The young king's fingers toyed nervously with a pile of shards. "The district stewards have their instructions. They know that requisitions of wine and oil and grain have been increased by half. Yet the records of receipts show less than the same month a year ago, when my father was alive."

Obadiah's square-cut features were expressionless. "The king speaks truly. His servant should remind him, however, that the stewards and deputies are only collectors. It is the people of the districts who do the paying. And—if they refuse—"

Ahab moved impatiently. "And why do you think *gibborim* have been installed in the key town of each district, if not to enforce the king's commands?"

"The king must forgive his servant," countered Obadiah gravely, "if he was under the mistaken impression that they were there for the protection of the people."

Ahab flushed. Abruptly he lifted a shard of soft brown pottery ornamented with a reddish slip. " ' In the second year,' " he read deliberately, " ' sent from En Nakurah to Gaddiyo, deputy steward of Manasseh District. Two jars of wine. To be credited to Ahzai.' And it should be three jars, not two." He frowned. "En Nakurah! Just across the valley! It's understandable, the people in farther districts rebelling. But for those who live in our very shadow, who have a chance to see Israel's strength—"

"Perhaps," said Obadiah slowly, "that is why they rebel. Because they *do* see."

Ahab looked startled. "What do you mean?"

The flint-gray eyes looked straight into his. "There was a time," said the steward, abruptly shedding his manner of impersonal humility, "when you yourself would have been a greater rebel than any of these." He picked up the shard which Ahab had pushed back into the pile. "Instead of sending two jars, like Ahzai, *you* would have sent none at all."

Ahab sprang from his chair, his swift motion toppling the pile of shards. "Are you daring to imply——" He choked, so angry that he could not speak.

"I am implying nothing, merely reminding the king that the instinct to rebel against oppression is inherent in the very blood and bones of the people of Omri."

"Oppression!" Ahab's features were rigid, "How dare you pronounce the word in the same breath with my father's name? Omri acted always for the honor of Yahweh and in the interest of his people. He saved them from a line of drunken puppet kings, united them under a strong government, built a city which can lift its head proudly with Damascus and Tyre and Thebes."

"The people of Israel have always looked askance at cities," said Obadiah slowly.

"Yes, and you know why, don't you? Because mentally they are still living in tents. If that fanatic Rechab and his followers could have their way, we'd actually be doing it." Eyes narrowing, Ahab leaned across the table. "Is it Rechab and his fanatics who are causing all the trouble?"

The steward looked thoughtful. "No. Rechab and his son Jonadab are naturally opposed to the king's policies, but they don't have much influence on the people."

"Then who is it?"

Obadiah avoided the king's gaze. "I am but the king's steward," he hedged.

As if to further disclaim responsibility, he drew his seal from his girdle, reached into a jar close to his elbow for a bit of moistened clay, and pressed the two firmly together. The impression appeared, deep and clear as if cut by a stylus: *Obadiah, servant of the king.*

"Where is Gaddiyo making his collections today?" demanded Ahab bluntly.

"At—Pirathon, I believe."

"Good. Less than an hour's drive. I shall go there at once."

The steward's fingers closed so tightly over one of the bits of pottery that its jagged edge bit into his palm. "I—would not advise it, my lord."

112

"Why not?" Ahab regarded him sharply.

A small drop of crimson oozed from the tightly closed palm. "I—am concerned for the king's well-being and safety. The men of Pirathon have a reputation—"

"I know. For brute strength and valor. Because they once produced a Benaiah!" Ahab's eyes flashed scorn. "It's time they learned that both David and his mighty men are dead and that another rules in Israel." His voice turned affectionately gruff. "Watch what you're doing, you balky donkey! You've cut yourself!"

2

"Drive more slowly," Ahab told his charioteer. "We're in no hurry."

Once the clatter of wheels and hoofs became muted, other sounds assumed clarity: the plaint of a shepherd's pipe, whirring of wings, the grating of a wooden plowshare on a stony terrace. The sky was a bowl of gold-washed blue, the olives on every slope a mist of silver. Only yesterday, it seemed, the hills had burst into green, as thick-sown with flowers as a clear night with stars. He reached out suddenly and seized the reins, drawing them taut with an impelling urgency. Then as suddenly he remembered. He wanted this springtime to pass. By the time its emeralds faded into duns and grays, please Yahweh, his son would have been born. He thrust the reins back into the hands of the charioteer.

"Pirathon! And be quick about it!"

His mood had changed. Scanning the landscape with a critical eye, he frowned at the sparseness of the barley fields below the little town, the scarcity of blossoms on the freshly pruned vines lining the terraces above. The rains had been poor this year, no latter rains at all. But it was from last season's produce that Gaddiyo was making his collections. There was no excuse for this dereliction.

He frowned too at sight of a cluster of black tents pitched close to a wide-branching sycamore, a company of half-clad *nabis* squatting in meditative posture in its shade. The unmistakable figure of Micaiah in their midst identified them as one of the bands connected with the temple in Samaria. Why, thought Ahab irritably, could they not be content to live decently, like Jezebel's prophets of Melkart, instead of roaming like ne'er-do-wells about the country?

Gaddiyo was in Pirathon. His oxcarts and pack donkeys, drivers and scribes and slaves and *gibborim* had pre-empted the tiny market place. Established on the elders' platform, the deputy was so intent on business that for several moments he remained unaware of the royal chariot's entrance.

"Lying son of a pig! You can't tell me the jars in your storehouses are all empty. Your olive presses were grinding fast enough when I was here last—yes, yours, Nadab, son of Elimelech. I remember seeing those bull shoulders bent to the pole of the millstone. Yet here you bring one measure when the king demands five!"

Nadab planted his bare feet solidly apart. "The *gibbor* will bear witness that my wine and oil casks have been drained and my grain pit is empty."

"Empty as a bone," vouched the burly policeman, "picked clean by the vultures."

The deputy's apoplectic flush turned an even deeper crimson. "By all the gods of every city from Thebes to Hamath! By the Egyptian Bast and Moabite Chemosh and Philistine Baalzebub—" But before the divine roster had been completed his eyes spied the royal chariot and his jaw sagged open. "And his majesty the king of Israel!" he finished lamely.

"You mean," demanded Ahab bluntly, "you think the men of Pirathon have taken their stores of wine and oil and grain to the hills and cached them in caves?"

Gaddiyo found the proximity of kingship even more disturbing than his previous frustration. A city man and by descent a Canaanite, respect for royalty was as deeply ingrained in his flesh as the network of tiny purplish veins which fed his flabby cheeks.

"If the divine lord had but forewarned his miserable servant—"

"Answer me," directed Ahab with curt brevity.

Gaddiyo glanced at his visitor and hastily complied. Yes, and not only the men of Pirathon but those of En Nakurah and all the other towns. There was nothing one could prove. The *gibborim* sent to search confirmed each taxpayer's contention that he could pay a certain proportion of his assessment and no more. And it was usually the same proportion. It was as if the townsmen had agreed on an amount which they considered just, and—

"Who is behind it?" interposed Ahab tersely.

The deputy extended pudgy hands. By all the gods and especially Yahweh, he did not know! At En Nakurah, there had been a band of *nabis* encamped and he had thought of asking them the cause of his misfortune, but when he left the town they had gone.

"If you knew this was happening in other towns," said Ahab, frowning, "you might have sent your *gibborim* ahead."

Ah!—Gaddiyo was triumphant—but he had done just that. There had been *gibborim* watching Pirathon all last night, and not a man had emerged from the gates. But, of course, the deputy pointed out with cautious shrewdness, when citizens rebelled it was not a matter for the police to handle. That was the army's province.

Rebellion! Army! In startled protest Ahab sprang to his feet. For the first time he noticed that the outer rim of the market place was lined solidly with people. Wherever he looked he saw their faces, grim, unsmiling, motionless. Then suddenly there was neither silence nor immobility. The air whined, and Ahab, staggering, fell to his knees, sharp pain piercing his shoulder. A woman screamed. There was a shuffling of feet, a flashing of sunlight on iron blades.

"You Rehoboam!" a voice shouted. "You who add to the yoke your father Omri put upon us! May Yahweh raise up for his people a defender!"

Lifting his head, Ahab could see only clouds of dust, and when the dust had cleared, the market place was empty. The captain of his *gibborim* appeared, leaning on the platform, breathing hard, a thirst for blood in his bold Philistine eyes.

"I sent men after the assailant," he reported with an intimacy inspired by emergency, "but they couldn't find him. However, they were careless enough with our swords to give these dogs a lesson. Shall I order them into the houses and—"

"No!" So violent was the king's prohibition that the captain, startled, let his sword clatter to the stones of the platform. "And next time wait for orders before you turn your sword against a son of Israel."

"Y-yes, your majesty. B-but—does my lord the king wish us to stand by and do nothing when—when his subjects rebel?"

"You'll do what your king commands," stormed Ahab, "no more and no less."

He knew he had acted like a fool. His reaction to the attack was as incomprehensible to himself as to the bewildered *gibbor* and the solicitous but furtively contemptuous deputy, the one a Philistine, the other a Canaanite. He did not deserve to be king. How could he make Israel great and Yahweh a peer of other gods if at a crucial test like this his emotions were those of a sentimental boy? He had actually identified himself more with the men of Pirathon than with their king, understood exactly how they felt standing there in grim silence. And that a Philistine should attempt to silence with the sword a free man of Israel!

But it was still not too late to act. Gaddiyo was right. The suppression of rebellion was the army's province. He would return to Samaria, dispatch a company of a hundred to punish the rebels and make them pay their taxes...seeking first, of course, the approval of Yahweh through the oracle of his priest.

The pain in his shoulder set his raw nerves throbbing with every jolting motion of the chariot. As it descended the hill toward the sycamore the black tents of the *nabis* swam toward him through a nebula of dancing sparks. Then suddenly the bright day went dark...

He awoke to the pungent odor of myrrh and the sound of harps and timbrels. He was lying on a pallet under a goat's-hair canopy, and nearby on the uncarpeted ground a man was squatting. The muted sunlight, slanting through the opening, picked out unmuscular but wiry arms, sensitive features, a shaven head with its forehead puckered into the livid contours of a branding mark.

"Micaiah," he said wonderingly.

The young *nabi* was at his side. "The king is resting more comfortably?"

"Yes. I can scarcely feel the pain. What did you do? Perform some magic?"

"No. Simply dressed the bruise with healing herbs."

The reminder restored Ahab's sense of urgency. "Do you know what happened? The men of Pirathon refused to pay their taxes. They accused me, the defender of Yahweh, of being another Rehoboam! And one of them threw a heavy missile—"

The eyes beneath the branded forehead darkened. "The casting of the missile was an evil thing," returned Micaiah gravely. "It was not the will of Yahweh."

The will of Yahweh! Ahab rose unsteadily. He must hasten to discover and fulfill that will. A pity precious time must be spent in consulting the priest! If he could dispatch the company of a hundred immediately on his return to Samaria, the punishment could be inflicted on Pirathon before sundown. Well—why couldn't he? Were not prophets interpreters of the divine will as well as priests?

An hour later, seated on a square of matting beneath the upraised tent flap, he tried vainly to curb his impatience. He had asked the prophets a simple question: if it was Yahweh's will that he should dispatch the army to punish the people of Pirathon and enforce the new taxation laws; yet instead of shortening the process of putting his plan into execution, they were prolonging it!

His gaze swept the medley of figures, some still leaping frenziedly, some so lost in ecstasy that they lay writhing and foaming at the mouth or prone as dead men...then came to rest on Micaiah, sitting motionless, apart from the other *nabis*, slender, unmuscular body in complete repose. Yet the impression it imparted was of strength rather than of fragility. It was not lack of virility which kept the man Micaiah from joining in the frenzied gyrations of his comrades. Nor was it indifference. In his serene aloofness he was as lost in ecstasy as they. What, then? Had he discovered some even more potent method of ascertaining the divine will than music and dancing and the imbibing of intoxicants?

The moment of climax was approaching. Out of the confused medley of sound and motion rhythm slowly evolved, words became intelligible.

"Hearken, O anointed one!"

"Hear, O heavens and give ear, O earth!"

Ahab settled back on his mat, smiling, the shrill pronouncement already filling his ears. So simple was the formula that he could almost repeat it in advance. Israel was the people of Yahweh. If they did what he wanted, they would prosper. And since increased prosperity depended on increased taxation, it followed that the execution of the latter, by whatever means necessary, would receive divine approval.

But it was Micaiah, not the master *nabi*, who delivered the verdict, and in no fever pitch of ecstasy, but quietly, as one man might speak to another. The smile faded from the king's face. A slow angry flush rose to his cheeks, mounted his high forehead.

"Hear this word which Yahweh the Eternal has put into the mouth of his servant. Let not the king send among my people them that wield the sword. Instead let him lighten the burden of taxation which he has put upon them, let him content himself with only as much as a free people will cheerfully and willingly give. Then only will his kingdom be blessed, and my name will be exalted."

3

"We are here, my lord the king."

Ahab started, glanced about stupidly, and stepped stiffly down from his chariot. He started for the palace entrance, then, changing his mind, walked slowly to the far end of the unfinished courtyard where a huge sunken pool was in process of construction. A lounging foreman sprang to attention, shouted curt commands, coiled his lash hastily about the slow-moving, naked limbs churning a mixture of clay and wood ashes into thick gray plaster. Ahab winced. Was he never to see a workman in a labor levy without remembering that once his grandfather—! Again he turned and walked, this time with unswerving directness, toward the palace entrance.

Deliberately Ahab composed his features, dispelled the worried frown, straightened his shoulders. Perhaps, with her bright dark gaze turned inward toward the son she hoped soon to bear, the queen would not notice this once that something was amiss. At least he could hide from her the monstrous suspicion which as yet he dared not admit even to himself—that the prophets of Yahweh were his enemies, were inciting his people to rebellion!

CHAPTER 2

1

"Aie, aie! My sweet little pigeon, rest gently now. It's all over."
She struggled up through the red sea of pain. Long ago she had lost
all sense of identity, become merged into that essence of suffering
womanhood which had borne almost as many shapes and names as
earth had borne lands and people. She had been Isis roaming the
wastes in search of her dismembered Osiris, Anath weeping for Al
Eyan and Ishtar for Tammuz, Ashtart struggling through the waters
of the swollen Adonis made crimson with the blood of her mutilated
lord.

The red waves parted, bore her gently to the surface. Now again
she was Jezebel, wife of Ahab, queen of Israel, and Jael's voice, softly
crooning, was telling her that at last she had borne her lord a son.

It was time. Seven sons she might have borne him already, and
until today she had given him but one daughter, a small replica of
herself, beautiful as a piece of Mycenaean pottery and as alien to her
environment. This son, please Melkart, would be different.

"Open your eyes, you can't fool Jael. I can see that little smile
playing about your lips. Open your eyes, pigeon, and look at your
first-born son."

Your first-born son. Why did the words flood her with a sudden
paralyzing coldness? With relief she turned her attention to the
swaddled mite in the curve of her arm. Coldness? A warmth such as
she had never known swept over her. There would be no sly
whispers, no eyebrows raised at the appearance of this child. He was
Ahab all over again, the same sharply molded features, high forehead,
strongly arched brows, already penciled with two black determined
strokes, and, clinging to his finely shaped skull, a few tufts of wiry,
curling black hair.

"Look at him, Jael! See how he moves his head already? Though
goodness knows the band is so tight he can't move anything else!
Isn't he beautiful?"

The nurse sniffed. "He'll do well enough. Though, if you take
my advice, you won't do much bragging before the proper sacrifices
are made. I'd better set some incense burning right now in the little

shrine. With your first-born son it's all the more important that no god or goddess is offended. By Ashtart and by all of her holy doves—"

The shrill monotone continued, but Jezebel heard no more. For with Jael's carelessly spoken imprecation the cycle of memory had become complete.

Your first-born son?... I promise... By Ashtart and all her holy doves...

2

But as the days passed and Meribaal gave no sign of remembering, the coldness receded. She began to breathe freely again, to take pleasure in the child.

Ahab's delight in his son was as spontaneous as a child's joy in a new toy, and as extravagant. He had been fond of his daughter, but Athaliah had always been an elusive child, quite the opposite of this tiny miniature of himself who, as soon as the tight swaddling cloths were removed, began waving chubby arms and kicking ecstatically at the first sound of his father's footstep.

Eliah, Ahab decided, his son's name should be. And Jezebel, opening her lips in protest, closed them again. What matter if for the present the child were called "Yahweh-is-God" instead of some name doing honor to her Baal? Easy enough later to change it. This was no time for protest. Better to have the new wall buried in its foundations before removing too many stones from the old!

Besides, during the first weeks and months after her son's birth, Jezebel took pleasure in yielding to Ahab. It was summer, and long days in the cool, upper palace apartment or, after the west wind had risen, beneath silken awnings on the roof, were followed by shorter, even more languorous nights when their cushioned couches were curtained only by the darkness. Nothing, she determined fiercely, should mar the perfection of these days of reawakened ecstasy. Let the new building projects—the extension of Omri's palace, the strengthening of the citadel, even the walls of Melkart's new temple—proceed more slowly for a time if necessary. Let the foreman from Tyre whip the conscripted laborers to greater activity—or less. Yes, even let the audacious peasants evade more and more taxes and go unpunished! This enchantment must not end. She would not let it end. But it did...as abruptly as the splitting of a chip of limestone beneath a stonedresser's mallet.

"The priest Meribaal," announced Eshmun the eunuch, imperturbably.

He was still ageless, as on the day he had taken her hand and led her up the hill. His skin, the color and texture of soft leather, had merely weathered with time into deeper richness. From long habit she remembered that he would never sit on anything so soft as a cushioned chair or divan.

"Bring a square of hard reed matting," she ordered Eshmun with surprising steadiness and, when it came, indicated a spot a good distance away from her chair.

Meribaal deliberately lifted the matting and moved it, so that her features would be clearly visible to his shortsighted gaze. But she noted with relief that his eyes were their usual warm earth-brown, not hard ebony.

"A letter came only today," she began lightly, "from my father Ethbaal. The castings have been made for the bronze pillars and the brazen altar and laver. For months goldsmiths have been fashioning lamps and candlesticks and cups and basins and—"

The priest interrupted the hasty flow of words with a simple gesture. "It is not of these things which I came to speak," he said gently.

Her voice trailed into silence. The trembling of her limbs beneath her mantle of rose-colored linen seemed visibly to set its interwoven threads of gold aquiver.

"Then why—" She forced the words through stiff lips.

"Surely the daughter of Melkart knows why I have come."

The trembling ceased then. She attempted to speak, but no sound came.

"The foundations of Melkart's temple are laid," said the priest calmly, and Jezebel began to breathe again. "Three of the walls are already rising. These blocks of soft limestone weld together so neatly that no mortar is needed, and once they harden scarcely a seam is visible." His dark eyes glowed. "It will be a house like a jewel, carved from one giant tusk of ivory. A pity it could not occupy the highest position on the hill—"

"It will yet," interposed Jezebel swiftly. "Be patient, Meribaal."

"It is Melkart, not I," returned the priest gently, "who is likely to become impatient. For while three walls of his house rise, the fourth is barely begun."

"Why not?" demanded the young queen hotly. "If it's for lack of workmen—"

"It is not for lack of workmen."

"Then why—" Her eyes fell before his steady gaze, returned, fascinated, like a bird to a cleverly laid trap.

"The queen knows why. The fourth is the front wall, containing the threshold of the god's house. Could its foundation be laid without—sacrifice?"

His gaze was still kind and warm, without a trace of anger. *A trap, she thought, need not have iron jaws. A bird can be caught just as surely in meshes of silk.*

"But—that can easily be arranged. A foundation sacrifice should not be hard to find. Why wasn't it done long ago? The new-born infant of a slave girl, or—"

Foolish words! The bird, too, would struggle, flutter its wings...

"The queen knows why I waited."

The priest's voice was gentle as a caress. *He really loves me thought Jezebel wonderingly. It pains him to have to do this to me.*

"I remembered the queen's vow and, knowing that she was with child, waited. And I did well to wait. Would Melkart be content with the poor flesh and bones of a slave, when the first-born son of a king is already his?"

The fluttering became frantic motion then, beating of terror-crazed wings. Didn't he know that if she had spoken such words, she had not meant them? She would do anything that Melkart wanted, anything—

"Except the one thing you have promised him?" reminded the priest quietly.

His eyes were still not angry, neither warm brown nor ebony-black but the bleak dead gray of a winter's dusk. *He too is caught in the trap*, she knew suddenly.

"Suppose I break my vow," she whispered. "What—what will Melkart do?"

The priest's voice turned strangely harsh. "Would to heaven I could tell you! What sort of being is he, this—this king of our city and our destinies? As capricious as his earthly counterparts? Or—is there some pattern in his deeds? And if so, what? Sometimes I think I will go mad if I can't find the answer!"

She stared at him uncomprehendingly. "You—you mean you're telling me what Melkart wants and yet—yet you don't know—?"

"Tell me"—the thin features turned sternly gray—"was there tenderness in the arms you saw lifted above the fire? Was there pity in his brazen visage?"

"No—no!" She lifted swift hands to her face.

"You think your father was permitted to break his vow?" Though her hands still covered her face she could feel the searing sharpness of his leveled finger. "Tell me, have you passed through the fire once—or a thousand times?"

She shuddered. "More than a thousand—"

"Would you condemn your son, then, to such a curse? Would you have him waken to the sunlight of each new day—"

"No, no—I'll keep my promise! I'll do what you say—anything—"

She closed her ears now as well as her eyes, covering them tightly with her hands, dropping to her knees beside the chair and burying her face in its cushions.

"He's—so little," she moaned. "And the stone will—be so cold—"

The priest's hand was gentle on her head.

3

"Don't you wish," asked Ahab softly, "that this night were never to end?"

His fingers, reaching along the parapet, touched hers gently, without passion. Dusk had long since fallen, and, though torches flitted like fireflies on the lower terrace and in the unfinished courtyard far below, up here no lamps had been lighted. None was necessary. The graceful parapet still held warmth and sunlight imprisoned in its whiteness.

"Yes!" she cried with sudden vehemence. "I wish it could last forever."

Ahab drew back, startled, laughed uneasily. "You know I was jesting. What! Never see our son take his first steps, come running to meet us—"

"Don't!" To soften the involuntary sharpness of her cry, she moved closer, laid playful fingers over his lips. Deliberately she pushed back the fillets of twisted gold thread, letting her hair fall loose—a trap artfully, shamelessly sprung to recapture the magic of the precious moments. His fingers reached out, were caught, enmeshed. There was urgency now rather than lightness in his touch.

"It's even more beautiful now than in the sunlight," he murmured, threading it through his fingers, mingling the curling blackness of his own hair and beard with its starlit strands. The moment was theirs again, to hold, to fill to the brim with sweeter ecstasy than they had yet known, to sip from, to drink thirstily, to drain, just as they might desire.

Why, then, should she choose to take it in her hands and crash it into bits?

When she had told him, he drew back so sharply that his fingers, still locked in the strands of her hair, caused her to wince with pain.

"You're—mad!" he whispered. "Or—" He leaned closer, and she felt his eyes raking her features. "No. You're not jesting, are you?"

"No." Now that he had disentangled his fingers, she felt no more pain, only a deep weariness and an aching satisfaction.

"But—you said—our son—you—you wanted to—"

"To give him as a sacrifice of thanksgiving. Is that so strange? Do not your people also make sacrifice to Yahweh of their first fruits?"

"Of our cattle and crops, yes. But—but not—"

"Not of the best. Is that it?"

He sprang up, his face an intense white blur in the starlight. "If Yahweh wanted us to sacrifice our sons, would we withhold them? We give him what he asks."

"What he wants or what he dares to ask?" Now that the moment was shattered, she took a fierce pleasure in trampling the sharp bright bits. "Why aren't you willing to admit that this god of yours is a weakling?"

"Stop!" He lifted his hand, and she thought for a moment that he was going to strike her. "How dare you speak so! What do you know of Yahweh, the Lord of Israel?"

She returned his burning gaze with cool detachment. "Are you sure," she demanded, "that you know him yourself? From all I hear, he's not so different from the other Baals. I've watched your people worship him, and I know. They sing him the same songs, honor him at the same festivals, pour oil on the same stone pillars on the same high places—yes, even practice the same spells to bring him back to life when each year he goes into the realm of death."

"You lie!" exclaimed Ahab hotly. "Yahweh does not die."

She shrugged. "Some of your people think he does. I've seen them each spring, weeping with their hair unbound, planting their Gardens of Adonis."

He was confused, she could see, for he turned from her and, moving to the parapet, stood looking out over the dimly illumined citadel, its outlines pale skeletons among the shadows. Swiftly she pressed her advantage. "You see? You're not sure yourself what he is like. How then can you know what he wants or doesn't want? Men of this country, men of Israel among them, have sacrificed their sons before now. Look in the foundation stones of Megiddo, of Taanach, of Beth-shan—"

He turned on her so swiftly that his motion left her breathless.

"If you do this thing," he spoke with a deadly quietness, "if you harm one hair of the head of our—of my son, I swear by Yahweh you'll go back to Tyre."

After he had gone she drew a long shuddering breath, then laid her head against the stone parapet and wept.

The subject of their quarrel was not mentioned again. Ahab seemed to take it for granted that his command would be obeyed, although there were evidences that he did not trust her entirely. Armed guards were placed outside the child's chamber, and his Tyrian nurse was replaced by a sturdy young woman of Israel.

"Someday he will be king," Ahab explained briefly, "and he must be taught from the beginning the faith and wisdom of his people."

Jezebel made no objection. She knew exactly how he felt. But his precautions were as unnecessary as they were useless. Until she made up her mind what to do about her vow, the son of Ahab was as secure in her protection as during the long months she had borne him, and once she should come to a decision, a dozen nurses and armed guards could not keep her from carrying it out.

Each morning Meribaal appeared outside her apartment, his very presence both an appeal and an accusation, and each morning she sent him a message of dismissal. The work on the temple of Melkart, she knew, was practically suspended. But should she perform the act which would speed its construction, there would be no need of a temple of Melkart in Samaria, for its builder would have returned to Tyre.

At night she was tortured by a recurring dream. She would climb the mountain again by the side of Meribaal, up and up, never arriving...then suddenly she would be standing within the cave, the hot breath of the pit leaping out to enfold her. She would see a woman—herself—emerge from the shadows, place a tiny form in the hands of the waiting priest, who would lift it to the bronze arms. Clearly she would see outlined in the red glow the familiar features, the shining black ringlets! But she could not cry out, could only stand dumbly, watching the arms slowly descend...

"Today," she would tell herself in panic, waking, drenched with sweat, "today I must decide."

But the days of summer passed. The huge double wall of the courtyard grew to twice the height of a man's shoulders. The tax collectors of the Manasseh District coming to pour their stream of wine and oil and grain into the maw of the palace treasury gave place to those of Dor and Naphtali and Asher and Ephraim. The green hills enclosing Samaria turned pale yellow, then a sickly brown. Vineyards came alive on all the rocky slopes. And the son of Ahab and Jezebel learned to clap his hands and to reach with chubby fingers for the curling black strands of his father's beard.

Then there came a day when it became plain to Jezebel what she must do.

4

"If it pleases the son and daughter of him who rides his chariot through the heavens, let this halting tongue describe the picture which this miserable servant of the blessed ones envisions." With eyes half closed, the Tyrian craftsman rocked back and forth. "A room impaneled with cedar and inlaid from floor to ceiling with such poor trinkets of ivory as only these wretched hands can carve..."

Jezebel's eyes gleamed. "I like that. A room all paneled with ivory! I'm sure no other court has anything like it. Our 'ivory room,' we'll call it. No, that's not good. I have it! 'Ahab's ivory palace!' Isn't that a fine idea, Ahab?"

The king started guiltily. "What's that? Oh—yes. It's a splendid idea."

"Let's see your patterns," ordered Jezebel.

The craftsman laid aside his humility like a superfluous garment. The cringing body straightened. The halting tongue sprang into glibness. The wretchedly inept fingers became, by their owner's admission, the world's cleverest, the poor trinkets of ivory in his goatskin bag the greatest masterpieces on earth.

Ahab was moody, restless. Seated close to the parapet on the stone terrace adjoining the queen's apartment, he found his eyes wandering to the small House of Records in the courtyard below, where at this time of day Obadiah would be making an accounting with the district stewards. The queen's request for his presence had been urgent—his "advice required on a matter of grave importance." Urgent! Debating whether the motif of a room's decoration should be palms or sphinxes, when one's kingdom was toppling?

"You may leave us now. I have looked at all the patterns I care to see today."

The wagging jaw gaped. Chagrined, the craftsman, ego again deflated, rewrapped his samples and by a series of prostrations maneuvered himself from their presence. Long fingers nervously tapping the smooth stone of the parapet, Ahab continued to stare down into the courtyard.

"For every ten measures of oil requisitioned," said Jezebel, watching him narrowly, "the people of Manasseh sent five. And now the people of Ephraim send only three. Is that what you are thinking, my husband?"

Ahab started. "How—how did you know? Are you a—sorceress?"

She laughed scornfully. "It doesn't take a sorceress to count the skins of oil and wine unloaded from a donkey train." Rising abruptly, she moved to the parapet, seating herself so close that if he lifted his eyes from the courtyard, her figure must capture his attention. "Well? What are you going to do about it?"

Ahab hedged. There were *gibborim* on duty in each district, he reminded her vaguely, assigned to assist the deputies in their collections.

"Assist!" Her lips curled over the word. "It's hardly the term we would use in Tyre. But—no matter. What orders have they been given?"

Ahab continued to gaze with studied intentness at the courtyard, "To seize the stipulated grain and oil and wine if they were not forthcoming."

"Good. Why, then, three skins of grain and oil and wine instead of ten?"

Because, he explained carefully, in most places they had found none to collect. The people of Ephraim had evidently decided upon concerted resistance to the deputies' demands. Both earthen casks and grain pits had been found empty.

Jezebel moved impatiently, her hands gripping the edge of the parapet behind her. But her voice remained cool and even. The armies of Israel, she trusted, had proven capable of handling such an emergency?

Ahab's lips tightened. "We—haven't sent in the armies—yet," he said firmly. "And the *gibborim* had no orders to lift the sword against the people of Israel."

She laughed aloud. "The men of Ephraim are rebels! What do you keep the army for if not to quell rebellion? And what, pray, are swords for if not to use?"

"To protect with, perhaps," returned Ahab slowly, still avoiding her gaze. "To safeguard the rights of the people."

Her eyes blazed, compelling his gaze to meet hers. "The people! I've heard nothing else since I came to this backward little country. Anybody would think to hear you talk that you thought the king existed merely to benefit and serve the people!"

Ahab's eyes met hers then, steadily. "I suppose it is hard for you to understand us," he said earnestly. "Perhaps it's our desert background and the communal life we used to lead, or—something else, harder to define. We had a leader named Moses. He taught us many things, about Yahweh and about—man."

"What things?" She returned his gaze with the same steady intentness.

At first Ahab spoke slowly, groping for words, then with a loquacity approaching glibness. "Every man is a *baal,* an owner, a master, entitled to Yahweh's free gifts—air, land, water, all the things which make life good—rights which no one, not even a king, can take from him. We are all subject to the law of *mishpat,* justice, and if anyone takes these rights from us, we have a right to rebel, to—" He stopped suddenly, frowning. "I—I wish you wouldn't sit there, so close to the edge. You might fall."

She broke into tender laughter, and, slipping from the parapet, sank to the carpet at Ahab's feet, hugging her knees and grinning up at him with the elfish pleasure of a child. "You don't really believe that," she chided. "You're just repeating things you've been told. You've been listening to that stupid Obadiah again—and the prophets of Yahweh."

"The—" Ahab looked startled. "What do you know of the prophets of Yahweh?"

The copper-brown eyes, just visible above the folded arms, were very bright. "Many things. For one, that they're causing all this trouble about taxation."

He flushed guiltily. "How—how did you know?"

She shrugged. "There are ways. The question is, what shall we do about it?"

"We?" He looked startled again, wary.

"Of course." So suddenly and radiantly did the inspiration come that she was afraid the light of it in her face would be too revealing. Hastily she bent her head and leaned forward, her forehead almost brushing the gold and blue embroidery of his purple tunic. "My lord must know," she murmured, "that his queen shares his dreams for the increase of his kingdom and—and his god. Let him remember the cities I have helped build, the new markets I have labored to secure, the—" She hesitated, then rushed on breathlessly. "Yes, and the children I have borne him for the future glory of Israel—" Sensing the sudden stiffening of his body, she continued softly, "and the child within me which I am yet to bear."

Her intuition had not proved false. She could feel the release of tension in his muscles, the hungry tenderness in the touch of his fingers on her hair.

"Can my lord not see," she continued hastily, "that whatever threatens the fulfillment of his dreams for the kingdom is not only his problem but mine also?"

"Yes. I do see that. But—this is one problem on which you can give me no help. You know nothing of our history, of the way our people think and act."

"I know the way kings should think and act, and that is more important."

"If you were king, what would you do?"

"I don't need to be king," she spoke with sudden directness, "to solve this problem. I can do it quite as well by being queen."

"You—surely you're jesting!"

Lifting her face with a smile half teasing, half challenging, she removed his seal ring and held it toward him in her palm. "Let me keep this for a single night, and I promise you the problem of taxation will be solved."

It was the teasing half of her smile which he preferred to recognize. "And just how do you think you're going to perform this miracle? By issuing an edict?"

"Perhaps."

"But, my dear child, I've already issued half a dozen edicts. One more—"

"You mean," she tried not to let her voice sound too eager, "you'll let me try?"

He picked the ring from her palm and, holding it between thumb and forefinger, regarded it soberly. "This is a dangerous toy for a child."

"I'm not a child."

"Perhaps it could be an even more dangerous tool—for a woman."

Her eyes glimmered up at him through thick lashes. "What time will there be for mischief in a single night if—if my lord is with me?"

He dropped the ring and, with a hunger long unsatisfied, swept her into his arms.

"Forget the taxes," he whispered. "Forget that we quarreled or that I berated you when your only offense was devotion to your god. Forget—everything—"

"Yes—oh, yes!"

Eagerly, joyously she yielded herself, lifted her lips to his in an abandonment of self-surrender...even as she groped in the deep pile of the carpet, searched for the seal ring and found it, closed her soft palm about its hard smooth surface.

CHAPTER 3

1

The moon was well past its full, and at the beginning of the middle watch the open spaces about the western gate were still shrouded in darkness. Nevertheless, the two men moved cautiously, hugging the blank walls with the tenacity of shadows.

"What if the captain of the guard forgot to unlock the postern gate?" whispered the shorter and slighter of the two. "Are you sure of the captain's loyalty?"

"I'm sure of nothing any more," muttered his companion, whose enveloping garments succeeded only in throwing into bolder relief the broad shoulders and unmistakable profile of the king's steward. "Hush! We're close to the market place."

Slowly, scarcely breathing, the two men picked their way among rude shelters of skins and sackcloth, tethered animals, and sleeping human shapes...slipped across the last unsheltered space, now faintly illumined by moonlight, into the darkness of the gate tower. The steward's fingers shook as they encountered, first the hard metal studs on one of the massive wooden portals, then the smoothness of an iron bolt, finally the fastening of the little postern door set in one of the lower panels. When it yielded, he made an almost inaudible exclamation of relief, changing to one of dismay as the door creaked noisily in its socket. The two men waited, frozen into immobility, for a guard's sharp challenge.

"It is well," whispered Obadiah finally. "The captain is our friend." He placed his lips close to the other's ear. "May Yahweh go with you, Micaiah!"

The shorter and slighter of the two figures slipped through the opening, moved swiftly across the space inside the gate, then at a stirring in the shadows stopped warily. The lepers! There were always some of them creeping from their wretched burrows into the shelter of the gate to spend the night. But they were sleeping heavily tonight. Even the creaking of the gate had not awakened them.

He moved less reluctantly now. The long ramp, every span of its inclined surface an easy arrow mark from the guardhouse, offered less hazard than the death trap of the gate tower. Keeping close to the wall, he made his way slowly until he reached the sharp turn; then, in spite of the barrage of moonlight, he moved more swiftly.

So still was it that once he thought he heard the creaking of the little postern gate as Obadiah closed it, and vainly waited, throat swelling painfully, for a shrill scream of warning. The lepers were indeed weary. Like the dogs and the vultures, they had found much to occupy them in the past three days. Even a prophet's poor possessions were meat for scavengers.

Crossing the valley northward, he walked swiftly, blessing instead of cursing the enveloping brightness which edged the nettles of each roadside thorn with silver and clearly outlined every camel's hoof mark in the dust. Leaving the road when it began to wind upward among the hills, he turned aside to a small hamlet, sought out a house at the end of a narrow lane, and knocked on the door.

"Who's there?" called a voice sharply. "Do you come in peace?"

"Hush, Jonas, not so loud! It's I—Micaiah."

The doorpost grated, and a man's face appeared, gray with terror.

"N-not here! Don't try to come in here. There were soldiers here only today—"

"I'm not staying," the prophet assured him quickly. "And no danger will come to you unless you bring it on yourself by your loud speaking. If you are a true servant of Yahweh, then this night you will have a chance to show it."

When Micaiah left the hamlet, his single garment of goat's hair was covered with a linen tunic and a cloak of striped wool, his prophet's brand and tonsure concealed by a large turban. And he rode astride the back of a little donkey.

When he came into the plain of Megiddo, dawn was breaking. Toward the east Gilboa lay crouched like an elongated beast warming itself before a blazing hearth, and on the north the sunlight had already reached the top of Tabor, turning it into a golden crescent. The valley looked less green than usual, for the winter rains were late in coming. Yet after the stony barrenness behind, it seemed a rich paradise, a country in which to relax and draw deep breaths of freedom.

But for Micaiah there was no loitering. Not until the road merged with the great highway crossing the plain from Megiddo did he relax tension, if not speed. To increase his safety, he hastened to overtake a donkey train of wheat growers from Sharon, their bulging sacks bound for some city market—Beth-shan, he hoped—then, keeping somewhat to the rear, adapted his pace to theirs. But at the next junction the Sharon farmers took the northward turn toward Tabor.

As he passed the side road leading up the lower slope of Gilboa toward Jezreel, he saw the gates open, and, to his dismay, a band of *gibborim* came riding out in full uniform, bronze shields and helmets glittering, crimson tunics flashing color.

"Please Yahweh, let them turn toward Tabor, not toward Beth-shan!" prayed Micaiah fervently. What should he say if they were to accost him, demand his business, force him to open the two goatskin bags?

"Remember," Jonas had enjoined, "you are a peasant from Manasseh—no, better make it farther, from Dor. You have heard that your brother in Jabesh-gilead is ailing, and you go to visit him, taking with you two bags of barley."

The *gibborim* did not turn toward Tabor. Before his donkey had taken a hundred paces, he heard the thundering hoofs on the road behind him. Then as he looked ahead where the road wound downward through the valley, his muscles froze. Even from this distance there was no mistaking the sackcloth garments, the unconventional postures. A band of *nabis* was coming up the road from Beth-shan, dancing to the music of pipes and timbrels. Was it possible that they did not *know*?

Let the gibborim stop me, he prayed, *let them ask questions. Let them take much time, that a miracle may take place and the prophets may turn aside...*

But the horses went thundering past, blinding him with clouds of dust. When they cleared and he was able to see again, he found that the path had dipped sharply, shutting off all view of the road. The little donkey was slow, and it was many minutes before he gained the top of the next rise. When he did, he paused, trembling from sheer relief, for, except for a few straggling caravans and some flying red-and-black specks which were the speeding *gibborim,* the road was empty. Thank heaven, his fears had been for nothing! The prophets had not been there—or, if they had, a miracle had happened and Yahweh had saved them. Perhaps the last three days also had been but a figment of his imagination. He would waken presently in the house of his guild back in Samaria, would go with his comrades into the court of the temple for morning sacrifice, after which they would eat their common meal together.

Then suddenly he rounded a turn in the road and saw them. They were lying, just as the *gibborim* had left them, each sackcloth-covered breast thrust through just once, expertly, with a spear, features frozen in intense, incredulous surprise beneath the branded prophet mark on each forehead.

2

"No." The householder of Jabesh-gilead shook his head. "The Man of Yahweh has not been here since the grape harvest. He went away."

"Where?" demanded Micaiah.

The man gestured vaguely. "Who knows? He is here—and then he isn't. But"—his features sharpened in the light of the small oil lamp—"if it is important—"

"It is, it is! A day and two nights have I traveled. Tell me where—"

The man turned wary, withdrew into the darkness of his courtyard.

"How do I know you mean him well? There have been rumors—of course no one believes them!—that there are those who would destroy the prophets of Yahweh."

Micaiah pushed back his turban, and the man groveled. "Have mercy, master. How could I know you were one of the sons of the prophets when—"

Micaiah shook his arm impatiently. "Just tell me where he is."

"You'll not call down a curse? In the name of Yahweh and his consort Anath?"

"In the name of Yahweh," responded Micaiah sternly, "who alone is lord of Israel and who has no consort."

"Aye, just as you say, master," agreed the man hastily. "Though I've worshiped them both side by side plenty of times in the temples of Beth-shan. Yes, yes, I'm going to tell you." He lifted his arm to avert the curse he thought he saw smoldering in the prophet's eye. "Not where he is, I don't know that, but where you can find someone who does know. Go up the river Jabesh to the Vale of Dancing..."

Abel-meholah. A month ago, at harvest time, the pleasant valley would have been alive with color. Now the vines on the hillside terraces were cut back to brown twisted trunks, and the fields below were bare save for a few farmers plowing.

Micaiah pushed wearily on down the steep hill. The man called Shaphat was maddeningly deliberate. Turning his plow over to his son, a sensitive-featured, keen-eyed boy of about ten, he pushed back his headdress, wiped his bald head slowly on one of its three loose corners, then with leisurely pains readjusted it, pulling the black goat's-hair rings well down over his massive forehead. All the time his eyes, sharp as his iron-tipped wooden plowshare and as expressionless, did not move from Micaiah's face.

"You have come to see the Man of Yahweh. You have brought him a message from the king's steward." There was an interminable pause. "He is not here."

"But we know where we can find him, Father." The boy who, goad stick in hand, had been unable to resist prodding the oxen and continuing the furrow, turned his head eagerly. "I can take him—" As the handle of the slender plow flew out of his hand, both words and boy were half buried in a barrage of earth.

"How often have I told you," Shaphat reminded his son absently without turning his head, "that if you once put your hand to a plow you must not look back?"

The boy spat hard and rubbed his eyes. "But I could take him, Father. It's only a few hours up the wadi, and I know—'"

"Quiet," returned Shaphat without raising his voice. "I have not decided."

And to Micaiah's dismay he gave no indication of doing so. Leading the way to his house inside the hilltop town, he set refreshment before his guest, then conducted him to a small room on the housetop.

"You are tired. Lie down and sleep."

"But—"

"When I have decided, I will awaken you."

Micaiah slept. When he awoke, it was as if his eyelids were being pulled apart by some resistless force. The clay lamp beside his bed was lighted, and the big man was standing looking down at him, the sharp eyes compelling his gaze.

"Come," he said.

Micaiah rose and followed him, relief changing to misgiving when his host conducted him down the outside stairway and into a small inner room crowded with men, flickering lamps casting highlights and shadows over their grave bearded faces. Panic filled him. These men of Gilead were different from those on the other side of Jordan—fiercer, less tractable, closer to their desert forebears. It was not danger he feared. It was lack of cooperation. Without the assistance of these stern-visaged men he could not fulfill his mission.

"These are my fellows," said Shaphat in measured tones, "all small landowners—*adonim*—like myself. You have come with a message for the Man of Yahweh. Before we can take you to him, we must know what that message is."

Micaiah looked around at the grim faces, some frankly hostile, others merely unfriendly, only one—that of the sharp-eyed boy crouched in a corner, thin arms hugging his knees—bright with curiosity. How much should he tell them? His orders had been to tell no one his mission except the Man of Yahweh. While he hesitated, a young man with burning eyes and a jutting chin burst into the silence.

"We know what he's come for. Didn't he say the king's steward sent him? And isn't our month for taxation and forced labor close at hand? What could be his mission to the Mahanaim District but to enlist the aid of Elijah in enforcing these new infamous demands? Are you cowards, that you sit here in silence? Have you forgotten your vows?"

The words were hot sparks in tinder. Forgotten! By their heads and beards, no! Three hundred bushels of fine flour and six hundred of meal must the king have each day for his table, together with thirty fatted oxen and a hundred sheep, and so many men for labor that there would be none left to tend the few remaining cattle and till the fields! Was it not because of these very burdens that their fathers had revolted against Solomon? So the stranger had brought a message from the king's steward! Then let him take one back from the men of Gilead. They would not pay the new taxes. They would not increase the number of their sons to serve in the labor levy. And if the king desired to know by whose authority they dared rebel, then let him inquire of the *nabis!* Let him—

All eyes were turned suddenly on the stranger, who had risen from his mat and was now swiftly unwinding his long turban, throwing aside coat and girdle and, with a sound like the grating of a saw against metal, rending his seamless linen tunic from top to bottom. Fascinated, their eyes clung to the white mark branded on his forehead, to the garment of rough goat's hair clothing his angular body.

136

"A *nabi!*" someone whispered in amazement.

"Yes," said Micaiah. "One of those who have encouraged brave men of Israel in rebellion. And I will gladly take your message to Obadiah, the chief steward, or to the king himself, even though there is less than one chance in a hundred that I can reach Samaria alive. But not before I have delivered my own message to the Man of Yahweh—that three days ago a decree was posted, sealed with the king's own seal, that throughout the land the prophets of Yahweh should be hunted down and killed. The *gibborim* are strong and obedient mercenaries. They have done their work well."

They did not believe him at first. A thing like this could happen in other countries—in Tyre, in Damascus, even in neighboring Moab—but not in Israel. They continued to stare, dumbly, until a voice from the corner broke the silence.

"And Yahweh let them? Have the *gibborim* killed Yahweh too?"

It was a child's voice, clear, penetrating, the voice of Elisha, the young son of Shaphat. Like a sharp knife, it ripped their incredulity into shreds. The squatting figures shuddered, moaned, beat their breasts, rocked back and forth on their calloused heels to rhythms as old as human suffering, as ageless as the frustration of injustice.

3

"The eagle leaves its safe eyrie on the high crags and makes for itself a soft nest among the reeds. Shall it fly back, then, on maimed wings to complain to its comrades because the hawker comes?"

Micaiah stirred uneasily under the fierce gaze. He had not yet recovered from his wonder at sight of the black tents clinging like lizards to the sheer side of a cliff in this lonely wadi far up in the headwaters of the river Jabesh.

"Rechabites," Shaphat had explained briefly. "You've heard of them?"

"Yes, of course, but—" How explain that Rechab and his half-fanatic followers had always seemed more legend than reality, that it was obviously fantastic in this modern age for any man to cling to the belief that an Israelite should be a nomad like his fathers, should build no house, sow no seed, plant and own no vineyard? Now, sitting here in the murky dimness of the tent, he was not so sure.

Rechab chuckled, a brittle sound like the crumbling of ancient papyrus. "Crack-brain, am I? Freak? What do you say now, Shaphat, you and your brethren who are smarting under labor conscription and high taxes? Didn't the seer Samuel tell you what would happen if you tried to ape the ways of the heathen city-dwellers whose stone houses and fields and vineyards—yes, and idolatrous high places— you so gleefully appropriated? 'You will cry out,' he warned you, 'on account of the king whom you have chosen, but Yahweh will not answer you.' "

Micaiah shivered.

"And you there, you little spindling Yahweh's man, who have come here whining because your king and his heathen wife have killed all your little comrades! What else did you expect? Will kings in Israel be different from those in Thebes and Damascus and Tyre? You come crying for the punishment of Yahweh, and I tell you, Yahweh will punish, yes, and not just Ahab and his godless wife, but all Israel."

Micaiah's eyes throbbed with pain. "What—do you mean?" he whispered.

"Lift your finger to the winds. Do they not still come from the north, even though it is long past their time of changing? Open your ears toward the paths of the air. Are they not full of the beating of wings? Does the stork returning from her home in the cedars linger in her favorite haunts? Look to the ways of the beasts. Watch their uneasy prowlings. Hearken to the laughter of the jackals. The birds know, the animals know, the earth knows, and even now she cries out in thirst. Only man does not know."

Shaphat gestured impatiently. "We did not come to listen to your curses, master. We came to find Elijah the Jabeshite."

"He has gone up the wadi along the Brook Cherith," volunteered the other occupant of the tent, a man with bony features and a very thick black beard, his hands constantly busy rubbing oil into the seamed surface of an old goatskin bag. "I have sent one of the colony to fetch him."

Again Rechab chuckled. "Aie, aie! Then make ready a tent for him, Jonadab, my son. And prepare for the ceremonies which will make him blood-brother of our clan. After he hears this news, our comrade Elijah will not be leaving us. He has been long enough halting between two opinions, making pilgrimages to Carmel, turning that lank body of his into skin and bones with fasting. He's been there now for a month, up the wadi in a cave, as dead to the world as a tree trunk. Would probably starve if some of my men didn't take him food every morning and night and fill his water skin. And I'll swear by my beard he doesn't know when they come. Most likely thinks it's the birds that have been feeding him. But this will show him."

The black-bearded man turned abruptly. "Show him what?" he demanded.

Rechab directed his gaze full at his son. "That our way is right. That there is no hope for Israel unless she returns to her tents."

"I'm not so sure." Jonadab's voice was stubborn, his moody eyes coldly resistant. "Our way is right, I grant you that. But does that mean we should turn our backs on all who refuse to follow it?"

The fierce old eyes shot sparks. "It is Yahweh, not we, who has turned his back on them."

Micaiah slipped out of the tent unnoticed. He was intensely disturbed. If the old man was right and the news he brought would be the deciding factor in causing Elijah to join the Rechabites, then his mission was doomed to failure. Melkart, not Yahweh, would become god of Israel—and without a struggle.

Unwittingly his feet carried him beyond the cluster of tents, traced a path which zigzagged in sharp V's down the steep hillside, then wound along the edge of a dried stream bed. Though his sandals were worn through, so that his steps left a trail of crimson on the stony ground, he was unconscious of physical pain.

This Man of Yahweh—what did he really know about him beyond the wild tales circulated among the gullible peasants? He had seen him only once, the night he had lain beside Ahab on the housetop in Jezreel and peered down into the courtyard, but Micaiah had sensed then, in spite of his vast strength, a certain timidity in the man. Stern though he was in defense of his ancestral God, would he prefer to retreat into the past rather than face this life-death struggle of the present?

"Then he's a coward," muttered Micaiah, kicking so hard at a stone that his bruised toes sent waves of pain pulsing through his body. "And Yahweh is a little god, less even than the Baals in their stone pillars. If he's like that, he'd better go back to his desert and let the world move on without him."

It was then that, looking up a little wadi, he saw them coming, the man walking with long, swinging strides, the boy leaping with the sure carelessness of a young animal from rock to rock. The boy saw Micaiah and waved.

"I've found him," he cried. "And I've told him what the king did."

"So the prophets of Yahweh are dead. And Melkart will soon be the god of Israel. Is that what you have come to tell me, Micaiah, son of Imlah?"

Micaiah gasped. A moment ago the amazing figure had been at least a hundred yards away. Now it was towering above him. He stole a furtive glance at the long limbs projecting from the sheepskin, half expecting them to reveal the rough hide and sharp hoofs of a mountain goat.

"Yes, my lord Elijah—I—I mean no, my lord Elijah. That is—"

"Yes—no! What kind of answer is that for a prophet of Yahweh? Are all his prophets as uncertain of the mind of Yahweh as of their own? Then no wonder he has washed his hands of you. Why shouldn't he prefer dead tongues to lying ones?"

Micaiah's senses swam and throbbed. The heat of the ovenlike gorge seemed to concentrate itself in the flaming tongues of tawny hair and beard, to leap out at him from the blazing eyes. Then they slowly steadied, and, after his first startled confusion, he faced the shriveling gaze without flinching.

"The prophets of Yahweh are dead, yes," he said with dignity, "but not all of them. That is why my answer was both yes and no. For this is the message from Obadiah, the king's steward. 'Say to my lord Elijah that I have hidden away a hundred of the prophets of Yahweh, placing fifty together in a cave, and am feeding them with bread and water from the king's table.'"

To Micaiah's dismay it was Elijah now who appeared uncertain. "Obadiah is a brave man," he admitted grudgingly. "But—why should he send such a message to me? In warning? But I belong to none of your guilds and have nothing to fear. In an appeal for help? Shall he who has warned others against a raging fire thrust his hand in the flame, to plunk a few foolish brands from the burning?"

Micaiah's dismay mounted to despair. He could almost hear Rechab's hoarse chuckle. *Ha! What did I tell you? Did I not bid my son Jonadab make ready a tent for Elijah? And you, my spindle-legged little city's spawn, had better join him!* Well, why not? What else was left, unless... He drew a long breath and wet his lips.

"Is your Yahweh s-such a little god," he stammered, "that he deserts his people the m-minute they get in—in trouble?"

Again the two fires engulfed him, but he sensed in them a new quality, a concentration of awareness which was like refreshing coolness.

"It is the people always who desert, not Yahweh."

"But—he can't be very big or—or strong."

"Why not?"

"He—" Micaiah gulped. Then a desperate compulsion possessed him, an audacity which brought the words tumbling. "He takes us, so our fathers tell us, out of tents in the desert and brings us into a land of houses and tilled fields, of markets and crowded cities. Then, because life becomes complicated and new problems arise, shall he take to his heels and flee back to his tents? Then he is more of a coward than we, his prophets, and I want none of him. We may as well be killed, for we have nothing to say to this generation. Is your Yahweh like you? Then take your little god and shut yourself up in a smoky tent and draw the covers of the past over your head. As for me, I'll go back to Samaria."

Turning, he stumbled down the stony path, throat swollen almost to bursting, sweat—or was it tears?—blinding his eyes. His muscles ached with intense weariness. Both body and spirit seemed drained of all energy.

He felt as his ancestor Jacob must have felt after wrestling all night with the Eternal. Except that Jacob, according to the old story, had won, had in some strange way compelled divinity to do his bidding. And he, Micaiah, had failed. It had seemed for a moment as if all about him there was a vast holding of breath, as if the future as well as the present were somehow hanging on the issue of his struggle. Absurd, of course. He was such a little, sorry apology for a man, having not the slightest importance in the long scheme of things. There was nothing left for him but to go back, but, if Yahweh was kind, he would not reach Samaria, perhaps not even Jezreel. There must be many bands of *gibborim* abroad today, and there was no longer reason to disguise himself.

A hand like a strong vise fell on his shoulder, transmitting sudden energy which went leaping through his body.

"Come," said the Man of Yahweh. "We will go back together."

CHAPTER 4

1

If he had found her standing, fully clothed and queenly and full of assurance of a deed well done, he might easily have struck her. But she was lying just as he had left her soon after dawn, hair tumbled, eyes dewy with sleep, one golden arm still circling the faint depression where his head had lain.

"You—*you*—" His anger was inarticulate at first, as incapable of release as the tight-locked muscles of his deeply hunched shoulders and knotted fists.

She yawned, stretched her arms, then smiled up at him ruefully. "I know. You've found out what I did—set your seal to an edict ordering all the prophets of Yahweh to be slain. You're angry, of course. I know just how you feel. All right. Go ahead and strike me. Strike us both—me and your unborn child."

Deliberately she threw aside the silken coverlet, exposing the soft gold vulnerableness of her body. Lurching forward, he stood looking down, stormy gaze raking her flesh, the muscles of his arms strained taut like drawn bows. Then slowly his arms fell. Revulsion instead of anger distorted his features.

"You—" he choked. "You—actually went from my arms—"

"Yes." Again she took the words from his mouth. "I slipped out while you were asleep and wrote the edict and sealed it and sent it to the captain of the *gibborim*. Don't you see, my dear—I had to! You would never have done it yourself."

"I—kill the prophets of Yahweh! Are you mad?"

"You see? You would have let them go on spreading their destructive ideas and wrecking your kingdom. Now it's done. The edict has gone out, stamped with the royal seal. Thanks to the laws of the kingdom, nothing you do or say can change it. And the responsibility is all mine. Their blood is on my hands."

Ahab gazed at her in stunned horror. "You—you've made me a thing accursed in Israel! I, servant of Yahweh, *killing his prophets!*"

She lifted herself slowly on her palms. "Not servant of Yahweh. His counterpart upon earth. His equal. Don't you understand yet, my Ahab? You're a king. A king isn't a servant of his god. He *is*—God."

"No! You lie!" Leaning suddenly over the couch, he seized her slender shoulders and, dragging her upright, shook her with all the devastating energy of his suddenly unleashed emotions. "Traitor, deceiver, daughter of ungodly Baals!" The words acquired rhythm with his violence. "Slaying the prophets of the God of Israel! Were justice done, Yahweh would surely strike you dead!"

She did not resist; rather, yielded herself as a pliant reed bends to the fury of a storm, then, when he had flung her back among the cushions, lay ruefully rubbing her reddened shoulders and smiling up at him without rancor.

"Good! I'm glad you did that. Now perhaps you'll begin to see reason."

Arms limp and trembling, Ahab stood staring at the two ugly red thumbmarks scoring the fragile shoulder bones. "Reason—" He choked.

"Of course. Your Yahweh won't strike me dead, my dear, and for a very good reason—because it was for his sake I did it. Can't you understand yet that the prophets were his enemies? They were standing in the way of his kingdom. You admitted that yourself."

"But—" The red marks beat against his consciousness with the rhythm of pounding pulses. "Suppose they were—one doesn't kill..."

She shrugged the dainty, bruised shoulders. "In what other way could they be so effectively silenced? Surely even your tenderhearted Yahweh knows how to deal with his enemies. If you don't believe it, go and ask him."

"What?" His vision steadied into startled awareness. "You—you mean—"

As she slipped from the couch, sheathing her soft vulnerability in an arrow-straight gown of blue metallic silk, her slender body discarded all its languor. Even her hair, bundled into a net of fine gold mesh set with winking emeralds, possessed no warmth or softness, and her copper-brown eyes were as gleaming-hard as jewels in a dagger's hilt. "I mean this," she said sharply. "Go to the temple and inquire of the high priest what is the will of your god. Then condemn me, if you can, for slaying the prophets of Yahweh."

2

As they opened the small packet from the queen, the soft pudgy hands of Melkiah, the high priest of Yahweh, trembled with anticipation. Even his nervous shock over the fate of Yahweh's prophets failed to quench his eagerness. A disturbing business, but, after all, the prophets had been indiscreet, meddling in matters of the kingdom which did not concern them. And—one must admit—their eclipse must presage a strengthening of the power and prestige of the priesthood.

He was not disappointed. The ivory medallion nestling in its bed of purple foam and depicting a handsome Adonis transfixed on a boar's tusk was not only a compliment to his fastidious taste but priceless. It would make a valuable addition to the treasures he—or, rather, Yahweh—had been accumulating in recent years.

"For the defender of Israel's prosperity," read the scrawled bit of papyrus, "And may his life prove as enduring as his inimitable taste."

Smiling, Melkiah passed his sensitive fingers over its surface, relishing its intricate detail, its satin smoothness—frowned as they encountered a rough jag in the spherical edge. Impossible that the queen should not have noticed such a flaw! His flabby cheeks turned suddenly as pale as the ivory. Impossible indeed! Impossible also that it should be there by accident, a tiny V-shaped gouge in the outer rim, undiscernible to the eye but instantly perceptible to exploring, sensitive fingers used to reaching into a leather pouch and shaping themselves to the contours of a black or white stone disk. The queen knew his secret! But how? Even to himself he had never dared admit—! Was she a sorceress that her eyes could penetrate thick leather, discover a tiny V-shaped flaw—

"The king is here!" announced Amnon, the second priest, his thin features nervously twitching. "He's come to inquire the will of Yahweh! Could—could it be about the—the prophets?"

As Melkiah replaced the treasure in its bed of purple foam, again his hands were trembling, but not with anticipation. Crushed in his perspiring palm, the bit of papyrus crackled noisily. *May his life prove as enduring...*

3

The oracle of Yahweh was rendered by Urim, the white stone disk, indicating approval of the killing of the prophets. Ahab was at first stunned, then angrily incredulous; finally he accepted the verdict with bitter resignation. He should have known that the God of this new world-conscious Israel would permit no obstacles to stand in the way of his increasing power and prosperity!

But at least even a docile and obedient king should be permitted to mourn—! Donning sackcloth and covering his body with ashes, he shut himself into his apartment and went without food and water for three days, continuing a rigid regimen of self-discipline and fasting until the customary seven days of mourning had been completed. So gaunt and hollow did his flesh become that when he finally appeared again in the House of Records to hold conference with his steward, even Obadiah's bleak and stony features softened.

"My lord, you have the look of death!"

"Well? And why not? Has not the whole land of Israel become a death's head?"

The steward's face again turned granite-hard. "Yes!" he retorted with unaccustomed boldness. "Impressed there by the king's own seal!"

Grimly Ahab regarded the clay jars and baskets and goatskins which filled the House of Records and spilled out into the great courtyard, leaving scarcely room to reach the low table piled high with shards. "What's the matter? Don't I furnish you with enough slaves to transport this—this booty to the storerooms?"

Obadiah suddenly turned his back. "The—storerooms are also full," he replied in a voice muffled by the folds of his headdress.

"Good!" Ahab picked a shard from the pile. "So it's the Mahanaim District this month. 'Ten casks of wine to be credited to Jered of Tabbath.' Ten demanded and ten paid. Yahweh should be well satisfied."

Obadiah's swift motion sent a pile of shards clattering harshly to the floor. "Yahweh satisfied!" The steely flints burst into hot sparks. "You have the effrontery to blame the Most High for your slaying of his prophets!"

The denunciation awakened in Ahab relief rather than anger. It gave him opportunity to rebuke not only Obadiah but the bitter doubts within himself. "Yes! And why shouldn't I? When Yahweh himself gives his approval—"

Obadiah gasped. "Will the king blaspheme as well as kill?"

"You mean," Ahab retorted with grim triumph, "you doubt the oracle of the high priest?"

"Yes, if he lent approval to this—murder. Like many others in Israel these last ten years, he speaks the will of Melkart rather than that of Yahweh."

Ahab leaned forward, his fingers closing so hard about the bit of shard that his knuckles showed white. "I might have known," he charged bitterly. "Whatever the offense, you'd manage somehow to make *her* the culprit. You've always hated her."

Obadiah's steady gaze did not flinch. "Can't you see what she's doing?" Suddenly his courage leaped all barriers. "Oh, for the love of Yahweh, Ahab, send her back to Tyre before she turns the just God of Israel into a brazen tyrant!"

Ahab sprang to his feet, hand and shard upraised. "In Tyre," he cried hoarsely, "a man could not speak such words to his king and live!" Then he sank back, shuddering, the shard slipping from his fingers. "Heaven help me, my old comrade, I—almost struck you!" Crushing his arms against the heap of broken pottery, he buried his face deep within them. "How can a man know the truth? If Yahweh's own priest cannot be trusted—and his prophets all dead—"

Obadiah rose suddenly, moved to the outer door and closed and bolted it. Returning, he seized Ahab by the shoulder. "Not all," he said succinctly. "Come."

At first, when the iron door of the storehouse cavern grated open, Ahab merely sensed their presence—uneasy shufflings, stench of unwashed bodies, fear. Then vague forms took shape. Dimly he discerned the pale flesh of a shaven head, the scar on a branded forehead. "Prophets of Yahweh," he muttered. "Alive—"

"A hundred," whispered Obadiah. "Fifty here and fifty in the grain storehouse. But I can't hide them here much longer. Her spies are everywhere."

Ahab's eyes glittered with excitement. Even before the iron door had again swung shut, he was outlining the daring plan to Obadiah...

4

Satisfied that Melkart had accepted her sacrifice of the prophets of Yahweh in lieu of her son, for the first time in many months Jezebel felt free again. The wall of Melkart's house was properly reared on the infant son of a slave girl, purchased for a few copper rings and buried, head downward, in a new clay jar. If Ahab, attending the ceremonies by her side, took it for granted that the sealed jar contained the usual Israelite sacrifice of oil and a lighted lamp, she considered it too unimportant to make the correction.

The single flaw in her triumph was Ahab's studied avoidance of her person. At times she detected in his gaze a distaste akin to positive loathing. Tormenting for the moment, but knowing her power over him, she could afford to wait! His constant insistence on her company was born, she knew, not from desire for her presence but from fear lest she discover his secret. It amused her to humor him, as when he insisted that she accompany him on his trip of inspection to Jezreel and Megiddo.

"I need your advice," he explained carefully. "If we're to make Jezreel our summer capital, our palace there should not be much inferior to this one in Samaria. I promise we'll not stay long enough to make your visit boring."

But it was he, not Jezebel, who proved the restless member of the expedition. Jezreel was too full of memories. Even the splendid new palace built on the site of his grandfather's house was haunted by old ghosts. The crackling of thorns beneath a pot of lentils, the smell of Haran's drying herbs, the sight of a dark cavity...

"Some loose stones in the old foundation wall," apologized the contractor profusely. "But it will be sealed as tight as the lining of the king's new bathtub."

Ahab stared into the opening, remembering the day he had dislodged the loose stones and discovered it, had crawled inside and found himself in a rude, rock-lined tunnel which he had explored in fascinated terror to its end, emerging finally from a well-concealed cave on the hillside outside the town wall. Besides Obadiah, whose horror of dark tight passages had kept him from exploring it, Ahab had told only one person of its secret. Rachel.

"Don't seal it," he ordered on a sudden impulse. "Put back the rocks as they were. It—it might make a good cooling niche for wineskins."

It was the encounter with Rachel, however, which brought his visit in Jezreel to an abrupt end. He had gone with Haran to inspect the vineyard hedges and, returning, passed close to the cistern overflowing with sparkling water from the spring, Ain Jalud. She was standing at the top of the steps, earthen jar poised in perfect balance on her head, slender figure attuned like a vibrating harp string to the tumbling beauty of the Valley of Jezreel. And suddenly it was as if the intervening years had never been. He had not gone to Tyre, nor become king, and she was most certainly not the wife of Obadiah. They were just Ahab and Rachel, a son and daughter of Israel

Look at me, he willed silently. But, though he concentrated furiously, she did not turn her head. Almost in a panic, for Haran was moving on and the chattering voices of the women were growing louder, he broke a small branch from a myrtle bush and tossed it lightly at her feet. She did turn then and look at him, unstartled and deliberate, scorning to steady the poised jar even by the tips of her fingers. Changing swiftly from sooty softness to a fiery black, her eyes delivered a verdict far more eloquent than words. *You—killer of Yahweh's prophets! Have you no shame, coming here to turn even your grandfather's house into the symbol of all he most despised? And once I believed I loved you! What do I feel for you now, you ask? Hatred? Contempt? Pity? Sometime, perhaps, but not now. And not hatred either. You can't quite bring yourself to hate one you loved. So that leaves—contempt.*

Then, as deliberately, she turned and looked away again, and Ahab followed Haran up the path. That same day the royal party moved on to Megiddo.

Here also it was Jezebel who was content, Ahab who was pursued by an unflagging restlessness. It was as if the evil spirit of the fever-ridden area had entered his blood, driving him to ceaseless activity. He must do great, and even greater, tasks for Yahweh to atone for the slaying of his prophets. There was no lack of outlet for his energy, for Megiddo, partially destroyed by the Egyptian Shishak some half a century before, was being entirely rebuilt, and Solomon's stables, capable of housing three hundred chariot horses, were in process of restoration.

But still he found the demands too small to consume his unrest. He wanted to burst all boundaries, not only of Megiddo, of Israel. It had become suddenly necessary to prove the superior strength of Israel's God, not only to others but to himself. And how better than to exploit another's weakness? In his eagerness to share his sudden inspiration, he went to Jezebel's apartment in the governor's palace, waiving for once his consistent avoidance of her company.

"Damascus?" Her eyes narrowed. "Are you sure you're in your right mind and not running a fever?"

Impatiently, almost angrily, he drew back from her solicitous touch. "Why shouldn't I go to Damascus? It's time Ben-hadad and I had a conference. Do you think it's fair to Yahweh—his power growing daily by leaps and bounds—yet still we have to pay tribute to a little city state like Damascus?"

"And do you think you can change the situation," she countered scornfully, "by paying its king a visit? Is Ben-hadad likely to wax so generous over a bowl of wine that he will give up advantages won from your father at sword's point?"

"I could bring him gifts—"

"Gifts! What else is the tribute you send him twice each year and in such abundance that your treasure rooms are each time nearly emptied! Go to Damascus, yes, but not now. Wait until you have military strength to make resistance."

Ahab did not agree. Furiously pacing the narrow apartment, he defended his inspiration with both heat and vigor. Was not Ben-hadad still trembling for fear of the Assyrian hordes who not so long ago had come sweeping down almost to his borders? And was not Israel his strongest ally in case such an attack should come again? Surely now the Syrian king would be in a mood to make concessions.

"Could it be"—Jezebel made the suggestion cautiously, bright eyes intent beneath carelessly drooping lashes—"Ashurnasir-apal of Assyria to whom you should be making diplomatic advances, not Ben-hadad?"

Ahab's reaction was both swift and violent. What! Play the traitor to all his Semite neighbors? Run to the enemy behind their backs as—yes, he would say it!—as Ethbaal her father had done, taking them presents and currying favor to get their trade? Counting profit of more value than his people's liberty—

Jezebel shrugged her shoulders. "You're probably right," she agreed with a languid yawn. "You know so much more about these stupid politics than I ever will. Why don't you go on to Damascus as you suggest? But I"—she stretched her arms lazily—"I'm tired of traveling, beloved. Why don't I just stay here, or, better yet, return to Samaria?"

Ahab gave her a startled glance. "I—I believe on second thought," he said slowly, "that you are right. This is not the time to go to Damascus."

When he had gone, she discarded her languid pose and laughed softly. Poor stupid darling, afraid to let her return to Samaria alone for fear she would discover his secret—his and his precious Obadiah's! Did he think she didn't know, had not known all the time? She must tell him of her knowledge soon, set his fears at rest. But not yet. There was still time for him to change his mind and go to Damascus, and a friendly alliance with Ben-hadad by no means accorded with her plans for Israel. Conquest, yes, but not appeasement. If there was to be any running with gifts, it must be to Assyria, not Damascus. For, though she was queen of Israel, she was also daughter of Tyre.

5

Jezebel lifted her hand and with one firm stroke pulled together the curtains of her litter—new curtains, made of the finest Tyrian purple, not like the shoddy draperies which had first screened her vision from the ugliness of this barbaric country. But with the same vigorous gesture she pushed them apart again. Barren and barbaric the country still might be, but she was queen in it, no longer a stranger. As with a scorned jewel come into her reluctant possession, its flaws had become objects, not of contempt, but of fierce shame and challenge. A stony, unterraced hill, an unplowed field, a vineyard grown wild and ragged, a loitering caravan...not a detail escaped her attention. Once she issued a sharp command to her bearers, who set down her litter and summoned to her side a peasant who stood gaping in the door of his stone hovel. He came running eagerly, eyes hopefully agleam above hollow cheeks, grimy fingers clutching the copper rings Ahab had flung him.

"Yahweh give you many sons!" he babbled happily, cupping his hands.

"Fool!" she reprimanded sharply. "Down on your knees, stupid oaf!"

He genuflected hastily, then with some bewilderment and the abrupt assistance of the nearest bearer prostrated himself in the dust.

"Good. Get up now. I wish to question you."

He stood, shoulders bent and head thrust forward, regarding her warily.

"Does that field belong to you?" She indicated a stony plot beside the road.

He muttered something unintelligible, but the motion of his head indicated assent.

"Then why haven't you planted something on it? Here it is only two months to harvest and what do you have? Nothing but weeds and nettles. How do you think you will be able to pay"—she caught herself swiftly—"to feed your family if you're too lazy to even plant a crop?"

He burst into a torrent of gibberish, and, frowning, she turned to one of her bearers. Even after all these years she found it hard to understand the harsh, clipped upland dialect.

"He says," interpreted the bearer with all too willing glibness, "how can he be expected to grow anything with the ground as dry as it was last grape harvest? Can a man set his plow into a block of limestone? It's no use. He will just have to wait until the baal of this place gets ready to send more than a few meager drops of rain. But with a few more copper rings such as the anointed one of Yahweh was gracious enough to throw him, he could buy for his children a few handfuls—"

"Enough!" ordered Jezebel furiously. "Proceed without further dallying. The king's chariot is out of sight already. See that you overtake it."

The bearers obeyed, moving at such an accelerated trot that she bruised her shoulder on one of the cedar columns. When she called sharply to them, they diminished their speed to maddening slowness. In Tyre she would have known well enough how to handle them, A few dozen strokes of the lash—a couple of days in a dungeon... But these men of Israel were different. There was a stiff-necked arrogance about them, even when their lean bodies were bent the lowest. Take that wretched peasant! She might have been an uncouth country wench for all the homage he accorded her. Small satisfaction in humbling a man's body to the dust if all the time an intangible something within him remained stubbornly erect! Still, there was one redeeming feature about the unpleasant episode. The man had acknowledged that it was the "baal of the place" who would send the rain, not Yahweh.

The litter bumped suddenly to the ground. She became abruptly conscious of excited voices and confusion on the road ahead, but, though she pressed her face close to the slender columns, she could see nothing.

"Open the door!" she called loudly. Fools! What do you mean by—" But she was shouting to the empty air.

Her fingers tore at the fastenings. Before she succeeded in loosening them, she had ripped one of the silk curtains and bruised her soft flesh. With hands trembling more from rage than fear she pushed back the sliding door and crawled awkwardly through it, wincing as the sharpness of rough stones penetrated her thin, porpoise-skin sandals.

The royal caravan was in confusion. Ahab's chariot, just ahead of her litter, was empty. Servants were shouting, running, a knot of them clustered like flies about some object on the ground. Jezebel's heart gave a quick lurch. Assassins? Murder would be easy on this lonely road to Samaria, with its sharp turns, its cave-ridden hills. Heedless of the stony ground, she ran forward.

"Ahab! My lord, where are you? Can you hear me? Where—"

Her voice was drowned in the clamor. Even the *gibborim* seemed to have lost their heads, for they were dashing about aimlessly, running along the road, climbing up the rocks, as if in search of something. Moving straight toward the tight cluster, she pushed vigorously with her small fists, pried with her elbows.

"Let me through, imbeciles, or I swear I'll have your heads! Let me—"

Penetrating the tight knot at last, she saw the familiar figure stretched on the ground. Uttering a little cry, she sank on her knees beside it, gathered the beloved head, with its crown of waving black hair, fiercely to her breast.

"Ahab! What have they done to you? Speak to me, open your eyes!"

His eyes did open, but only to stare up at her vacantly. His lips babbled. "Find—man—Yahweh—do anything—remove curse—forgive—"

His flesh, burning through the linen folds above her breasts, spoke more clearly than his lips. She sprang to her feet.

"Fools! Don't you know fever when you see it? While you stand there gaping and running about, your king may die." She uttered clipped commands, punctuating each with a stamp of her foot. "Lay him on the chariot floor. Take cushions from my litter to place beneath him. Call the captain!...Well? Will you obey your queen, or just stand there with your tongues hanging!"

The attendants stirred themselves to belated action, but still confusedly. Even the captain appeared too excited to salute properly.

"Shall—shall I just let him go, your majesty?"

"Let whom go?"

The soldier's mouth fell open. "Her majesty didn't—see him?"

"See whom?"

"Why, the—the—" The captain threw up his hands. *"Him!"*

A half-dozen officers and attendants rushed to explain, all incoherently:

"...wasn't there and then he was...rocks seemed to open...head of a man and body of an animal...at least seven feet tall... No, by Anath, nine!... Eyes like coals of fire...stood there in the road and the horses were turned to stone...scarcely uttered his curse before the king fell down as if dead...was there and then he wasn't...earth swallowed him...looked everywhere..."

Jezebel's eyes narrowed into thin slits. Curtly she gestured them to silence, turned again to the captain with peremptory abruptness. "Divide your company. Send half with us to Samaria under your lieutenant. You stay with the other half and—*find him!*" The words leaped out like two strokes of a lash. "It's a matter of life or death—*your* life or *your* death. You understand?"

A sickly pallor overspread the captain's sunburned skin. "B-but—your majesty—he—he uttered a curse—from Yahweh. The soldiers are afraid—"

"You understand?"

"Y-yes, your majesty."

6

Over and over in the ensuing days Ahab would start up from his couch, eyes fever-glazed and staring.

"It's—you—Man of Yahweh! I know you. You're the—spirit of all the dead prophets—But it—wasn't I that—killed them—helped to save them—a hundred—ask Obadiah—faithful to Yahweh—built him temples—named my children for him. And suppose—their blood is—on my hands—it was for Yahweh's sake—make him greater. He can't do this—to my people—send no rain—don't leave me—wait—"

And over and over Jezebel would gently but firmly press him back against the cushions, then with her cool hands place soothing poultices against his burning flesh. "Hush, beloved! Lie quietly. I'll find him for you."

For long days and nights she did not leave him. But the morning when the fever broke and he fell into his first untroubled sleep, she rose from beside his couch, stretched her deadened limbs, and cast off her gentleness like the garments she dropped when she stepped down into her blue-tiled bathing pool.

"Tell Obadiah to come at once," she ordered with curt abruptness.

She had prepared for the interview as carefully as if the steward were a high-ranking ambassador. Enough regal authority to impress yet not imply that the audience was of great importance. A simple coronet of flat gold disks patterned with small leaves and lotus blossoms; a dress of pure white Sidonian weave, straight cut to make her look tall and slender. And she would receive him standing, here in the central court of the downstairs winter apartment, her back to the entrance, so he must apprise her of his presence.

For ten years she had waited for this opportunity, and she intended to savor it to the full. What satisfaction to make those stonelike features crumple, not all at once, but slowly, as one would chip away the surface of a piece of limestone! She was unprepared therefore when, turning at the whisper of an agitated footstep, she found the steward's square features already contorted with anxiety.

"The king—my lord—is he—"

So identically did his agony of concern mirror her own that she was thrown off guard. "The fever is almost gone," she assured him quickly. "For the first time in days—" Then, remembering, she drew herself up haughtily.

The steward's figure also stiffened, and he bowed with formality. "The wife of King Ahab has commanded the presence of her lord's most loyal servant."

"Of her own servant also," corrected Jezebel swiftly. "But whether loyal or not to the mutual interests of his king and queen, that remains to be seen."

Moving to the far side of the brazier, her white-sheathed figure catching and absorbing all the blues and golds and ochers of the painted walls and striped columns, she extended her hands carelessly to its warmth. She could feel his gaze upon her, hard, warily alert, steady. There was no hurry now. The ten years had been a long time. Their compensating moments must be prolonged to the limit.

"I've been considering the matter of space in the new palace, Obadiah. Queer, isn't it, how one never plans quite enough room, like our having to use part of the great court for the two storehouses for wine and oil receipts! There's another thing we failed to take into account. So silly of me, since I was born in a palace and should know the necessities of a royal court—not like my lord Ahab—"

She paused only long enough to flash him a swift glance and to fit the first of her carefully sharpened darts to the curved bow of her lips. "Imagine our carelessness, Obadiah! We never even thought of a dungeon!"

"A—dungeon, my lady?"

"One does need dungeons, of course, in a palace. So many things are likely to happen. A revolt, perhaps—even disobedience among the servants! Dungeons are indispensable. And we haven't any, Obadiah. What shall we do?"

"I—could not say, my lady. It seems rather late now, does it not, to alter the plans for the palace?"

"Oh, but they don't need altering!" Flashing a bright smile, she drew a whole handful of barbs from her quiver. "Do you know what I've discovered? We have a dungeon already. I found it on the old plans of Omri's palace. It's under the inner court, just to the east of this one where we're now standing—an underground chamber, maybe a cave originally, running back into the solid limestone of the hill. There—are such caves hereabout, are there not, Obadiah?"

If any of the darts had reached its target, the stony features gave no sign. "So I have been told, my lady."

"Then you don't know? What a pity! Because I had been depending on you to help me find this one. There must be an entrance to this chamber somewhere, perhaps in one of those little rooms near the sunken pool." Drawing the two last and sharpest darts from her quiver, she set one of them to her pursed lips. "You're going to help me find that little chamber now, Obadiah."

To her annoyance the steward inclined his body in a perfunctory bow which hid his features. "The queen has only to command her lord's—her servant. But—is she sure it might not be better to wait until the king—"

"Very sure."

"Then—if the queen will excuse me, I shall go and summon servants—"

"No need of that, Obadiah." The last little dart was tipped less with acidity than with sweetness. "I have already summoned some of my own attendants to assist us. They are waiting now outside this court with torches."

Since the pronouncement of the crazed apparition on the road from Megiddo, Jezebel had known what she must do. The prophets of Yahweh were more dangerous even than she had thought. She should have followed her first impulse, exposed the steward's treachery as soon as her spies had reported it, dispatched a band of *gibborim* to destroy the concealed remnant. But she had thought she could afford to be lenient. The peasants of Israel had obviously learned their lesson. So, presumably, had the handful of terrified, half-starved fugitives. Besides, leniency had been the ransom price for restored understanding with Ahab. Now, regretfully, she must relinquish it to the exigency of the moment. She had taken a chance to wait this long. Without the constant vigilance of her private espionage system, headed by Eshmun, she would not have dared to do so. But the *gibborim* had been always close at hand, within a few instants' calling distance. One incautious movement on the part of Obadiah...

The steward's straight back was as stonily enigmatic as his features. He led the way silently as the small procession, the torch-bearing slaves augmented by a half-dozen sturdy *gibborim*, made its way along the unfinished court, past the sunken pool, into the first of the two small chambers. Its carefully cut stone walls revealed no possible opening save a low doorway near the left-hand corner. Passing through this, they entered a second cubicle, empty save for a dozen or more goatskin bags piled in one corner.

Pausing to accustom her eyes to the flickering shadows, Jezebel darted swift glances about the walls. Her muscles tensed, then relaxed. Ah! The door was there, just as she had expected, and in the right place, in the east wall facing the inner court of Omri's palace, its brass studs gleaming in the torchlight like the eyes of a small wary animal.

"Open it," she commanded tersely.

The door grated, exposing a black rectangle of emptiness. Her nostrils quivered at the assaulting odors, partly in distaste, partly with

156

the sensitive alertness of an animal scenting its prey. For there were man-smells mingled with others in its tomblike breath, of that she was sure.

"You see, Obadiah? It's just as I thought. There is an underground chamber."

The stony features remained inscrutable. "The queen is a clever woman. And now that she has found what she was seeking, I trust she is satisfied?"

"Almost, Obadiah. I know it is there, yes. But I must see it with my own eyes."

"I—would not advise it, my lady. The passage is no doubt difficult."

Her eyes danced. "Oh, but I don't mind difficulties. You should know that by this time. And you'll go with me, of course. With my lord's most faithful servant to protect his queen, why should I hesitate to venture into even the deepest of tombs?" She issued sharp commands. "Let two slaves go first to light the way. Then half the *gibborim,* with weapons held in readiness. Then myself, with Obadiah. After us the rest of the *gibborim,* with hands to their sword hilts." Laughing lightly, she shot the steward another quick glance. "You never can tell what you're going to find in the earth's bowels—can you, Obadiah?"

"I—I—" The square features had turned a sickly gray. "If it pleases the queen to let her servant remain outside—"

So abrupt and complete was the change in him that Jezebel found the triumph of it disconcerting. It was to have been a contest won with adroit skill against a worthy adversary, not a coward. Her appraising gaze turned suddenly contemptuous.

"Very well. If you're so frightened at what we might find, remain outside. And I'll leave one of the *gibborim* to protect you."

"It's—not that I am frightened, my lady, just that dark, narrow places—"

"You needn't explain," interposed Jezebel curtly. "Remain outside by all means. I'm sure the *gibborim* can give me adequate protection."

Her triumph had already lost its savor. The procession crawled at a snail's pace through the narrow, sloping tunnel, for the two slaves in the lead were terrified, and without the prodding spears at their bare heels would not have budged. Every sound was magnified and distorted, the slaves' whimpers, the oaths and clicking spears of the *gibborim*, the shuffling footsteps. Jezebel was soon wishing she had merely ordered the occupants of the hiding place slain without investigation. Obadiah's gray terror had been proof enough of their presence.

The tunnel seemed endless. She had not supposed it would be like this...the same choking darkness which had surrounded her that day long ago in the cave, the same stone walls pressing in on either side. In a panic she reached out her hands and found them even closer than she had expected, less than an arm's length.

There was a terrified scream, followed by a sound of falling. One of the *gibborim* swore loudly. Others broke into excited speech.

"Snakes of Anath, look out! There's a sharp drop there."

"Fool! Hold the torch steady. Your comrade isn't dead. He's just fallen and bumped his shins."

"I can feel the floor with my spear. It's a long step, high as a man's waist."

"Down with you, or, by Yahweh, I'll run you through the belly!"

The tunnel came to an abrupt end. Beyond, the two torches flickered feebly in a dark abyss. Jezebel hesitated, but only for an instant. Dropping to the floor, she hung her feet over the edge, explored vainly for a footing, then gingerly let herself down. The floor was solid stone. It took but an instant for its ice-cold dampness to penetrate her thin sandals.

"Slaves!" She was startled by the shattering loudness of her own voice. "Here with your torches! Fools, hold them steady!"

Impatiently she seized one of the torches and, holding it high, peered sharply into the shadows. Moving to the right, she encountered another solid wall of rock, roughly scarped and edged with tool marks. The place was, as she had expected, half natural cave, half rock-cut chamber. And—*it was empty.*

She could not believe it at first, had circuited the space three times to assure herself that there was no deceptive angle or adjoining passage. Had Eshmun and his spies double-crossed her? Had Obadiah been forewarned; had he maneuvered a hasty transfer of his fugitives to some other hiding place? Not too hasty, for the place had been swept clean. Yet they had been here, and recently, of that she was sure. The very air throbbed to the rhythm of tensely beating pulses.

She was still carrying the torch when, minutes later, she stood in the small store-chamber and confronted Obadiah. Hand trembling so that she could not hold it steady, bewilderment turning to fury, she threw caution to the winds. "Where are they? What have you done with them?"

The light, flickering over the steward's stonelike features, struck not a single spark from the flint-gray eyes. "Done with what, my lady?"

"You know what. The prophets of Yahweh whom you hid in this cave. My spies reported every movement you made. Deny it if you can."

"I deny nothing. Why should I? If the queen has proof—"

"Of course I have proof. Weren't you seen only last night by my slave Eshmun entering this chamber with a basket and a goatskin?"

Obadiah bowed gravely. "He may very well have seen me."

Her eyes shot triumph. "Then you *do* admit it!"

"Admit what, my lady?"

She was confident again now, her hand steady on the tapering iron handle. "That you have been harboring enemies of your country, condemned to death."

"No. That I was bringing to the chamber a basket and a goatskin."

She laughed contemptuously. "Proof enough. For what other reason—"

Obadiah pointed to the goatskins neatly stacked to the ceiling in one corner of the chamber. "If the queen looks inside those bags," he said quietly, "she will find grain—wheat and barley—which I have been storing there for the king's household against the famine which is already upon us. It is possible that the slave Eshmun observed me in the act of rendering this service to my master."

"Then why—" But suddenly she realized that he had told her why, and she like a fool had not believed him. It was sickness, not fear of her, which had turned his features gray. And she had pampered him in his weakness, spared him the only torture it had been in her power to administer!

Her first impulse was to fling the torch in his face. Instead she tightened her fingers on the iron handle until the skin strained white above her knuckles. He had won a major battle, yes, but the war between them was not over. She had waited ten years. She could wait another ten if necessary. And it was worth this brief discomfiture, discovering his weakness. This stone giant who refused to blink an eye in the face of her royal power over life and death was actually afraid of the dark!

She laughed lightly. "Thanks, Obadiah. I found exactly what I was looking for. Sometime I'll prove to you that this place will make a perfect—dungeon."

CHAPTER 5

1

The sons and daughters of Israel were puzzled and aghast. What had gone wrong? Had they not performed the same rites, made the same offerings as in other seasons when the rains had been abundant? Indeed, more rites, more offerings, for in the new temple of Yahweh the ceremonies of each feast day became increasingly elaborate, the demands of his priests greater and greater.

Nor had they neglected those Canaanite gods whose sacred stones and wooden posts were still to be found on every high hill in the land. For Samaria with its new temple was far away from most of them, and the two golden bulls, one at Bethel and the other at Dan, while no doubt potent sources of fertility, could be visited at best but once or twice a year. And, besides, how did a man know it was Yahweh who caused his wheat to sprout and not the *Baal* who dwelt in the stone pillar on a neighboring hilltop? Better to take no chances.

That first spring festival after the dwindling of the rains they flung themselves into its observance with feverish abandon. Had they angered Yahweh by the omission of some small detail? Then this time they would rectify the mistake, though they mingled their own blood with the wine filling the round libation cups. Had the dead lord Adonis failed this once to rise again? Then their women would mourn him with a loud voice. They would plant gardens with their precious seed, cause them to sprout quickly, fling them into scant-flowing streams, proclaim their lord risen from the dead! Had the *Baal* who dwelt in the stone pillar grown cold with desire toward his Ashtart who languished in the nearby tree trunk? Ah, then gladly, by sheer power of example, would they reactivate his slumbering emotions. Fiercely, with an urgency born less of desire than of desperation, for the nights of the festival were short, they stretched themselves in his shadow and sought to re-enact the terrible, strange drama of creation.

But it was not so in the second spring, nor in the third. Though they went through the customary motions, they were like puppets wearily propelled by strings. Energy was too scant and precious to be expended in song and laughter. Besides, what was festival without feasting, and of what use the sowing of seed in starved loins, whether of earth or woman, with the fruits of last season's sowings long since turned to dust? Even desire for desire was dead.

Strange, Ahab thought as he looked at his first-born son, Eliah, to see such normal development in a world from which all growth seemed to have fled! In a torture of delight and guilt and apprehension he watched the child change from toddling infant to a sturdy creature who climbed fearlessly to the highest turrets of the palace, whose small feet, unwilling always to remain shod, were never still, and whose lithe body, topped by black curls and clean features amazingly like his father's, might be seen darting about the palace at all hours and in all places, usually shadowed by his adoring but despairing Hebrew nurse Almah, a plump calf in pursuit of a gazelle.

Remembering the children haunting the roadside where his chariot passed, Ahab found in these glimpses of his son more of torture than of delight. If the famine continued and Obadiah's fast-dwindling stores must be still more carefully rationed, would Eliah become one of those scraps of skin and bones? And if they were consumed entirely... He could not face the thought. Surely, no matter how great his anger, Yahweh could not be so cruel.

Yet sometimes it was less the anger of Yahweh which he feared than that of his own people. How long would they endure the sight of well-fed princelings when their own children were dying? Often, looking at his two small sons, he surprised an emotion in himself of bitterness and resentment. It was his fault that his people were suffering. Elijah had told him so. Why, then, should his children be spared and those of his innocent people be permitted to starve? He would even feel a fierce urge to strike the laughter from their eyes and the bright chatter from their lips. Then, conscience-stricken, he would snatch Eliah in his arms, joining in his carefree laughter, burying his face in the black curls, exulting in the energy of the hard, wriggling little body.

He gave no utterance to his fears, indeed scarcely admitted them to himself, until the day when he returned from Jericho.

2

Here, deep in the Jordan Valley, in the lush oasis watered by its ever-living spring, one could almost forget the starved uplands of Israel.

162

Seated on the imposing reviewing stand which had been constructed on a high knoll overlooking the walls of the new city, Ahab looked about him with satisfaction. This laying of the gates of Jericho was the climax in the long series of triumphs which had attended his southern tour. Surely the propitious events of the past days could indicate but one thing—that Yahweh's favor had been restored to Israel. Expansive, almost exuberant in his hopefulness, Ahab leaned toward the man who had made this latest triumph possible,

"A notable achievement, Hiel," he commended heartily.

The wealthy contractor, a Canaanite from the hill stronghold of Bethel up the mountain pass to the northwest, reflected neither the heartiness nor the exuberance. "I have endeavored to do my duty," he responded with the proper deference. The man's transformation puzzled Ahab. In the months since he had commissioned Hiel to rebuild Jericho, the Bethelite had grown drawn and haggard. His untrimmed beard looked like wisps of straw, his skin the color of the leprous mounds lining the Jordan river bed. It must be the heat, Ahab decided. Few types of vegetation thrived in this tropical hotbed. Or could he be still worrying about that old curse he had mentioned when the king had first asked him to undertake the assignment? There was power in the spoken word, yes, but surely no sensible man like Hiel would take seriously an idle threat uttered nearly four centuries ago! Still—he had at first obstinately refused the commission.

"You'll not regret this act of loyalty," Ahab assured him with sudden urgency. "It would have been a crime to let this treasure house remain a mound of refuse, as it has been these four hundred years. Think of it, Hiel! That everlasting fountain spilling its wealth into the sand!"

"Its waters are bitter," replied Hiel tersely.

"Then," retorted Ahab with more gaiety than he had exhibited for months, "keep a set of weights beside your goblet and weigh your gold before you drink of them. For you're going to be a rich man, Hiel. The moment these gates are raised"—he spoke the words on an impulse—"I am appointing you governor of Jericho. Not a caravan will leave this rich valley but you will have your share of it. Now aren't you glad I compelled you to build the city?"

Except for a mumbling which might or might not have been thanks, the contractor was silent. Ahab's perplexity turned into anger.

Any courtier in Samaria would have given his right hand for the opportunity just conferred on him. It would make him rich and assure the future of his three sons, whom Ahab remembered from his trips to Bethel as unusually clever and attractive children. He could even recall their names—Abiram, Haltiel, and Segub—the latter a mischievous lad of five or six with an impish grin which had revealed the lack of two front teeth.

"How—" began Ahab, then stopped, his inquiry for the health of Hiel's sons suppressed behind tight lips. His mounting resentment was the one irritation in an otherwise perfect sequence. His reception in Jerusalem had been that of conqueror rather than visiting monarch. A happy contingency which had driven Jehoshaphat, king of Judah, to seek Ahab's aid in repelling an invasion from Moab and Edom! And, as it turned out, the appeal had been unnecessary, for the invading armies had been ambushed by wild tribes long before reaching the border towns of Judah. But, fortunately, Jehoshaphat's concessions to Israel had already been made, and during Ahab's recent visit the alliance had been further sealed by a contract betrothing Ahab's daughter Athaliah to Jehoshaphat's oldest son, Jehoram.

And this raising of the gates of Jericho was the crowning triumph of all. Ahab refused to let its perfection be marred by the sulkiness of a little Canaanite from Bethel. Deliberately he turned his back on Hiel and directed his full attention to the drama fast approaching its climax, the laying of the final stones into whose deep sockets the huge bronze-plated doors of cedar would be fitted. Already the great stones had been dragged up the ramp and removed from their wooden sledges. An army of slaves stood ready with the hoisting ropes. In the space between the two massive gate towers the throng of workmen was augmented by a group of white-robed *kedeshim* and *kedeshoth* from the temple at Bethel, prepared to celebrate the historic moment in song and dance. Ahab tensed with excitement, his whole being pulsing in anticipation. For three hundred years this lush valley had been waiting for this sleeping mound of earth to waken. *Now* ...

As the anticipated climax failed to come, he frowned. Finally he turned impatiently to Hiel. "Why—"

But there was that in the Bethelite's ravaged features which compelled even a king to silence. Wonderingly he followed the man's tortured gaze, saw the crowd in the gate part, making way for two figures bearing between them the naked, lifeless body of a boy...saw them lower it slowly into the waiting cavity...heard then but did not see, for his eyes were closed in sudden horror, the grating of iron wedges and the straining of ropes, the sharp impact of stone against stone as the great rock slipped into place.

He was conscious of a faint moan, a brief shuddering as of the earth recoiling beneath his feet. Then, as shoulders heaved and ropes strained and the huge, bronze-studded gates were hoisted high, the air burst into shouting and song.

> "Lift up your heads, O gates!
>   and be lifted up, O ancient doors!
>   that the King of Glory may come in!"

> "Who is the King of Glory?"

demanded the *kedeshoth* in ecstatic trebles, and the *kedeshim* replied,

> "Yahweh, strong and mighty,
>   Yahweh, mighty in battle!"

But Ahab's ears were attuned only to the raw harshness as Hiel tore his linen tunic from top to bottom, to the beating of clenched fists against a bared breast and an agonized cry which seemed to rip open the very earth beneath them.

"O Segub, my little one! My son, my son!"

> *"Cursed before the Lord be the man that rises up and*
> *rebuilds this city, Jericho.*
> *At the cost of his first-born shall he lay its foundation,*
> *And at the cost of his youngest son shall he set up its gates?*

The words beat against Ahab's consciousness with the rhythmic pounding of the horses' hoofs on the road up through the Valley of Michmash. The chariot labored through waves of heat, from which even the ascent into the cooler uplands brought no surcease. Nor did the bare bones of a town clinging to a hilltop serve to dissipate his emotions, for Ai—the ruin—was but another reminder of the fabulous Joshua, reputed to have uttered the ancient curse. Was it possible that a few idle words, spoken in the heat of passion, could survive by almost four centuries the lips which uttered them? Or, even if the words had power, was Yahweh the sort of God who would wreak vengeance on the innocent, bearing a petty grudge for four hundred years?

No! Ahab wet his lips, the better to shape his silent disavowal. It was Hiel, not Yahweh, who had fulfilled the ancient curse. Hiel was a Canaanite. It was the custom of his ancestors to make foundation sacrifices, even of their own sons. If he chose to take the old saying seriously, to assure the success of his enterprise after the custom of his people, it was his, not Ahab's responsibility.

"But—I *am* responsible," some stubborn instinct persisted in rejoining silently. "It was I who commissioned Hiel to rebuild the city, I who commanded him after he refused. It was I who rebuilt Jericho, not Hiel. If there was any power in the curse, *it should be my son, not Hiel's...*"

The waves of heat through which the chariot labored turned to sudden coldness. With a swift gesture Ahab seized the reins from the hands of his charioteer.

3

Jezebel, sitting within the lattice projecting from her high square tower, saw his chariot emerge, a twinkling speck, from the cleft in the hills toward Shechem and cross the intervening plain. Ahab himself must be driving, she decided, noting the headlong yet remarkably smooth pace of the splendid Arabian horses. Even at a great distance she could sense the poise of the upreared heads, the superb rhythm of the rippling flanks, and unconsciously her nostrils quivered and distended.

"He's like Melkart, king of the city," she thought exultantly.

For an instant she knew almost complete happiness. Then she remembered that Ahab seldom drove except to seek release from profound disquiet. Had something gone wrong during the visit to his new vassal kingdom? Nothing, she trusted, affecting the betrothal of Athaliah to the young prince of Judah!

Turning slightly, she darted a swift glance at her daughter, head bent dutifully to the task of embroidering a garment of fine white weave. Already, Jezebel noted with satisfaction, the pink breasts beneath the sheer bodice were budding into roundness.

"What are you doing?" she asked suddenly.

"Making a garment for Ashtart."

"And who is Ashtart?"

"She is mother-sister-wife," replied the girl dutifully but without emotion. "She who conceives but does not bear, who is to the Lord Melkart as darkness to light, as wood to fire, as earth to the sprouting seed."

"And who"—though the queen did not raise her voice, the words seemed to leap like a flame between them—"is Melkart?"

The girl lifted her face then, meeting her mother's gaze. Every fiber of her slender body seemed to quiver.

"Melkart," she said with a fierce fervency, "is the sun up in the sky. The moment I wake I run to the lattice to look for his chariot. When he goes away at night I cry and lie down and cover my face. Melkart is the fire which keeps me warm. He's bigger and stronger than Yahweh. Someday the whole world will belong to Melkart. And—listen. Mother!" The girl's voice sank to a whisper, and her small fingers gripped the white cloth as if about to tear it in pieces. "I'm not really making this for Ashtart. I'm only pretending."

Jezebel looked startled. "Of course you're making it for Ashtart."

"No. It's for me I'm making it." The child spoke with a furious intensity. "Ashtart doesn't like the Lord Melkart the way I do. She can't. I—I'd do anything for him. I—I'd burn myself in the fire and let him walk on my ashes. She doesn't like him like that."

"Hush!" warned Jezebel. "Don't let Ashtart hear you say such things."

But as she turned back to the window, there was a smile of satisfaction on her lips. There would be no conflicting loyalties for Athaliah. She would never be torn until her very being seemed riven apart, as was Jezebel now, watching the chariot of Ahab whirl in its cloud of dust across the plain, wondering if this time he would come first to her apartment as he used to do, excitement choking her so she could scarcely breathe. Better, in case he should come, not to seem too eager, to remain here quietly...

But she could not. When the chariot rumbled into the great court, she was leaning over the parapet of one of the lower terraced roofs, her pounding heart keeping pace with the clattering hoofbeats. A half-hundred officers and slaves sprang to their duties, unbuckling the horses and leading them, still aquiver and prancing, to their stables, rolling the light two-wheeled chariot to the great pool at the north end of the courtyard to wash its cedar frame and gold trappings clean of dust, crowding about with basins of water, flasks of cool wine, fresh garments.

Curtly Ahab gestured back the slaves, waved aside Abijah, his keeper of the wardrobe, and strode toward the palace proper—not, Jezebel noted with an even further quickening of her pulses, in the direction of his own quarters but toward the court containing the inner stairway leading to the women's summer apartments. She felt a fierce, sweet exultation. It was again as it had been in the first days of their marriage, when he had been so in haste that he had taken the stairs two at a time...

"Eliah!" The small stairway amplified the sharpness of his voice, sent it echoing through every corner of the palace wing. "Where is my son Eliah?"

When he emerged on the housetop, she turned and faced him, such a fury of jealousy consuming her that she could only cling helplessly to the parapet.

"Here I am, Father! Look! Up here!"

Following the sound of the shrill, piping voice, she lifted her eyes and, drained of all other emotion, was struck dumb again, this time with terror.

"Hush!" muttered Ahab. "Don't make a sound to startle him. I'll go up the inside stairway and come on him gently. Pray Yahweh nothing happens!"

He disappeared, and she began an eternity of waiting, her gaze clinging, horrified, to the tiny figure poised on the parapet edging the topmost terrace, towering at least a score of feet above the next lower court of stone and, beyond the sharp angle less than a yard from where the child stood, plunging sheer to the rock foundations of the palace a good hundred feet below.

"See me, Mother? I'm waving my arms like a bird. On you see me?"

"Yes—yes, darling, I can see you." She knew she must speak, must somehow stop that violent waving with which he was trying to attract her attention, but her voice was a mere croak. *Yahweh protect him*—no, what was she saying!—*Melkart*—no, better perhaps if Melkart did not see him. It might remind him—

"Look, Mother! See how tall I am? I'm a statue!"

"I see. You make a lovely statue. They have to stand very still, you know." *Dear Ashtart, let him keep on being a statue. Let him*—

"No, I don't like being a statue. I like to move. Watch how fast I can move, Mother. Look at me, I'm running!"

Stopping her mouth with her clenched fist to keep from screaming, she watched, agonized, while he ran lightly along the parapet. *Not the corner,* she prayed silently to any gods who might be listening, *don't let him turn the corner!* But he did turn it, hesitating barely an instant, and, still running, disappeared from sight. She closed her eyes then and sank down in a huddle, her forehead pressed hard against the stone, as if, hiding her face, she might not be able to hear his scream. When Ahab turned her gently and placed the child in her lap, her arms were so numb that she could not hold him.

"Did you see me, Mother, how high I was? Father came, and I jumped down into his arms, and he scolded Almah, and now she's crying."

Slowly the life flowed back into her deadened limbs, and with a smothered cry she strained the small wriggling body fiercely to her breast.

"Let me go, Mother. You hurt!"

Later, when in the privacy of her apartment Ahab had told her the reason for his fear-crazed flight from Jericho, it was his head that her arms encircled.

"He's safe now," she comforted. "Nothing is going to happen to our son. And if there was power in the curse, it has already been fulfilled. Hiel has seen to that. Can't I make you understand? He's safe, beloved."

Their lips clung together, first with sweet relief, than with an urgent hunger which they had not known in many months.

"I wouldn't have told you," whispered Ahab, "if I hadn't discovered today that you love him as much as I do."

Suddenly she struggled to free herself from his imprisoning arms. "Blessed Ashtart! Surely you don't think—"

Then as abruptly she ceased to struggle. What difference what he thought? Moments like these were too precious and infrequent to jeopardize with argument. And yet—how blind could a man be? Believing that because she had suggested sacrificing their son to her god, her love for him had been less instead of greater!

CHAPTER 6

1

The famine continued as inexorably as did Ahab's search for the Man of Yahweh. On the terraced hills about Samaria the vines lay strewn among the stones like drying bones, and the wine vats, which should have been echoing to the cheery tread of crimson-stained feet and the rhythmic "Ho, ho, ho!" of the harvesters, were as vacant as eye sockets burned empty by long staring at the sun.

Slowly the dry northwest winds shifted to west and southwest, but there was no moisture in them. The time for plowing came and passed, and the wooden shares hung, gathering dust, on their pegs. Even the Vale of Dancing across the Jordan lay brown and lifeless beside a starved driblet, and in the town on the nearby hilltop the son of Shaphat watched the brooding faces of his neighbors and pondered on their conversation.

"Never in the age of a man has there been such a famine. I was up beyond the camp of the Rechabites looking for grass for my cattle in the wadi where flows the Brook Cherith, and it was dry as a barren woman's breast."

"So? They say that's where the Man of Yahweh went. Did you see—"

"Not a sign. Nothing but a dried-up brook and an empty cave."

"Last week a camel driver from up near Sidon told a queer story about a worker of magic who caused a poor widow's oil cruse to remain ever full and her grain jar never to become empty. His description sounded like Elijah."

"May his lying lips crack with thirst! Think you Elijah would be filling the jars and cruses of strangers when ours, his own neighbors', are empty? You know the tales they tell about him. They all need to be taken with a grain of salt."

"But he must have gone somewhere. And without magic how could he have kept clear all this time of the king's sleuths?"

"Jonadab and his father are right. Israel should never have had a king."

"Aye, aye! Even with this drought we'd be having grain now in our pits if we hadn't had to pay half of it in taxes."

"May Yahweh have mercy and deliver us!"

"Aye, but how? By strengthening the spears and bows of our enemies in Damascus? By raising up a rebel who will kill Ahab and all his—"

"Hush! For Yahweh's sake! The very stones have ears!"

Jezebel was as diligent in the search for the Man of Yahweh as Ahab, but for a different reason. Ahab sought him for purposes of consultation, to discover how the anger of Yahweh could be averted. She wanted to destroy him.

But the search continued to be unsuccessful. *Gibborim* had combed the country. Officials dispatched to each distant court had been permitted to return only after receiving the king's oath that the troublemaker had not been seen within its borders, and these had been followed by spies, to check on the oaths. Jezebel had her own spies operating throughout the realm, as well as in neighboring kingdoms.

When the rumor reached her that the Man of Yahweh had been seen near Sidon, she was furious. But an urgent and indignant message to her father brought no results. Ethbaal was sorry, but he was unable to discover any such person. But if it was the famine which worried her, he could set her fears at rest, for he was preparing a great rain-making ceremony, when he himself would make intercession to the Baal. And if she would see to it that there was a slight increase in the Tyrian imports of oil and wine, together with a slight decrease in price, he would be glad to request the deity to include Israel in his resumption of fertilizing activity.

Though she dashed the small roll of papyrus to the floor and stamped on it angrily, Jezebel's eyes turned, first thoughtful, then shrewdly calculating. If Ethbaal could do it, why not she? And what a triumph for Melkart! If she could only make it sufficiently dramatic, something which would command the vision of all Israel as awesomely as the white crests of Hermon or the bold flank of Carmel...

"I want to do something to help," she said earnestly to Ahab.

"You remember that old altar on Mount Carmel where I sacrificed to Melkart? I would like to go there again with some of my priests and prophets. My people have a rain-making ceremony."

He lifted a harassed face from the wooden tablet he had just received. "You know you have the right to practice your religion as you wish. But—"

Her eyes sharpened. "I see you have a letter—"

"Yes." He seemed relieved to talk about it. "From Nimshi, keeper of the horses in Megiddo. He writes that there is no more forage for the horses. Already ten of the best Arabian chariot steeds have died, and the rest are slowly starving."

"But—we can't let them!" Jezebel's cheeks flamed crimson. "Don't you realize that the nation's security lies in its horses and chariots?"

"Of course I realize it," returned Ahab bitterly. "But what do you expect me to do? Horses eat grass, not cedar furniture and expensive ivories."

"But the first cuttings throughout the realm are requisitioned for the horses," she reminded him sharply, "and some grass grows even in time of famine." She regarded him narrowly. "The first cutting *was* collected as usual?"

He avoided her gaze. "Yes. Or at least as much as could decently be taken. When all a man has between his children and starvation is a little dried grass—"

"Then it wasn't collected. Is it possible that you're trying to tell me a few babes in arms are more important to a nation than her chariots and horses?"

He gave her a strange, half-startled glance. "No. I—I suppose not."

"Then don't act as if they were. How long do you think Benhadad would wait before attacking you—or Mesha—or even your dear brother Jehoshaphat—if they knew you were without defense?"

Ahab rose reluctantly. "I suppose you are right. I—I shall take Obadiah, and we'll search the land from one end to the other for fountains and brooks. Perhaps we can find enough grass to keep the beasts alive. I—I shall summon him at once."

But he did not go immediately to keep his appointment. Instead he stood on an upper balcony staring moodily down into the inner court where his two small sons, Eliah and Ahaziah, were playing, gleefully rolling white marbles in an attempt to knock down a row of tiny ivory pylons. Babes more important than chariots and horses? No. Jezebel was right. Not to a nation slowly but surely increasing in power as its neighbors grew weaker. Not to a God who punished the innocent for the sins of the guilty, who remembered and demanded the fulfillment of an idly spoken curse after four hundred years. *But to a father...*

2

"Think, Meribaal! Can't you see it? A splendid procession of four hundred of Melkart's priests and prophets, all marching in a mighty army to Carmel from Samaria—no, from Jezreel! There won't be a soul in the kingdom left unaware of Melkart's triumph."

The priest watched her broodingly. "And you really believe, my child, that Melkart will listen to the prayers of his priests and prophets and send rain?"

She stopped her nervous pacing only long enough to dart him an impatient glance.

"Why not? Don't tell me you have so little faith in your rain-making ceremonies! But to make sure, we'll choose the very day that my father the king is making supplication in Tyre. Then it can't possibly fail."

There was an edge of anger in her voice now. She was offering both him and his god such power and triumph in a single moment as neither of them could have expected in many years' time, and what emotion was he showing? None at all.

"And you expect me to conduct these ceremonies?"

She stared at him. "Of course. Are you not the high priest?"

"Then I shall be forced to refuse."

Her anger stormed about him with the fury of a tempest beating against a rock. Refuse his queen? Did he know the price of insubordination? She would devise some punishment more devastating than any yet invented. She would—

"Why?" she asked finally with the helplessness of a frustrated child.

"Because," replied Meribaal with infinite patience, "I could not approach my Lord with worthless substitutes, knowing that he is denied the one thing he asks."

Even then she failed to grasp the significance of his words. "You mean you know something more efficacious than the rain ceremony? Then in Ashtart's name tell me!"

"It is you, my child, who should tell me. Surely you have not forgotten."

"Forgotten—what? "

"The vow you made to him long ago and have not yet fulfilled."

She stopped pacing, as if turned suddenly to stone. "You—don't mean—"

"That the famine is a punishment for your broken vow? I mean just that."

"But"—even her lips felt rigid, stonelike—"but—that's impossible. The Lord Melkart was fully satisfied when—when—"

"Was he? It was you, not he, who said he was."

"But—he must have been! See what he has done—given me another son—blessed our nation with prosperity—"

"You call three years of famine prosperity?"

"No—no!" Jezebel clapped her hands over her ears. "I shan't listen to you. I—I shall have you hung head downward in water. I shall have ten skins of oil heated and poured over you!"

The priest's eyes remained the same warm brown, only sightly deeper than the soft wrinkled leather of his skin. "Do with me what you will," he said gently. "Only"—a faint gleam appeared in the earth-brown depths—"unless you are prepared to keep your vow, I would advise you not to make such waste of good oil and water."

As soon as Ahab and Obadiah had set out on their search for forage, Jezebel embarked on a program of furious activity. Her plans completed, private agents were dispatched to all parts of the country. In market place and hostel, around shepherds' and camel drivers' and even bandits' campfires, there were the casually loquacious lips of merchant or muleteer, bard or goatherd or wandering peddler.

"I hear her majesty the queen is going to persuade her Baal to send us rain!"

"Aye. On the Burning Place of Carmel, at the full of the moon."

"Rain or not, by my beard and eyebrows, it will be a spectacle worth seeing!"

"But don't plan to get home the same night. Have you seen the plain of Megiddo after a hard rain? The River Kishon goes mad. You'll be drowned!"

"Ha! Drowned! I'll settle for a full goatskin!"

They came. From the hills of Ephraim and Southern Dan and Benjamin and the coastal regions of Dor. From Naphtali and Issachar and Zebulon, far to the north, and Asher, close to the borders of Tyre. From Ramoth-Gilead and Mahanaim beyond the

Jordan. They came in litters and carriages and oxcarts, riding upon asses and camels, and astride human backs. Mostly walking. For the energy of animals, what few were left, was less expendable than that of human beings.

They came for different reasons, to mock, to pray, to steal or beg food from more frugal fellow pilgrims, to be on hand in case the unexpected happened; but mostly because there was nothing else to do—no fields to plant, no harvests to reap, no grain to grind. It took almost as little energy to drag oneself along a road as to sit brooding in one's empty courtyard or in the doorway of one's house, shivering in a patch of weak sunlight because it seemed better to eat than to burn the little dried grass which was available.

And so they came.

3

Proceeding toward Jezreel ahead of her priests and prophets to meet Ahab in Megiddo, Jezebel saw them coming and felt a surge of triumph, changing to something akin to fear. There were such crowds of them, swarming the road so thickly it was almost impossible for her litter bearers to make headway! And there was something vaguely frightening about the deep-hollowed eyes, the gaunt faces. She rode with the curtains drawn all the way to Megiddo.

Here, since Ahab had not arrived, time hung heavily. One could not continually partake of the governor's cakes and wine, nor stand on the palace roof gazing with nostalgic yearning toward the sea, nor perform constant worship in Solomon's exquisite little temple of Ashtart. In fact, one visit here was enough.

It was a mistake to take Eliah with her. He was frightened by the shrill din of the great bronze sistrum. He objected to the donning of the worshiper's long byssus robe with its clumsy linen stockings, and he wept aloud during the slaying of the victim and the draining of its blood into the cuplike depressions beneath the altar. Worst of all, when at Jezebel's request the priest of Ashtart endeavored to place on the young prince's black curls the head of the slaughtered animal, he screamed in terror and rushed into the inner temple where the gold image of the goddess sat enthroned above her sphinx-carved altar, the fiery gem at her forehead shining like a monstrous eye in the darkness.

"A bad sign." The priest shook his head solemnly. "It will take much spilling of blood to placate the goddess. And not, I fear, the blood of sheep and goats."

The child was still sobbing when they returned to the governor's palace. "W-why did you let that old man put that—that thing on my head?"

She explained it to him sternly, her arms, yearning to comfort, hugged stiffly against her breast. "It's ourselves we should really be giving the goddess as a sacrifice, but she accepts the sheep in our place—that is, unless we do something to make her angry, as you did tonight."

He planted his small feet stubbornly apart. "I don't care if she is angry. She can't hurt me. Yahweh won't let her. And—I'm never going to that hateful temple again."

She was less furious than frightened. The impulse which had prompted her to bring the child on the journey seemed suddenly the compulsion of an inexorable purpose. Had the simple instinct to assure his safety by keeping him beneath her own protection sprung from some deeper and darker urgency?

The small palace suite became unbearable. After a sleepless night and hours of pacing, the rows of bronzed pillars supporting the encircling balcony throbbed against her aching eyes. Wherever she turned, the child was there, above him a brazen figure towering accusingly. She must escape or go mad. But where? Into the lime-paved inner courtyard and up the stairway to the flat roofs of the soldier's barracks? But Eliah would be sure to follow. He loved high places, and it would be so easy... In a panic she fled in the opposite direction, down the outside staircase to the great central courtyard, where on the tiled floor in a secluded angle a group of the governor's officers were tossing dice. They started up guiltily.

"Y-your majesty! Is—is there anything the queen desires? A s-slave to bring wine or sweetmeats? Her l-litter—"

"No. I've been drowned in wine and buried in sweets. And where would I go in a litter? Where is there to go in this reeking, fever-ridden town except—" Her eyes gleamed. "Yes. I shall visit the stables. Have Nimshi, the keeper of the horses, summoned. And—and tell him to bring with him his little grandson. The one called Jehu."

4

From the moment she stepped into the lime-plastered passage leading to the rows of stalls, Jezebel felt swift excitement and release. And the boy at her side was her kin, as was no other human being she had ever encountered. Even their physical reflexes appeared to flow in unison: the upflung head and dilating nostrils, the cocking of ears at each whinnying challenge, the way their fingers curved caressingly before reaching out to touch the glossy flank of a horse.

Jehu was no longer the child she remembered from previous visits. The fierce scowl, the shock of straight black hair, were still there, but the chubby child's body had lengthened into a close-knit blending of lean flesh and hard muscles, almost as tall as herself, whose nearness she found at times oddly disturbing.

"You should see Midnight and Stormcloud," he said eagerly, in total disregard of his grandfather's signals. "They're colts and— something to dream about. That is, they would be if they weren't half starving. Grandfather let me name them."

Nimshi bent almost double in his effort to distract the queen's attention. "Her majesty must forgive my grandson's boldness. He is still hardly more than a child," he quavered, missing entirely the smile of secret amusement they exchanged over his bent head.

"We will go to see them," said Jezebel. "Now. This minute."

Jehu was right. The two colts were—or could be—something to dream about. From silken manes to prancing feet they were black as midnight, except for a white patch the size of a man's palm on Stormcloud's forehead. They were the softness of velvet, the richness of ebony, the smooth swiftness of quicksilver. The sight of their hollowed bellies and protruding bones was almost more than she could bear.

Utterly fearless, the youth moved about in their stall, slipping their halters from the holes in the corners of the two stone pillars and fastening them about his bony brown wrists. His dark eyes challenged hers across the glossy flanks.

"Come inside! They won't hurt you if you're not afraid."

"No, oh, no!" groaned Nimshi. "May Yahweh have mercy on us!"

With not an instant's hesitation she went inside the stall. Again Jehu was right. Because she was not afraid, she knew there was no danger. The sharp hoofs pranced harmlessly without touching her soft sandals. Feeling a gust of hot breath on her neck, a slippery tongue tickling her cheek, she laughed aloud.

"They're beautiful, Jehu," she cried aloud, mourning, "Oh, what shall we do! We can't let them die!"

When her hand, stroking one of the hollowed flanks, touched his, she did not draw away but let her own close over it, startled to feel a pulsing warmth flow from it through her finger tips. But it gave no response to her quick, involuntary pressure, and presently he withdrew it deliberately from her grasp.

"They're not going to die. Yahweh won't let them." He spoke with an intensity akin to the fierceness of his scowl. "I'm going to drive them. And when I do, when I'm standing in the chariot with the reins in my hands, there'll be nothing on earth can stop me. I'll be like—"

His voice, starting with manlike vigor, took a ridiculous upward thrust. But Jezebel did not laugh. "You'll be like Melkart riding the waves," she said, "with a bow in one hand and the reins of a flying sea horse in the other."

"No." The simple negative was as deliberate as the withdrawal of his hand. "I won't be like Melkart. If I'm like any god, I'll be like Yahweh."

She wanted suddenly to hurt him, to break the web of kinship which had bound them so subtly together. "Perhaps you will drive them," she said clearly. "But only if your lord, the king, permits you."

Their eyes met in sudden bold antagonism which, strangely enough, seemed only to intensify their kinship. "I shall drive them," he repeated stubbornly.

Emerging from the stall, Jezebel drew from her bosom a small clay image of Ashtart. "Here," she told the boy casually. "A token of your queen's favor."

He took the little image, his fingers shaping themselves slowly to its seductive curves...stood holding it while she watched him, a tiny smile hovering behind her lips. Then suddenly he raised it high and dashed it to the stone floor.

"No! I won't take it. I'll have nothing to do with it. I—I wish I hadn't shown you the old horses. Go away, why can't you, and leave me alone!"

Turning with a choking sob, the boy ran precipitately from the stable.

The horrified Nimshi was rendered almost inarticulate. "Heaven protect—" he mumbled, fairly groveling at her feet. "Fairest of earth—forgive—"

Jezebel cast him a brief contemptuous glance. "Driveling coward!" she thought absently. "Probably thinks I'm going to order his head struck off."

Well—and why didn't she? She should be consumed with fury, racking her brains to think of some fit punishment for a boy's unforgivable audacity. But instead she stood looking after him, her whole being athrill to his very defiance, while on the stones at her feet the severed head of Ashtart lay vacantly smiling.

CHAPTER 7

1

"What's this I hear?" So disturbed was Ahab that he did not wait to bathe and take refreshment before coming to the women's suite. "The report is all over the kingdom that Baal Melkart is to end the famine on the day of the full moon! And half of Israel is swarming to Carmel. The road from Beth-shan was alive with pilgrims."

"Was it?" Jezebel came at once to greet him, concern softening the contours of her perfectly chiseled features. "My dear, what a journey you must have had! And they say you found no forage for the horses! Come, sit here among the cushions, and I'll order fresh wine and fig cakes. And warm your eyes as well as your feet at this brazier. See—it's shaped like an altar and carved with little cherub heads. Much too fine a piece for the palace of a little governor!"

But Ahab would not be diverted. "It was Yahweh who sent the drought," he interrupted hotly. "How then can it be Melkart who removes it?"

Jezebel shrugged her slim shoulders, their golden curves glimmering beneath her gossamer-fine Tyrian purple robe. "My ancestors, remember," she replied composedly, "have prevailed on the Baals of this land to send them rain for many centuries."

"And what if you fail?" Ahab's eyes blazed in his haggard face. "What will you do then with all these hordes whose false hopes you've raised?"

"Why—" For the first time Jezebel felt a hint of misgiving. Returning to the brazier, she idly touched the tip of her finger to the head of a smiling cherub, then, finding it hot, withdrew it with a sharp exclamation.

"Have you ever seen a mob hungry and desperate?" he persisted harshly. "Do you think they'll just return quietly to their homes, with food still being hoarded in the royal storehouses, with the person who raised their false hopes riding past them in a cushioned litter?"

Coming close, he towered above her, the smell of his dusty and sweat-soiled garments shamelessly invading the delicately perfumed aura about her. Wrinkling her nose slightly, she withdrew to the other side of the brazier, lifted the smarting finger and let her trembling lips close about it.

"I'll take the chance," she said lightly.

* * *

They were in the banquet hall when the news came.

Jedediah, the governor, had bidden all the city elders to a great feast in honor of the king and queen. Secret caches of fine flour and imported wine had been reluctantly produced, the best remaining lambs and bullocks of the protesting peasants requisitioned. Frivolity lay on the surface like a brittle crust, beneath which flowed dark, ungauged depths into which no man quite dared to look. But so thin and brittle was the crust that when Ahab, on receipt of a secret message, started from his couch, face pale with excitement, it splintered into bits. So sudden and complete was the silence that the king's low response, intended for the messenger alone, penetrated to every corner of the banquet hall.

"Returned? You say he's seen—! Then in Yahweh's name tell him—"

The voice dropped abruptly. Immediately Ahab rose and left the room.

The mood of frivolity did not return. The guests ate and drank and conversed but with an air of strain and urgency, muting their voices and casting uneasy sidelong glances at one another. Jezebel thought she would go mad with waiting. As soon as she could do so gracefully she left the hall and went straight to Ahab's apartment. He was not there. An attendant was folding the king's hastily discarded festive garments, but he could tell her nothing.

Hurrying to her own chamber, she found that, too, empty. All was in order, a fire burning in the brazier. The little cherub heads were tantalizing in their indifference. Where were Jael and Tanath? She opened her lips to call sharply, then, conscious of a slight noise, closed them again.

Swiftly she crossed the room to the adjoining chamber where Eliah presumably lay sleeping, and froze in unbelieving horror. A dark cloaked figure was bending over the couch, its upraised hands casting a grotesque and sinister shadow on the wall above the child's head. Its curved fingers seemed to close about her own throat. She heard herself scream.

The figure turned swiftly, the light from the open lamp full on his face.

"Oh! It's you!" She wept aloud in relief. "Blessed be Ashtart! I thought—"

She stopped just in time, unwilling to admit even to herself that first horrifying suspicion that he was an instrument of her own dark conjuring, willed into being to fulfill a fatality from which there was no escape.

"I was giving him my blessing before leaving, after the custom of my people."

The room slowly steadied. She saw the child's nurse Almah sitting among the shadows, eyes glued in doglike devotion to the sleeping figure, a twisted end of her headdress clutched in the outflung fingers.

"What do you mean—leaving? And why these clothes? No wonder I mistook you for a marauder. You're dressed like an odorous sheepherder."

Ahab tried to be evasive. It was nothing, he said. Merely an official matter requiring his attention.

"Nothing? When you leave a banquet hall in haste and depart on a journey in disguise in the middle of the night?"

With persistence she discovered the truth. A message had come from Obadiah. Er—no, his chief steward had been no more successful than he in finding provender for the horses. The land was as bare of good forage as a leper's skin of hair. But—he had found something—

"Yes?" In another moment, Jezebel thought, she would scream.

"The Man of Yahweh," blurted the king.

"Ah! I—see." Her mind moved with lightning swiftness. Strange that after three years of scouring every rabbit hutch, every rathole in the kingdom, he should appear now of his own accord! And on the very eve of her triumph! Disconcerting? Dangerous? Or—excitingly challenging? "You know where he is?"

"I—" His eyes were wary. "I know where I can find Obadiah."

"Then go to him. At once. Make him take you to the man's hiding place. If you wait an instant, he may be gone again."

His relief was instant and complete, "That's what I plan to do. The messenger is waiting for me now, outside the palace. It's all arranged so I can slip out by a secret exit. If the people knew, there would be a furore."

"Wait!" Her voice intercepted him sharply. "I shall go with you."

"But—"

182

She was beside him, fingers gripping his arm. "Can't you see? I must go. This concerns me too. And in the darkness no one need know who I am, not even Obadiah. They'll think I'm just a servant."

She had her way. When Ahab emerged from the palace by the secret exit, she slipped after him like a shadow. Soft slenderness swathed in a voluminous cloak, bright hair bundled into a turban, she might have been any nondescript peasant lad dogging the steps of an equally nondescript companion.

2

"And when I saw him there in the path ahead of me, I fell on my face, so startled was I. 'Are you really my lord Elijah?' I asked him. And he said, 'I am. Go, Obadiah, tell your lord that Elijah is here.' "

"And then?" prompted Ahab in a cautiously lowered voice.

He isn't sure he wants me to hear all this, thought Jezebel, digging the heel of her sandal into her donkey's lean flank to urge the plodding beast closer.

"I said to him, 'How have I sinned, that you would deliver me into the hand of my lord Ahab, to slay me! Is there a nation anywhere in the world where he hasn't sent messengers to hunt for you, not even taking their word when they said, "He is not there!" but requiring an oath of them as well? And now you say to me, "Go tell your lord that Elijah is here!" Suppose I do so and then you disappear, the way you have a habit of doing, and when Ahab comes to look for you, he does not find you. Then he will slay me!' "

"Fool!" Ahab's guarded voice was chiding. "You know I would do no such thing."

"Do I? How can a man of Israel be sure any longer how his king will act?"

Jezebel frowned. Had a steward spoken such words in Tyre—! She dug her heel so hard into the small beast's flank that it squealed with pain.

" 'Have I not served Yahweh all my life?' I said to him. 'Was it not told my lord what I did when Jezebel the queen slew the prophets, how I hid a hundred—' "

"Sst!" Ahab hissed, to Jezebel's amusement. "Remember my— my slave!"

She pulled hard on the reins, so that when he cast a surreptitious glance behind, she was well out of earshot. She had heard all that was necessary. They could tell her nothing new about the salvaged prophets who, she was as well aware as they, were scattered harmlessly through the country, cowering and silent, telltale brands hidden beneath peasants' rags.

The sudden awareness of blackness ahead and sloping earth beneath brought that swift panic which always came when a hill loomed unexpectedly. They were climbing straight up the side of a mountain. Which one? Carmel? Tabor? One of the slopes of Gilboa? She tried desperately to remember which way they had turned on leaving Megiddo, but she had noticed only the pale thread of the path in the moonlight. What a fool she had been! Here they were proceeding to a rendezvous with a man they had been hunting desperately for three years—a dangerous enemy—and not an armed soldier or *gibbor* within miles! She should have put Eshmun on the trail of the two men with a small band of soldiers, then, having discovered the man's hiding place, ordered his swift capture. But it was too late now.

The path became so steep and rough that the two men dismounted, and with relief she followed suit, thankful for the toughness of the cowhide sandals which she had appropriated from one of her slaves along with the cloak.

"Are you all right, boy?" Ahab asked once solicitously, and she muttered a gruff assent.

The path burrowed through a thicket of myrtle and carob and juniper, and both sky and moonlight abruptly disappeared. Snatching at something to steady her, she felt a branch give way in her hands. Attempting to hasten, she stumbled over a root and fell to her knees, then, finding she could feel the path better with her hands, continued up the steep incline in a half-crouching position, eyes closed and body tensed against the invisible reaching fingers.

She forgot the presence of the men ahead. It was the same as on that other day when she had mounted the hill beside Meribaal...yet not the same. For this time she knew where and why she was going. And there was no hand to hold. If there had been, she could not have grasped it, for, to keep her burden secure, she must hold her left hand tightly to her breast and with her right feel her way along the path, testing each stone to see if it offered solid hold.

The burden seemed hard and unyielding, yet she knew if she touched it she would feel the softness of a baby's silken hair and the warmth of human flesh. Athaliah? Eliah? Ahaziah? She could have told by feeling. The little girl's skin had been smooth, like rose petals. And Ahaziah's short tufts were straight instead of curly like Eliah's. But it did not matter. All which mattered was that the burden was there and that she would not have long to hold it.

Emerging from the thicket, she was not surprised to see the dark entrance of a cave outlined by the red glow of a fire. Yet the scene was not as she remembered it. There was no white-robed priest. And the brazen figure which towered in the background... He was tall, yes, just as she remembered, and there was the same sternness in the chiseled, firelit features, but... Surely the brazen Melkart had not worn so long a beard, nor a great sheepskin.

"Is that you, oh, you ruination of Israel?"

With the sound of Ahab's voice, harsh and bitter yet filled somehow with a child's aggrieved plaintiveness, she was abruptly restored to the present. She smiled to herself, partly from sheer relief, more because of the revealing tone of Ahab's question. Who did he think this Man of Yahweh was? A doting nurse who, as soon as he started to cry, would fix his little kingdom and hand it back to him as good as new? Even she, hating and despising him as she did, knew better. One did not go to meet a lion with the curved stick used for bagging crows. She was almost exultant when the stern voice whipped through the darkness.

"It is not I who have been the ruin of Israel, but you and your family, by forsaking the Eternal and following Baal."

The words cut through the languor of the night like the cry of a wild beast stalking its kill, and within Jezebel, crouching outside the circle of firelight, some primordial instinct responded to the challenge. Her pulses quickened. Tides of energy came pounding, wave upon wave, through her veins, and she waited in an agony of impatience for Ahab to move boldly forward and answer the ringing challenge.

"My father!" Falling on his knees, the king spoke with the humility of a slave addressing his master. "Thanks be to Yahweh, I have found you! Tell me, I pray, what I must do. Tell me—"

At Obadiah's sharp exclamation he lifted his head, turned it in the direction of the steward's gaze, and was stricken speechless.

She moved forward into the circle of light with the consummate grace of an animal sure of its strength and exulting in it. The tentacles of the thicket had pulled back her turban and loosened the tawny mane of hair. Her eyes gleamed like yellow flames. Even the shapeless cloak could not hide the fluid rhythm, the splendid leashed energy of the slim body. She was like a creature of the jungle which, after a lifetime of being tamed and stroked and petted, comes suddenly face to face with one of its own kind.

If the statuesque figure commanding the center of the circle noted the addition to his audience, he gave no sign. His stern gaze remained fixed upon Ahab.

"What must you do? This. Send now and gather all Israel to me at Mount Carmel, with the four hundred and fifty prophets of Baal who eat at Jezebel's table. I will meet them there on the day of the full moon."

Jezebel gasped. That this vagabond should issue orders to his king, speak of his queen as if she were a peasant wench—these were bitter enough insults! But that he should deliberately seize upon her plan of gathering her prophets at Carmel and attempt to appropriate it to his own ends! She turned fiercely on Ahab.

"Tell him"—she choked. "Tell him—"

But she could see by the king's face that he would tell him nothing. Nothing, that is, except a beggarly acquiescence. He was groveling at the feet of this unlettered mountebank. Very well! She did not need his help or want it. Eyes shining, nostrils dilated, she wheeled to face her antagonist.

"*You!*" She spat out the word in a fury. "You dare to summon my prophets—"

But the space where the tall figure had stood was empty.

"He has gone," said Obadiah impassively. "I have looked in the cave and all about the hillside. It is no use searching further."

"You mean you actually explored the cave? *You?*" Jezebel could not resist the bitter jibe. "How far? To the entrance of its first dark passage?"

"It has no passages," returned the steward without emotion.

Jezebel clamped her lips tightly. She must not let him know how infuriating she found his stubborn calmness. Turning to the space just beyond the fire, her eyes scored Ahab's sleeping figure. Lying beneath Obadiah's cloak, one arm flung toward the warmth, he looked as secure from worry as his son Eliah. Trusting that now he had found his precious Man of Yahweh, all his troubles were ended!

The steward, stooped to lay more fuel on the fire. "We must remain here until morning. If the daughter of Melkart wishes to rest—"

"I wish nothing," she retorted curtly, "except to find that—that dirty sheepherder who was here but a few minutes ago."

The fire flared, throwing into bold relief the stonelike features. "If the queen refers to the Man of Yahweh, she knows both where and when she may find him."

She fell into the trap. "Where? When?"

"On the slopes of Carmel. On the day of the full moon."

She forgot her restraint then. "You think I'd let him interfere with my plans or claim for your miserable little Yahweh any share of Melkart's triumph?"

"Could it be"—the slate-gray eyes were suddenly aglow—"that the queen fears our Yahweh so greatly that she dares not match the skill of her Melkart against him?"

"No! May the vultures eat your flesh through all eternity, how dare you suggest such a thing!"

"Then why—?"

Why, indeed? Her foot ceased its nervous tapping. What a fool she had been! Spurning the very tool which would insure the success of her plan! For how could there be contest without a striving of rivals, or conquest without an antagonist to suffer defeat? She should bless the Man of Yahweh instead of cursing him.

"You are right. I have nothing to fear. We will meet your little champion, I and my prophets of Baal, on the day of the full moon on the slopes of Carmel."

The steward's face remained inscrutable. "Since the wife of my lord will not rest, at least let his servant relieve her of her burden."

Only then did Jezebel look down, to see that her left arm was crooked about a small dead branch of juniper. She gazed at it for a moment with horrified fascination, then, slowly loosing her hold, let it fall into the fire.

CHAPTER 8

1

But Jezebel was not with her prophets at Carmel on the day of the full moon.

When she lay down on her couch the preceding night, every preparation had been made. Her new purple gown with its cloth-of-gold overdress hung over a high-backed chair directly beyond the lamp stand, so that when she half closed her eyes, its threads caught the gleam of the flame and danced and quivered as if shot through with fire. A swift camel train had been ordered to the palace gate at dawn, capable of conveying her the twenty miles from Jezreel to Carmel almost before the elaborate rites should be initiated.

Ahab, as well as her priests and prophets, had made the journey on the preceding day. Seeing the long chain of his caravan, the jeweled pendant of his chariot, swinging on the plain's withered breast, she had known a moment of fierce jealousy that he had not invited her to ride with him. A pity that on this eve of her greatest triumph they must be rivals! But it would be his triumph too. She would make it so. Once he had seen the power of Melkart and acknowledged his supremacy, there would be no more barriers between them. They would ride back together side by side.

"Don't stay in my chamber tonight," she said suddenly to Jael, who was, as usual, fussing interminably over her covers.

"But—suppose the beloved of Ashtart wishes something?"

"The beloved of Ashtart will wish nothing."

"Then suppose—someone comes—"

"Who could possibly come, Jael!" Jezebel was amazed at her own patience. "I merely said I—I want to be alone." To her further surprise her voice rose on a note of hysteria. "*Alone!* Do you understand?"

"Yes, yes, of course Jael understands." The crooning accents soothed, the stumpy fingers patted, but the black eyes remained stubborn. "She will lie on her mat beyond the threshold and make sure her lamb sleeps as sweetly and safely as Eliah."

"Eliah!" Jezebel started up from her couch. "Why shouldn't he be safe?"

"It was your safety I was talking about."

"Then why did you mention Eliah?"

"But I didn't. I mean I did, but—Oh, by Anath, how did this start!"

"Go, Jael, into the adjoining chamber and see if Eliah is safe and well."

"But—why shouldn't he—"

"I said—*go!*"

"Merciful Ashtart, all right!" The nurse sniffed. "But I don't see—!"

She was back promptly, still sniffing, a silver goblet in her hand. "There! All that fuss for nothing. Sleeping as sweetly as a closed lotus bud, and his nurse wide awake beside him. Here! I've brought you a little wine and a potion."

"A—potion?" Jezebel's eyes were wide and bright.

"Here in this silk bag. It's a powder I bought from a sorceress in Tyre. There's enough to make one sleep without dreams through two night watches."

After the nurse had gone, Jezebel fingered the little bag of purple silk. Untying it, she held it poised over the wine, then slowly retied it and thrust it into her bosom. Still slowly, she sipped the crimson liquid until the goblet was empty.

She awoke—or did she dream?—to see the figure standing not far from her couch, face lost in the shadows, brazen contours reflecting the glow of the pit of fire which must lie somewhere beneath.

"So you have come."

She did not speak the words, did not hear them, yet they were there, as finished a reality as if she had shouted them; just as the reply was there also.

You knew I would come sometime—have always known.

"What—do you want?"

You know that too.

"I—I don't know what you mean."

Then why did you take the potion and hide it away unopened?

"It—it was just a foolish impulse."

You did it because you knew you could postpone your duty no longer.

"That isn't true. You're forgetting all I've done—that tomorrow is to be your day of triumph!"

If tomorrow is to be a day of triumph, you must make it so.

"No—no!" She struggled then, blindly. Without realizing that she had left the couch yet conscious of hard tiles beneath her bare feet, she thrust her hands over the blazing pit, pounded furiously at the brazen figure, then, finding it amazingly yielding, tore at it with her fingernails. The fire from the pit rose higher and higher, licked hungrily at her hands, and still she struggled... But it was no use. It was like beating a rock, tearing at a smothering cloud of sand...

"Your new robe! Merciful Ashtart, it looks as if a wild beast had clawed it!"

"Does it?" asked Jezebel without emotion.

At the same time Jael uttered an anguished cry. "Blessed mother and sister of the god! What has my lamb done to her hands!"

Jezebel contemplated them impersonally. So they were the cause of the agonizing pain. "I must have walked in my sleep and held them too close to the lamp."

She suffered Jael's duckings and anointings without comment.

Only when the tender ministrations were finished did she say abruptly, "I shall not be going to Carmel today."

"Not going—! But—"

"Don't look so shocked. My priests and prophets can manage quite as well without me. And ask no questions. I've merely changed my mind, that's all."

Now that it had become plain what she must do, there was no more indecision. To Jael's extreme vexation she insisted on donning the vestments she had once worn as a priestess of Melkart.

"B-but—why? You're in Jezreel—have you forgotten?—not Samaria. There's no temple here yet. The foundation's barely laid. And besides, I'm not sure we brought that coarse old robe and those ugly linen stockings."

But she located them finally at the bottom of the wardrobe chest and, still sputtering, draped the coarse folds about the oiled and scented body.

"The day you were going to wear cloth-of-gold and a crown on your head! And instead you look like one of the temple underlings who kill the goats for sacrifice!"

Without tasting food, Jezebel went immediately to the highest terrace where the palace was still in process of construction. Nowhere were the walls of what was to be the top story ready for the roof beams. None of the courses was complete, those in one wall ending with headers, those in another with stretchers, so that they mounted one upon the other in a series of stairs. Huge bossed blocks of limestone were strewn over the area, and the floor was littered with dust and chips. Not a workman was in sight. Such dereliction of duty, normally a stimulus to swift disciplinary action, today elicited only a cursory glance of approval.

She took time to look across the plain to Carmel, focused her eyes on a small area of the wooded slope close to the jutting northern rim of hills, and frowned. The rain-making ceremony should have begun at dawn. Surely she should be able to see the smoke of the morning sacrifice from this distance! What had gone wrong? Had the old altar again needed repairing? Yahweh's would, she had seen to that!

Summoning an attendant, she issued two brisk commands. A mounted *gibbor* with six runners was to be dispatched immediately to Carmel, there to observe proceedings and bring news to Jezreel each hour. Second, a place was to be cleared here on the terrace and suitably furnished to contain the royal presence.

Scarcely had she made one circuit of the terrace when she heard the gates clang below; and by the time she had finished the second, the dust of the horses bearing the *gibbor* and the six runners was leaving a trail across the plain. But by then sweepers, furniture movers, and other menials had converted the eastern end of the terrace into pandemonium, so she made no more circuits. Instead, resting her elbows on one of the flat stretchers in the unfinished southern wall, she peered over the edge and down into the stone courtyard far below, where the foundations of the new temple of Melkart were still scarcely above floor level.

For an instant her heart lurched sickeningly, and she clung to the stones for support. Then her pulses steadied.

"Bring Eliah to me," she ordered the sullen Tanath, "with his nurse. Tell her the fresh air up here will be good for him."

The child was radiant, bursting with energy and excitement. He adored his mother, and to be summoned to her presence in the middle of the day was an unexpected privilege. But he eyed the white garment with distaste and, when she would have drawn him with sudden fierce affection into her arms, he held back.

"Eliah doesn't like dress. Scratches. And your face looks hard when you wear it, not soft like flowers. Tomorrow, when you have other dress on, you hold Eliah."

Eluding her grasp, he circled in a wider and wider orbit, bouncing on the cushions of her couch, tasting the fruit and sweetmeats on the loaded tray, holding up the silver wine goblets to see them sparkle in the sun; finally venturing farther afield to hoist himself to one after another of the strewn slabs of limestone.

"Look, Mother! Look, Almah! I'm a gazelle! See how I can jump!"

"Careful," warned the nurse, dogging the small figure like a too bulky shadow.

"Catch me!" he teased gleefully. "You're a wolf, Almah, and I'm a gazelle."

He led her a merry chase, jumping from one to another of the stone slabs with the sure-footed grace of the animal he aped, but finally she brought him back and dropped him, squealing with delight, among the cushions. Jezebel, negligently holding a brimming goblet, turned suddenly to the breathless and disheveled nurse.

"Here, Almah," she offered smilingly. "You need this wine more than I do."

The young woman gasped, her plain face flushing more deeply from this unprecedented favor than from all her strenuous exertion.

"I want some too, Almah. I'm thirsty. Let me drink first."

"No!" So sharp was Jezebel's protest that both child and nurse, about to share the cup, turned in startled amazement, and some of the wine spilled on the floor. "Not that cup," she continued lightly. "That's Almah's. But you shall have more than just a taste. You shall have a little goblet all your own."

She filled it herself from the tall silver ewer and held it to his lips, her bandaged hands as steady as the tiles of inlaid marble on which her feet rested, and almost as stone-cold...then poured another goblet for herself and drained it.

The child smacked his lips. "It's good. I like it. Will it make me strong, Mother, like Father? Now that I can drink a whole cup, am I almost a man?"

She must have gulped her own wine too fast, for suddenly she choked. "Yes, darling, you—you'll never be my baby any more."

She tried to catch him in her arms, but he was off again. Carefully she replaced her goblet beside the ewer, then fixed her gaze thoughtfully on the nurse...saw the plain features relax and the eyelids droop.

"Don't go to sleep, Almah," she admonished her. "It's your business to watch the child." She yawned deliberately. "I feel a bit sleepy myself. You will watch him, won't you, Almah? I can trust you?"

The girl's eyes flew open, dazed and startled. "Yes, oh—yes—I'll—watch—" She made an agonized attempt to stir herself.

"Almah!"

This time the sharp appeal elicited not even a flutter of the lashes. Jezebel cast a swift glance about the terrace, looked up once at the high watchtower and noted that no guard was in evidence. Then she leaned back and waited.

Later...a moment?...an hour?...she turned her head just enough to see the small agile figure boost itself up the side of one of the huge stretchers in a lower course of the southern wall, balance for a precarious second on its stomach, then slowly but surely pull itself to the top, scamper along its surface, take a running leap for the one next higher, boost itself... Yes, she had counted on his choosing the south wall, where the steps of the unfinished courses rose higher, mounted more steeply, ended in a long ledge of smoothly dressed stone broken abruptly in the center to make room for a lattice. Strange, how well she knew exactly where and when his impulses would lead him, as if he were still part of her flesh!

After another eternity she turned her head again. He was almost at the top now, pulling himself up over the last huge stretcher...No, this time he didn't quite reach it. He must run back and try again. His steps seemed a little less steady. The fever of the strong wine had entered his limbs. With his second attempt her own muscles ached and strained, and she clenched her fists so hard that the long nails bit through the bandages, but she was conscious of no pain.

There! He had pulled himself up at last, was squatted on the top of the stretcher, nursing his knees. Poor lamb, he must have scraped them on the rock! She wished she were close enough to see if they were bleeding. Her mind functioned automatically, as if unrelated to the hard coldness which was her body, and suddenly she felt a wild desire to laugh. *She was worried because he had scraped his knees, had scraped—*

When he reached the break in the long straight ledge where the deep rectangle had been left for the lattice, she was standing beneath, eyes sharply calculating each movement of the agile little body. So well did she understand his every instinct that when he turned and ran back, bare feet pattering on the smooth stone, she knew that it was not in retreat from the unexpected barrier, only in preparation for its conquest. She even knew that he would be too intent on gaining his objective to look down and notice her presence.

"Mother! Look at me!" he called shrilly without turning his head. "Watch me jump! I'm going to fly like a bird!"

He ran lightly along the ledge, poised for an instant on the edge of the deep rectangle, gauging the distance across it. *Now!*

"Look out!" she screamed sharply. "Don't jump or you'll fall! For the sake of Melkart—"

Already in the act of springing, the small figure wavered, swayed for an instant, then, without a cry, only a wild startled motion of its arms, disappeared.

"For the sake of Melkart!" she repeated over and over, her voice rising to higher and higher notes of shrillness. "For the sake of Melkart, for the sake of—"

Then finally the words ceased, and there was only the sound of a scream. Her own? Please Melkart, no! Had not Meribaal said there must be no crying out, or the god would be angry and reject the offering? She strained to hold her breath, gripped her throat chokingly to quench the sound... Then it too ceased, and there was only silence...blessed blackness...emptiness...

She was conscious first of a painful throbbing in her hands, followed by an agonized awareness, as of dead limbs slowly awakening. Then sound penetrated her ears, shouts and screams, that shrill wailing peculiar to women in the presence of death. She opened her eyes, looked up at a vacant rectangle between two empty walls of stone.

As memory functioned she closed them again, tried desperately to plunge once more into the flood tide of unconsciousness, but again and again she was drawn back to the surface by some inexorable compulsion. Finally she ceased struggling and in obedience to its imperative struggled up out of the abyss, set her knees on the hard tiles of the floor, lifted herself...

Crossing the terrace with steps which became increasingly decisive, she grasped the sleeping nurse by the shoulder and shook her violently. "Almah! Wake up! How dare you go to sleep! And where is the child? You promised—wake up, I say!"

As the slouched figure remained inert, Jezebel's efforts became more and more frantic. Enough for two night watches, Jael had said, but she had emptied only a small part of the little packet of powder into the goblet!

The nurse stirred at last, opened dazed eyes.

"Where is he, Almah? What have you done with him? You promised to watch him, and here I find you asleep!"

"I—I—Where am I—the child—"

"Yes, where is he? I doze on my couch and awaken to find him gone, and you lying here asleep. You promised to watch him, Almah. I trusted you. What have you done with him—my son, my son—"

She kept repeating the phrase, unable to stop, though her purpose was now fully accomplished. The girl was running about the terrace frantically calling and searching, wringing her hands, loudly proclaiming that if anything had happened to her precious lamb, it was her fault, and would Yahweh have mercy on her!

"My son, my son, my—"

Perhaps Jezebel would have kept repeating the words interminably if she had not suddenly noticed the maid Tanath just inside the arch leading to the inner stairway. She was standing very still, as if she might have been there a long time, and there was a look of bright-eyed, intent awareness on her face.

2

It was over at last. She had done all that Melkart could possibly require. Her first-born son? She had given him. The sacrifice of herself? That too. For in the hours of this day she had died, was still dying, not one death, but a thousand.

Nor could she, like her son, enjoy the compensations—inactivity, sleep, oblivion. First there were the small unfinished details: the message to Ahab at his encampment below Carmel, informing him of his son's accidental death, due to negligence of his nurse; the order that the child's body be placed beneath the foundation stones of the new temple of Melkart, on whose threshold he had fallen-, the brief, enigmatic dispatch to Meribaal in Samaria: *Promise fulfilled at last. Pray Melkart to end drought.* And, of course, the maid Tanath.

"Perhaps you can help me," she told the woman earnestly. "You see, I'd like to know exactly what happened. You were standing there on the edge of the terrace. You must have seen the whole thing. *Did you?*"

The maid gasped, her pale cheeks flushed. "Oh, no, your majesty, I didn't. I—I'd only just come to the terrace when—when you—began to shake Almah by the shoulder. I—By Anath, I didn't see a thing!"

"You—seem very sure." Jezebel's eyes bored through their lashes. "Why do you hate me so?" she asked the maid curiously.

Tanath gasped again, and for an instant her blazing eyes were nakedly revealing. "I—Surely the beloved of the gods doesn't know what she is saying. How could her servants feel anything but"—she choked—"but love—"

Jezebel regarded the woman with a new interest, tinged almost with respect. *She does hate me,* she thought with no emotion other than amazement. *I wonder why.*

"How would you like to return to Tyre?" she asked bluntly.

"No—please!" The maid was on her knees, pleading, the color again flaming high in her cheeks. "I'll do anything. Only let me stay here with—"

"With whom?"

"With—you, my mistress."

Jezebel studied the flushed face. "Very well," she said finally. "You shall stay. Unless," she added significantly, "I find reason to question your loyalty."

It was foolish. The woman should be returned to Tyre—or rendered even more inarticulate. But if she sent her away, she might never discover why—or who...

She did not weep. Time enough for tears when the day's cycle should be complete...a whole lifetime. She took off the coarse garments, donned the regal robe of purple and cloth-of-gold which, when properly draped and covered with its embroidered girdle, did not show the torn places too badly; added an elaborate frontlet of gold and a high crown set with emeralds. For she had finished her duties as priestess and was about to mount beside the lord Melkart to his throne of conquest. She went up again to the housetop—not the highest terrace—turned her face toward the distant slope of Carmel, sat down, and waited.

The first of the six runners returned soon after midday.

"Well? Are you as slow of speech as of limb? I watched you run. A child chasing a butterfly could do better."

"May the—beloved of the gods—forgive—"

"Enough. Save your breath. And if you would save your head at the same time, don't keep me waiting. What is happening on Carmel?"

The messenger, breath partially regained, was voluble but vague.

"Yes, yes, of course there are crowds. Do you think I'm a fool that I don't know that? What are my prophets doing? Have they started the rain-making ceremony?"

The ceremony? Why, yes, the messenger supposed they must have started it. When he left, they were all doing their limping dance about the altar. That is, he supposed they were doing it. He hadn't really noticed—

"Hadn't—!" Impatience rendered her almost inarticulate. "Then in the name of Melkart what had you been noticing?"

The messenger was nervous now as well as breathless. Why, he—he supposed, like everybody else, he had been looking at the Yahweh-man, listening to him—

"Ah!" Jezebel's voice was smooth and soft as silk, sheathing silk, hiding a sharp blade. "And how did the Yahweh-man look? What did he say?"

Deceived by the smoothness and softness, the man waxed eloquent. How could anyone help looking at the Yahweh-man? Like the mountain he was, and his voice like thunder.

"Yes? And what did he say with this voice that was like thunder? Did you hear?"

Even then the messenger sensed only the silk. Of course he had heard. Loud enough it had been to carry even to the camp on the plain, or to the high crag above where the king sat watching. How long, it had demanded, would the people go limping along between two gods? That was the very word the Yahweh-man had used—"limping," and that was how he knew the prophets must have already been doing their dance. If Yahweh was their god, they should follow him, but if Baal Melkart...

Here the messenger may have sensed the blade's cutting edge, for he hesitated, paled, and stammered. He—he wasn't sure just what had happened then. The—the Yahweh-man had told them to get ready two sacrifices, he thought, one for Melkart and one for Yahweh, and the one for Melkart had been placed on his altar.

"Then why wasn't it offered?" demanded Jezebel. "The smoke of it would have been plainly visible from here, and *my* eyes, at least, have not been so enamored by a barbaric uplander that I could see nothing else!"

The servant was terrified. He knew now what his blunder was likely to cost him. The sacrifice had not been offered, he mumbled, because—because—Why, yes, he remembered now! Because the Yahweh-man had said it was to be a thanksgiving sacrifice to whichever god should send rain and—

Too absorbed in furious thinking to devise proper punishment, Jezebel ordered the messenger taken away and flogged. Then she began pacing the western end of the terrace, eyes boring the brazen clearness between Jezreel and Carmel.

So in her absence the sheepherder had seized the center of the stage, believing he could render Melkart's prophets powerless by making them postpone their sacrifice! She laughed, loud and bitterly. How little did these boorish uplanders know of the King of the City, believing him, no doubt, most easily persuaded by the blood of bulls and goats! Fools! Famines had been broken in Tyre by the shedding of human blood before this little Yahweh had ever been conceived!

"Come down and rest," pleaded Jael. "It's wailing and weeping you should be, not laughing and parading the roof like a bride decked for her wedding night. Come! It's enough to drive anybody a little mad, what you've seen today. Let Jael put her lamb to bed and rub soothing oils into her aching forehead."

But Jezebel vouchsafed her not a glance. Only when the second messenger appeared did she halt her pacing. This one was as meticulous with detail as the other had been negligent. So many *dudim,* filled with corn and fat, each oval in shape and possessing two handles, had been planted in the ground in so many rows, with networks of canals, and so many libations had been poured into each. All through the morning hours the priests and prophets had danced their limping dance and called on their god, cutting their bodies with knives and lances until their blood poured forth...

Suddenly the messenger chuckled. And all the time the Yahweh-man had been urging them on, he continued with unmistakable relish, deriding their efforts and taunting them with such jibes as, "Come on, shout! Shout louder, why don't you? Maybe your god is taking a nap and needs to be wakened! Maybe—"

At the look of sudden fury on the queen's face the messenger's mouth fell open.

"How dare he!" stormed Jezebel. "Fool! Surely he knows that a rain-making ceremony is a long procedure. Does he think Baal is a maudlin god who sends rain after just one or two circuits of the altar?"

"Not—rain! Fire—"

"Fire! What fire?"

The man was maddeningly slow. Why, the fire to burn the sacrifice, the bullock which the prophets had cut into four pieces early in the day and put on the altar with no fire beneath. The queen of heaven must know about the agreement—

"What agreement?"

She punctuated his detailed recital with terse interruptions, and when he had finished dismissed him abruptly, so engrossed in thought that she neglected to order him flogged for his untimely amusement.

Then she paced the terrace like a caged tigress. If she had been at Carmel, this never would have happened. It would have been she, not her opponent, who did the challenging, and the issue would have been that of wresting rain from the sky, not manufacturing fire by some magician's trick! Or—perhaps this little desert god was capable of sending fire. Weren't there old tales of his thundering and playing lightning about his sacred mountain? Suppose he was. What did that prove? It was rain that Israel needed, not fire. And did not the life-giving waters have their sources in the holy hills where for generations the Baals of this land had dwelt? It was infuriating, maddening! If only she had been there... But if she had, she reminded herself swiftly, the favor of Melkart would not have been obtained. What good to win this little skirmish if she had lost the battle?

On the distant slope across the plain she suddenly saw smoke ascending—first a thin vapor, then a black spiral shot through with tiny threads of flame. Her heart leaped. There was fire at last upon Mount Carmel, sacrificial fire! But—*by whose hand had it been kindled?* It would be at least two hours before the fastest runner, leaving the scene now, could reach Jezreel. And—she could not stand here and wait quietly for two hours. She had to know.

3

The charioteer kept casting wary, sidelong glances, his curiosity a marked hindrance to efficient handling of his horses. His orders had been to drive a high-ranking officer to the king's encampment. But the king's soldiers seldom covered their short tunics and coats of mail with a cloak reaching from shoulders to ankles, nor muffled their faces in the hanging folds of a turban.

Jezebel noted the glances with grim impatience. It was all she could do to keep from snatching the reins into her own hands. Even these half-starved beasts had plenty of speed held in leash. She could feel it in the staccato pounding of their hoofs. Yet she could not speak. Or—could she?

"You may as well understand," she said suddenly, "that you are driving the queen of Israel."

His dismay was ludicrous. "You have nothing to fear," she continued, "as long as you attend to your business and obey orders. And the first one is—get me to the king's encampment—*fast.*"

There were no more sidelong glances. The charioteer drove as if his life depended on his expert manipulation of the horses—as, indeed, he knew it did. And in spite of their wasted strength, the animals responded to the urgency in both voice and fingers. Jezebel clung tightly to the carved railing. The pounding of the horses' hoofs, the jolting of the leather-tired wheels on the uneven ground set her teeth chattering and her temples throbbing, yet satisfied some urgency within her. Flinging back her head, she yielded herself to the swift motion, taking a fierce solace in its very discomfort.

She thought: *How Eliah would like this! I must ask Ahab to take him—*

The charioteer turned a startled face. "Did—the daughter of Melkart speak?"

She gripped the wood of the railing, pulled herself up firmly from the pit of blackness. "If I spoke, it was only to tell you to go faster."

Somewhere along the way they passed the third messenger and the fourth, one so close on the heels of the other that it seemed impossible there should be an hour's running distance between them, but she made no effort to stop them.

The cloud seemed to come all at once. She closed her eyes, opened them again, and there it was, white and tenuous, as if someone had blown gently on a brazen bowl. Her heart gave a great leap. She had watched just such a cloud dozens of times from the palace roof in Tyre, seen it rise from the sea a mere speck, scarcely larger than a man's hand, and in a few moments...Such fierce exaltation swept through her as she had never before known. Melkart had accepted her offering.

"It's going to rain," she said calmly to the charioteer. "Drive faster. We must reach the king's encampment before the storm breaks."

She could sense the incredulous dropping of his jaw. Before they had driven another five miles clouds were filling the whole horizon above the outthrust flank of Carmel...light and delicate at first, edged with flame from the lowering sun, but turning swiftly dark, billowing upward like the smoke from a thousand sacrificial fires. There were distant flashes of lightning, and even the rumbling of the chariot wheels did not quite drown the subsequent thunder.

The jaw of the charioteer was now tightly clamped, and, glancing sideward, she could see lines of strain radiating from his lips. Good! Within minutes there would be thousands of just such awe-struck faces in Israel. In fact, their chariot was already passing some of them, for as they approached the jutting headland, close to the narrow trench where the starved driblet of the Kishon lay hidden, the exodus from Carmel was beginning. Scanning the faces closely, Jezebel tried to analyze their diversities of emotion. Terror? Awe? Relief? All of these—and something more. Could it be—No, these were men and women, not beasts. Why, then, should they remind her of a tame lion she had once seen licking its lips, the blood of its last meal still moist on its whiskers?

The rain came, not timidly, but with the brisk decisiveness of a marching army. Many of the pilgrims stopped in their tracks, threw down their bundles, danced and sang and shouted, cupped their hands to receive the precious drops, flung aside cloaks and headdresses and sandals that the life-giving rain might come in contact with their bare flesh.

The chariot was barely crawling, but Jezebel felt no impatience. It was a moment of triumph which she wanted to savor. Pushing back her own headdress, she lifted her face to the rain, exulting in its rapidly increasing violence; almost yielded to the impulse to jump down from the chariot and whirl with the dancing pilgrims, to blend her voice with their exultant chants...until suddenly she heard words.

"Sing to Yahweh, sing praise to his name,
    extol him who rides on the clouds...
O Yahweh, thou didst pour down a generous rain,
    reviving thy land as it languished..."

Bewilderment came first, then bitter self-denunciation, then devastating anger. Impossible that these stubborn fools should not know yet which deity had sent their precious rain! Had they not all been there on Mount Carmel, witnessed her prophets' rain-making ceremony? *Yes, and the trickery of that clever mountebank, Elijah!*

Stubborn fool herself, not to have foreseen that he would turn the success of Baal's prophets to his own advantage! Easy enough for him to pretend that it was Yahweh and not Melkart who had sent the rain—as easy as for Ethbaal to be smugly congratulating himself at this moment that by his prayers he had prevailed on the god to end the famine! Oh, she had been both blind and stupid!

"No, no!" she screamed. "Not Yahweh! Melkart!"

She had been right about that something in the surging sea of faces. It had been a satiated thirst for blood. She saw it again as groups of pilgrims came crowding about the chariot, only now it was unsatisfied. One of them clutched the hem of her long cloak in an attempt to pull her from the chariot. Others clung to the leather tires and the frame of the wheel base to keep the vehicle from moving. But, though Jezebel sensed her danger, she felt no fear, only anger and outrage.

"Get away!" she screamed. "Every one of you shall pay with your lives for this. Do you know who it is you're threatening? Then let me tell you. I—"

But her voice was drowned in other screams as the chariot gave a sudden lurch and she was almost thrown from her feet. When they had left the group of threatening pilgrims far behind, she turned to the charioteer, sharp rebuke on her lips. But, "If they had known who you were, they would have killed you," he said simply. And she remained silent, knowing it was so. But—why? Even if the Man of Yahweh had persuaded the people that it was his Yahweh and not her Melkart who had sent the rain, why that bloodlust in their faces?

The crowds thinned suddenly as the road approached the narrow pass leading from the plain of Megiddo into the plain of Accho. Ahab's encampment, she knew, was somewhere close to this pass. She wished now she had asked its exact location from one of the runners, for twilight would come soon, and the steadily driving rain had already dropped a thick curtain a few yards in front of the horses.

"You—know where you are going?" she asked once, uncertainly.

The charioteer nodded. "The camp is on the other side of the Kishon. An hour ago we could have crossed anywhere. Now it's better to trust the ford."

The water, crawling through its twisted channel like a sleepy serpent, reached almost to the hubs. "Will we be able to return?" she inquired anxiously.

Oddly their positions seemed to have reversed. It was the charioteer now who was confident, even a little arrogant. "If it does not rain too hard," he replied, "and if we do not wait too long."

It was soon after they climbed up out of the river bed that she saw them. Glimpsing their vague white shapes through the driving rain, she thought at first they were bundles of wool from some caravan which had missed the ford and come to grief. Then, as they drew closer, she saw the faces. *"Stop!"*

Leaving her sandals buried in the slippery, clinging mud, she waded through it in her bare feet to the nearest of the sprawled, white-clad figures, and, kneeling beside it, uttered a little cry, harsh and unintelligible, like that of a wild creature which finds its young despoiled. When she half lifted it in her arms, the head lolled to one side, and there was a gush of blood from its lips. The familiar features of one of her prophets stared up at her, frozen in grim terror. The flesh was still a little warm, the knife-wound in the breast moist with blood. Hastily she closed the eyes, moved the white headdress so the rain would not fall on the still features, and straightened clumsily to her feet.

But there were other staring faces being drenched with rain— hundreds of them. Frantically she ran from one to the other along the bank, closing the eyes, straightening the distorted limbs and sodden garments, inspired by no other motive than a terrible urgency. When the folds of her headdress got in her way, she pulled it off and flung it to one side. The same with her cloak. But she could not minister to them all. There were too many, piled one atop the other, and the bank was far too steep. She stood helplessly, trembling from cold and exhaustion, until finally she felt a touch on her shoulder. Pushing a tangle of wet hair from her eyes, she saw that it was the charioteer.

"The king is not in his encampment. He was here, but he returned across the river with the Man of Yahweh, after—" He gestured wordlessly toward the bodies.

She stared at him dumbly, only half comprehending.

"The water is rising," he continued urgently. "If we don't return now, we may find crossing difficult. And—if the queen will forgive the presumption—"

"What is it?" Her lips only half formed the words.

"I—wouldn't advise the queen to show her face now among the men of Israel."

She was in the chariot again, the sodden coat about her shoulders. This time when the horses lunged down the bank and into the stream, they barely found a foothold. The serpent was now fully awakened. Writhing and twisting within his narrow confines, he lashed furiously at the straining flanks, tossed the iron-bound vehicle upon his coils as easily as if it had been an insect. But the chariot finally emerged, its occupants drenched to the waist, and in the wake of the struggling horses reeled up the slippery bank. Twilight was now fast approaching. The loose red soil of the plain was churning into mud. But the charioteer was equal to his task. Selecting one of the firmer wheel tracks in the sprawling breadth of paths, he directed his course toward the distant battlements of Jezreel.

For Jezebel only one moment in that long tumultuous ride stood out clearly...when with a great rumble of wheels and pounding of hoofs the royal equipage swept past them, Ahab himself was driving. She saw him standing straight and tall, alone in his chariot, his mien that of a soldier returning victorious from battle. And ahead of his horses, preceding even his footmen and other attendants, ran a wild, ecstatic figure, long beard streaming in the wind and rain, huge ungainly body clad only in a sheepskin.

CHAPTER 9

1

"Don't grieve so," said Ahab. "It couldn't be helped. It was meant to be."

From her seat on a square of reed matting, body clothed in sackcloth and head strewn with ashes, Jezebel gazed up at him. Through the heat waves rising from the glowing brazier, his tall figure seemed to waver, to mingle its substance with the unreality of surrounding shadows.

"I've been afraid of it," he continued with tight-lipped brevity. "It was I who rebuilt Jericho. The curse was meant for me, not Hiel."

She laughed then, could not help it. The sound of her laughter rose high and shrill, seeming to emanate from her body yet becoming instantly a thing apart from herself. She saw Ahab's face, grave and concerned, and thought, *He thinks I'm hysterical with grief*—and only laughed the harder. Then, as abruptly as her flesh turned from hot to cold, she stopped, and shivered.

"It's not only for Eliah that I'm mourning," she said dully. "That happened ages ago. It's for the prophets of Melkart."

His features compressed into a stern mold, "Then—you know."

She regarded him steadily. With the coldness had come decision and clarity. On the issue of the next few moments hung the future of all her hope for Israel, possibly her own future as well. She must gamble for her very life.

"Tell me what happened today on Carmel," she said deliberately.

It was not what she had meant to say. Words of accusation had been ready on her lips, as ruthless and uncompromising as those she had dispatched not an hour ago to the Man of Yahweh: *As surely as you are Elijah and I am Jezebel, may the gods kill me and worse if by this time tomorrow I do not make your life the same as any one of theirs.* But she knew suddenly there were weapons more powerful than anger.

"So you really think," she said contemptuously, after he had finished, "that it was your Yahweh who sent the rain—just because a clever conjuror makes you think he can draw down fire from heaven!"

He lurched toward her. "That isn't true. I saw it. Can a man doubt the evidence of his own senses?"

"Yes. Sometimes. In my father's court I once watched a magician saw a woman in two, then put her together again. But I knew he didn't really do it. It was a trick."

"This was no trick." His eyes flashed their scorn, dark and hot and furious. "Listen! Let me tell you again what happened as I saw it."

"From where?" she interrupted coolly. "Where were you standing? Beside Elijah?"

"Well—no. I was on a high crag above the hollow, so I could get an even clearer view. I saw his every motion, saw him cut the bullock in four parts, saw—"

"What kind of knife did he use?"

"Why, a—a flint one, I suppose. Bronze knives aren't used for ritual."

"But you don't know?"

"Well, I—I wasn't close enough to see."

"Oh? But you did see him cut it into four parts? You're sure of that?"

"Yes. And he placed it on the altar and ordered a deep trench to be dug—"

"I know. And then he ordered water to be brought. One, two, three goblets—or skins—or barrels, depending on who is telling the story."

She signaled to an attendant, and the fifth and sixth runners, who had been waiting outside the door, were brought into the room. Since her interview with them an hour ago they had been fed and wined, and both men were in excellent spirits. They retold their stories glibly and with obvious embellishments. Several times Ahab would have interrupted, but Jezebel gestured him to silence. She waited until the sixth runner had finished.

"Aie, aie!" Turning to Ahab, she threw up her hands in a deprecating gesture. "I don't know what to think, I'm sure this man said before that it was two pitchers of water which the Yahweh-man poured out in libation, and now he says two goatskins."

"Not two. Three," interrupted the fifth runner. "And it wasn't goatskins. It was barrels. I saw with my own eyes. By my hair and whiskers, I swear it!"

"It was neither," put in Ahab firmly. "And it was no libation. It was—"

"And you're sure, both of you, that it was water?" interposed Jezebel. "Somehow I got the impression from one of you that it might have been—oil."

By Anath, of course it had been water! The fifth runner ought to know. *Ah! Then he had actually seen it drawn?* Well—no, but he supposed they had brought it from one of the springs there on the mountain. *What! In time of famine and so much water—so many barrels?* By Ashtart, that was true! But—well, it had surely looked like water. And, after all, what else could it have been unless—well, yes, he supposed it *could* have been oil...

"You see?" Jezebel probed gently after the two runners had been dismissed. "No two stories agree. One thought he saw a stroke of lightning. The other was sure the fire sprang from within the altar itself. Already the amount of water has swollen like the river Kishon. How can you be sure what actually happened?"

Ahab's face was drained of its usual ruddiness. Within its ashen contours his eyes glowed like two live coals. "I'm sure of only one thing," he averred with slow, emphatic vehemence. "Yahweh made himself known to his people today as the God of Israel—their only God. It doesn't matter how he did it. What matters is that we know now it is he, and not the baals, who sends sunshine and rain and quickens the seed in our fields and in our loins, who—who is the author of our life itself. We haven't been really sure of it before. Now we are. And that's the thing which makes this day important for Israel. Not what may or may not have happened on Carmel."

Jezebel gazed at him for a moment in silence. The interview was not proceeding as she had expected. It was not like Ahab to be so sure of himself.

"How can you be so certain?" she temporized. "What makes you think it was Yahweh and not Melkart who sent the rain? I tell you it wasn't. I know it wasn't!"

"It's not only I who am sure. It's my people. If you could have seen them—"

"I did see them. Stupid, loutish peasants!" All the bitterness and ignominy of her experience on the plain below Carmel swept over her. "I hate them all. I've always hated them. They killed my prophets and my priests and—"

"I know. I didn't want them to do that. I swear I tried to stop them. But—you must admit it was only what you did to the prophets of Yahweh."

"Because they were traitors," she insisted desperately, "because they were destroying all that we were trying to do for—for Israel."

"And just what were we trying to do?" he shot back sternly. "Make Israel great. Make her God honored and feared above all others. All right. At last we've succeeded." His voice turned suddenly harsh. "Haven't you complained all these years that Yahweh was a weakling? Well, you can't complain any longer. He has been thirsty enough for human blood today. And I challenge even Melkart to remember and fulfill a curse of vengeance after nearly four hundred years!"

His features vanished into a thick red mist. "Don't leave me!" she cried. "My child gone and—and now you! The—the fire—it's all about me—save me—"

Strong arms reached out to draw her back from the throbbing pit of flame into which she seemed to be falling. They were not the arms of Ahab, but of Jael.

"There, there, lamb. Merciful Ashtart! You have a fever. And no wonder, coming back soaked through, and your head and feet all bare. Your flesh is on fire!"

2

The night wore on. Snug in the homes of their peasant friends or huddled in crude shelters on the hillsides above the plain of Megiddo, innumerable pilgrims, unable to sleep for sheer ecstasy and excitement, listened to the thundering waters of the Kishon and relived the day's strange happenings.

"Hear that rain! The drought is ended, thanks be to Yahweh!"

"Aye, thanks be to Yahweh! And let's see that we remember to keep on thanking him. It's Yahweh who makes our crops grow, not the other baals."

"Hear, hear! Better perhaps to tear down the stone and sacred tree?"

"Well—no. I'd say not—yet. Let's wait a bit and see if Yahweh continues to bless us. Besides, who says it's not Yahweh we worship on the high places?"

"Listen to the river! This morning a dried-up worm—now a raging serpent!"

"Remind you of anything? Some story the bards sing?"

"Aye. Deborah and Barak. 'Listen, O kings, O rulers, hear!' "

"That's it. Remember how it goes—that part about the Kishon?

> " 'The very stars in heaven were fighting,
>   fighting Sisera from their spheres;
> Kishon's torrent swept the foe off,
>   Kishon's torrent in their faces!' "

"By Anath, what times those must have been!"

"Who knows? The thing that happened today may be just as long remembered."

"And by the way, just what *did* happen today? Does anybody really know?"

3

The night wore on. In the palace of Ethbaal in Tyre revelry and feasting continued long after the king, tired out by the rain-making ceremonies, had left the banquet hall and gone to bed. But his son Baalazor was equal to the occasion. In fact, he was assuming more and more of his father's duties of late. Not enough, however, to suit the young—not so young, either, any longer—prince's ambition! There were whispers in court circles that if the king did not die a natural death pretty soon or abdicate quietly, fate, in the form of a fortuitous accident, might intervene to change the course of Tyrian history.

But tonight the king's popularity was at an all-time high.

"A miracle if I ever saw one! Scarcely did the king's prayer have time to ascend in smoke before the rain came and our year-long drought was broken."

"Let's hope the favor of Melkart extended over the border into Israel. They say the drought there has lasted three years!"

"I believe it. I've forgotten what a cake of good wheat flour tastes like."

"Wine, too. I've missed that vintage from Samaria. It's as good as Lebanon's."

"To the king, and may he live longer than we expect!"

"Yea, and to Israel! May she keep our stomachs full!"

Lolling on his couch, restive eyes gauging the depths of this evanescent loyalty with the accuracy of a plumb line, Baalazor endured this hour of his temporary eclipse with tolerant good humor. Let his father enjoy his brief triumph.

4

The night wore on. Under cover of its darkness two men slipped through the gate of Jezreel, descended the ramp, and made their way south past the foothills of Mount Gilboa toward the pass leading to the plain of Dothan. There was nothing to guide their steps but the feeling of the worn paths, now slippery trenches of mud. Still, the taller of the two moved with such unerring swiftness that his companion, in spite of his wiry slenderness, had to take two steps to his one. Although they met no travelers, when they spoke it was in near whispers.

"You're—sure this is the—wise thing to do, my father?" asked the younger man breathlessly. "Why the south? Why not the road to the east, beyond Jordan?"

"Not there," replied the other briefly.

"Why not?"

"That would be the first place her long-nosed hounds would come to search. The south is safer. And besides, I—must go where—I can think."

As the older man fell silent, apparently already immersed in thought, his long steps slackened, and his companion regained his breath. Though it was too dark to see, the latter's keen young eyes probed the other's features.

"You are afraid, my father. Why?"

"And why should a man not be afraid when a powerful enemy threatens his life?"

"Yet you were not afraid a few hours ago on the mountain. You were a tower of strength. You molded the will of a nation in your bare hands."

"That was—a few hours ago—on the mountain."

When the younger man spoke again, it was with great humility and hesitation. "Could it be that—it is Yahweh, not Jezebel, of whom my father is afraid?"

"What—What's that?" So agitated was his companion that he stopped short, forgetting to speak in a whisper. "I, Yahweh's champion, afraid of—!" He plunged on through the darkness, then stopped again. "Why in heaven's name should I be afraid of Yahweh? Is it not to me that he reveals his will?"

The younger man ran to overtake the striding figure, slipped, fell flat in the mud, picked himself up and ran again. "My father seemed—certain of the will of Yahweh—on the mountain," he panted, "so certain that he—had no fear—of any man or woman— on earth. Could it be that—that he was not so certain in the valley— when he killed the priests and the prophets?"

"Why shouldn't we have killed them? Did not that queen-devil kill *our* prophets? In the name of Yahweh, what should I have done!"

Again the younger man, in order to overtake, was forced to slip and flounder. "Isn't that—just what my father—wants to find out— why he is running away now—afraid—why—he sets his face— toward Yahweh's holy mountain?"

"Micaiah!" The word burst in a great cry from Elijah's mighty throat. "Will you not even let me run from my enemies in peace? What are you! A scourge? A goad? A fiery brand clinging to a man's flesh? Is—is it Yahweh who sends you to torment me?"

The two men journeyed on through the night, silent now, one plunging like a tortured animal, the other stumbling after him.

5

The night wore on. In response to a knock on the gatepost of the house of Naboth, in Jezreel, an old man hobbled through the rain- drenched outer court, turned the flat wooden key, and swung the door wide in its metal socket.

"Peace to you, stranger, whoever you are. Come in and welcome."

A tall, heavily cloaked shape slipped inside, waited until the square bolt had again been shot, then followed the hobbling figure across the outer court into an inner room, where in a small clay pit an open fire was burning.

"Obadiah?" asked the stranger in a muffled voice. "I—have a message—"

The old man grunted, then chuckled. "I'll call him. But he's likely to pay about as much attention to a message right now as to the bit of bread and cheese I just took him. Sit by the fire, stranger; warm yourself."

Relieved that he had not been recognized by old Abner, Ahab crouched by the fire and stretched out his stiffened hands. Faint curls of steam rose from his soggy garments, and the raw smell of wet wool became mingled in his nostrils with the even more acrid aroma of the ashes matted beneath his drenched headcloth. Why had he come here? He could no more have analyzed his motive for this than for any other act of this terrible night...his frantic beating and clawing at the freshly fitted limestone blocks beneath which, he was told, the body of his son lay buried... *Bring back the masons and stonecutters, for Yahweh's sake get it out of that heathen— No, no matter. What difference*...his furtive slipping from the palace, a cloak flung over his mourning garb...his walking for hours through the streets until finally his feet had brought him without his volition to this familiar door.

Obadiah? The name had sprung unbidden to his lips, no more than an excuse for entering. Deborah, the wife of Naboth? It would not be the first time he had turned to her for comfort. But Deborah could have no salves nor splints, no cleansing herbs for the healing of this hurt. Nor words of solace. *Yahweh bless his poor lamb!* Yahweh a shepherd? Hardly. Not the Yahweh he had met today upon Mount Carmel, who had goaded his people to slaughter, who, in fulfillment of an ancient curse, had taken Ahab's own son!

Strange, how little the room had changed! The same blackened fire-pit set in the same floor of hard-trodden limestone chips; the same clay water jars and cooking pots and round cover over the sunken grain pit, where Daniel, the boldest of Naboth's sons, had hidden one day and almost suffocated; even the same bustling, chattering females, concerned, of all ironies, with their favorite preoccupation of bringing a new human being into the world!

"The salt—you're sure it's been crushed?"

"Stupid! What else would I have been pounding all this time in the mortar!"

"And the dried myrtle leaves—and swaddling cloths?"

"They've all been ready for hours."

"And should have been needed hours ago, if you ask me."

"I tell you, I don't like it. Even with the rain coming, it has been an unlucky day. That accident at the palace—"

"You should see Obadiah! Running about like a goat with its head in a bag! You'd think it was he bearing the child instead of his poor Rachel!"

Beneath Ahab's musing gaze the fire burst into splintering sparks. He knew suddenly why he had come to the house of Naboth. Not Obadiah, not Deborah. *Rachel.* In this hour of his extremity he had turned to her as naturally, as inevitably, as a flower to sunlight or a bird to its nest. It had been, would always be so. As comprehension swept over him, it was followed by a sense of irreparable loss. He had been doubly bereft this day, first of his son, now of his love. No, trebly. For at this very moment Rachel was crouched somewhere within this house, within the sound of his voice, struggling, perhaps in an agony deeper than his own, to bear to another man the child which might—which should—have been his.

How long he sat there motionless, hands outstretched to a blaze which held no warmth, he could not have told. Even when the first tiny wail came to his ears and the household burst into that tumult of rejoicing accompanying the advent of a man-child, his limbs remained frozen beneath him.

Squatting bulkily beside the fire, the wife of Naboth cast one penetrating glance at the motionless figure, uttered a cheerful "Welcome, stranger!" and settled herself to her favorite occupation, the swaddling of her latest grandson.

"Tell that witless Obadiah," she ordered lustily, as if in answer to his agonized, unspoken question, "he can stop his pacing now. Both his wife and son are as sound as new green olives."

Life coursed painfully back into Ahab's limbs. Again he stretched his hands to the fire and felt warmth tingle through their numbness. He marveled anew at the gentleness of the big, deft fingers, the skill with which they sponged and patted and sprinkled, finally rolled the red wriggling shape, arms pressed to its sides and feet stretched full length and close together, in the great square swaddling cloth.

"There!" pronounced Deborah with satisfaction. "A stout shoot of the tree of Naboth if I ever saw one! Hold him, friend. Give him your blessing. A good sign it is in Israel to have a stranger in the house when a man-child is born, especially if that stranger be"—her voice melted to a whisper—"the anointed one of Yahweh."

Obediently Ahab took the small trussed bundle, cupping the wobbly little head gently in his left palm. So soft was it, so light, so fragrant, that a melting warmth stirred through all his body. His son was dead, yet through some strange beneficence as inexplicable as the sprouting seed, he was alive again. Yahweh was not all destroyer. Beneath the ugly red tide of the swollen Kishon the earth was already quickening into life. As Yahweh lived and as he, Ahab, was king of Israel, he would see to it that no curse ever came near this child!

Rising, he lifted the swaddled bundle high and raised his face.

6

The night wore on. And a scream sounded through the palace.

Hearing it, Jezebel started up from her couch, reached out in a terrified gesture, and felt her hand clasped in stumpy, calloused fingers,

"I'm here, little lotus blossom. Jael's here. Don't be afraid."

The fog of delirium, parted momentarily, drifted in again. A scream... *Look out! Don't jump...* No, that wasn't right. She had already heard the scream. It was over. She was lying on the cold tiles, sinking into blessed forgetfulness. But—she mustn't! There were still things to do... *Wake up, Almah! Where is he? What have you done?...*

"Hush! Lie still, my poor lamb. It's all over now."

But it was not all over. There was still Tanath standing in the arch of the stairway, only there wasn't any arch behind her now, and her face surely had not looked like that, tearful and terrified and—yes, accusing.

"It's Almah! She's dead. Thrown herself from the high terrace. It was her screams you heard. She's dead, I tell you, and it was you..."

"No, no, don't let her! Take her away!" Screaming, Jezebel struggled up out of the fog. Through the last lingering wisps she saw the girl being dragged away, beaten by Jael's stubby hands. It was all right then. Her secret for the moment was safe. She had nothing to fear, unless... Her vision suddenly cleared, and she found herself looking up sharply into Ahab's face.

"I—guess I haven't been myself. Did—did I say anything strange—?"

His eyes were inscrutable but kind. "No, nothing strange at all after the day you have experienced. It's natural you should blame yourself for the accident. But it wasn't your responsibility to watch the child. It was Almah's, and she has tried in the only way she knew to atone for her negligence. Don't blame yourself. If either of us is at fault, it is I, for rebuilding Jericho without remembering the curse, or for believing that Yahweh—" His lips tightened. "I shall pay for it with remorse all the days of my life."

"No, no, it wasn't you, it was—" In her anxiety to comfort him, she almost said too much. "It was Almah's fault," she finished carefully.

"I know. And it's all over now. There's nothing more you can do."

Gratefully she yielded herself to the cushioned embrace of her couch. He was right. The day was finished. She had fulfilled her vow. The drought was ended. She had paid for its ending with the death of her son. And Ahab did not guess her secret. He even believed himself responsible. What more in Melkart's name could she ask? Melkart... Better not to even think his name, or the canker of doubt which she had tried all these hours to disregard might grow, become a hard living core. Or better, perhaps, to repeat it, to keep on repeating it until the rankling canker had been fully diagnosed, torn out...

Melkart. Where had Melkart been when his priests and prophets were being killed? Why had he not saved them? He had sent the rain, yes—or—*had he?* Suppose—suppose, if her child were still alive, sleeping safely in the next room with Almah by his side, *it would have rained just the same!*

PART THREE—JEZREEL

1

Melkiah, the high priest of Yahweh, was a mountain of quaking uneasiness. As he shrugged and grunted and twisted into his long blue robe, its border of golden bells tinkled an agitated accompaniment to his nervous pulses.

"Be quick," he ordered his second priest, Amnon, whose trembling fingers, attempting to adjust the shoulder straps and embroidered girdle of his linen ephod, seemed all thumbs. "The king must not be kept waiting."

The younger priest's thin face acquired a pasty hue. "Has—has the king come to inquire again what—what to do about the Syrians?"

The high priest grunted. "For what other reason should he come to the temple at this time of day? And, judging by the sounds, half the city is with him."

Amnon fumbled with the jeweled breastplate. "They say the Syrians have come even closer to the city," he babbled. "Their armies fill the whole valley to the south. And the peace terms these new messengers propose are worse even than those the king agreed to after he consulted Yahweh before. What will you—I mean what will Yahweh tell the king to do?"

Melkiah ran a moist tongue over his dry, protruding lips. He felt sweat gathering in his pudgy palms. "That," he returned piously, "is for our Lord Yahweh to say."

So crowded was the great court that his transit of it was robbed of its usual impressiveness. Even the huge tank of cast bronze was so densely surrounded that only the massive necks and upflung heads of its four supporting bulls were visible. Half the city, had he said? Nearly all of it.

Under his regal garments the legs of the high priest were trembling like aspens. It was because of his drawing of the sacred lots two days before that the king had agreed to the insolent demands of Ben-hadad, king of Syria, who with his armies and allies had swept down through the pass from Megiddo and settled like vultures in the valley below Samaria. Now, it seemed, Yahweh was to be called on for another decision. Yahweh? The high priest groaned aloud. He wished fervently that there were no way of distinguishing between the two round pieces of stone in the leather pouch hung from his neck. It was only by accident that, one day long ago, he had discovered the tiny nick in the edge of the white disk. He should of course have disregarded the knowledge, continued to draw out the first object which met his hand as embodying the will of Yahweh. But the temptation to please the king had been too great.

Now, whatever judgment he rendered, tragedy was likely to follow. The Syrian king had demanded a complete looting of the city. If the high priest advocated further appeasement, his name would be scorned by every red-blooded young patriot in Samaria. All about him he could hear their voices raised excitedly.

"Ransack our king's palace, would they, take the women and children? Never!"

"If Yahweh gives such counsel, he's a god for weaklings. We'll follow Melkart."

"Not Melkart. Did not the Tyrians run to Assyria with gifts?"

"Chemosh, then! If Yahweh fails us, Chemosh will lead us into battle!"

But they had not all lost their heads, Melkiah noted swiftly. In the ranks of the older, more solid courtiers were grave, bearded men, their grim features hiding memories of the terrible Syrian onslaught in the time of Omri. Better pay double tribute for the next twenty years, they would counsel, than see Samaria reduced to dust! The country was unprepared for war. Ahab had been a builder and a trader, not a fighter. Even the seven thousand men in his regular army, though well trained, were inexperienced except for border skirmishes. These old men knew that resistance was but another name for suicide.

The prophet guild would be for war. They had always been hotbeds of patriotism. There was still a remnant among them of that rabid hundred who had escaped the scourge of Jezebel. In one swift glance he could almost pick out their faces, deeper lined and of a weathered toughness reminiscent of the old days when prophets had not lived in luxury as retainers of the king but had still roamed the country. At least the troublemaker Micaiah was not among this group. But another face in the front row caught his eye, narrow, sharply chiseled, and so darkly scowling that even in the hot glare of sunlight its features seemed drawn into shadow.

"Don't think you can fool all of us," the dark gaze scorned, "by that pretense of dignity. Underneath those rich robes I can see your fat legs shaking."

Melkiah hastily turned his back on the scowling features. Eyes which could penetrate the defenses of a man's pride might also detect the flaw in a white disk hanging in a bag from his neck.

There was a blare of trumpets. The guards at the eastern gate had barely sprung to attention before runners burst through its portals, bronze shields glittering. At their heels, with an impressive rattling of armor and flourishing of spears, came the *gibborim,* so splendid and heartening an exhibition of strength that a tumultuous cheer burst from the crowd, to be followed by such a dismayed silence that the whimpering of a child outside the temple area was plainly audible.

For the king was wearing neither his ceremonial garments nor the high conical crown adorned with twisted bands of gold. Clothed in rough sackcloth, the long black ringlets of his hair gray with ashes, his tall figure moved in sharp contrast beside that of his queen, sword-straight and slim in a sheath of rich purple overdraped with cloth-of-gold, scornful eyes glittering among the winking gems studding the black mesh veil which only partially concealed her face.

Why was the king wearing sackcloth? Bewilderment accelerated to dismay and dismay to panic. Melkiah knew why, and as he moved toward the dais the trembling in his limbs increased. He was to receive no help from the king in making his decision. Whichever way the lots fell, the king's garb silently proclaimed, Israel would be clothed in mourning. Bitterly the high priest cursed the skill so carefully engendered in the tips of his sensitive fingers.

Amid a silence as palpable as the wisps of smoke still spiraling upward from the great brazen altar, Ahab rose to his feet.

"An enemy has come to Israel," he said simply. "Two days ago Ben-hadad of Syria sent messengers to me demanding tribute. 'Your silver and your gold are mine,' he said. Complying with the oracle of Yahweh, I replied to him, 'It is as you say, my lord, O king. I am yours, and so is all I have.' "

An angry murmur arose among the younger courtiers, but Ahab silenced it with a gesture. "Today the messengers of Ben-hadad returned with still greater demands. Says the king of Syria, 'At this time tomorrow I shall send my servants to you, and they shall ransack your palace and the palaces of your officers. Whatever they see that pleases them, they shall seize and carry off.' "

This time the murmuring was not to be silenced. It swept over the courtyard like a rippling wave. "Never listen to him!" "Never agree to it!" "An insult to our nation and to Yahweh!" But, though the protestations were glib, there was more of panic in them than of anger.

Again Ahab gestured for silence. "It is for Yahweh to say what we must do," he announced with finality. "Let the high priest give us his answer. Shall I yield to these further demands of Ben-hadad, king of Syria?"

With trembling fingers Melkiah removed the pouch from his neck and with his left hand held it high for all the people to see. Panic seized him. Frantically he scanned the king's face for some indication of his will, but the royal features remained enigmatic. A foot of space was an interminable distance...but at last his hand traversed it, reached through the opening, fumbled about and found one of the smooth disks. Slowly, by long habit, his fingers passed over its outer edge, encountered a barely perceptible nick. Good! It was the white disk—*yes!* Yahweh too was becoming less adventurous with the years. He had chosen the safer, more cautious course.

He was about to draw the disk from the bag when his eyes encountered those of the queen, so intensely brilliant that they seemed to have absorbed all the brightness of the winking gems...then fell instinctively to the only moving object within view, a scarf of black mesh wound carelessly into a circle, idly swinging with each negligent motion of her hand.

His fingers opened, swiftly groped, closed again, then with a firm gesture drew the black disk from the leather pouch. Israel would defy Ben-hadad!

2

The hooded lantern on the roof of the guardhouse surmounting the high tower of the citadel cast scarcely enough light to outline the motionless figure crouched beside the parapet. But Ahab needed no light for his bitter brooding. As well as if it were daylight he could see the wide rim of encircling hills, and in the valleys between, clustered like predatory birds forewarned of a killing, the gaily striped tents of Ben-hadad and his thirty-two little feudal kings.

So this was the way it was to end—the fine kingdom he had so proudly reared for Israel and Yahweh! He had failed again, like the youth who had stood spellbound while his enemy escaped. Yes, and for the same reason, because he had foolishly believed it more godlike to create than to destroy. Well, he knew better now. Yahweh had made it plain enough today.

Rising abruptly, Ahab plunged his fingers through his disordered hair, blinding himself in a fine deluge of ashes, and found relief in the necessity of weeping.

"It need not have been!" he groaned aloud. "I swear it need not have been!"

For Ben-hadad, Ahab was convinced, had come for a more ulterior purpose than the looting of Samaria. For months now he had been pressing Israel to join him in a confederacy aimed at repelling the aggression of Assyria, and, had it not been for his alliance with Tyre, Ahab would have done so long ago. Even now it might not be too late. Were he to dispatch another envoy, or, better yet, go himself to Ben-hadad... But no, it *was* too late. Ahab's lips twisted grimly. Remembering Carmel, he should have known the verdict. Yahweh's honor must be defended, his supremacy maintained, regardless of how much blood was shed.

"Afraid?"

He wheeled, his pulses leaping. "How did you get here? Obadiah promised to wait at the foot of the stairs——"

"And see that no one disturbed you. But—I've always managed to make myself persuasive, even with granite obelisks like Obadiah. And"—her eyes peering through their protecting veil were copper gleams of challenge—"the reception my lord accords is sufficient proof that I no longer have power to—disturb him."

He uttered a harsh exclamation, then suddenly she was in his arms, his cold lips plunged into the warm magic of her hair, every nerve in his body come suddenly alive and quivering with awareness—yes, and with self-contempt because, even though he had known for ten years that his emotion toward her was not love, she still had such power to enslave his senses. Would he become free, he wondered sometimes, when she had lost her beauty? But she had grown more beautiful, not less, with maturity. If there were lines in the deeply yellowed ivory of her skin, they seemed but more convincing evidence of that fineness of detail which was the mark of the master craftsman. And, like the sea to which she had always been akin, she was never for two moments the same. Even her hair was as constantly changing as a lifetime of sunsets.

He pushed her from him abruptly. "Why did you come here?"

"I asked a question first," she replied calmly. "I'll repeat. Are you afraid?"

He moved back into the shadows by the parapet. "Why should you think that?"

"Your ridiculous garb, for one thing," she countered sharply. "It's only the coward who mourns over the threat of death rather than its reality."

"And only the fool," retorted Ahab, "who boasts when he girds on his armor, rather than when he takes it off."

"You should tell that to Ben-hadad!"

"I did. Not an hour ago."

She moved to his side, the lantern-gleam still in her eyes. "What did he say?"

"He said," replied Ahab evenly, " 'The gods kill me and worse, if there is sufficient dust left in Samaria for each of my followers to have a handful!' "

They stood in silence, looking down at the innumerable little blades of camp fires.

She made a blurred impatient gesture. "You were actually sorry, weren't you, when your Yahweh told you not to accede to Syria's infamous demands?"

Ahab hedged. "Ben-hadad didn't come here with his thirty-two kings to plunder."

"You think I didn't know that?" she returned scornfully. "Of course his real purpose was to force you to join the confederation."

"Well—and why shouldn't I?" Ahab's lips set stubbornly.

"Oh!" She stamped her foot angrily. "Sometimes you're so blind! Can't you see that Assyria need not be our enemy?"

He wheeled toward her. "You think I should have been running to Shalmaneser, the Assyrian, with gifts as did your precious Tyrians? Remember—?"

They were both silent, recalling the somber procession they had seen on one of their infrequent visits to the court of Jezebel's nephew Matten-baal, who had come to the throne after the suspiciously sudden death of Baalazor: in its lead two merchant princes in their long clinging double robes and gaily wound turbans, necks already bowed in meek subservience, in their wake an army of slaves bearing half the wealth of Tyre. Down through the winding streets to the northeast harbor the procession had passed, followed by a wailing populace; into the fleet of long narrow boats the treasure had been poured—bales of wool and purple linen, white woven stuffs, ivories, ingots of gold and silver and lead and copper—until the proud camel figureheads at prow and stern were plunged into the sea to their necks. Out of the harbor the boats had slipped, up the coast toward the far Orontes to keep humiliating tryst with Shalmaneser, sitting beneath a cheerful parasol beside the sea.

"They'll get it all back a thousandfold," argued Jezebel furiously.

"I don't doubt that," retorted Ahab bitterly. "Your Tyrian traders would as soon sell cedar logs for instruments of torture as for temples."

"And why not?" She stamped her foot again angrily. "You stupid Israelites! Look at you now, staring into the dark and brooding when you have a war on your hands! What difference does it make why Ben-hadad is here or what are the issues involved? He's here, and for once your Yahweh has shown the courage of Melkart and told you to go out and fight him. Why don't you do it?"

Stung to the quick, Ahab seized her shoulders in a viselike grip. "Confound you and your Melkart, we will! I'll have you know we are no cowards. We'll defend our city until every drop of blood is shed."

She laughed her scorn. "Of course you can *defend* the city. Omri knew what he was doing when he built Samaria. I said—why don't you go out and fight him?"

Ahab gasped. "That would be suicide!"

Wrenching herself free, she stamped her soft sandal with furious futility. "Oh, What's the use trying to turn your insipid little Yahweh into a red-blooded Melkart! Even when you get him—" She bit her lip. "Even when he finally makes up his mind to render a bold decision, what good does it do? Oh, if only just once a man worthy of the name of king would show his face in Israel!"

"A prophet of Yahweh?" Ahab frowned. "But I told you I wanted to be alone. You—" He made a harassed gesture. "Oh—very well, Obadiah. Have your way."

Jezebel had scarcely time to withdraw into the shadows before the member of the prophet guild appeared on the roof. Briefly, as he passed the lantern, she saw his features outlined, narrow, sharp, intense, the black scowling brows a startling contrast to the white-shaven scalp above, and she drew a quick breath.

"My lord!" The newcomer went straight to the king, speaking with the barest apology of an obeisance. "I had to come. I was lying on my couch, and suddenly it was plain to me how Yahweh plans to deliver the Syrians into your hand."

She could not hear Ahab's reply, but it must have been in the form of a question, and a skeptical one, for the answer came, swift and furious as the dashing of a clay image to a hard stone floor.

"You mean you doubt the oracle of Yahweh, you, the Lord's anointed? What do you think the giving of the black disk meant, if not that the enemy was to be delivered into your hands!" The young man waved his arm in a wide gesture which included city, valley, Ben-hadad and all his camp. "You see this host? I shall put it all in your power, says Yahweh, and you shall learn that I am the Eternal!"

"How?" demanded Ahab tersely.

Jezebel's ears sharpened. The young man was outlining a plan for conquering the Syrian army, so daring and mad a plan that only an idiot—or a genius—could have conceived it. When he had finished, she waited, foot impatiently tapping, for the motionless figure still leaning on the parapet to awaken to its possibilities.

"Who—who is to open the attack?" asked Ahab slowly.

"You are," replied the young prophet with explosive directness.

Still the king remained motionless, considering, while Jezebel, nails pressed hard in her palms, thought she would go mad with impatience. But at last she saw the hunched figure stir and straighten.

"It's—an audacious scheme, but—it might work. You're right. It's the thing to do. We must act with the utmost secrecy and with the greatest haste."

Once Ahab had made up his mind, there was no lack of swiftness. He was across the enclosure and halfway down the stairs before the visitor started to follow. Abruptly Jezebel moved out of the shadows. *"Jehu!"* she called softly.

The man wheeled, just where the rays of the shaded lantern fell full on his face. "How—who—you know my name?"

As she moved into the circle of light, she saw his somber features become suffused with crimson, springing first into the hollows of his thin cheeks, racing to his temples. His eyes darted to the floor, as if half expecting to see the fragments of a clay statue lying on its stones.

"How are Midnight and Stormcloud?" she asked with disarming eagerness.

The self-consciousness dropped like a mask. "You should see them now! Their coats are as glistening black as polished ebony and as smooth as—as—"

"As a woman's oiled and perfumed skin?"

His eager lips clamped shut and the scowl reappeared.

"Are they still at Megiddo?" she hastened to inquire lightly. "If so, I must stop and see them when we go to Jezreel. We have another palace there."

Chattering on brightly, she saw the tight line of lips soften, the still boyishly vulnerable features relax their scowling guard.

"They're still at Megiddo," he admitted a little sullenly.

"While you," she continued pointedly, "who were going to drive them up to the gate of the palace, dance yourself into a swoon or shake a rattle. Why?"

She could hear his swift-drawn breath. "I—I am in the service of Yahweh."

"So are the captains in the king's army, his archers and—his charioteers."

She could almost see his fingers twitch, tighten on invisible reins. "Tell me, grandson of Nimshi, wouldn't you rather be riding with the king into battle than dancing yourself into a frenzy trying to find out whether or not he's going to be victorious?"

His answer was in every lineament of his body—dilating nostrils, upflung head, quivering reflex of muscle in forearm and throat and temples. And as if in response, the brisk night wind whipped hard against his face, and, snatching at the hooded flame, tore about the high enclosure in a frenzy of racing shadows.

"Suppose—suppose that when King Ahab rides to battle it should be Midnight and Stormcloud who draw his chariot and Jehu who holds the reins? Would you like that?"

"Yahweh in heaven, would I like it!"

Again, as over Stormcloud's quivering velvet flanks, their glances met and mingled in inescapable kinship. Would it always be so, wondered Jezebel, when they met? Was this attraction—or was it antagonism?—which leaped unbidden between them, compounded of such elemental instincts, common to them both, that their very conjunction must give birth to accompanying elements after their own kind: winds, racing shadows, stamping hoofs, swiftness, passion, perhaps violence?

His hand, resting on the stone lamp base, moved gently back and forth, palm cupped slightly as to the contours of a horse's velvet flank. Impulsively she let herself sway with the wind, reached out her hand to steady herself by the lamp stand, slid it along the round stone... Deliberately, for a second time, he drew his own away, but not before she had sensed the spasmodic tightening of his fingers, noted the convulsive twitching of the little muscle above his shaven temple.

She laughed amusedly. "The wind is strong, isn't it—makes you lose your balance! I'll speak to the king at once," she continued briskly, forestalling his instinctive retreat by arriving at the stairs ahead of him. "He needs a new charioteer, and I've never fancied his choice of horses."

"I—I'm not sure—"

"Don't tell me that. If there's one thing you and I could never be, it's unsure of ourselves. You don't believe me? Then wait until you find yourself in the king's chariot behind Midnight and Stormcloud, the reins in your hands."

She had won. She knew by the way he stood, bracing his body against the wind, outstretched fingers curled and tensed. Descending slowly into the darkness, she smiled with satisfaction, then halted suddenly.

"Oh, by the way, Jehu! Whatever became of Elijah?"

"Elijah?"

She had the full advantage now, for, while she was quite immersed in darkness, he was still standing close to the lantern. Her narrowed eyes detected his first startled motion, followed by a guarded tightening of his features,

"Yes. That strange creature they used to call the Man of Yahweh—remember? I just thought you prophets might know whether he's still alive."

"He's—alive, I know that. I—I believe he lives somewhere on the edge of the desert. If—if it's important that the queen should discover—"

"Heavens, no! It's of no importance. I was just curious."

She went on down the stairs, soft sandals making no sound, eyes gleaming in the darkness. She knew very well that the Man of Yahweh was alive, could have told, after a little checking with her spies, exactly where he might be found. Once she had changed her mind about destroying him, choosing a more subtle technique for supplanting his Yahweh with her Melkart, it had amused her through the years to play with him as a cat plays with a mouse, allowing him plenty of running space but keeping him forever aware of the sharpness of her claws.

So Elijah was maintaining contact with certain of the prophets. How? Not through the wanderings of the guilds, for of late years the *nabis,* habituated to sedentary comfort, had lost their taste for wandering. By outside infiltration? If so, by whom? Brows furrowing, she remained motionless, one small foot poised beside the other on the shallow shelf of stone. That queer member of the guild in Samaria who kept coming and going, the one Ahab used to fume about because his prophecies were so unfavorable? Micaiah. That was his name. A little man with thin arms and small, fine skull bones. Not a weak man, however. A steel rod could possess the same thinness as a reed. Yes, she must watch Micaiah...

Seeing the shadow at the foot of the stairs, grotesquely elongated by the slanting flare of the torch suspended by the guardhouse door, she froze, pressed herself flat against the outer wall. Fear tightened her throat. Whose was the figure standing just beyond the turn, and what was it doing with its hands upraised and curved, as if in readiness...?

Obadiah! He has always hated me, she thought mechanically, before remembering that the steward must surely have gone with Ahab. Where was Eshmun? Waiting, probably, as she had told him, in the guardhouse, playing draughts and getting himself drunk with the soldiers. Suppose she called him! Granted that he could hear her through the thick walls and above all the other sounds, could he get to her in time? Not as quickly, surely, as that waiting figure, only a few steps away! Return up the winding stairs to Jehu? No—better to remain here where she could see what was approaching, than be swept back into that spiral of darkness!

When her ears detected the sound of measured steps and the dull clinking of a spear shaft against stone, she almost sobbed with relief. Thank heaven, the guard! At his approach the figure wavered, became absorbed into the shadow of the guardhouse wall. Jezebel waited until the pacing guard was opposite the stairway,

"Eshmun!" she cried sharply. "Where are you?"

"Here, my lady." His welcome voice came promptly, soothingly, and presently the lamp illumined his figure at the foot of the stairs, bowed low with his usual faultless decorum. She descended to him gratefully.

"Where were you, Eshmun?" In spite of her relief, there was a hint of panic in her voice.

"Did not my lady tell me to await her coming in the guardhouse? If this poor slave has failed in his duty to the mistress of men's destinies—"

"No, no, you've done nothing amiss." Relief turned her tone almost affectionately bantering. "What's the matter? I've never seen you look so upset. And your hands are trembling! What happened, Eshmun? Did you lose at draughts?"

"The eyes of the queen of women are too keen. She even knows when the humblest of her slaves has played a game and—lost."

Following him down the outer stairway of the great square tower, she still looked back nervously, but she could detect no pursuing shadow, and the eunuch's tall figure outlined against the even-spaced flares of torchlight was reassuring. She noted gratefully the strong curves of the fingers lifted in a brief steadying gesture.

Suddenly she frowned. "You came very promptly when I called you, Eshmun."

"It is a slave's duty, my lady, to be always waiting."

"As you came from the guardhouse, did anyone brush past you?"

"Not—not that I recall, my lady."

"And you saw no one in the shadows?"

He hesitated only an instant. "No one, my lady."

She placed light fingers on his shoulder. "How fortunate I am to have such a faithful servant, Eshmun! How could I ever do without you!"

Casual and fleeting though her touch was, she could feel him tremble.

The discovery she made in that moment caused her to stop short, turned her weak, first with outrage, then with suppressed merriment. Why—*Eshmun was in love with her!* It was as worshiping devotee that once, long ago, he had invaded her privacy. And all these years she had believed him an enigma, had wondered what complex emotions lay hidden beneath the opaque surface of his perfect decorum. A good joke on Jael, who had suspected such dark and treacherous depths! When all the time there had really been nothing there—nothing at all except a simple and doglike devotion!

CHAPTER 2

1

It was an utterly foolhardy plan. Its one chance out of a hundred for success lay in its very madness. Yet when at dawn Ahab flung himself, fully clothed, on his couch, his sleep was dreamless and untroubled. For three days and nights he had labored, scarcely closing his eyes. Now the preparation was complete. His final order had been given—save one. Before evening his kingdom would have been either lost or won. Until the appointed hour, there was nothing further he could do.

Awakened by his armor-bearer, Joel, he donned cuirass, helmet, and bronze greaves, buckled on his sword in silence. Proceeding to the tower of the citadel, he let his critical gaze sweep the city's enclosure. The chariots were horsed and manned, a good hundred of them, crowding the space between citadel and city gate. What appeared to be a dense melee of spearsmen and swordsmen and archers, swarmed inside the citadel without plan or purpose, was in reality a well-designed pattern, capable of conversion into orderly marching ranks at an instant's notice. And the motley handful of infantrymen looking more like rabble than soldiers, crowded into the city gate...

Ahab smiled grimly. Could the crafty Ben-hadad possibly be stupid—or drunk—enough to fall into the trap? Senses sharpening to even greater acuteness, he turned his attention to the camp of the Syrians, submerged, like the city, in the apparent quiet of the noon siesta. All signs of activity had ceased. The mounds of earth and stones being erected for bombardment of the walls by siege-engines and battering rams were deserted, the tethered horses grazing, unattended, beyond the chariot area. So straight overhead was the blazing sun that the shadowless hills seemed limned on flat canvas. With an abrupt gesture he drew his sword from its sheath and swung it in a wide arc.

The handful of two hundred-odd poorly armed and apparently ill-trained infantrymen poured from the gate through the narrow angle beneath the flanking tower and down the ramp with a silent efficiency oddly at variance with their shuffling step and unmilitary bearing. No ram's horn announced their departure. Rigidly alert, Ahab waited only until a cloud of dust indicated the passing of an alarmed sentry across the plain toward the camp of his Syrian general. Then he plunged into action.

Down in the courtyard he sprang into his waiting chariot. "Now! And may Yahweh perform the miracle that can save us!"

"You doubt the wisdom of Yahweh?" demanded the scowling young man at his side, his charioteer for only a matter of hours.

"No," retorted Ahab curtly. "The stupidity of Ben-hadad."

However, as the superb black horses arched their necks, uncoiled their velvet flanks, and flowed through the gate of the citadel, he knew a few moments of exaltation, of almost complete confidence. This bold young son of Israel, who was so certain that he knew the will of the Eternal and in whose fingers reins became connecting nerves, must hold an even more indomitable energy than that of these two splendid horses in his grasp!

But as they charged down the narrow channel between the tides of grimly silent swordsmen and spearsmen and archers, his confidence waned. What were seven thousand men unversed in warfare beside Ben-hadad's twenty—thirty thousand? And this meager display of chariots, crowding easily into the small area of the market place... How many minutes before they would be reduced to dust and rubble?

The chariot thundered through the gate, wheeled with a screaming of leather tires to negotiate the angle between wall and guard tower, and rattled down the long ramp, the rumble of its wheels already drowned in the roar of chariots close behind it. There was no turning back now. The scales were plunging sharply. Ahab waited grimly for the sharp turning which would give the first clear view of the valley and the verdict of life or death for Israel.

2

"What!" Ben-hadad, king of Syria, reared himself on his elbow and set down his wine bowl just long enough to ogle the sentry in mock alarm. "At leasht two hundred of them, you shay? Marching down the ramp and preparing to sh-storm our camp? By Hadad, I'm overcome by thish dish-display of strength!" He lifted the silver-rimmed bowl in unsteady hands. "Brother kings, a toast! To the flower of the army of Ish-Israel—and shweet may be our plucking!"

The monarch's flushed face disappeared within the upreared bowl. With loud guffaws his companions followed suit—all but one. A beardless Hittite with two long locks of hair falling on either side of his tall, pointed cap remained erect on his couch and set down his full bowl untasted.

"This Ahab doesn't sound like such a fool as that," he ventured. "Shouldn't my lord Ben-hadad at least investigate—"

The king rose resignedly from his couch and floundered across the carpet to the entrance of his tent. "By Hadad, he's right! I can see them. We'd better—" For an instant caution sharpened both voice and vision, then he rubbed his eyes, looked again, and laughed uproariously. "At leasht two hundred—and we a mere twenty thoushand! By Hadad, what will become of us!" He turned unsteadily toward the sentry. "Dispatch a half-dozen chariots and round up a whole company of fifty—no, better make it a hundred. What do you shay, brothers? Shall we take them dead or alive?... Alive, you shay? Good! Bring them here to our tent. We want to shee thish mighty host—pride of Ish—of Ish—"

The thirty-two princely allies of Ben-hadad shouted loud agreement—all but one. Quietly the Hittite slipped out of the pavilion, ran to his own less gaudy tent on the fringe of the circle, issued a brisk command, and within moments was pounding across the plain in his chariot, a detachment of his own mounted warriors close behind. Arriving at the scene of skirmish only seconds behind the company of a hundred dispatched by Ben-hadad, he immediately cursed himself for his undue anxiety. Why, the approaching enemy detachment was a mere handful, ill-armed and so inefficient they could scarcely keep in step! The guards at the outpost could have handled them alone. He had been a fool...

Then suddenly he stared, horses rearing and reins frozen in his hands, as the full strength of Israel's *gibborim,* smuggled into Samaria on a series of moonless nights from every one of the eleven provinces, discarded their roles of inefficient bravado and sprang into action. So swift was the transformation, so devastating the onslaught, that Ben-hadad's company of a hundred were taken quite off guard. Totally unprepared for hand-to-hand combat with an outnumbering band of physical champions, they fell like grain beneath a sharpened sickle. Within moments every man of the *gibborim* had picked his victim. Those who were not at once impaled on spears or hacked with shortswords found themselves pursued in their frenzied retreat by shapes which wore the limbs of giants, arms which elongated their brandished weapons into twice their length. Before the Hittite could calm his rearing horses, the small area of the skirmish was a screaming shambles. Reaching for the silver trumpet at his girdle, he blew a long shrill blast.

"Forward!" he shouted. "Forward in the name of Hadad! They're only a handful. A gold piece and a slave girl to every Hittite who gets his man! Follow me!"

But his warriors, seeing what had escaped his attention, the advance chariots of Israel's army pouring down the ramp and across the plain, were in full retreat toward the camp. Wheeling, he understood instantly the significance of the approaching menace as well as his own peril. So he had been right! King Ahab was not the fool Ben-hadad in his fuddled drunkenness had thought him. What a masterly coup—choosing an hour when he knew the Syrian monarch and his henchmen would be drunk and idling, clearing the stage of all obstacles by this clever preliminary skirmish! And how easy it would have been to stop them!

Since he was not a man to turn his back on danger, the arrow struck him square in the forehead, between the two long sidelocks of hair.

3

Pouring out of the high western gate of the city and down the ramp like the swollen Kishon let loose, Ahab and his seven thousand took the idle, drunken Syrians completely by surprise. Before dozing archers had time to fit arrows to their bows, or infantrymen to buckle on their swords, they found themselves face to face with furious-eyed fanatics whose hoarse shouts, "For Ahab and Yahweh!" were but seconds in advance of their spear thrusts. Scalps were sundered and breasts thrust through while hands were reaching for shields and helmets.

Within minutes the camp of Ben-hadad and his allies was a shambles. Wine from overturned goblets mingled its crimson with that of human blood. Horses, as crazed as their drivers, reared and plunged and floundered, the hands which had half harnessed them to their chariots locked in a death grip to their traces. The sturdy two-wheeled chariots which had been the army's proudest assets became its worst liabilities, imprisoning both men and beasts in an impossible tangle of wreckage.

The soldiers of Israel were unequaled in valor when they knew that Yahweh was with them. No need today of close wedge formation or of stout walls of shields to protect advancing archers! No need at all for defense, merely for courage to advance and swift certainty of stroke, whether with bow and arrow, battle ax, spear or shortsword. Each Israelite acted for himself and killed his man, driving his weapon home with the sure aim of a stonecutter pounding his mallet.

"For Ahab and Yahweh! Blessed be Yahweh, our deliverer, the Lord of hosts!"

Into the wreckage they plunged, and the Syrians fell before them like ripe grain before the reaper's sickle. Those who had the power to escape and flee, the soldiers of Israel pursued, the swiftest among them reaping a second crop of death and even a third, and the slower following after them like gleaners despoiling any clinging roots of life their comrades might have left.

When finally Ahab rode back toward the city gate, the sun hung toward the western hills. In its path the whole long valley with its uprooted tents, its twisted heaps of rubble, lay bathed in crimson. His soldiers, tireless even after the long pursuit, were already busy with the job of salvaging—despoiling the tents of furnishings, stripping the corpses, heaping gold goblets and royal vestments indiscriminately with shortswords and scabbards, helmets, jeweled daggers, shields of bronze and leather, blood-caked tunics. They were drunk with victory and the taste of blood.

"Hail, Ahab, son of Yahweh!"

"Ride to victory over the slain bodies of your enemies!"

"Let Yahweh drink the blood of his foes and be filled!"

He forced his lips to smile, acknowledged their hoarse croaks with waves of his hand. But his fingers clinging to the gilded rail of the chariot were strained white. What in heaven's name was the matter with him! This was his victory, as well as Yahweh's. He should be returning home as proudly triumphant as these two superb horses which yesterday had been smuggled into his stables from Megiddo and which were now drawing his chariot, heads erect and black manes tossing. Instead he stood with bent head and twisting stomach, eyes smarting less from the brightness of the sun than from a sense of pitying loss for the strewn bodies which were the symbols of his victory.

Not so the man at his side. The dark eyes beneath the charioteer's bronze helmet gazed full at the sun with unblinking intensity, their narrowed pupils mirroring its crimson. Ahab's gaze lingered on the rapt face, the exultant figure. In the presence of such self-confident fulfillment, he was all the more conscious of his own frustration.

"You—have performed a great service for Israel today," he said grudgingly.

The dark eyes flashed. "Not I. Yahweh."

"But without your counsel we would never have thought of such a bold maneuver."

"A prophet," replied Jehu sternly, "should never take credit to himself for interpreting the Eternal's will."

"Nor a king for following his interpretation," retorted Ahab somewhat testily. He was not sure he relished this new relationship—a charioteer who assumed for himself the authority of a prophet. If the man had not shown himself to be such a wizard with horses and if Jezebel had not requested his promotion...

"If the king had seen fit to follow my counsel a little further," said Jehu boldly, "it would have been better both for him and for Israel."

Ahab's hand tightened on the chariot rail. "What do you mean?"

The charioteer looked straight ahead, his firmly braced body an arrogant line of defiance. But his words were deferent enough. "As his servant ventured to suggest, we might have overtaken the son of Hadad."

Ahab's cheeks suddenly throbbed with the glare of the setting sun. "What good would that have done?" he demanded with tight-lipped calmness.

"Ben-hadad will be back next year," replied the younger man with the bold vigor of authority, "at the time when kings go forth to battle. Since he has let his enemy live, the son of Yahweh should consider well and strengthen his position."

Ahab's long fingers circled the carved rail with a crushing grip. It was all he could do to keep from seizing this young upstart by his arrogant, unbending shoulders and dropping him from the chariot. The sheer insolence of a charioteer's presuming to censure his king's techniques of military strategy! Just because he had devised one daring maneuver and proclaimed it in the name of Yahweh...

In the name of Yahweh! And was he still speaking in that name? Ahab ground the rim of bossed cedar more deeply into his palms. Was Yahweh really displeased with him because he had refused to pursue Ben-hadad, had let him escape on horseback after that last noble attempt to rally the Syrian forces? And indeed, just what had restrained him? Certainly not fear. At sight of the fleeing king on his black Cilician mount, leaping a solid wall of spears, Ahab had felt the very blood leap within him. He had forgotten for the moment that the possessor of this kingly courage was his enemy, just as that day long ago on the mountain...

"Look out!" The cry exploded from his lips like a missile shot from a sling. "Watch where you're going! That man on the ground..."

In one sweeping gesture he seized the reins from Jehu's hands, snapped them taut with an iron strength, at the same time swinging his right arm in a swift arc which almost tore it from its socket. The horses screamed, swerved sharply to the right and straight up into the air. But the sickening lurch of the wheel told him it was too late even before he had flung the reins again to Jehu, sprung from the chariot, and knelt beside the twisted shape which had been blocking their path. The hand he had seen frantically signaling was now a limp reed, the upreared head with is panic-stricken eyes a mutilated fruit dangling from a broken stem. Gently he closed the staring eyes, wiped the boyish features clean of blood-caked dust, then drew a long sidelock of hair over the slender column of neck, scored deep by the wheel rim. When he sprang again into the careening chariot, he was as unnerved as the quivering beasts Jehu was still endeavoring to bring back under control.

"You saw the man lying there," he said in furious accusation. "You must have seen his hand waving, known he was alive. Yet you made no effort to stop."

Scowling, the young charioteer pitted his stubborn strength against that of the plunging blacks, nursed them slowly but surely into unwilling submission.

"Why should I have stopped?" he countered sullenly. "The man was a Hittite, wasn't he, fighting with the Syrians? It was Yahweh's will that he should die."

Before Ahab's vision the round red sun exploded into tongues of flame, one of them searing his own throat. "Then hereafter follow Ahab's will instead of Yahweh's," he spat out hotly, "at least when you're driving his horses. You may be Yahweh's prophet, but you're the king's charioteer, and don't forget it."

The words of defiance brought a sense of relief, almost of cleansing. The mood of melancholy, of frustration, was left behind with the mutilated human remnant which he had been prompted by some inexplicable impulse to save. It was as if, by exerting his will on Jehu, he had mastered also some alien quality within himself. Indeed, as they approached the city and were met by an acclaiming populace, it was Ahab now who stood boldly erect in the chariot, the charioteer who struggled, fumed, and sweated in desperate endeavor to control his headstrong horses.

Up the long ramp they crept, breasting the reluctantly parting crowds like a frail craft navigating a flooded sluiceway, through the choked opening beneath the high square gate tower, with missiles of spring flowers instead of stones and arrows impeding their progress along the narrow, twisting passage, through the great gate and up into the citadel beyond.

"Hail, Ahab, beloved son of Yahweh!"

"Sharp are your arrows. Nations fall before you!"

"He has made you taste the flesh and drink the blood of your enemies!"

Flushed with success, Ahab received their tributes. There was life now, not death, in his path. These were his people, and he had saved them. Jehu was wrong. Yahweh was not displeased with him. At last, Ahab exulted, his mood still one of defiance, he had wiped out the stain of his old cowardice. Was it power for which the God of Israel hungered? Then he had it, for today Hadad, rival lord of the mountain and the storm, had been leveled in the dust. Was it the blood of his enemies for which he thirsted? Then tonight he was filled to repletion.

"Sing your songs to Yahweh," he commanded, lifting his gold-circled helmet. "It's his victory, not mine."

They obeyed with alacrity and vigor.

"Yea, sing praises to Yahweh, our deliverer!"

"He who each year goes down to his death!"

"And lives again to take vengeance on his enemies!"

"Yahweh, who regains his youth in the fire of battle!"

"Sing to Yahweh, King of the City!"

The words spun against Ahab's consciousness with the soft barrage of spring flowers and leafy sprays and garlands, then turned to cold, stinging pellets. Confusion seized him. Where was he, in Samaria or Tyre? *King of the city! He who goes down to his death...*

Feeling sudden brightness smite his eyes, he lifted his gaze to the highest point of the citadel where Yahweh's temple glittered, its two bronze pillars twin strokes of flame, its white stones turned blood-red by one last sword thrust of the setting sun. And slowly his senses steadied. It was Samaria, not Tyre. And it was Yahweh's temple which crowned the crest, not Melkart's. Yet even as he watched, the red glow faded. The white walls changed from crimson to purple to gray. The two strokes of flame burned out like guttered candles.

CHAPTER 3

1

Seeing it standing in the audience chamber, Jezebel knew it only for a jar of unguent, the gift of Osorkon of Egypt—not an omen of the one disaster she feared above all others.

Its beauty almost took her breath away. High as a man's head and fashioned of pure alabaster, it gathered into its milk-white depths all the sunlight streaming through the high grilled windows. In spite of its great size, it was a thing of perfect symmetry, its two enormous handles as gracefully proportioned as those of a small cosmetic jar. The fragrance of its precious unguent filled the chamber like a breath of incense.

The king having gone to Megiddo on military business, she went reluctantly to the audience chamber to receive the envoys in Ahab's place; reluctantly, because she knew the mission was another attempt to persuade Ahab to join the confederation against Assyria. But at sight of the jar her reluctance vanished. She feted the envoys for nearly a week, trusting from day to day that Ahab would surely return before their departure. Finally, when they insisted that they must take back an answer to the Pharaoh's letter, she permitted it to be read in her presence, fortifying herself for the boring recital with as many physical comforts as possible. But the platter of sweetmeats placed close to her elbow was never tasted.

"To the king Ahab, my brother, son of Yahweh and lord of the land of Israel, speak, saying: I, Osorkon, son of Amon-Re and lord of the two lands, bid him greeting and am happy to assure my brother that the gods of Egypt have bestowed divine approval on his marriage with my daughter, fairest and most beloved of all our princesses, and as soon as I receive word that my brother also has secured the approval of his esteemed god..."

Jezebel managed somehow to hold herself still, even to stifle a yawn with delicate, rose-tipped fingers and, when the letter was finished, to turn to the scribe with just the right blending of diplomatic interest and personal unconcern.

"Write a message from Ahab, son of Yahweh, divinely anointed king of Israel, to Osorkon, son of Amon-Re and all the rest—you know how to phrase it. Tell him that his brother Ahab appreciates his gift and that as soon as he has consulted with his deity as to the matter of their previous correspondence, he will send messengers to the court of his brother Osorkon apprising him of the decision."

She continued to wear the smiling mask during the subsequent final banquet, and only after she had escaped to her apartment did she lay it abruptly aside.

"Bring me a mirror."

Holding the bronze oval close to the lamp stand, she studied her features dispassionately, noting the faint grooves above the finely molded cheekbones, the unmistakable slackening of muscles beneath the turquoise-tinted lower lids. With an impatient gesture she thrust the mirror back into Jael's hands.

She had known always that this moment would come. The wonder was that she had not had to face it long ago, for Ahab was unique among the world's monarchs in having taken but one wife. What she had not expected was her own reaction. She had supposed the furious fires of jealousy which now swept her had long since burned to ashes. She wished she were an animal with raking claws, a huge rock with the power to crush—anything but a woman who must act subtly, shrewdly!

The next morning she went to the Temple of Yahweh and summoned Melkiah, the high priest, to meet her in the king's porch. He came, flushed and puffing, mitered headdress awry, ephod dangling from one jeweled shoulder strap.

Swiftly she put his fears at rest. "I have come to offer sacrifice to Yahweh," she said, smiling, "in the absence of my lord the king."

The priest regained his confidence before his breath. "The queen must forgive—humble servant—was not expecting—knew the king was away—hour when the queen usually goes to make sacrifice to Melkart—"

Jezebel shrugged. "That can wait for once. After all, it is Yahweh who is lord of this land, not Melkart."

"Yes, yes." The flushed face beamed. "If the queen will excuse her servant, he will go and make ready. A sheep—or perhaps a bullock—?"

"A bullock," said Jezebel, her eyes resting speculatively on the sagging features, the eagerly pursed lips. "Wait a minute. Sit here beside me for a little, Melkiah. The sacrifice can wait."

As he sank into the cushioned armchair, she noted a hint of wariness in the narrowed eyes half hidden within their fleshy pouches. Was he, perhaps, cleverer than he seemed? Better to proceed cautiously.

"What a lot of worry I must have caused you," she said ruefully, "in those early days when I was so insistent that Melkart, and not Yahweh, should be supreme in Israel! I must have given you many sleepless nights, Melkiah."

The priest cleared his throat. Well—yes, he didn't mind admitting that he was finding life more comfortable in recent years. "Less—"

"Hectic?" supplied Jezebel sympathetically. "I'm finding it that way, too, Melkiah. Do you suppose all brides are like that before they settle down? Look at Ahaziah's new wife from Ekron! Insisting on having a temple here in Samaria for her Baalzebub! Let's hope the new bride from Egypt doesn't make as much trouble."

The—the new—Melkiah must ask her pardon...

"What! You hadn't heard the king is taking a new bride from Egypt?" The queen's eyes were wide and innocent. "Then he hasn't asked Yahweh's approval of the marriage? Oh, but he will soon, probably when he comes back from Megiddo. I do hope"—she shot him a swift glance—"she will be more reasonable about her gods than I was. She'll bring them to Samaria, of course—Isis and Osiris and Amon-Re and all the rest. No telling how many temples she'll insist on building. That is, provided, of course, Yahweh gives his approval to the marriage."

Melkiah pursed his lips and rolled his eyes piously toward heaven. At the same time his fingers slowly stroked the edges of one of the round jewels on his breastplate. Yes, he agreed, all these predictions would undoubtedly come to pass—that is, provided Yahweh gave his approval.

His eyes, returning earthward, met the queen's, then looked hastily away.

2

But Ahab was not in Megiddo. He was crouched on the stone floor of a lower terrace in the palace at Jezreel, playing at skittles. His companion, a boy of about ten, watched with bated breath while he carefully aimed the thick ivory disk, slid it along the surface of polished inlaid cedar and between the tiny wooden columns at the far end, expertly downing the three remaining cone-shaped figures.

"Good! Bravo, Uncle Ahab!" The boy clapped his hands. "Aie, aie! Never as long as I live will I be able to play like that."

Ahab laughed modestly. "Yes, you will. Wait awhile. Your father and Uncle Dan and I were shooting skittles when we were half your size."

"But you used to beat them. Father says so. Show me again how you hold it, will you? Wait! I'll set the ivory figures up again."

As the small figure hung poised over the game board, Ahab watched each eager motion with a hungry intensity. Sometimes, as now, he found the depth of emotion he felt in the presence of this son of Obadiah almost frightening. Suppose his love for this boy, as for his own first-born son, should hold in its very essence not a blessing but a curse! Better, perhaps, if when the servant had come to him two years ago with that complaint of a disturbance...

"It sounds like some kind of animal, my lord, in the wall behind the big earthen storing jar. I would have ordered the thing moved except that the king gave orders nothing in that lower storeroom was to be touched."

A foolish whim that the old secret must be protected! He had opened his lips to order the jar removed, the hole behind it cleaned out and closed with masonry...

"An—animal, you say? Impossible! But—I'll go down and have a look..."

Conscious of the servants' curious, gaping faces, he had traversed the lower court and the kitchens and, taking a lamp, entered the small dark storeroom, closing the door behind him. And instantly the damp earth floor beneath his bare soles, the stale familiar odors, had dissolved all sense of time. Then, as now, remembering, he was a child again, tugging and straining at the great clay storing jar which hid their secret, surprised to find how small it seemed, and thinking that it must be empty, for it moved so easily. The hole, too, seemed small, hardly big enough to squeeze through.

He was not even surprised when, stooping and giving the familiar signal—one long whistle followed by two short—he received the sepulchral response; nor when, following a series of muffled tappings and scrapings, a small black curly head thrust itself through the opening.

"Hist!" he warned in accordance with the once familiar pattern.

"Hist yourself!" The young newcomer climbed nimbly through the opening.

Ahab frowned. This was no incorporeal figment of his imagination but a flesh-and-blood entity with dirty hands and knees and one front tooth missing.

"Who are you?" he demanded abruptly, wondering where he had seen those eyes before. Jet black they were and set wide apart, and, though obviously frightened by his sudden sternness, they did not waver.

"Jeshua, the son of Obadiah."

"I—see. And what are you doing here, Jeshua, son of Obadiah?"

"Finding the secret passage." The gap in the front teeth had disappeared now along with the engaging grin, but the straight line of lips hiding it did not tremble.

"And how did you know there was a secret passage?"

"My mother told me."

Of course. Rachel's eyes. And this was Rachel's son, the swaddled mite he had held in his arms the night after his own son had died. The memory stirred in him a painful awareness, like life prickling in a long-numbed limb.

"She said you and she used to crawl through under the city wall. That is—you *are* the king, aren't you?" He might have been speaking of the gardener.

"Yes. I am the king."

"I thought so. I knew you by your hair, black and curly like mine, and because you look so stern. My mother says you used to laugh and have fun, but not any more. Why not? Isn't it fun being king?"

"I—Does your mother know you're here?" demanded Ahab abruptly.

The steady eyes wavered, but only momentarily. "No. I didn't ask her. She said it was a secret. But nobody saw me, at the other end, I mean, outside the city wall. And I didn't mean to come clear through. I wouldn't have if you hadn't whistled the signal."

The prickling awareness had become warmth now, tingling through his whole being. "And you weren't afraid?" he demanded with a sudden fierce urgency. Obadiah had been afraid. The day they had discovered the hole, he had refused to enter it, had stayed behind in the little storeroom while Ahab, alone and terrified yet following some inexorable compulsion, had groped his way through the clammy darkness.

"Of course I was afraid. I almost died, I was so scared. But— when you see a hole going somewhere, you—you have to find out where it goes!"

Ahab flung back his head and laughed. "Yes, son, yes. You certainly do."

The word "son" had come as naturally to his lips as if he had been speaking to Eliah. For in the exultant discovery of that moment he had known that this *was* his son, as none of the living seed of his loins could ever be...his and Rachel's, born of his spirit though not of his body...

"Show you how to hold the skittles? Sure! Come here, son. See, hold it like this. Here! Let me hold your fingers in mine."

The hand cupped within his was longer, slenderer than it had been on that day he had led the boy from the storeroom, chiding the bewildered kitchen servants for letting an errant waif from the streets slip past them...and more confident. For since then the two hands had been joined in partnerships far more adventurous than a game of skittles—journeys through the caves which honeycombed Gilboa, climbs to remote glens in search of rare spring flowers, even a swift ride in the king's chariot from Jezreel to Tabor, their fingers linked together on the reins.

"I did it! Look, Uncle Ahab. I knocked them all down at once!"

The woman watching in the pillared portico stepped quietly forward. "It's time to come home now, darling. That is, if our lord the king pleases."

"All right, Mother." The boy was casually cheerful. "Just one more shot. But why do you call him our lord the king? I thought you and he used to play together."

Ahab rose quickly from his knees. For an instant his eyes and those of the woman clung together, then hers turned deliberately away. "Because he is our lord the king. And what happened long ago is—as if it had never been."

"Is it?" Suddenly Ahab was at her side, his voice as roughly insistent as the grasp of his fingers about her slender wrists.

"Let me go!" She tried desperately to draw her hands away, but he held them fast. "You have no right—"

"No right!" His voice was tense. "Have you forgotten all the times I pulled you up the last steep slope of a mountain, dragged you

246

through tight places in a cave, guided you through the steps of *meholah*—yes, and held you in my arms—"

He could feel her pulses leap through the knots of his fingers, even while her muscles strained. "No! It wasn't you who did all those things. It was a simple peasant boy of Israel, not a king."

Unable to draw away, she pushed back into the space between the courtyard wall and the tall fluted pillar, its unyielding straightness matched in the taut defiance of her slender body.

"And now," returned Ahab, his voice dropping almost to a whisper, "I am neither peasant boy nor king. Only a man who has known for a long time that you are the only woman he has ever really loved."

He was so close to her that he could smell the fragrance of her hair, compounded, not of perfumed oils, but of clean winds and mown grass and sunshine. At that moment, he knew, he could have taken her again in his arms and she would not have resisted, for through the pulsing wrists he sensed a sudden letting down of all barriers. But he did not do it. Their love, he knew swiftly, was too precious to be cheapened by furtive embrace or stolen kisses. Instead he let the hard fury of emotion resolve itself into tenderness, slipping his fingers slowly downward to enfold her small palms, absorbing through his hungry gaze all the beloved, familiar lineaments. She had changed very little with the years. Time, finding her molded of warm clay instead of ivory, had used none of his finer instruments upon her, only filled in the hollows beneath the too prominent cheekbones, softened the too generous curves of mouth, added a ripeness of fulfillment to the chastely immature breasts. The wide-set black eyes, kin to the vibrancy of midnight hair, had been left untouched, for they were not of the essence of time. They returned his gaze now, honest and unabashed as usual, concealing nothing.

I know, they replied steadily. *And I love you—have always—shall always...*

When he finally released her hands, it was to draw a long breath of fulfillment.

Deliberately the woman moved from the shelter of the fluted column toward the boy, who, still hunched on the floor, was struggling stubbornly with the ivory disks, "Come, Jeshua," she said calmly. "It's time now to say good-bye to—to our lord the king. You will not be seeing him again."

The child looked up, startled and distressed. "But—why—"

247

"She means until I come again to Jezreel," explained Ahab. "You see, kings can't spend all their time playing skittles. I must return to Samaria tonight."

"No," said Rachel. "I meant just what I said." Still deliberately, she moved between him and the child. "You will not be seeing each other again."

Ahab's new-found tranquillity exploded like a bursting bubble. Amid the ensuing emptiness he heard her voice continuing quietly. "Before he was born, I promised him to Yahweh, even as Hannah once promised her son Samuel. Before you return to Jezreel he will have gone to be with a band of prophets who live beyond Jordan."

His relief was so great that he broke into boyish laughter. "Is that all? Of course you must fulfill your vow. And it's time the boy was properly educated. But not beyond Jordan." He waxed suddenly eager. "I'll take him to Samaria. He'll be taught with my own sons in Yahweh's temple. Yes, and you shall come—"

But the words died unspoken before the look on her face. "It is Yahweh to whom I vowed my son," said Rachel with scathing coldness. "Not Baal."

Her words were like a plunge into freezing water. "What do you mean by that?"

Her gaze remained unwavering, though she reached one hand behind her to place it reassuringly on the boy's curly head. "It is not Yahweh whom you worship in Samaria."

His anger choked him so that he could scarcely speak. "How—how dare you—"

"Speak the truth to the king? I'd dare anything for the sake of my son."

"But it's not true!" Words came pouring now, hot, as from an erupting volcano. "Once, I'll admit, there was too much of Baal in Samaria. But not since that day of Yahweh's triumph on Mount Carmel. For ten years, I swear, Yahweh has not had a rival in Samaria. He has been King of the City—" He stopped short, staring at her in sudden consternation.

"Yes," she said. "Exactly. King of the City—Melkart."

"I—I shouldn't have used those words—" stammered Ahab.

"Why not? They were the truth. It's because they are the truth that I must send my son away."

"No!" It was fear that activated him now, as well as anger. "I won't let you take him away! I tell you he's going to Samaria to be educated with my own children, as a prince, in the temple of Yahweh."

"And have him grow up like your sons, a sot and a wastrel? Yahweh forbid!"

He could have taken her by the shoulders, as he had done more than once when they were children, and shaken her. "Do you know what happens to those who defy their king?" he demanded loudly.

"In Tyre and Moab and Damascus—yes," she replied steadily. "They hear knocks on their doors at night and are never heard from again. Is that what happens now in Israel?"

He had seen such scorn in her eyes only once, the day he had passed her by the well here in Jezreel after the killing of Yahweh's prophets. But, bitterly though the sight of it rankled, it was not her appraisal of him or of his kingdom which mattered most at the moment. It was her child. To have him taken away, he knew suddenly, turned into a sack-clothed fanatic who might speak his name only in denunciation—it would be more than he could bear!

"You can't send him away!" he cried hoarsely. "I won't let you. Do you hear? I can force him to come to Samaria and you to come with him, if I just speak the word. I'm the king of Israel, I tell you!"

She made no reply, merely took the child's hand and moved with her usual swift but unhurried rhythm across the marble terrace and through the arch leading to the outer stairway. She did not look back, but the boy, according to his custom, turned just inside the arch and waved his hand.

"Good-bye, Uncle Ahab. Leave the skittle board just as it is, won't you? We didn't finish our game!"

3

Before Ahab had time to remove the dust of his journey from Jezreel, he received a note scrawled on a bit of papyrus: "Come to me after the hours of siesta. I'll be waiting in the ivory palace."

He frowned, being in no mood either for entertainment or for subtle prodding as to his duties in running the kingdom. All other matters—even the Syrian war threat and the defense plan which had occasioned his visit to Megiddo—seemed trivial beside the compulsion which now stirred him. Until he had talked with Obadiah and insured the achievement of his purpose, he would know no rest.

But Obadiah, it seemed, had gone to Shechem and was not expected in Samaria until evening.

Rigid with tension, he lay on his couch, every fiber of his long body resistant to the soothing wiles of the little Egyptian masseur.

"If only the good God, the anointed one, would make himself less like his country and more like mine! Not like the golden sands of the blessed Nile, I do not expect that! But, by the eye of Horus, how can one massage a block of limestone!"

Ahab sprang upright, like a bow released from the pull of the bowman's fingers. "Then don't try. Take yourself and your stinking perfumed oils away. I'm in no mood for them. And send Nadab, my scribe, to me," he ordered abruptly.

Of course. Better far to send a letter to Obadiah than run the risk of an interview. By the time Nadab was squatted on the carpet, a reed pen behind each protruding ear, palette hugged lovingly against his bony chest, words were already besieging his lips. Nadab was interminably slow, deaf too, and half blind. But he had been Omri's secretary from army days, and Ahab seldom had the heart to summon a more efficient scribe.

"To Obadiah, chief steward of the king's household..."

Patiently, his urge for swift action only partially appeased by his restless traversing of the carpet, Ahab adjusted the pace of his thoughts to the painstaking crawl of the reed brushes across the fragments of blue pottery, stopping for frequent exchange of black for red ink and vice versa, for the extraction of fresh ostraka from the leather bag, for the maddening repetition of words for the deaf old ears.

Obadiah, beloved brother of the king, was at last to reap fitting reward for his long service. He was to be given a palace within the citadel, where his family would be maintained as part of the king's own household. His wife would become one of the queen's own ladies in waiting. And his son—here the crawling pace of Nadab's brushes set Ahab's nerve tips quivering—his son was to be favored above those of all the king's other courtiers. In fact, he was not only to be elevated to the rank of *prince*... Yes, Nadab had heard aright, the word was prince...but he was to be made an equal with the king's own sons, sharing their priestly tutors, their royal apartments, and... No, the king was not out of his mind, he had no fever, and Nadab's ears were not wells of emptiness into which no stream of truth ever poured...the son of Obadiah was to share, according to his age, the right of the king's sons to the succession of the throne.

Now for the capping stone, the final sentence. "It is for Yahweh's sake, and Israel's, that I ask you to yield to me in this desire, for it has been made clear to me that Yahweh has a purpose for your son. We must make him ready to fulfill that purpose. I am trusting that you will put no obstacles in his way."

It was done. All that remained now was to wait. But even after the scribe was gone, he continued to pace the carpet, fingering object after object, stooping once to blow the coals into a flaring vigor which matched his own increasing restiveness...caused also the golden leopard skin, the subtly ironic gift of Baalazor, to leap out from the shadows of the east wall of his chamber. Again he laid his hand on the smooth, glinting flank—to his consternation felt fire speed through his veins. Hungrily he caressed it, buried his face within the vibrant softness which was like a woman's tawny hair.

So he was not free, after all. Even though he had stopped loving her, he was still her captive, as on that day he had first seen her dancing, her bright head a flaming altar demanding his human flesh as its sacrificial victim.

Come to me after the hours of siesta. I'll be waiting in the ivory palace.

4

Jezebel spent the full siesta period in front of her dressing table, fingers curved about the ivory lotus stem of her bronze mirror, while Jael fussed over her with ointments and perfumes, bone spatulas and kohl sticks and little jars and vials. The daughter of Osorkon was reputed to be young as well as beautiful.

But at least there could be no competition between them in the matter of dress. Egyptian linens were like washed-out moonlight beside the vivid suns of Tyrian purples. She regarded with satisfaction her new long-sleeved ankle-length robe of glistening white, with its overdress of rich cerulean. Her hair, too, still as shining bronze as her polished mirror, defied competition. Only her face showed the impress of advancing years, and Jael's skill in blending and applying just the right amounts of kohl and powdered turquoise and red ocher succeeded, unless the light was too strong, in minimizing, if not concealing, its defects.

The light was not too strong in the ivory palace. Sifting in long skeins through innumerable grooves, it wove a soft web of muted beams and shadows. The suite of rooms with its central court open to the sky was now completed, every inch of its cedar-paneled walls and fluted columns inlaid with delicately carved patterns of ivory: chains of full-blown lotuses and buds; sphinxes and cherubs with lion bodies, the grooved feathers of their wings filled with rich overlays of gold and red ocher and turquoise and lapis lazuli; bright plumaged birds and battling lions and griffins set among drooping palms and thickets of papyri. Half reclining on her cushioned couch, Jezebel felt treasured and secure, like a gem in a jewel box.

Her heart leaped when she saw the sudden lighting of Ahab's face. It had been months—years—since she had detected such demanding hunger in his eyes. He would have come to her side at once, but she gestured him to an ornate cedar chair, its outstretched arms curving into two crouching ivory lions.

"Sit there, my lord. The fire will feel good after your long ride from Megiddo. I suppose it's still raining." Hugging her knees cozily, she smiled up at him across the glowing brazier. "I'm still not reconciled to your soggy upland winters. But—they have their compensations. This hot spiced wine, for instance."

"And the warmth of a woman's arms," said Ahab softly. "I'd much rather warm my hands at the fire of your hair—"

Again he moved toward her, and again she stopped him with a gesture. Reluctantly he sank into the embrace of the outthrust ivory arms and extended his fingers to the glowing coals, but his gaze continued to caress her hungrily.

Her eyes sparkled back at him. "It's this room," she chided. "There's always been something magic about it."

"You're like a piece of ivory yourself," he murmured, his eyes refusing to follow her inclusive gesture, "lovelier by far than any of these."

"Nonsense!" She laughed a little harshly. "Once, maybe, but not any longer. The deeper the lines graven in an image of ivory the better, but not so with the face of a woman. I'm growing old. No wonder I no longer satisfy my lord."

"No longer—what—I—" His eyes were startled, wary.

She laughed lightly. "Here! Try some of this spiced wine and a honey cake."

Waiting until Ahab had taken a few slow sips from the goblet, but not until he could relax sufficiently to withdraw his features from the arc of light surrounding the brazier, she said calmly, "The embassy arrived from Osorkon. They brought an unusual gift, an alabaster jar of ointment, also a message."

The ruddiness of the glowing coals suffused his features. "Did—did they—"

"Yes. They told me all about the agreement you and Osorkon have been contemplating. At least the letter did. Including your coming marriage with the Pharaoh's daughter." She made an appreciable pause. "A splendid idea, I think."

"You—you do?" His relief was ludicrously apparent.

"Of course. Surely you didn't think I'd oppose it, did you, after all the alliances I've urged you to make?"

"But—"

Though she wanted desperately to know what he had been about to say, she did not press him. Why had he been so afraid of her opposition? Because he was secretly determined to join the confederation or because he wanted another wife? Had he finished, his words might have given her a clue. Now she might never know.

"The Pharaoh is in a hurry for your decision," she said with apparent dispassion. "Not that you'll need to consider. But—I suppose Yahweh must be consulted."

"Yahweh?" She saw his eyes narrow in sudden alert concentration. "That's the first time you've ever suggested—"

"Just as a matter of form, of course," she interrupted hastily. "He has shown remarkably good judgment of late in his oracles. If he keeps on developing, he'll be quite as fit to govern the destinies of a great nation as Melkart or Hadad."

Ahab gripped the arms of his chair. "You—sound as if Yahweh, the Eternal, were capable of changing!"

"Well?" Her copper eyes caught the gleam of the coals. "Surely the deity who presides over all the complicated concerns of a great world power like Israel has *grown* since he rode in from the desert in his little wooden box!"

Ahab frowned and sipped again from his goblet. But it was the intoxication of her nearness, not of the heady, pungent wine, which kept his mind from functioning clearly. "Perhaps—perhaps you're right. But—"

"Of course I'm right. Listen, my darling." As she leaned forward, he was conscious of the subtle fragrance of myrrh and cassia and aloes blending with the faint aromas of incense scattered on the coals. "I have a confession to make. When I came to Israel, I thought that your Yahweh wasn't a great enough god to lead a people to national preeminence in this modern world. I—I deliberately tried to destroy him and put Melkart in his place. Do you hate me for it?"

"Hate you!" His hands, gripping the ivory lions' heads, showed white about the knuckles. How could a man know whether the emotions which tore his vitals sprang from love or hate? "Why are you telling me this now?" he asked abruptly.

"Because I've changed my mind," she replied simply. "I know that Yahweh is great enough, and it's we, you and I, who have made him so. I wanted you to know this, so you would understand that, even more than in the past, we are working together for Yahweh and for the greatness and glory of Israel."

"You—you really mean that?" He tried vainly to sharpen his judgment to a keen edge. "You believe we are—working together?"

"Of course. Has my lord forgotten that I am his queen, his— wife?"

"*My wife—*" Uttering a smothered cry, he started from his chair, but before he could bridge the distance between them, she clapped her hands and a slave appeared.

"The master's wine has grown cold. Bring me a fresh goblet so I can pour him another. And don't go. Wait here beside us. I may need something else."

Ahab watched the thin crimson stream pour beneath her steady fingers. "Baalazor called you a leopard," he said suddenly. "Leopards are beautiful and—cruel."

Her eyes darkened. "Only to those who try to hurt them," she replied quickly, "or to take away something which belongs to them." She held out the goblet. "After you've gone to the temple to consult Yahweh about the alliance with Egypt, come to my apartment and— tell me the outcome."

"Why should I go now?" he demanded roughly. "Tomorrow will be time enough."

She yawned and stretched lazily, with deliberate feline grace. "Better not keep such important people as Osorkon—or his daughter—waiting."

***

Jael admitted him late that night to her mistress' apartment, then discreetly vanished. Lying on her couch among the shadows, Jezebel watched him cross the room slowly, as far as the lamp stand, where he hesitated a moment, the light flaring on his features. But she could read nothing in them.

"Well?" she prompted gently.

"You'll be disappointed in Yahweh this time," he said abruptly. "He did not display the wisdom you ascribed to him."

"You mean he—disapproves of the alliance with Osorkon?"

"Yes. Both the alliance and the marriage."

"Ah! What a pity! That is, it seems so at the moment. But we'll discover, I'm sure, in the end that Yahweh knows best."

"Will we?" He withdrew from the orbit of lamplight and came toward her. "Then you haven't changed your mind about Yahweh being great enough to guide our nation? "

She shrugged her shoulders, letting the diaphanous robe of gold thread slip down to reveal their curves. "Silly! Of course not! It won't affect our trade with Egypt. Osorkon will be glad enough to exchange our imported horses for his chariots. But"—she wished she had not arranged the lighting with such subtle scheming for effect, since it left his features completely in shadow—"it's too bad for your sake, my lord. I'm getting old and ugly. And you might have had the young and lovely Pharaoh's daughter for your wife."

She could detect no motion of his figure, not even the movement of his lips. "I did not want the Pharaoh's daughter for my wife," he returned quietly.

It was what she had wanted him to say, yet for some reason the act was not being played as she had planned. If only he would display some emotion!... And then suddenly he did. A harsh, incoherent sound escaped his lips.

"What's the matter?" Her bright eyes gleamed up at him like two disks of copper. "What are you looking at so intently?"

"*You!*" he cried hoarsely. "With your hair unbound like that, and in that gold robe with the light falling through the slits in that pierced marble screen, you look for all the world like—like—"

"Like a leopard?" she prompted mischievously. "Well—why not? I may as well live up to the comparison. And you may find that leopards have other qualities than cruelty—or even beauty." Eyes still gleaming and lips parted, she held out her arms.

But to her amazement the space between her couch and the lamp, set crazily aflare by the swift motion of his robes, was empty.

CHAPTER 4

1

The merchant appeared as disreputable as he did crafty. The straggly red beard was stained and flea-bitten, the turban, wound askew to half obscure the one good eye, a filthy tattered rag. A rich aroma of stables, stale inns, and staler kitchens caused Jezebel to bury her nose in the folds of her scarf. But the fingers which moved in and out of the unsavory goatskin were clean-nailed and delicate of touch.

"Show me more," she demanded, entranced. Already his dirty pouch bulged with gold and silver rings. But the long-necked vase which looked like a single gem of hollowed sapphire was a jewel for which any queen would have bartered her crown, the silver Ashtart with the ruby breasts and onyx eyes a collector's item.

The solitary eye peering beneath the rakish flap of turban held a roguish glint. "Ah, the flower of women would see more?" The merchant's voice sounded thick and furry. "There is one more treasure, yes. Like Tyrian purple to this homespun." The red beard wagged regretfully. "But it is not for sale."

"Show it to me," ordered Jezebel imperiously.

"The queen commands? But—the sight of such treasure is too great a temptation for slaves. It must be for our four—our three eyes alone."

Jezebel hesitated. Dismiss all her attendants? Ten to one the scoundrel had a knife concealed beneath his odorous *simlah*. A will, too, as adamant as her own. Already the well-groomed fingers were drawing the string taut about the neck of the goatskin. "Leave us," she ordered her attendants abruptly.

Once they were alone, the merchant solemnly winked his one good eye, picked from his mouth a wad of matted wool, removed the *simlah* to disclose a spotless linen coat, unwound the ragged turban, discarded false red beard and eye patch, and to Jezebel's amazement stood revealed—

"*Eshmun!*" she exclaimed incredulously.

"I have executed your commission, my lady."

For once speechless, Jezebel sat staring at the enigmatic features. So this was the secret of his uncanny success in performing difficult commissions! Was the facade of faultless decorum but another one of his disguises? The eunuch drew a bulky parcel from the goatskin, removed the wrappings of heavy yellowed linen, and revealed several small rolls of animal hide, each tied with strips of faded silk.

"Two I purchased at the price of a king's ransom, another I exchanged for an ivory bauble, a third I stole from the chamber of the high priest in Jerusalem."

"You have—done well, Eshmun." In vain Jezebel searched the inscrutable eyes for but one flicker of the roguish glint. "You—may go now."

Summoning her litter, she went straight to the temple of Melkart, and, passing the curtained entrance of the dark chamber where towered the bronze image of Melkart, sought the high priest's chamber. As usual Meribaal was crouched on his mat, shoulders hunched, lips mumbling, filmed eyes thrust close to the faded script of an old papyrus. Lost in his reading, he paid no heed to her presence.

"Fulfill then thy desire, O man, whilst yet thou livest. Anoint thy head with oil, and clothe thee in fine linen adorned with gold. For the day will come..."

Jezebel looked over his shoulder. "What is it, Meribaal?"

Regretfully the priest rerolled the fragile manuscript. "I was reading from an old Egyptian dirge, 'The Song of the House of King Antef.'"

"And why do you read such drivel?"

The weak eyes swam with tears of exertion. "No words of a seeking soul are drivel. And if one reads enough words, there is always a chance of finding—"

"Finding?" Her voice was sharp. "Finding what, Meribaal?"

The soft crackling of the papyrus died. "Who can tell, my child?"

"Here! I'll give you something more practical to read." She thrust the leather rolls into his hands. "Look, I got them at last. All the sacred writings of these disgusting barbarians. Ugh! Even their books smell of animals."

The bloodless fingers quivered. "Writings, you say?"

"Yes. Read them, Meribaal. Find out all you can about their little desert god. Then we'll know better how to change him into Melkart."

The earth-brown eyes turned ebony. "How many times must I tell you this is madness, blasphemy! You cannot change one god into another."

"Can't I? But I already have!" She crouched on her knees before him, triumphant gaze on a level with his. "At least I'm well on the way. Watch the daughters of Yahweh plant their gardens of Adonis. Count the images of Ashtart. Go into Yahweh's temple and up on the high places and see what rites are performed. It may be Yahweh's name on their lips, but it's Melkart they are worshiping—yes, and they even call him *Melkart,* King of the City. Kill the prophets of Baal, would they, and exalt those of Yahweh? All right. Then I'll make the prophets of Yahweh those of Baal. What matter by whose name their ecstasies are induced as long as they say what I want them to say? Give me ten more years, and I tell you Yahweh will *be* Baal, Samaria another Tyre."

But the priest was not listening. With eager fingers he was picking at the frayed knots, gently unrolling one after the other of the ancient leather strips. "Old, old," he murmured devoutly, holding the faded script close to his eyes to read the titles. " 'The Book of Jasher.' I've heard of it. Poetry... 'The Book of the Wars of Yahweh'... 'The Ten Words of the Covenant.' "

Then suddenly the frail body tensed. The fingers unrolling the last and stoutest roll of leather began to tremble. "The ink is still fresh! The man who wrote this is still alive, and—and he had no doubts! I can't wait—"

Already the weak eyes wept from the strain of focusing. The shoulders hunched. The lips began to mumble. " 'In the day that Yahweh the Eternal made earth and heaven, when no plant was yet in the earth and no herb of the field had yet sprung up...' "

Smiling, Jezebel rose to her feet and tiptoed out of the room.

But she was not smiling when, stepping from her litter in the palace courtyard, she glimpsed a man and a boy climbing, hand in hand, to one of the higher terraces. Even at that distance she could see that the head of the man was crowned with a narrow circlet of gold and that of the boy with black, curling hair.

2

Spring came again to Israel and with it a sudden burst of green on the barren hills and little red and yellow and blue flowers interlacing the grass like the pattern in a woven carpet. With it also came the time when kings went forth to battle.

Had it not been for this threat of war, Ahab would have been well content. The presence of Obadiah's son in Samaria, with the opportunity of stealing a few moments with him each day, had lent warmth and color to the drab, chill winter which even the displeasure of Rachel, who had refused to come, had not been able to extinguish. But the shadow of Syria loomed large. Could he have secured the approval of Yahweh, Ahab was sure he could have dissipated that shadow long ago. An embassy to Damascus offering Israel's support in the confederation... But always Melkiah, with his oracle, had prevented. Or Jehu.

Since his brilliant strategy in defeating the Syrians, Ahab had somehow permitted the bold young prophet-soldier to become his chief adviser. Why? Because he possessed such uncanny military insight? Or because as a prophet he claimed to speak the will of Yahweh? Ahab was not sure. But at the behest of his erstwhile charioteer, now a captain in his army, he had mobilized all Israel to make ready for Ben-hadad's possible attack, ordered new chariots from Egypt, enlarged the stables at Megiddo, stepped up requisitions of grain and oil from all eleven districts until the warehouses in both Samaria and Jezreel were full to bursting.

As a result the country was near to bankruptcy. The rich trade which had elevated Israel from an obscure province to one of the world's great powers was almost at a standstill. And the peasants, smarting, hungry, were close to rebellion.

"I have had my ear to the ground," reported Jehu one day in the early spring. "And I have heard the things which Ben-hadad's officers are saying to their lord."

"What things?" inquired Ahab sharply.

"They are saying, 'The gods of the Israelites are hill gods, and so they proved too much for us.' They have also given the king of Syria this advice: 'Set aside the kings, every man of them, and fill their posts with satraps. Then muster an army equal to the army that you lost, horse for horse, chariot for chariot; we will fight the enemy on the plain, and we shall certainly prove too strong for him.' "

Ahab was both astonished and crestfallen. "How in heaven's name did you get hold of such information! I have heard nothing of this from my spies."

Jehu shrugged. "There are ways. And—perhaps my lord has forgotten—I am still a prophet of Yahweh."

"But—this changes our whole strategy. It means that we have to fight them on their terms rather than ours."

"Not if we make the terms first," said Jehu bluntly.

"What do you mean?"

"Only that the king of Syria can't fight us on the plain," returned the captain tersely, "if he finds us waiting for him in the hills."

"You mean—start the war ourselves?" Ahab's features tightened. "Force him to attack us even if he does not plan to?"

"He plans to." Jehu's voice was as brusque as if addressing an equal. "And the soldiers of Ahab are as capable of marching as Ben-hadad's. You know the route he will probably take—the west side of the Sea of Chinnereth."

"But—suppose he should come the east side." Ahab sparred for time to think. "Then he would sweep into the plain of Megiddo from the north, meet no resistance at the pass, and find Samaria unguarded."

The sullen lips curled. "Surely the king has spies sufficiently clever to discover and apprise him of the direction an army of twenty thousand troops is marching!"

Ahab accepted only part of Jehu's plan. Secretly, he transferred the bulk of Israel's army to Megiddo and other points close to the great northern plain. But beyond this he refused to take the initiative. Only when swift couriers apprised him of the movement of Ben-hadad's troops from Damascus did he give the marching order. Yet so carefully had every detail been organized that scarcely an instant was wasted. Leaving only small detachments to guard the other passes, Ahab led the remainder at double-quick march down through the valley of Jezreel, past Beth-shan, along the snakelike twistings of the Jordan to the southern end of Chinnereth. And here again he refused to follow Jehu's plan, to gamble the whole future of Israel on the assumption that Ben-hadad must take the eastern route. The young captain sulked and fumed by turns.

"I tell you, you'll be sorry. If we marched on now, we could choose our battleground. Now who knows where they may overtake us? Perhaps right here on the plain in just the setting they intended. Their chariots will cut us down like ripe barley!"

Ahab opened his lips to rebuke the insolence, then closed them. It had always been a man's right, he remembered, to speak his mind in Israel. "Nevertheless," he said, dismissing the young captain abruptly, "we remain here until the message comes."

But the message did not come. Ben-hadad also must be biding his time. Ahab chafed under the suspense. By day he paced his tent and by night, donning over his soldier's leather tunic the homespun cloak which had belonged to his grandfather Joseph and which for some reason he always carried with him into battle, he prowled incognito from fire to fire, listening to the grumblings of his men. Once, squatting in the midst of a complaining group, he tried to remonstrate. Where was their patriotism? Did they want a foreign king to overrun the land, lay waste and pillage, seize their crops, take away their wives and daughters and impress their sons into slavery? Where was their loyalty to Yahweh?

One man shrugged. Another spat into the fire. A third laughed aloud.

"Patriotism! You think we came here for love of country?"

"Why should we fear Ben-hadad any more than Ahab? The king's tax collectors take all we have now!"

"Yahweh? *Our* God, you say? Ours—to make sacrifices to twice a year when we go to Dan or Bethel or Samaria? As long as he gets his tithes, we can starve for all he seems to care!"

In spite of his fear of detection, the hot words poured from Ahab's lips. "Fools! It would serve you right if Yahweh delivered us up to our enemies! Suppose you had to live subject to a ruler who knew nothing of Mishpat, a ruler to whom men were commodities to be bought and sold and the land inherited from your fathers was as likely to be taken from you as your tithes of wheat or barley!"

Again the fire hissed gently before shooting out a mocking tongue of flame.

"Fool yourself, brother! Where have you been?"

"I take it you haven't had your children taken into slavery because you couldn't pay your debts."

"Or one of those big city landlords foreclose your mortgage."

"I say, who are you, anyway? We'd better hush up, comrades. He may be one of the king's snooping spies."

Ahab walked no more among the fires that night. Deciding suddenly to seek the sympathy of his son Ahaziah, he turned aside to the other royal tent.

Approaching, he became conscious of bright lights and jangling music. Stooping to peer through the low entrance, he saw his son and a dozen other young officers making merry around a makeshift banquet table, piled high at each end with half-empty platters, all pushed back helter-skelter to make room in the center for a half-naked dancing girl who, with slow, seductive motions, was exhibiting her charms for all to see, obviously with the intention of auctioning them to the highest bidder. Other dancers either awaited their turn or, already auctioned off, lolled on the cushions or in the arms of their patrons.

"Two silver rings—one for each of those rosebud breasts!"

"Three—and a real ruby big enough to fill that pretty little navel!"

"The same—plus an alabaster jar of spikenard!"

"I'll top them all! A crown of gold leaves to wear as long as she lies—I mean liezsh—beshide me!"

"Bravo! Ahaziah wants her. Our bids are all off, comrades."

Ahab pushed his way into the tent, a haze of red swimming before his eyes. Only one thing stood out clearly: the soft round amiable face of his son Ahaziah. He stared at it aghast, conscious for the first time of its resemblance to that of Baalazor. "*You*—" His horror made him inarticulate.

The young prince wavered to his feet. "By the fish-tailed Dagon! It doeshn't look like him—looksh like common sho-soldier—but it is! Look, fellows! It's my fa-my father, the king of Ish-ra-el! There, I shaid it!" Smirking, he turned to the other officers for approbation, encountering only tense faces and dead silence. "Whatsh the matter? Can't you shee it's my—my fa—" This time the word would not come. He stood grinning foolishly.

Ahab found his voice. "*You*—my son! And *you*—officers in Israel's army! I tell you to be in instant readiness for battle, and what do I find you doing!" He turned to the dancers, huddled tightly in a corner of the tent. "Get out! Go back to whatever village or town or city you came from. And if you show your faces again in this camp, I'll have those painted heads severed from their necks!"

He waited until they had scuttled out, whimpering, then turned again to the officers, sharp voice ripping through the silence. "If you're the flower of Israel's army, then Yahweh help us! It would serve us right if Ben-hadad marched in on us tonight. Do you know what they would have done to you in the old days for breaking the vows of soldiers? Run you through with your own swords!"

For a moment he seemed about to perpetrate the act himself. Then slowly the rigidity of his body relaxed.

"Go to your tents," he ordered with more weariness than anger. "In the morning we will make sacrifice, and you will go through the necessary rites of cleansing. And—Yahweh pity us if the Syrians come too soon!"

Back in his tent Ahab dismissed his servants, flung himself face down on his cushioned pallet, bitter and despairing, fully expecting the Syrians to come before dawn. With the army in its present mood, Israel was defeated before the battle was even begun. He had failed. But how? Had he not made Israel a mighty nation in the world? Had he not given his sons every advantage, from a palace nursery equipped with every luxury to the best Hebrew tutors the temple schools afforded? And how did they repay him? The people—by grumbling about their taxes! His sons—by turning into stupid sots and libertines! He groaned aloud.

He slept as if drugged, wakened to find the sun shining beneath the tent flap full into his face, in his ears the din of excited voices, and he sprang to his feet conscience-stricken. Just in time he remembered that he was still wearing his common soldier's disguise and waited in an agony of impatience for Joel, his armor-bearer, to prepare him for public appearance.

"Ben-hadad?" he queried sharply. "He's attacking?"

"No." The officer guarding his tent looked disgusted. "It's just a band of prophets!"

Moving to the forefront of the noisy crowd of spectators, Ahab regarded the spectacle in dismay. Prophets here! Surely their presence could bode no good. Time was, back in the days of Samuel and David, when the prophet guilds had followed the troops into battle, whipped their flagging courage; but those days were past. Most of the members who had survived Jezebel's purge were too timid or old for adventure, and the new recruits were of a different caliber. As he watched their labored attempts to induce a state of ecstasy, his lips curled disdainfully. These soft, panting creatures looked like pirouetting caricatures of the lean impassioned figures he remembered watching in his youth. Was Israel also becoming soft and decadent?

His eyes fixed suddenly on a slender whirling figure close to the center of the group, and his disdain vanished. Here was no weakling. In the wake of this man's fierce zeal the rhythms of both strings and percussions seemed to lag. Studying the rapt features beneath the bare expanse of scalp, pale pink as if freshly shaven, Ahab frowned, discovered to his amazement that the man was Jehu.

Slowly, in response to the passion of the central figure, the flagging energy of the prophet band was whipped into a semblance of the ancient holy frenzy. In the glazed eyes was reflected the red glow of desert campfires. The crashing of cymbals became the thunders of the holy mountain, the shrill blast of a ram's horn the battle cry of Joshua, the call to arms of Deborah, the victory shout of David.

It was with a certain diffidence, almost a sense of shame, that Ahab saw the climax coming: first the eulogy of his predecessors, Jeroboam, Nadab, Baasha—a noticeable omission of the insignificant Elah and the bloody Zimri—then extravagant praise of his father Omri, finally the bony, prophetic finger leveled at himself:

> "Your right hand will find out all your foes;
> The Eternal will consume them in his wrath,
> devouring them in flames of rage.
> You will sweep their children off the earth,
> destroying their offspring among men!..."

Covertly Ahab glanced about at the faces of his soldiers, saw the craggy, hard-bitten features suffused with emotion, the smiles of derision consumed in kindling fires of patriotic fervor. What! Not even a cynical wariness? Surely these canny peasants must see that their emotions were being roused simply for expediency! Last night, around the campfire, they had been able to think for themselves, and, angry though it had made him, he realized now that some instinct deep within him had exulted in their boldness, that even at this moment he was searching fearfully yet eagerly for some sign of doubt or rebellion in their rapt faces. But there was none. They had let themselves be played upon as if they were sheep's guts.

"For the glory of the Lord and of Ahab!"

"May we pursue the Syrians until there is none left!"

"Until their rivers Abana and Pharpar run red with blood!"

"Until their seed is destroyed from off the earth!"

Triumphantly Ahab was borne back to his tent on a litter made of interlacing spears, a hundred eager soldiers vying, at the risk of scratched wrists and pierced palms, to have a hand in the carrying. Thanks to Jehu, a near-miracle had been performed. The lost morale of the troops had been regained.

Good heavens, what was the matter with him! He should be glad they had acted like sheep, crowded together and led without a dissenting "Baa" through the narrow aperture which should lead to victory. Why, then, this vague but persistent conviction that he was witnessing, perhaps helping to hasten, the very death throes of what had once been the peculiar genius of his people?

3

So great was his relief when the message came demanding action that Ahab's low spirits rebounded and soared. When he stood facing his hastily summoned captains of fifty and a hundred, it was the sword-sharpness of his features, the terseness of his speech, which compelled their attention, not the thin gold circlet wreathing his bronze helmet. Grizzled veterans who had followed Omri into battle saluted with a well-remembered leaping of the pulses. Young officers who had mumbled behind his back about "Tyrian vassalage" and "the woman's hand which held the scepter" met his keen gaze with pure respect.

"The Syrians are on their way," he announced crisply, "a hundred thousand and more of them, the runners say. They are marching by the road which crosses Bashan to the east of Chinnereth."

Deliberately he sought out the scowling features of Jehu, saw the narrowed eyes shoot sparks of triumph. "You see?" their arrogant gaze seemed to reply. "I told you they would come that way. Now it may be too late."

Except for an involuntary tightening of muscles, Ahab ignored the challenge. "We will march at once," he ordered with curt brevity, "as soon as the evening meal is served. And see that every soldier eats it standing, with belt tight around his waist, sandals on feet, weapons in hand."

It was dark before the hasty preparations were completed. Ahab himself rode at the head of his troops, to set the pace, and on horseback because he knew that chariot travel by night would be too slow. The moon, approaching its last quarter, had not risen. Passage across the river valley, a good four miles at this point, was easy, but once they reached the uplands it would be a different matter. They must crawl through narrow winding gullies or along the edge of dizzy cliffs. To meet the enemy here at almost any point would be suicide. Nevertheless, he welcomed the slowing of pace, the flexing of powerful muscles beneath the bridle rein, which indicated the beginning of the steep ascent. His own muscles tightened. Every sense sprang into alertness. It was his problem now, not Jehu's—no, nor even Yahweh's—to discover within the next few hours and in almost complete darkness the place where he might successfully withstand the enemy.

The knowledge filled him in turn with grim elation and sheer panic. To follow Jehu's advice, take it for granted that Ben-hadad would pursue the eastern route, would have been foolhardy. And yet... In spite of the increasing coolness Ahab's tunic beneath his leather waistcoat was drenched with sweat. Suppose the ragged moon should climb higher and higher, should be drained of its brightness like a slice of lemon sucked dry of juice...and still they found no place...

His eyes were by now so used to the dark that he could discern the curved sickle of a lizard's tail on an outcropping of limestone.

And suddenly he saw it, almost too good to believe—the narrow pass above the great gorge where two hills, descending in broad arms, reached toward each other on the south and almost came together, the purpling shadows indicating a similar narrowing toward the north, where the Syrian army must enter! He sounded the order for encampment with a pounding like drumbeats in his ears. Dawn found the army ensconced behind the two hills, so well concealed by scrub and thicket and rock outcropping that its presence was almost undetectable.

Ahab could not resist the temptation. He summoned Jehu to his tent. "You will take your company of a hundred," he ordered brusquely, "and go north along the ridge, ready to cover the enemy from the rear after they have passed into the valley below. There will be a thousand men ready to join you, and another thousand will be detailed to a similar position on the opposite hill. You should have no difficulty in guarding it against the enemy's retreat."

For once there was only admiration in the sharp dark eyes. "I see. And there will be similar detachments on the south, guarding the pass there. The enemy will be trapped, like water poured into a vessel. By my hair and beard, we have done it, my lord and master!"

Ahab's long fingers snapped at the edge of one of the metal disks on his bronze cuirass. In spite of the wide eyes and the frank humility of "my lord and master," the "we" rankled in his breast. "We have done nothing yet," he reminded crisply. "And you would have more hair to swear by if you had kept to your duties as soldier and left prophesying to others. Suppose the sons of Hadad had come while you were dancing yourself into a frenzy and hacking your flesh to pieces?"

"And suppose," countered the young captain, "the sons of Hadad had come when the sons of Yahweh were grumbling in their beards. What then?"

Ahab conceded the point, grudgingly. "Israel owes you a debt," he admitted with perfunctory gratitude. "The morale of the troops was low, and your summoning of the prophets was a masterly stroke. It may give us the victory."

"It is Yahweh who gives the victory," shot back Jehu with savage fervor. "And I speak now as his prophet. Thus says Yahweh: 'Because the Syrians believe that I am a hill god and not one who has dominion also in the valleys, I will put this huge host into your power, to let you see that I am the Eternal. You shall destroy them utterly, so that not a man of them remains. Like a vine ravaged by the locusts, like a dry branch consumed in a hot oven, so shall this host be which I have given into your hand.' "

4

Ben-hadad, marching at a furious pace to surprise the enemy in their encampment on the lowlands south of Chinnereth, swept between the narrowing hills and into the widening valley without suspicion of an ambush. His coming was like the bursting of a flood, flowing wave upon wave, flecked with the sunlit foam of plumed crests and glittering wheels and harnesses and silver spear points. Watching from a rock covert on the northerly ridge, Ahab was swept with a complexity of emotions...awe, admiration, triumph, and, strangely, compunction. They were so splendid in their strength, their arrogance—yet so vulnerable!

Ben-hadad's crowned helmet and crimson cloak were as conspicuous in the moving flood as a bright, bobbing sail among a fleet of scows, and, though his fingers tightened automatically on the shaft of his spear, Ahab noted with inexplicable relief that the royal chariot of his enemy was well beyond the range of his hidden archers' arrows. Enemy? With the blood of common ancestors flowing in their veins? The sons of Rachel falling on the sons of Laban, snarling, killing, when they should be falling on one another's necks like brothers!

Horrified, he came to his senses. Yahweh help him, was he going to play the coward *again!* Forcing himself to action, he lifted his spear, and the shrill blast of the ram's horn rang out, to be drowned in the fierce battle cries of the fifties, of the hundreds, of the thousands. The dry skeletons of the two barren hills sprang into life, the valley into confusion.

"For Ahab and Yahweh!"

"The God of Israel is with us!"

"Let him drink the blood of his enemies!"

Ahab stared, fascinated more by the impassioned fervor of his own troops than by the tumult in the flowing stream below. What had entered into them to change them from complaining drones to these zealots obsessed with a mad lust for blood? The spirit of Yahweh? No! The Eternal himself forbid! Melkart, yes—Melkart, whose temples were reared on the flesh and bones of little children, within whose sacrificial fires one glimpsed distorted human features! But not Yahweh!

Again he had almost waited too long, the uplifted spear which was to signal the attack remaining barely breast-high in his hands. The moments of reprieve had given the disconcerted forces on the plateau below time to rally, to make ready for the expected onslaught. And Ahab, once again all general, knew that it was not the time. Better to wait now, to tighten their coils slowly, relentlessly, before the final springing of the trap. He lowered his spear.

For seven days the armies encamped opposite each other, the black tents of the Israelites clinging like flocks of goats to the two rocky hills, the Syrians swarming over the tableland below. Each morning Ahab assembled his troops with a great fanfare of trumpets, giving the enemy the impression that attack was imminent, and each

269

night, conferring with his captains, issued the same curt, enigmatic orders.

"Prepare your men for action. Spare no smallest detail. Proceed to the moment of attack even to the battle shout. Then bid them return to their tents."

He took a grim sort of pleasure in the face of Jehu. Baffled, scowling, it questioned and accused him silently: Why don't you act! You lost one big opportunity. In Yahweh's name, what are you about?

Ahab knew what he was about. Daily he sensed the slow slackening of morale in the ranks of the Syrians, the mounting tension. Just so, he understood suddenly, must the inhabitants of Jericho have watched from their stout wall the strange circuits of Joshua and his ragged desert rabble, hooting at first, contempt and derision giving place to baffled wonder, to vague uneasiness, to panic.

On the sixth evening his conference with his captains was as brief as his terse command: *"Make ready. The time has come. At the first sound of the trumpet—strike. And—"* the pause was barely perceptible— *"may Yahweh go with you!"*

On the seventh morning they joined battle with the enemy, and in a single day the Israelites killed a host of the Syrian infantry, a full hundred thousand, some conjectured. The rest fled up the valley to the town of Aphek, high on the plateau, where the Israelites, pursuing, laid siege to the town and slew, it was reported, twenty-seven thousand of the survivors.

Ahab drove in triumph up toward the gates of Aphek, through a world flaunting crimson. Wherever his eyes turned they caught the reflection of his own scarlet tunic...in the bright plumes surmounting the jeweled crests of his horses, in the banner streaming from the hands of his standard-bearer, in the beady eye of a swooping vulture. The chariot crawled through a turned furrow of blood-spattered human flesh. Even the gray-white turrets of Aphek glowed red in the lowering sun's reflection, and the bronze nailheads gleaming like bloodshot eyes in the great gates seemed to spot his chariot and follow its progress with a baleful intensity. The valley was like a temple court in time of festival, bathed in the altar's glow, the victims killed and heaped in readiness for the holocaust. *And I told Baalazor that Yahweh was different from Melkart, that he took no pleasure in human sacrifice.*

Jolted suddenly from his musings, he drew his sword hastily, eyes boring the clouds of dust to discover the identity of the figure just to the right of Stormcloud's outthrust head. Of course. Jehu. He should have known by the excited whinnyings.

"Come up," he said a little grudgingly, replacing his sword in its sheath.

The young captain sprang into the chariot. He was breathing hard from running, and sweat was pouring from his helmet.

"I saw the chariot of my lord and master coming, and I hurried to meet him in the name of Yahweh, who has blessed him mightily this day."

"Where is your company of a hundred?" demanded Ahab curtly.

Jehu's eyes gleamed like the bronze nails. "Surely it is more fitting for a hundred men to be left alone under the command of a subordinate than for the lord of the world to drive his own chariot up to the gates of a newly conquered city!"

"I'm not the lord of the world," objected Ahab testily, "only of a very small part of it. And now that Ben-hadad is no longer alive to maintain a strong buffer against the Assyrians, it may soon be even smaller."

Nevertheless, he delivered the reins into the eager fingers. Jehu was right, of course. He should not have left the camp so hastily without summoning his charioteer. He noted with some annoyance the swift response of Midnight and Stormcloud to the new touch on the reins. They swept up the long ramp toward the two stone towers, now gray-white as corpses, with the blood of the setting sun quite drained away. The great gates, closed to entrap the fleeing enemy, swung open with a loud clangor, huge posts grinding, nailheads as vacantly staring as the sightless eyes in a death's-head.

It was a dirty little town, one of those hamlets whose loss to Syria had long rankled in the breast of Israel. Ahab felt no triumph in its conquest. The looting had barely begun. Indeed, the carnage itself was not finished. On all sides pursuer and pursued were still playing their game of life and death. Eyes stared emptily from the ground. A severed head, helmet tipped rakishly over one horror-stricken eye, rolled in the gutter. Miserable hovels, their doorless openings spewing death, lined every street. For once Ahab welcomed Jehu's furious driving.

Then—"Stop!" he commanded suddenly.

The horses reared and swerved, their hoofs barely missing the two figures, bodies naked except for strips of sackcloth wound about their loins and strands of rope circling their heads. "Syrians!" hissed the young captain. "Devils! If they think they can escape the vengeance of Yahweh by assuming the garb of slaves! Here! If my lord will hold the reins, I'll make short work of them." With one continuous motion he thrust the reins into the king's hands, swept a bronze dagger from its sheath on his upper arm, and jumped down from the chariot.

"No!" cried Ahab sharply. "Stand where you are. We'll see what these men want."

The two Syrians crawled toward him on their bellies. Finally one of them reared himself to his elbows and began speaking hastily, one eye fixed warily on Jehu.

"We have heard that the kings of Israel are merciful kings, like their god Yahweh, and we come in the name of your servant Ben-hadad to beg you for his life."

Ahab felt a sudden inexplicable lifting of the spirit. "Is he still alive?" he exclaimed in surprise. "My brother Ben-hadad?"

"Yes." The cringing suppliant seized on the word eagerly. "Your brother Ben-hadad." Then swiftly he ducked again, just in time, for there was a flash of bronze metal and a sudden tingling in his scalp.

"Heathen dog!" muttered Jehu furiously. "I should kill you now, but I'll wait till you lead me to your master. So he's alive! By Yahweh, he won't be for long!"

"Put up your dagger, Jehu," commanded Ahab curtly. "Didn't you hear these men appeal to Yahweh for mercy? What can we do but spare their king's life?"

"Spare—! The king is mad! Surely he knows the custom in Israel—"

"I know it is not the custom in Israel or any other nation," retorted Ahab, "for a captain to defy the order of his general. *Put up your dagger.*"

He waited until the captain had sullenly returned the bronze weapon to its sheath, then turned to the two sprawled suppliants. "Bring your master to me," he ordered. "Tell him that Yahweh is indeed merciful and that the kings of Israel are, as he has heard, generous kings. Let him come and stand beside me in my chariot."

When he turned again to look for Jehu, the young captain had disappeared.

5

Ahab drove back to Samaria in a mood both exultant and defiant. The terms which he had arranged with the Syrian king left nothing to be desired. Ben-hadad was to restore to Israel all the cities lost by Omri, Ahab was to be permitted the same commercial rights in Damascus, with quarters in the bazaars, which the Syrians had enjoyed for years in Samaria, and Ben-hadad, the master-organizer of the confederation, was still alive to provide a bulwark against the threat of Assyria.

The defiance was wholly for Yahweh. Was his deity really displeased because he had shown mercy to an enemy of Israel, violating the ancient custom—or was it divine decree?—of wholesale massacre? Just what sort of being was this God of Israel to whom he had striven to be loyal? Would he have done as well to honor Melkart?

"Justice, O king! I beg of you—"

His musings were abruptly ended by one of those roadside interruptions common to a king's daily experience—the demand of some petitioner or group for the rendering of a verdict. This time it was not the usual clamorous quarrel, only a single figure by the road, bawling out its urgent appeal as the chariot passed.

"In the name of Yahweh, justice!"

Rigidly conscientious, Ahab reluctantly ordered his charioteer to stop, and waited with grim impatience, carefully concealed, for the wretch, to declare his grievance. This suppliant seemed to be a worse crank than most, and, though Ahab listened courteously enough, he gave the figure no more than scant attention, noting only that he was in soldier's uniform and apparently a victim of the conflict, for the upper part of his head and his chin were swathed in bandages. The loose lips and empty, heavy-lidded eyes bespoke no great intelligence, and the voice was high-pitched and whining.

"Your servant went into the thick of the fight," he whimpered, "and a superior officer turned suddenly and brought me a prisoner, saying, 'Guard this man; if for any reason he is missing, it shall be your life for his, or else you must pay me four hundred pounds in silver.' "

"Yes," returned Ahab curtly. "Go on. I'm listening."

"Ah, woe is me!" the man whined. "Your servant was busy attending to other matters, and when he looked again the man had disappeared."

Ahab could not conceal his impatience. "Why come to me with your problem? Your superior in the army has already pronounced your sentence. So be it."

The loose lips tightened, the heavy-lidded eyes flew open and flashed fire. With one swift jerk the man tore off his bandages, revealing the dark fierce features of Jehu. Springing to his feet, he leveled an accusing finger at the king.

"You are the man, not I," he cried in a loud voice. "Thus says Yahweh, 'Since you have spared the man I doomed, it shall be your life for his, your people for his people!' "

Speechless, powerless, Ahab listened, knuckles whitened on the gilded chariot rail. Twice, three times, the denunciation was repeated before the king could signal his charioteer to proceed. When they passed Beth-shan, he was scarcely aware of the crowds which came streaming in a serpentine line from its gates, of their acclaiming shouts of adulation, of the lush garlands of roses and lotus and oleanders crushed beneath his horses' hoofs. Nor, save for an involuntary shiver, did he realize when the valley's steaming heat gave place to vigorous coolness. It was his charioteer who, checking the pace of the horses and shifting both reins to his left hand, lifted the crimson cloak girdled about the king's waist and wrapped it about the shaking shoulders.

"Yahweh in his mercy destroy all your enemies!" he muttered piously.

The words penetrated Ahab's impassivity, and he smiled grimly.

CHAPTER 5

1

Jezreel at last! Jezebel breathed in the sea-borne air as if she could not get enough of it. Already the magic of the spring was past. The ephemeral green tinting the barren hills was mottled with parched, drying flakes, and on the plain the tiny emerald squares of wheat and barley and millet were tipped with gold.

Even for what beauty there was left Ahab seemed to have no heart. Instead of rushing off with each dawn to his precious gardens, he sat brooding in his chamber or paced aimlessly upon the palace roofs. She could not understand his apathy. He had come home from the war victorious. Yet, though he made no attempt to avoid her company, even seemed to seek it, he returned evasive answers to all her questions.

Except that Jehu had not returned to Samaria after the Battle of Aphek, she had been unable to discover anything amiss. Her suspicion that the scowling young captain was in some way responsible for the king's sullen brooding was based on a single outcry Ahab had made in his sleep on one of the few nights they had spent together.

You—I should have known! Those bandages—nothing but a trick—to hide your prophet's tonsure!

To penetrate his lethargy she planned small surprises and entertainments—breads and pastries baked in fantastic shapes; a troop of jugglers and sword swallowers from Damascus; bevies of dancing girls from Tyre; an incredibly old minstrel who sang songs to the accompaniment of a quavering *kinnor* with half of its ten strings broken. Only the latter aroused in him some degree of interest.

"I heard a story once," said Ahab, leaning forward and fixing his eyes on the parchment features. "An old man recited it one night as we sat around a campfire. It was about the"—his voice sank to a whisper—"the Beginnings of Things."

The old man's eyes kindled. "Did it go like this?" he inquired with hushed reverence. " ' In the beginning Yahweh created the heavens and the earth.' "

"Yes," said Ahab. "Go on. Sing it to me."

Jezebel watched the plucking fingers, listened to the gusty voice with mounting anger. The insolence of these barbarians, daring to claim, even in story, that the world had been created through the magic of their little desert god! A vision of Meribaal rose before her eyes, spare figure curled over one of his precious manuscripts, the story of the creation issuing from his bloodless lips. There had been no such presumption in his gentle voice—no, nor assurance.

"Dark was the air with cloud and wind and turbid chaos, until at last the wind produced Desire, the beginning of creation. From Desire came Mot, the primeval slime, and from Mot every germ of creation..."

"Say that again." It was Ahab's voice, sharp and insistent.

" ' So, Yahweh created man in his own image, in the image of Yahweh he created him, male and female he created them. And he saw that it was good.' "

"You're sure?" Ahab was leaning forward in his chair, hands gripping the two gold lions which tipped its curving arms. "That was exactly the way the story came to you from your ancestors? It said, 'Yahweh created man'? Not 'Israel,' not 'his own people'—but *man?*"

Startled by the intensity and, he feared, disapproval in the king's gaze, the minstrel hesitated. Yes, he insisted finally, he was sure. That was exactly the way he had received the story from his father, who had been a bard before him. But if the anointed one would contain his displeasure, his servant would endeavor to recall another story of the Beginnings which he had learned from a certain bard in Judah. Hastily, trembling fingers almost dropping the plectrum with which they plied the strings of the battered *kinnor*, he launched upon it.

" ' In the day that Yahweh made the earth and the heavens, when no plant of the field was yet in the earth, and there was no man to till the ground...' "

It was only when the child Jeshua paid his daily visit to the palace, accompanied sometimes by his father Obadiah, less frequently by his mother Rachel, that Ahab's sullen moodiness was for a little broken. Then with tightened lips Jezebel would watch the two withdraw into a small, exclusive world of their own. From a distance she listened with sharpened ears to their merry laughter, their silly quips; watched with intent but studiedly amused eyes each carefree motion in a game of marbles or skittles. Once, when the two heads of black, curling hair were bent close together over a game board, her eyes darkened in keen, furious speculation.

But she said nothing, did nothing, until after that other night when she heard Ahab cry out again in his sleep.

Rachel! Why do you look at me like that? I haven't made you break your vow! It's for his good—you'll see. Can't you understand, my darling? I must have him. I love him—like my own son—my son—my son...

2

"But you can't!" wailed Jael. "Queens don't do such things!"

"This one does," retorted Jezebel. She looked again in the mirror, to make sure the flowing headdress hid every thread of bronze. A further inspection of her features proved satisfying but unflattering. They might have belonged to any ordinary and definitely aging kitchen wench. She turned to Tanath. "Are you ready?"

She passed through the palace unrecognized, the maid tagging with dutiful humility some three steps behind. "Walk beside me," she commanded sharply, "and talk to me as if I were one of the servants."

The woman edged forward with cowering bravado. "Should—I come—this far?"

"Fool! Not like that! And speak to me exactly as if I were one of your fellow servants, a new one just come to the palace."

The bright eyes turned sly. "The mistress—will not punish—?"

"I'll punish you if you don't! Can't you get it through your stupid head? I wish to go to the well, and I wish no one to know who I am. I want them to think—"

But Tanath was no longer the cringing menial who walked three steps behind. She straightened, broadened, assumed a blowzy confidence. At the gate of the kitchen courtyard she picked up a clay water jar, balanced it in the crook of her arm while she chose two others, then thrust one of them into Jezebel's hands.

"Here, girl! Carry that on your head. Since this is your first trip, you may take just one. I said your head, dolt, not your shoulder!...What, you can't even balance a water jar? Was your mother a stupid donkey that she taught you nothing? All right, carry it as best you can, and come along."

With a glance scornfully contemptuous, Tanath lifted one clay vessel to her head, balanced the other on top of it with perfect ease, and walked away with a swagger of rounded hips. Jezebel's first furious anger was mitigated by her painful attempt to keep the jar upright with the help of both hands, at the same time watching her step. It was no use. The jar fell to the stones with a crash.

"Clumsy idiot! You'll get a beating for that." Tanath's scorn was obviously tinctured with pleasure. "Here, you'll have to take one of mine."

The new jar clutched awkwardly but tightly in both arms, Jezebel followed meekly, picking her way gingerly with her bare feet. Once they emerged from the paved court into the narrow street, the small stones cut cruelly, but she could not look to see where she was going. Wedged finally between a pair of shrilly bargaining hucksters and a screaming street vendor, she succumbed to panic.

"Tanath!" she screamed. "Come back—"

The maid's capable hand pulled her roughly between the bargainers' gesticulating elbows. "Slow snail! Can't you even find your way in a little village street?"

"Don't go so fast! Please, Tanath—"

"But I was only crawling. Our mistress is a"—the black eyes shot fire, then turned suddenly wary—"a hard woman to serve. She permits no dallying."

Jezebel's lips twitched. "I promise not to tell her," she assured.

It was easier once they passed through the town gate. The path down the hill to the well had been worn smooth by many feet. The warmth of the earth felt good under her bare soles, and the smell of ripe grain and fresh-mown grass was sweet in her nostrils.

"We're coming to the well," warned Tanath.

Jezebel sprang instantly alert. Swiftly her eyes scanned the buzzing groups of women at the top of the steps leading to the cistern. "You take my jar," she said hurriedly, "and fill it. Take a long time doing it."

Tanath obediently took the jar. "A fine state of affairs," she announced in a piercing treble, "when the king's household must employ donkeys for servants. Look at this one, sisters! Too clumsy to carry a water jar without spilling it, and too old to trust her brittle bones on the slippery steps of a cistern!"

Conversation ceased momentarily, while a dozen pairs of eyes lingered on the stranger with avid but brief curiosity. Left alone, Jezebel moved with apparent diffidence from one group to another, drifting finally to the far end of the curb where a withered old woman was crouched, half asleep.

"Clacking tongues!" she murmured with a little shudder.

The sleepy eyes blinked open. "What's that? Oh—it's you. I heard that Tanath—she's a spiteful wench." To Jezebel's distaste a knotted hand grained deeply with earth reached out to pat her knee. "What's your name, dearie?"

"Rachel."

"Ah, a good name for a woman to bear in Jezreel."

"You—mean you know others by that name?"

"More than I could count on these old fingers." To Jezebel's relief she removed the hand, the better to count. "There's Rachel the wife of Abner the goldsmith; and Rachel the daughter of Simeon, she who married the weaver from over Tabor way; and of course Rachel the daughter of Naboth, the wife of Obadiah—"

"I've seen her," interrupted Jezebel quickly. "Isn't it her son who comes often to the palace—in fact, lives in the king's household in Samaria and has become such a favorite that some say he may usurp the right of the princes—" She stopped abruptly, warned by a sudden stoniness in the withered features.

"For one come so lately to the palace kitchens," remarked the old woman tartly, lifting her stiff bones from the curb, "you have seen and heard much."

"Don't go—please. I'm so lonely." Stifling her repugnance, Jezebel reached for the hard, earth-stained fingers. "And I meant no harm. Everybody in the palace talks of this son of Obadiah—that is"—her grasp on the hand tightened—"if he *is* the son of Obadiah—? I've heard it whispered—"

"And for one who despises clacking tongues," the old woman said, detaching her knotted fingers with strength and finality, "your own is an unruly servant of a lazy mistress."

Jezebel viewed the stooped but rigid back with mingled rage and consternation. Turning, she encountered leering features and a strong odor of bad teeth and garlic.

"So the king's servant has been hearing tales about the fine daughter of Naboth! By Anath, that's not so strange as Naboth's old mother would like to think!"

Jezebel managed to conceal her distaste. "You—know this woman called Rachel?"

The loose lips curled inward over the rotting teeth. "She and her high and mighty airs! Just because she was once betrothed to the son of Omri! It's no great honor to share the king's bed. You notice she never got a chance to share his throne!"

Jezebel's stomach twisted. "Are—are you sure—"

"Sure she's shared the king's bed? Well, what do you think? Have you ever seen that son of hers? Does he look like Obadiah?"

"No, nor like Ah—like the king," protested Jezebel faintly. "Except—"

"His hair! Exactly!" The loose lips ejected one parting whiff of triumph. "Well, isn't that enough?"

Long before they reached the palace kitchens Tanath had lost her swagger and, aghast at her recent bravado, shrunk again into a cringing menial. Her gaze kept sliding furtively to her mistress' tight lips and smoldering eyes.

"My lady will not forget—that she swore—?" she broached once anxiously.

But Jezebel gave the maid even less notice than the rag doll which some servant's urchin had dropped in the palace courtyard and which she kicked impatiently out of her path. It was the sight of the doll, rag stuffing spilling and limbs grotesquely twisted, which gave Tanath her idea. Her dull eyes brightened, and her sullen lips curved into a smile.

3

Jezebel glanced about the banquet hall with satisfaction, glad that Ahab's moody indifference had relegated to her all preliminary plans for this annual feting of the elders of Jezreel.

For once, she had resolved, these rustic little dignitaries so prudishly convinced of their own importance should be given a taste of cosmopolitan society. Now she studied their reactions with a grim relish, watching stiff, bearded faces relax, stern disapproval melt like snow in a brazier-heated room. By the time the wine bowls had been refilled a half-dozen times and the second troop of musicians had appeared, with a bevy of male dancers from Gath, garlands were awry, stiff limbs dissolved into the most informal of postures, tight lips loose and garrulous. The mischief in her gleaming eyes demurely hidden behind her long lashes, curled lips obscured by the rim of her silver goblet, Jezebel let her gaze travel from one to another of the flushed, disheveled figures, ears savoring far more of spice and flavor in the conversation than her already sated tongue could discover in the wine.

"Not bad, not bad at all, these sons of Dagon—if you can call them sons!"

"Here! Toss each of them a couple of these golden halves of honeyed apricots. Apply in the right places, and you can call them daughters!"

"Sons or daughters, What's the odds?"

Only one of the elders, Jezebel noted, failed to enter into the spirit of the occasion, a dried-up shell of a man with a sparse sandy beard and skin the color and texture of a shriveled walnut meat. He reclined on the couch next to Ahab's, garland and banquet robe as circumspectly neat as when he had assumed his position, straight line of lips as immobile as a crack in the parched earth of cheeks and chin. His homespun robe of unbleached linen reminded one also of earth, for it was the color of turned furrows steeped long in the sun. She leaned toward Elhanan, her companion on the right, a man with bold eyes whose sight had been apparently quickened, not dulled, by the many bowls over which he had smacked his lips.

"Who is the man sitting next to the king?" she inquired curiously.

"The queen refers, no doubt, to Shemuel, chief of the elders... Not Shemuel? Ah! Then the one on his other side. The man's name is Naboth."

Jezebel's fingers tightened on her goblet. "You said—Naboth?"

"No wonder the queen has not heard of him. Though he is one of the elders of the city, he spends little time in the gate." Elhanan flipped the wing from a butterfly-shaped oaten cake, dipped it in a savory concoction of pheasant breasts smothered in tiny Ashkelon onions, and ground it between large white teeth. "Naboth is a nuisance," he spat with unexpected venom. "If Jezreel is still a little town where a young man has no chance to get ahead, it's more his fault than anybody else's."

Jezebel hid her smile of triumph in her upturned goblet. "Oh, come now! He can't be that powerful. Why, he looks like nothing but a peasant!"

"He might as well be. Spends half his time cultivating his little plots instead of enlarging his holdings and putting tenants on them."

Jezebel shrugged. "If he's pruning vines and driving oxen around an oil press," she retorted, "at least he's not sitting in the gate obstructing progress."

"You would be surprised! I mean—" The bold gaze had the grace to drop in confusion. "The gracious consort of the anointed one—"

"You mean I'd be surprised," interposed Jezebel dryly. "Go on. I'm listening."

Elhanan's discomfiture was only transient. "Naboth has more influence," he continued bitterly, "than any three other elders put together. He comes from one of the oldest families in Jezreel. His sons were playmates of the king himself. That's why he's sitting in the place of honor, second only to Shemuel. He may not come often to the gate, but—believe me, what he says *goes.*"

"And what does he say?" Jezebel's amused tone belied her sharp attention.

"That the customs of the holy fathers must not be changed one jot or tittle. That because a man's grandfather thirteen times removed owned a piece of land back in Gideon's time, he and his descendants have a right to it forever!"

"But—that's absurd!" So sharp did her voice sound in a sudden lull that Jezebel hastily lowered it. "Why, a man couldn't even foreclose a mortgage!"

"Ah! The queen is beginning to see. How can the noblemen of Jezreel reap the benefits of this modern civilization the queen has helped bring us if they cannot even take a poor man's land for debt?" Elhanan's face was flushed and furious. "Look at the noblemen of Samaria, joining field on field, filling their storehouses through the labor of their tenants and slaves—and then look at us! And all because of a few crackpots like Naboth!"

"I—see," said Jezebel.

The graceful but disappointingly curveless little males from Gath yielded the space beneath the fringed canopy to a troop of dancers from the temple of Anath in Beth-shan. Jezebel could see from Ahab's startled expression that he was not sure of the wisdom of this innovation. But he need not have worried. A bevy of Ashtart devotees would have shocked these prudish sons of Yahweh into a dither. But Anath's! Had not many of them visited her ancient altars close to their own Yahweh's in Beth-shan? Was there not a bronze image of Nehushtan, her serpent symbol, in the great temple at

Jerusalem? Whatever name they bore, she counted their presence here a triumph. As well call Ashtart by the name of Anath as Melkart by that of Yahweh! It was what gods did and said and were that mattered.

The *kedeshoth,* naked save for braided garlands of long-stemmed lotus blossoms coiled snakelike about golden loins and twining upward to cup the lips of their half-opened petals over pink-tipped breasts, were mistresses of allure. Once the first startled moment was past, the elders of Jezreel were voluble in approval.

"By my hair and beard, I see where I take more frequent trips to Beth-shan!"

"Snake charmers, eh? This time it's the snakes that do the charming."

All but Naboth. Jezebel watched the skin about his pale lips tighten until the straight slash of mouth was barely visible. His gaze was as intent on the dancers' motions as that of any of the elders. Like theirs, it stripped the garlands from their flesh, embraced every minute golden curve...but objectively, with a cool, dispassionate scorn, not with the crude fumblings of desire.

She frowned suddenly, unable to believe her eyes. The earthy figure was no longer reclining beside Ahab. It was standing upright, turning on its heel, brushing past the royal couch with as little reverence as if it had been occupied by a slave, striding from the banquet hall without a backward glance. And Ahab, lost again in one of his fits of moodiness, seemed unaware of the insult.

Jezebel lifted her silver bowl, clamping her lips hard over its edge. The rare, snow-cooled vintage from Lebanon tasted blood-warm and bitter on the tip of her tongue. She stifled an almost uncontrollable desire to spew it out of her mouth.

4

It was Haran who finally penetrated the armor of Ahab's brooding indifference. Each morning the gardener appeared at the door of the royal apartment and cheerfully delivered some small token into the hands of a disdainful slave.

"Tell the king these are the first figs from the tree at the corner of the upper vineyard, the one he used to like to climb..."

"Take this little box of olive wood to your master. Tell him I carved it for him with my own fingers after letting the wood ripen for seven years..."

"Give the king this spray from the styrax bush he planted with his own hands. Let him remember that it was of this tree that Moses made his staff...

But it was the little cutting from the almond tree, bearing seven delicate white blossoms, like a seven-branched candlestick, which brought the look of sudden awareness to the king's eyes. "What! An almond tree in bloom now? That Haran—what is he? Another Aaron that he can cause a dead rod to blossom? Get me my coat—not that gaudy purple thing. The old homespun browned with walnut dye, something that I can get stained with earth."

It was wonderful to feel alive again. The gray mists in which he had moved since his journey back from Aphek parted to reveal clear vistas of blue sky and sun-dappled mountains. Here in the family gardens little had been changed since his boyhood, and with Haran at his side, gnomelike body bent as grotesquely as a branch of one of his ancient olive trees, Ahab began to feel again that youthful exuberance and zest for physical labor which he had known as a boy. The vines, he discovered, had not been properly pruned in years, and foxes and jackals had played havoc with the hedges. Haran's eyesight was getting poor, and the underlings were lazy. Compared with those of his neighbor Naboth, the royal vineyards were a sorry sight.

For some reason the sight of Naboth's stout stone walls topped with neat hedges rankled like a thorny herb beneath the thong of a sandal. There was no sensible ground for this resentment. He owned plenty of well-dressed vineyards on the slopes near Samaria and the headlands of Carmel, with an army of vinedressers. He had purposely left these holdings at Jezreel under Haran's direction, counting the old man's peace of mind well purchased at the price of a few inferior orchards and vineyards. Why, then—?

He was standing one day looking up at the neatly clipped hedge when the round, jolly features of his boyhood chum Daniel rose like a full moon above it, accompanied by a smaller satellite. It was the boy Jeshua who spied him first.

"Ho, Uncle Ahab! Look at me! I'm up here on a ladder helping my uncle—my real uncle, I mean—clip the hedge."

"So I see." For no reason at all Ahab's reply was edged with irritation.

The eldest son of Naboth, always the irrepressible wag and tease, had never been impressed with Ahab's royalty. He waved a grimy hand.

"Ho, neighbor! If it isn't his highness, the anointed one himself! Pardon me, please, if I don't prostrate myself. It would be painful on this thorn hedge."

Ahab's laughter was genuine and spontaneous. "If you ever prostrated yourself before me," he retorted swiftly, "it was because you were looking for a bird's nest to rob and stubbed your toe in the process."

"Or because you dared me to wriggle through a wormhole!"

"Huh! Any worm whose hole you could wriggle through was an oversized python!"

They halted the merry badinage to laugh uproariously, not, at once, at their own scintillating wit, but at the agreeable discovery that the old robust affection had endured years and crowns unchanged.

"Remember—" When the word leaped from both pairs of lips simultaneously, they stopped and laughed again.

"Remember the time I got stuck in the cave?" This time Daniel achieved the head start. "And you stayed with me all night trying to pry me loose?"

Ahab was not far behind. "Yes. And the time I ran howling from a bear..."

The reminiscences flew thick and fast, as each attempted to outdo the other.

"And remember how we used to hide under this very hedge," recalled Daniel, chuckling, "listening to our grandfathers quarrel over this very bit of vineyard where I'm now standing? I can see them now, can't you, leaning over the wall, shaking their fists and shouting names no good Israelite should mention! How we used to laugh at old Joseph's popping eyes and white, bobbing beard! Remember?"

Ahab did not smile. "Yes," he said slowly. "I remember." The memory of his grandfather's death was still a knife-twist in his breast, and it seemed suddenly like sacrilege to hear his name spoken lightly on those laughing lips.

Jeshua clapped his hands. "Tell some more about the funny man, Uncle Daniel!"

Leaning his stout elbows on the thorn edge, Daniel laughed until the tears streamed. "Anybody would have thought," he chortled, "that they were going to slash each other's throats with their pruning knives! But they were really very good friends. Joseph knew there was no more chance of his getting this field than—"

"Than of his son's becoming king of Israel?" supplied Ahab quietly.

"Ha! Exact—Daniel's happy acquiescence faded into bewilderment. "But—but his son *did* become the king of Israel."

"So he did," replied Ahab mirthlessly, and swung on his heel.

A little later, directing the heightening and strengthening of the watchtower on one of the upper terraces, he found his gaze following the zigzag lines of the stone walls topped by their neatly clipped hedges. No wonder his grandfather Joseph had argued that the vineyard in question should belong to his family! It drove a jagged wedge straight into the heart of the ancestral holdings.

"Didn't my grandfather take the argument to the elders in the gate?" Ahab demanded of Haran abruptly.

The wrinkled features puckered into even deeper furrows. "The—argument—?"

"About Naboth's vineyard."

"Oh, that dry bone those two old dogs used to worry? Did he take it to the elders? Aie! Aie! He certainly did!" The old gardener chuckled in happy reminiscence. "There were witnesses from all over Israel, some even from Judah. You'd have thought it was a case over a national boundary. But it was finally decided on the testimony of one old man who claimed he had actually taken part in the conquest of Jezreel from the Canaanites. He established the accuracy of the boundary stones beyond all doubt. Your grandfather didn't have a leg to stand on. But did that stop his arguing? Not by one jot or tittle! He was at it that very day before he left for—" Glancing furtively sidelong, Haran lapsed into silence.

To the rhythm of a builder's chant, the slaves who were repairing the watchtower coiled back up the winding stair, flat baskets heaped high with field stone on their heads, breath hot with sour wine and garlic, and prepared to lay another course on the round wall. But Ahab had lost interest in the project. Elbows gouging the fresh mortar, he leaned over the half-finished parapet, and stared moodily at the terraced level far below where the stone wall with its stout hedge thrust its jagged wedge into the geometrical patterns of the royal vegetable garden.

5

Ahab's brooding despondency was back again. Jezebel took a meager comfort in his frequent visits to her own apartment until she began to suspect that its fascination lay in its position on the eastern side of the palace, where its latticed windows projected over the city wall. No sooner had he become comfortably settled on a couch, or in a cushioned armchair with a ewer of frosted wine at his elbow, than he was up and across the room so swiftly that the resilient pile of the crimson carpet had scarcely time to spring back into shape before he reached the window.

Once, attempting to move noiselessly after him, she was annoyed when, a fold of her skirt catching beneath a leg of the low table, her quick motion upset the heavy tray with a great clatter of silver plates and goblets. But he took no notice and, even when she stood by his side, seemed unaware of her presence.

Frowning, eyelids narrowed against the hot glare, she scanned the scene vainly for some unusual feature. The road beneath, which widened into an open space just under the combined palace and city wall, was churned into a foam of dust and strewn with the usual litter of human and animal flotsam; beggars crouched against the wall, hugging its sliver of shade; lank dogs wolfing the dust for refuse flung from the lower palace windows; the usual huddle of lepers bawling their "Unclean!" at an approaching string of pack donkeys. She cast a speculative glance toward Ahab's stern profile. If she could only find out what—

"He wouldn't sell it," burst out Ahab petulantly.

In her surprise and relief Jezebel almost laughed aloud. Expecting those stern regal lips to give utterance to some heroic melancholy, perhaps some secret guilt...then to see them pout and quiver, for all the world like those of a child deprived of his favorite toy! But she did not laugh. Moving closer, she placed a sympathetic hand on his arm, the hand of a mother, caressing, indulgent.

"Wouldn't sell what?" she asked gently.

"The vineyard. See it down there?" His arm, tensed hard beneath her fingers, moved to point. "That dark patch shaped like a triangle, between the road and the palace vegetable garden?"

"Yes. I see it. Rather a nice little vineyard, isn't it? Well kept."

"Surely you can see why my grandfather wanted it, why he should have had it. Yes, and why I must have it."

She was still inclined to be amused. "But, my lord, you have so many vineyards! And, anyway, all these vineyards around Jezreel yield red grapes, not the rich purple vintage you like the best."

She was unprepared for the intensity of emotion which burst from his lips. "Great heavens and earth, it's not for the vineyard I want it! Can't you see? It's a part of my ancestral heritage—or should be if some blundering fool who lived a hundred years ago hadn't meddled with the boundary stones. I wouldn't leave it as a vineyard. If it were mine, I'd have it bearing good fresh vegetables, melons as big as a harvest moon and as sweet as date honey, spicy herbs so fragrant—"

As he turned toward her, she noticed that his eyes glowed with feverish eagerness. "That's what I'd do with it—make it an herb garden. Solomon had one, they say, just south of Bethlehem. The queen of Sheba brought him rare plants for it, and so did caravans from the far lands of the Indus. It is said the perfumes of it were wafted on the south winds clear to his palace in Jerusalem. If Solomon had one, why not Ahab?"

Jezebel agreed soothingly. "An herb garden would be very practical." All desire for laughter had fled. It was not the whimsy of a child which prompted those impatient gestures, those pouting lips. She wished she dared put her hand to his forehead, but—no, it was better to humor him, treat the matter lightly. "Well, why not? If you want the vineyard, why don't you get it?"

"I told you, that's just what I tried to do." The stern lips curved again into a petulant pout. "I offered him a good price for it, in silver, or a better vineyard to take its place. And what was his answer? 'Yahweh forbid,' he said, 'that I should give you the inheritance of my fathers!'"

"And what did you say to that?" Jezebel asked, her lips compressed.

Ahab left the window and returned to his chair, his feet scuffing the rich carpet like those of a disgruntled child. But the feverish glint had left his eyes. "What *could* I say? The man was within his rights, of course. The vineyard is part of his inheritance." He lifted his foot gingerly and frowned. "The floor is wet!"

"It's nothing." Jezebel dismissed the circumstance with an impatient gesture. "That stupid Tanath set the tray table too close to my skirt, and when I rose from my couch it upset. The clumsy fool is always making blunders."

Clapping her hands, she issued a curt order for fresh wine and a basin and cloth, only vaguely aware of the venomous fury which leaped to the maid's eyes. There was no time now to deal with Tanath. She knew suddenly that on the issue of these next few moments depended the success or failure of all her years as queen of Israel.

"So—he refuses to sell you a piece of land, and you say this is an end to the matter—he, a common citizen of a little country town, and you the king of Israel!"

Her words came to his ears plainly enough, pelted against them with the coldness and solidity of hailstones. It was only her features, gestures, which dissolved into vagueness. "But—you don't understand—"

"I understand all too well." The cold accents pelted. "You are a king, and in every court in the world if the king fancies a piece of land belonging to any of his subjects, it's his for the taking. Yet when one of your stiff-necked Hebrews has the audacity to say, 'I will not sell,' you sit down and twiddle your thumbs helplessly. Oh, yes, I understand well enough!"

"No, no, but you don't!" Beneath him on the soft carpet he could feel his feet moving stubbornly, like those of an ox treading the worn path about an oil press. "You see, Israel is different somehow from these other nations that have kings. It's all bound up with our law of Mishpat—rightness in the relationship of a man to his God and of one man to another."

His tongue, it seemed, was as weary as his feet. He had no means of measuring time and distance except by one thing: wherever he stopped on the carpet, there was no sign of that patch of dampness.

"What you mean is," said Jezebel bluntly, "you're trying to fit your little desert god, who belongs in a goat's-hair tent, into the solid structures of a civilized world, and it can't be done."

"But—you still don't see—" Ahab's feet stopped moving. He lifted his hands to keep the pelting hailstones—hot they seemed now instead of cold—from beating against his face.

"It's you, my poor deluded husband, who fail to see. How long would your throne stand if this Mishpat were really the law of the country? What would happen to our prosperity if landowners weren't permitted to increase their holdings or a creditor to take a man's children as slaves in the payment of debts—if the peasant became a mouth to feed instead of a pair of hands to labor? Can't you see that such ideas of equality among men are axes laid to the very roots of our society?"

"But"—stubbornly Ahab forced his feet to move over the deep-piled carpet. "If Mishpat is the law of Yahweh—"

"And what makes you think it is?" Though he kept his hands to his face, he could tell by the sound of her voice and the fragrance of roses and delphiniums and myrrh that she was close beside him. "Is your Yahweh different from other gods, from my own Melkart, who blesses with wealth and prosperity those who please him and condemns to misery and poverty those against whom his wrath is kindled?"

Ahab was silent. She pressed her advantage. "Are not both the slave's iron ring and the peasant's lean belly badges of the god's displeasure?" He felt cool fingers laid against his forehead. "Come, my darling. I think you have a touch of fever. Don't try to think any more. Just tell me this one thing. If you had a treasure which you called your own, and you knew your lord Yahweh desired it of you, would it be yours or Yahweh's?"

"Yahweh's, of course." He was grateful that the answer was so obvious.

"And if you refused it to him—of course you wouldn't, but just suppose you did—would he not have a right to take it from you?"

"Yes, yes. If I deny my Lord anything he desires, let him not only take it from me. Let him slay me for my sin in withholding that which is rightfully his!"

"Well spoken, my lord the king, whose slightest word and wish are as the word and wish of Yahweh."

Gratefully Ahab let himself sink into the soft cushions. Vaguely he felt that there was something more he should say, some protest he should make, but he was too weary to make the effort. The gray mists were inside him now, hot in his throat. It must be the fever. He hoped so. Fever was unpleasant but bearable, especially when one could lie like this with soft petals of roses and delphiniums falling about one's face. There was only one thing wrong. It wasn't the fragrance of flowers he wanted, but something more provocative and pungent.

"Herbs," he murmured. "If the vineyard could only be made into a garden of herbs. Grandfather would have liked—would have liked—"

"You shall have your garden of herbs," Jezebel said, to soothe him. "Aren't you the king of Israel? Come, take a little of this cool spiced wine and a bit of this wheat cake. Let your heart be cheerful."

"But he wouldn't—sell it. I told him I would give him another better vineyard or pay him good silver for it. He's as stubborn as his father Abner."

"Who?" Jezebel's voice came to him from far away, cool and soothing as the spiced wine. "Who wouldn't sell it, my husband?"

Almost against his will he could feel his lips curling, distending into an aggrieved pout. "Naboth," he replied bitterly. "It was Naboth who wouldn't sell—"

"Naboth." Jezebel turned the word on her tongue as if it had been a morsel of sweet wheaten cake. Dropping on her knees beside the couch, she laid her cheek against his. "Don't worry, my darling," she consoled him gently. "Just leave everything to me. I will give you the vineyard of Naboth the Jezreelite."

When she rose to her feet, she held his seal ring enclosed in the palm of her hand.

CHAPTER 6

1

All Jezreel was in a furore of excitement. The elders' platform in the market place, always a popular place, was this morning so densely surrounded that litigants and witnesses had difficulty in making their way to the stand. Even though a caravan from Damascus had just been cleared at the gate, it was awarded scant attention. And few of the dozens of little booths, whose proprietors usually did a thriving and clamorous business while judgments were being administered, had yet been opened.

The appearance of the crowd, too, was unusual. While few, like the elders, wore sackcloth and ashes, simplicity in dress approached severity. Coats were of the coarsest native homespun. Girdles displayed no embroidery. Not a scrap of jewelry was to be seen. Yet no one knew the reason for the fast which had been proclaimed by Shemuel, the chief elder, starting on the preceding day at sunset. Obviously some sin had been committed, a sin of such enormity that, to atone for its corporate guilt the whole town must observe a period of mourning. Men looked askance at their neighbors, as if half suspecting one of them to be the guilty person. The usual voluble lusty exchange was terse and hushed to whispers.

"Think you the accusation will come from the platform or—"

"Man or woman, do you suppose? If the one, it's sacrilege. If the other—"

"I picked up a few stones on the way, just in case—"

"Sst! Another case coming up! Maybe this—" But it was only the complaint of a tanner named Amoz against his apprentice about the theft of two small goatskins, and when this matter had been settled to the satisfaction of all except the defendant, who had been ordered to restore eight for the two stolen, a heated argument ensued between one Abijah and his neighbor Paitiel over the damage done to the former's wheat field by the latter's donkey, ending with Abijah's being awarded three measures of barley (Paitiel not owning any wheat) and the donkey ten lashes.

With three exceptions, the elders appeared as uneasily apprehensive as the onlookers. Shemuel, stout and florid, grizzled locks circling his face like a halo, occupied his central stool with his usual stolid serenity. Elhanan, in spite of his garments of mourning, looked well-groomed and perfectly at ease. His bold eyes swept the crowd constantly until, after lighting on two nondescript figures hovering about the edge, they subsided into good-humored boredom.

The other exception was Naboth. Since he always wore a coat of brown homespun and his sand-colored hair and beard were almost the hue of ashes, the sober garments made little difference in his appearance. As usual, he sat straight as a dried reed on his stool, just to the right of Shemuel, listening with almost fanatical absorption to the arguments of the litigants. On these rare occasions of his presence it was Naboth to whom all the other elders turned as a source both of canny wisdom and of legal authority. His was the last word in defining the axioms formulated by ancient precept and custom. And seldom had the justice of any of his decisions been challenged, even by the losing litigant.

"Hist! It's coming!"

There was a stir of excitement as an angry man and a sullen woman pushed their way to the space before the platform. But a second glance excited only a ripple of laughter. Issachar the Jabeshite had for years been accusing his wife Bilhah of unfaithfulness, with no other proof than the rumor of a stolen kiss or the indiscreet swagger of a pair of lively hips. Snickering, the crowd heckled both plaintiff and witnesses, anticipating the verdict long before it was given.

"Let the accused go to the priest," proclaimed the singsong voice of Shemuel. "Let him pour water from an earthen vessel, put into it some earth from the floor of the sanctuary, and give it to her to drink. If she is innocent, it will not harm her. If she is guilty, it will cause her belly to swell and her thighs to rot."

As the man stalked out and the woman scuttled away there were loud guffaws and good-natured chaffing. Bilhah had already imbibed such an unsavory potion at least twice without damage either to figure or to vitals. The tension of the crowd had relaxed. Therefore they were unprepared when the moment of disclosure came. Even when they saw Elhanan rise impressively and turn toward Shemuel, they had no expectation that it was at hand. Not until his voice, unctuous and rich with tremolo, had been flowing about their ears for some seconds did they accord it a startled silence.

"Let Israel rend her clothes and gird her body in sackcloth. Let her unbind her hair and sit in the gate with dust and ashes on her head! Let the men of Israel lift their voices in the wail of those who have seen Yahweh's name trodden in the dust!"

The crowd quivered. *Blasphemy.* The most deadly of all the deadly sins a man could commit, the punishment of which was death by stoning. No man dared look at his neighbor, for more than one Israelite standing in just such a crowd had with horror beheld the accusing finger leveled at a face scarcely a hand's breadth from his own. Not a man present but had suffered nightmares in which he had seen it leveled at himself. Sometimes a person said things unwittingly, waking from sleep or drifting into it, turned a bit giddy by old wine, things which might be construed as discourtesy, even insolence, to deity. It would take only two witnesses...

Tongues wedged their tips between dry lips. So deep was the stillness that the second clearing of Elhanan's throat sounded as loud as the shaking of a dry gourd.

"Since the beginning of this day, at sunset, the whole city has been fasting by order of the anointed one of Yahweh. Let it not be accounted to us as sin that one of us has committed the unforgivable offense, has cursed both Yahweh and the king!"

The crowd shuddered. Bodies began to rock and sway. There was the harsh sound of the tearing of garments. The shudder became a groan, swelled into a rhythmic wail, carefully muted, however, to insure the audibility of further disclosures.

"Show us the vile culprit!"

"Let justice be meted out to this worker of iniquity!"

"May his flesh be torn by vultures and his bones consumed with fire!"

"Show him to us! Show—"

The exclamations were clipped as abruptly as a handful of grain by a sharp sickle. Eyes stared with horrified incredulity at the target of Elhanan's sternly leveled finger. The crowd was too stunned even for a quick-drawn breath. In dead silence it permitted the two nondescript figures passage through its midst. Not Naboth! Rather expect a virgin to give birth to sons, or palm trees to yield grapes! Naboth break the law? Impossible! He *was* the law. Time and again, when the other elders would have bent the rod of justice ever so slightly in the interest of leniency or expediency, Naboth had kept it unerringly straight. But finally, like the first winter rains seeping into the stubborn pores of the earth, the words of the two witnesses penetrated the stupefied group consciousness.

294

"I was walking along the road outside the hedge bordering his vineyard when I heard the sound of voices. Peering through the hedge I saw this elder of Jezreel, who now sits before you, raising his fist toward heaven. I heard him say—But I can't speak the words, lest the wrath of the Name he cursed consume me to ashes."

"Then I'll say them for you, brother. I'm not afraid. A good honest son of Israel I am, and I'll challenge any man in Jezreel to dispute my word."

The second witness glared about him before proceeding. "I heard what this Naboth said. By my hair and beard, I expected to see a bolt from heaven come down and strike him dead for the blasphemy he uttered! If there are among you men of faint heart, then close your ears before I repeat the words..."

Again the crowd shuddered, but no man stopped his ears. The dread words which, having been repeated by two witnesses, established the guilt of the accused beyond question, unless he could prove himself innocent, were absorbed to the last syllable. The very enormity of the horror made it the more credible. While they would have choked upon a crumb of rumor imputing some minor offense to this scion of virtue, they swallowed this fat loaf with never a hint of gagging.

Naboth himself was too stunned by the charges to respond with any adequate defense. Assisted forcibly from his stool and relegated to the defendant's position at the right of the elders, he exhibited at first grim disapproval, believing the whole thing to be an ill-conceived and highly sacrilegious joke. When finally he was convinced of the seriousness of the accusation, being the sort of man he was he could only calmly protest his innocence. Surely his brother elders could see, surely his fellow townsmen could see, that there was no truth in these absurd charges. Most of them had known him all their lives, whereas these witnesses were practically strangers. He for one had never seen them before. Would his friends take their word against his? Surely the men of Jezreel knew him well enough by this time to be satisfied that he would never curse either his God or his king! He would sooner relinquish his heritage as a freeman of Israel, put on the manacles of a slave, let his body be beaten to death by stones...

The latter reference was unfortunate, a grim reminder of the end awaiting any man accused of blasphemy if he could not prove his innocence. Naboth's firm voice faltered. No doubt he realized in that moment that any attempt he might make to save himself was hopeless. Two witnesses had spoken against him. Even though he knew and the elders knew—yes, even though every man in Jezreel might know—that they were liars, he had no way of proving it. The testimony of his sons was of no value. He himself would have been first to discount it. The fast had already been proclaimed. Last night at sunset he had adjured his sons and grandsons: *An impiety has been committed. The sin of the transgressor is on our heads. Let no food pass your lips until Yahweh is avenged.* His spare frame seemed to shrink further into its shriveled shell. His thin lips lapsed into tight silence.

"Not just Naboth!" a voice shouted. "Are not the sins of the fathers to be visited on the children to the third and fourth generations? Then let Naboth's sons suffer also for his impiety—yea, and his sons' sons!"

The crowd held its breath, stunned into silence. Naboth's sons also? But the bold accuser had henchmen to render loud support. "By Yahweh—yes!"... "Shall the tree be uprooted and the saplings left to grow?"... "Are you loyal men of Israel or no? Shall the father be punished for his sin and the sons go free?"

Feebly at first, but with increasing lustiness the crowds averred their loyalty.

"Yea, his sons also, and his sons' sons!"

"Let this sin be upon him and upon his children!"

Shemuel lifted a plump hand and wiped the sweat from his ash-streaked forehead. Shifting uneasily on his small stool, he beckoned the other elders closer and conferred with them in whispers. It was obvious that he had no liking for the proceeding and wanted to get it over with as quickly as possible. He cleared his throat.

"Men of Jezreel, you have heard the evidence—"

But it was unnecessary to proceed. The men of Jezreel, as well as their elders, had heard the evidence, had seen it confirmed to their satisfaction in the silence of the shriveled figure. And, though it might be the province of the elders to deliver the verdict, it was theirs to enforce it. Already hands were fumbling in coat folds and girdle pockets, stones and bits of brick were being slipped from palm to palm.

"Deceiver! Enemy of Israel!"

"Hypocrite! Pretending all these years to be an upholder of the law!"

"Let his blood be poured out as atonement for his sin, yea, and the blood of his sons and his sons' sons!"

296

"To the gate with him! Blasphemer!"

The gate was conveniently near the platform in the market area, the place of execution only a few yards from its two square towers. And of all natural resources with which Israel was blessed, stones were the most plentiful...

Elhanan, who as the accuser had been the first to throw a stone, returned to his house well satisfied with the day's proceedings. Suffering his slave merely to remove his sandals and give his feet the most conventional of washings, he ordered writing materials brought to an inner room and, when he had assured himself of privacy, set to work at once. The message, when completed, bore no salutation and no signature. And it was brief.

It is done as you commanded. Naboth and all his sons are dead.

2

By nightfall the fires of violence had died, like the blistering sun, to a heap of blackening ashes. But even much later, close to midnight, the man hurrying through the darkened streets of Jezreel dared not run the risk of recognition. The town was still restless, like a gorged animal whose belly stirs uneasily, and there were many late rovers about. Whenever he saw a torch approaching, he hugged the walls, hunched his tall body, and pulled the ends of his headdress across his face.

At the palace gate, however, admittance depended on proof of identity, and he faced the exploring torch squarely, thankful that the guard was not a Jezreelite. The exchange of passwords was a mere formality.

"Enter, servant of the king."

The guard knocked three times with the end of his spear, and the huge doors inched open. Again the man hunched his shoulders and hid his face, for the gatekeeper had known him since childhood. But the bleary eyes were drugged with sleep. Forgetting caution now, he moved swiftly across the darkened outer court.

"Obadiah!"

Groaning silently, he turned aside toward the bobbing flame of a tiny lamp.

"I knew it was you. I could tell by the way you walked, even in the dark."

"Hush, Haran! You'll wake the whole palace. Why aren't you asleep?"

"Sleep! After this day?" The earth-stained fingers clutched at the steward's trailing headdress. "Tell me, Obadiah, is it true? Are—are they all dead?"

"I'm afraid so, Haran. But, for Yahweh's sake, not so loud!"

"She too? His daughter? And—the child?"

Obadiah struggled with his impatience. "I—I don't know yet, Haran. I hope not. But let me go now—please! I have an errand—"

The fingers clung all the more tightly. "They say—the king signed—I can't believe— He—he wouldn't, would he, Obadiah? Not our Ahab!"

The flame flickered against stony features. "Ahab is—sick, Haran. He has been sick with fever for a long time. We must both remember that."

"Sick—yes. A long time. But—not with fever."

It was easy now to detach the clutching fingers. They were like a vine's dead tendrils. "Give me your lamp, will you, Haran? I—I left something in the palace and must go and find it... No, no! You're not to come with me!"

When he reached the low, arched doorway leading to the kitchens, he crept cautiously and hid the tiny lamp, flame and all, within the palms of his big square hands. But he need not have worried. Old Nathan, the watchman, was sprawled across the threshold, snoring. The kitchens, as he had hoped, were dark and empty, and, heart beating fast, he flung caution aside. However, after stumbling over a grinding stone and turning his ankle in the depression of a stone mortar, he moved more carefully, holding the lamp low and picking his way through a litter of clay pots and baskets and grain sacks. For, like most of Jezreel, the palace servants had neglected their labors for the day's excitement.

The door to the little storeroom creaked in its socket. Heart pounding and hands trembling, he slipped inside and closed it firmly behind him, his lifelong fear of dark, close places for once negated by an even greater terror.

"Rachel!" he whispered hoarsely. "Jeshua!"

The chill, musty chamber was taunting in its emptiness and silence. His heart almost stopped beating. But still he forced his numbed limbs to move across the earth floor toward the huge clay grain jar.

She was crouched in the angle between the jar and the wall, head leaning against the stones, the boy cradled in the crook of her arm.

Both were fast asleep. Uttering a muted sound that was half cry, half sob, Obadiah fell on his knees beside them, gathered them into his big arms. "Safe!" he muttered. "Thanks be to Yahweh, safe!"

The boy sprang wide awake and full of questions. "Father! Why did you wait so long? And why did you tell us to come here? Where—"

"Hush, son. Don't talk above a whisper. Old Nathan might hear."

"Where's Uncle Daniel, Father? Why did the man come and take him away?"

"I can't tell you now, son. You had no trouble? No one tried to stop you?"

"Of course not. Why should they? All the guards know us here at the palace. And we waited until the servants had all left the kitchen, just as you said. Then we came in here and hid. We've been here for hours, all cramped up."

The woman wakened more slowly. "It's—all over?" she whispered.

Their eyes clung together in the pale lamplight. "For them, yes, my dearest. Not for us. It's the second watch already, and we have a long way to go."

She moved her cramped limbs, straightened. "I am ready."

Obadiah handed her the lamp and set his shoulders to the great clay jar. But it was not the physical effort which choked his throat, turned his features gray.

"I'll go first, Father, and carry the lamp. I know the way."

The woman's hand was steady beneath the small clay saucer, her eyes bright with understanding, pity. "Your father will not be going with us through the secret tunnel, Jeshua," she whispered. "He will meet us later, outside the gate. It—it isn't that he is afraid. It's just—"

"I know. You told me, Mother. My father has a sickness."

Relief swept over Obadiah, wave upon wave. Strength flowed into him so that he was able to lift the great jar in his arms and set it down on the floor, a good two feet away. He could even inhale the dank, sour breath of the tunnel's open mouth without flinching. Of course. It was dangerous only for these two to be seen at the city gate. He could make some excuse to the gatekeeper, tell him that he was going to the stoning place to search for—for the body of his son before the vultures... It would take but a little longer, make the risk just a little greater.

"No," he whispered. "We go together. Now. There is no time to lose."

He lowered the boy into the dark, yawning mouth, handed him the lamp, steadied the woman's hand while she crawled awkwardly between the broken stones which were like angrily parted rows of teeth. Her fingers were ice-cold to his touch. Was it possible that she also was afraid of the long, winding darkness?—that she had played the brave and eager explorer only out of love for the intrepid Ahab?

Stripping off his girdle and unfolding it, Obadiah tore it lengthwise, tied the two pieces together, and passed the lengthened strip about the belly of the earthen jar. Then, squeezing his big frame down through the opening in the wall, he reached out for the two ends. Fortunately the girdle was strong. It stretched but did not break. Slowly, inch by inch, the huge cask slid back, hiding the entrance to the passage. Releasing one end, he pulled the girdle through the aperture.

Only then did the terror lay hold of him. His head reeled. His body dissolved into sweat. The darkness tightened about him like the coils of a snake. The stench of dank earth twisted his stomach and clutched at his throat, shutting off all power to breathe. It was no use. Frantically he fumbled to find the opening, pushed at the cask in panic, only to find that with all his strength it was impossible from this awkward angle to budge it even an inch. Very well, then. He would die here. Not even for those he loved could he endure such torture, for Jeshua and Rachel...

Rachel! She was somewhere in the darkness between him and the boy, frightened perhaps, unable to cry out. Heedless of his own sickening terror, he plunged into the darkness, feeling his way along the chill, moist passage until he found her, closed his big palm about her small cold hand, enfolded her securely in his strong arms.

"There's nothing to fear, my dearest," he assured her tenderly.

3

With the cooling of the day and of hot passions, men began to think, to remember, to ask questions. By the time the shadows of the high, wheeling shapes had merged into one descending shadow, there were little groups drifting together, looking at each other aslant from sheepishly grim faces, speaking in guarded whispers.

"Naboth! Fools we were to believe—"

"Those witnesses! Riffraff, ne'er-do-wells! Anybody's tools!"

"But—why Naboth? To be sure, few men in Jezreel liked him, but—"

"Remember how he told us once the king had tried to buy his vineyard?"

"You—you don't mean—you couldn't possibly think—!"

"Didn't Shemuel say the order for the fast was stamped with the king's seal?"

"It's impossible! Impossible! We live in a country where a man has his rights!"

"You mean *had* his rights, don't you—not *has?*"

"But—Mishpat—"

"After today, I tell you, there will be no Mishpat!"

As night approached and the shadow cast by the palace walls of Jezreel crept farther and farther eastward, past the mooted vineyard of Naboth, down into the deep, full bosom of the valley of Jezreel, the darkness which had been conceived and given birth within those walls traveled with it. But not slowly, creeping inch by inch like a shadow. Rather like a fire in the desert, leaping from one dried clump to another, tearing through underground tinder and through the tops of wild junipers and acacias. And not eastward only, but westward along the starved driblet of the Kishon and southward through the passes leading to Dothan and Shechem and Samaria, northward toward the steep brown wall of the Galilean hills.

"Have you heard?"

"Naboth, a man of Jezreel. He owned a vineyard—"

"The king, you say? Ill news you bring!"

"Yahweh have mercy, then what is to become of a man's rights, if the king who should be their defender..."

"Is there no voice to speak for us—no one who *cares?*"

4

The Vale of Dancing looked silent and deserted. Wearied from his long night's journey, Micaiah sat down on the hilltop for a few minutes' rest. Just so, and in this same place, he had sat down with the Man of Yahweh after their long journey northward from the southern deserts—but not for rest.

"There he is," Elijah had observed with satisfaction. "See him? That tall one with the white oxen?"

"But—how—" Micaiah had marveled, for his companion had not seen the boy for five years, and at that distance the group of at least a dozen plowmen, each with a yoke of oxen, had looked no bigger than toys.

"I know him by the way he walks and lifts his head."

They had gone down into the valley then, and Elijah had taken off his rough sheepskin and thrown it about the shoulders of the tall young man who had been plowing with the yoke of white oxen. Even now Micaiah could not quite forget the pang of that moment when he had realized that not he but this rawboned youth had been chosen as the prophet's companion and successor. He had tried to give himself to the beloved leader in constant and selfless service, and Elijah had been grateful. That first night of his deepest despondency when he had sat under a broom tree and wished to die, and Micaiah had brought him a goatskin of spring water and an unleavened loaf baked on hot pebbles covered with live coals, and bidden him rise and eat, the prophet had called him a ministering angel! *Why?* Was it because he had made of himself, not a staff on which to lean, but a goad, at times even a whip?

"You think I'm afraid to go back," the prophet had accused him once. "Tell me, was it an act of cowardice to slay the priests and the prophets of Baal?"

Micaiah had returned the burning gaze with candor. "I'm not sure," he had replied honestly. "I've wondered about that. Which takes the more courage—to win a battle by killing your opponent, or by proving him wrong. The first way is, of course, easier—if you can really call it winning."

Elijah's gaze had turned from fire to steel. "Does the son of Imlah dare imply that Yahweh did not win the victory over Baal at Carmel?"

Micaiah's gaze had remained unwavering. "Forgive me, my father," he had continued humbly, "but does not the answer to that depend on what issue the battle was waged? Was it fought to settle the question: Is Yahweh or Melkart to be supreme in Israel? Then— yes. Yahweh was the victor. But if, on the other hand, it was fought to prove that Yahweh is greater and nobler than Melkart... No. As well say, my father, that the assassin's knife proved Zimri a better man than Elah."

Elijah's anger had been terrible to see—terrible as the storm which that night had swept the desert. But in the morning the prophet had come to him and said, "You were right, Micaiah. Yahweh was not in the thunder and lightning upon Mount Carmel. He was not in the flashing of the knives nor in the crimson flow of blood on the banks of the Kishon. And—we shall not find him here."

Even now, after almost a decade, Micaiah could feel the swift, exultant leaping of his pulses. "Where, then, my father?"

"I—am not sure yet, my son. I only know—we must go back."

Go back, yes, together—to help lift their people's burdens! All the way from the sacred mountain to this hill the dream had gone before him like the storied pillar of cloud by day and the pillar of fire by night. Then they had descended into the valley, and the dream had come abruptly to an end.

"Peace to you, stranger."

Micaiah regarded the somber, unfamiliar features with bewilderment. "Shaphat?"

"My cousin Shaphat has been dead these three years."

"Then—Elisha, his son?"

"Gone. Shaved his head and put on the *nabi's* hairy coat and gone roaming like yourself. I can't tell you where. No more can half the householders of Abel-meholah tell where their sons have gone." The somber features lighted with recognition. "I know you now. You talked to us one night in this very house. Remember how bitterly we complained? We thought we had misfortunes then, but we didn't know the meaning of the word. Come in, *nabi*. My house is yours."

Micaiah accepted the man's hospitality only long enough to partake of a bit of unleavened bread and goat's milk and to lend a sympathetic ear. Abel-meholah had indeed fallen upon hard times. Demands of palace and army had drained more and more of its resources. For two seasons a blight had fallen on the wheat. The great purple clusters of grapes which had been its pride had turned small and sour. Its women had borne few children. The Vale of Dancing had turned into a Vale of Mourning, and there was no one in all the world of men—no, nor of gods—who seemed to care.

303

"Elijah—" Micaiah suggested, trying to conceal his eagerness.

No, not even Elijah. They did not know where he was. Some said in Carmel, some in the southern desert. But more believed him dead. He must be dead. Surely if he knew how the poor of Israel, like themselves, were suffering—!

Could he find it? Would his endurance be equal to the search? The valley of the river Jabesh was a boiling cauldron, its heat so intense that even sweat seemed to evaporate in steam before it could bring coolness to the flesh. The stony wadies snaking from it looked all alike, and he could not possibly explore every one. Not only was his food supply hazardously low, but he dared not risk many nights alone in this barren country. A fire bright enough to keep prowling jackals and leopards at bay would be not only an invitation to an equally dangerous band of Arab bandits but a peril of widespread conflagration.

The second night he dared build no fire at all. He crouched in the shelter of a rock, wrapped in his goat's-hair cloak, eyes boring the moonless darkness for prowling shapes. At noon that day he took the last of his barley meal, mixed it with river water into a small cake, and baked it on hot pebbles covered with a few live coals. When he reached the headwaters of the river high up on the edge of the eastern desert, he knew that, though he had gone too far and missed the turn, he was close to his goal.

There came a desperation now in his searching. Though his hands and feet were torn and bleeding and his sandals ripped to shreds, he felt no pain. Up one wadi...back again...up another...back... Over and over the continuity was repeated. Until suddenly toward the end of the third day, when the upper rim of the cauldron was edged with fire from the setting sun, he lifted his eyes, saw the landmark. He could almost hear again the boy Eiisha's excited treble.

See that thorny acacia growing straight out of the rock, with the hump on its trunk like a leopard crouched ready to spring? That's where we turn.

There was still enough twilight an hour later to reveal the outlines of the black tents clinging like bats to the bare rafters of the canyon far above his head.

"The ax will be laid to the roots of that evil tree which has sprouted in the soil of Israel," said Elijah calmly. "Already the keen edge is being sharpened on the whetstone of divine wrath, and out of the bones and sinews of human flesh shall the handle be turned. Is that not enough, O son of Imlah?"

It was not only the smoke of the fire of thorns in the tent which blurred his vision. The features of the prophet, Micaiah noted with a foreboding akin to panic, had with the years assumed a vague and nebulous quality, as if already the spirit imprisoned behind them had withdrawn into a distant and less material sphere.

He wet his lips. "No, my father. It is not enough. Israel is not a land to be stripped clean of ungodliness. It is people—can't you see them—huddled now behind the closed doors of their little houses wondering how soon their sons will be made slaves in payment for their debts, or when their little plots of grain or orchards or vineyards will be taken away? What of them, my father?"

"What of them?" The voice of the Man of Yahweh lost its emotionless detachment, was touched with impatience. "It's like you to ask such a question. You've never been able to see things with the long view, Micaiah. Always concerning yourself less with the stone of evil which must be overturned than with the poor wretch who may happen to be in its path! Can't you see that's why I chose Elisha in your stead? And now you come to harass me again—just when I find peace in the assurance that the will of Yahweh shall be fulfilled in Israel."

"And meanwhile," persisted Micaiah, fixing his eyes on a small lizard clinging stubbornly to the black goat's-hair ceiling, "a free man of Israel dies because he stands upon his rights as a son of Yahweh. And no voice is raised in protest."

The face of Elisha took shape among the shadows, stern and coldly disapproving.

"You should not have come," he reproved Micaiah. "The Man of Yahweh has found peace at last. He and Jonadab the Rechabite have reached an agreement on the program that is to be followed for the saving of Israel. I can tell you only this much. When it has reached fulfillment you will have no more to fear from the wicked dynasty of Ahab. Even as he was triumphant on Carmel, Yahweh will again reign supreme."

With painstaking slowness Micaiah moved his gaze from the bravely clinging lizard to the young man's determined features. "What kind of Yahweh?" he demanded.

"What kind—" The disapproval congealed into horror. "You blaspheme, son of Imlah! There is only one Yahweh, one Lord of Israel."

"One Yahweh, yes," agreed Micaiah, fixing his gaze on the thin straight lips. "But what *kind* of Yahweh? One like Melkart, whose people are tools to satisfy his whims? Then we may as well call Melkart our god."

"*You*—" The lips parted explosively.

"Or one who cares what happens to his people?" continued Micaiah with inexorable but hopeless persistence. "All of them. Poor peasants as well as kings and courtiers. One who keeps Mishpat and expects his people to keep it, not because it's some ancient outmoded body of customs belonging to a desert society, but because Yahweh is in his very being Mishpat—*justice!* Can't you see? It's what a god is that matters, not what his people call him."

"You mean," demanded Elisha bluntly, "you'd as soon worship Melkart as Yahweh?"

Micaiah looked straight into the cold, reproving eyes. "Yes. If by some miracle Melkart should turn into a god who cares, and Yahweh into one who is indifferent."

"You hear that, my father?" Elisha's voice was harsh. "Tell this blasphemer, this traitor, to be gone! Tell him—"

But Micaiah had not finished. Somehow his burning gaze compelled the young prophet to silence. "Remember, son of Shaphat, how when you were a child and your people in the Vale of Dancing were suffering injustice at the hands of the king, you asked a question: 'Is Yahweh dead?' "

"I—" For the first time the straight line of the thin lips wavered. "I don't—"

"Yes, son of Shaphat, Yahweh is dead in the Vale of Dancing, for there is none who cares if its fields lie barren and its grapes grow sour and its little children hunger and its men grow old before their time. And I say to you, he will die also in Israel if a man can be stoned unjustly and there is none to care. Most of his people will not even know he is dead, for though they worship Melkart or some other baal, the name of Yahweh will still be on their lips. Nor will those know that are yet unborn, unless sometimes they may see in their dreams the reflection of a light or hear the echo of a song. For how can a bird born in a cage sing of the wide skies, or a man conceived in a dungeon vision the pure sunlight of freedom?"

He could not have spoken another word. The black walls of the tent with its flickering lights and shadows swam confusedly. Desperately he lifted his eyes toward the tiny spot of stability, only to find that the bravely clinging little lizard had disappeared. Into the fire? What matter? What difference would it make in the long look of things—a lizard dropping into the fire, or a man stoned outside a city wall? But it did make a difference—*perhaps all the difference for all ages to come, between despair and hope, between slavery and freedom!*

And suddenly he saw that the lizard was still there, a tiny curl of jade, high up near the topmost tent post. He felt a hard, steadying hand gripping his shoulder.

"Rest a few hours, my son. We shall have to be starting for Jezreel at dawn, and we have a long way to go."

CHAPTER 7

1

The gray mists were peopled with accusing shapes and shadows.

"...send word to Hiel, tell him for the love of heaven not to build...curse meant for me, not him..."

"...should have killed him, you say? But he was my brother, my brother Ben-hadad! Are you sure Yahweh wants..."

"Yes, yes, you were right, Grandfather! Any fool could see. . .wanted to get it for your sake...but he wouldn't, Naboth wouldn't—"

"You! Found me again, my enemy?... Thought you were dead... Man of Yahweh...why do you look at me like that, what have I done? . . ."

But it was over at last. The gray mists parted, and Ahab found himself lying on a couch in the queen's apartment, attended by an army of zealous physicians hotly arguing the efficiency of their several techniques and remedies.

"You see, his fever has gone down. I told you I knew the magic words—"

"Nonsense! It was that potion I gave him to drink, the head and wings of a beetle boiled in snake fat. An old Egyptian prescription against witchcraft."

"Fools, both of you. It was I who exorcized the evil spirit by bringing the goat, transferring the disease to the beast, and then killing it."

"You lie. The inhalation of this brewing of herbs—"

"Where am I?" demanded Ahab, rearing himself so abruptly that the steaming flagon held close to his nostrils fell to the floor with a clatter.

Jezebel, the relief in her eyes sparked by a glitter of triumph, dismissed the physicians. "You were taken sick with the fever, my husband, here in my apartment. It seemed best for you to remain here until you recovered. Just a little longer—"

Because of his weakness he yielded, but the day came when his strength proved equal to his will. "Call Obadiah. Call Abijah. What am I, eunuch or new-born babe, that I should be coddled in the women's quarters?"

"Very well, my lord. Tomorrow, then."

"Not tomorrow. Today. There is business to be done."

"What business? Tell me, and I'll send a servant—"

"No." He turned from her abruptly, sensing that she would approve of none of the impelling purposes which motivated his sudden urgency for action...to see the boy Jeshua, to hasten negotiations for the alliance with Ben-hadad, to approach Naboth once more on the matter of selling his vineyard. The acquisition of the latter had now become obsession rather than desire. He must have it for Joseph's sake. If only he could satisfy the old man's whim and restore the rightful bounds of their patrimony, he told himself stubbornly, he might in part atone for the wrong he had done him.

"Tomorrow, then," he assented grudgingly.

Because his back was turned, he failed to notice her little smile of triumph. "Tomorrow. And shall we celebrate your return to health, my lord the king, by breakfasting together on the terrace overlooking the Valley of Jezreel?"

2

He was staring moodily down at the terraced gardens, when she greeted him. He turned and stared. She knew then that the days of careful preparation, the long hours spent since dawn before the little altar of cosmetic jars, submitting to the ritual of the devout priestess Jael, had been worthwhile. It had not been a mistake, either, to wear the new purple robe with its girdle of shining gold to match her crown, and its bodice embroidered with sapphires.

"Did you say—breakfast?" Beneath his tone of cheerful banter she detected a wary alertness. "I'm only a husband, my dear—not a foreign dignitary."

Her response to the cheerful banter was a tone of corresponding lightness, to the wary alertness a proudly upflung head. "You're a king," she retorted gaily. "And when a woman breakfasts with a king—a *real* king—she shouldn't wear the garb of a poor handmaid or shepherdess."

Ahab cast her a sharp, covert glance. Could she suspect his negotiations with Ben-hadad and be pursuing some scheme to deter him from his purpose? But the features below the glittering gold-and-sapphire circlet were innocent as a child's. He looked ruefully down at his plain linen coat, its sole decoration a wide blue fringe. "You should have told me you were expecting a king for breakfast."

"It's what a man does that makes him a king," returned Jezebel swiftly, "not what he wears." Detecting again in his eyes that startled wariness, she added lightly, "Don't worry, my lord. You look quite kingly enough just as you are." With teasing gaiety she pushed him down on one of the couches. "And when I want to kneel beside you, like this, and lay my cheek against yours—like *this,* I don't want any bothersome scepter, especially one shaped like a shepherd's crook, getting in my way."

She carefully maintained the tone of affectionate good humor when, after finishing her dainty meal of fresh figs and apricots, with little loaves of white bread baked in the form of small birds and butterflies, and submitting her fingers to a silver bowl of scented water and a wisp of linen, she leaned casually toward him.

"I have a surprise for you, my lord the king. This morning you're going down to take possession of the vineyard of Naboth the Jezreelite, which he refused to sell you. It is all yours, my husband. You shall have your garden of herbs."

Ahab's delight was as genuine and spontaneous as that of a child unexpectedly presented with a long-coveted toy. "I might have known!" he exclaimed. "I've seen you practice your bargaining wiles on merchants. What did you have to do to persuade the obstinate old goat to sell it? Promise to make him governor of Jezreel?"

Unable to hide his elation, he sprang from his couch, jostling the low table so that wine spouted from a silver ewer on the white damask cloth. Unheeding, he moved swiftly to the parapet and, shading his eyes against the blinding morning sun, picked out the tiny wedge of green. *His* now! No, not just his. A part of the patrimony of the house of Joseph. Surely the stubborn old bones of his grandfather must be turning exultantly in their grave! Ahab could almost hear a faint chuckling. Then suddenly he turned.

"No," he said. "It wasn't the governorship. I offered him that long ago and he refused it. What did you do to persuade him?"

With a long polished nail Jezebel calmly traced the outline of the crimson stain. "One doesn't have to persuade the dead," she replied composedly.

"Naboth—*dead?*" Ahab moved slowly back toward the table, looked down at her in sudden horror. "You don't mean—*you*—"

"Killed him?" She supplied the words coolly, almost with amusement. "No, my dear husband, of course not. Naboth was accused of blasphemy before the elders and condemned to death. He had a fair trial."

"Blasphemy—Naboth!" Ahab's head was whirling. "He could no more be guilty of cursing Yahweh than—than—"

"Than of defying the wishes of his king, who is Yahweh's human counterpart?" Jezebel's voice remained light, almost bantering. "But he did do that very thing, didn't he, and in so doing he scorned both his god and his king, which is exactly what they accused him of before the elders."

"But—they could not have done this thing of themselves! Who—how—"

"You promised to leave it all to me, remember? A small enough thing for a king to ask, certainly, a little piece of land to plant some herbs, when all that his subjects own could be his for the taking!"

"But—" The whirling in his head had become pounding now, hammer strokes against his temples. "You know very well I didn't mean—"

"That you had the courage to prove yourself a true king?" His fingers closed about the slender neck of the silver ewer. "It was you who did it!" he accused in sudden panic. "If Naboth is dead, it was you who killed him, not I! The guilt is yours, all yours, do you hear? Yahweh bear witness, I'll have no part in it. Let his blood—his red blood—be upon *you!*"

Though the weakness of the long sickness turned his limbs to water, his voice into a shrill treble, there was no lack of strength in his hands. He flung the contents of the ewer with such violence that the tongue of spurting crimson, overshooting its mark, licked the scalloped edge of the pink silk awning and dissolved in ruby sparks. Horrified, Ahab looked down to find the dribble from the inverted vessel overspreading his own coat with an ugly bloodlike stain.

Slipping unscathed from her couch, Jezebel laughed softly. "You see, my lord? We're in this together. You can't play the coward this time, even though you try."

With an exclamation that was half cry, half groan, he lunged toward her. "I—ought to—kill you—"

"Spoken like a true king, who can do what he will with his subjects. All right, my lord. Go ahead. See, I'll make it easy for you. It's a long way to the stone-paved court. You can even make it look like an accident." Still smiling, eyes tauntingly agleam, she seated herself with casual ease on the parapet, even leaned suggestively backward and, hands lightly curled over the edge, swung her slender feet high off the floor.

But this time Ahab refused to be diverted. "—to kill you," he continued, coming steadily toward her, "as you have killed all that I once held most dear. First my grandfather Joseph. It was you who made me fail him. Then the prophets of Yahweh. You tricked me into giving you my seal, just as this very moment you are trying to trick me again... But I won't let you, do you hear? It's Naboth's dead body I see, not your soft golden flesh. It's my grandfather Joseph and Yahweh's prophets—yes, and the love of a good woman of Israel. You've killed them all—everything I ever really loved—" Seeing him lurch toward her, feeling his tense hands grip her shoulders, Jezebel knew a moment of dizzying panic. But her reason remained clear and lightning swift. "And your son"—she spoke the daring words with indulgent lightness—"whom we both loved best of all—was it I who killed him?"

Uttering a harsh cry, Ahab turned from her and sank down on the couch. "No—no"—he groaned. "If either of us was to blame for that, it was I. Yahweh help me, what have I been saying!"

"Only the things a king has every right to say!" Suddenly she was at his side, as vibrant with energy as a slender flame. "Do you want to know the real reason why I dressed like this today—not like a wife going to meet her husband, but like a queen fit to occupy the throne beside her lord? Because, for the first time since coming to your miserable little country, I knew I was about to take my place beside a real ruler. I've waited a long time for this. I've loved you, yes. My flesh would have burned for you if you'd been a sheep-herder or a camel driver. Now give me the right also to *respect* you! You're a king, my husband, do you understand that at last? You have no obligation to your people except as it furthers your interests to protect them. Everything they have is yours if you want to take it. A man has no value in himself, and the sooner you get that strange idea out of your head, the better!"

A man has no value in himself! Silently Ahab stared at the white cloth with its bright crimson stain. Blood it might well be, he thought, the blood of Naboth. Was it only by accident that, spurting from the ewer, the wine had flowed in a straight line, then curled to one side like a shepherd's crook—or a king's scepter? Fitting emblem of royal power, a scepter fashioned of a dissenter's blood, and surely one not unpleasing to Yahweh! He should have learned that by this time, after Jericho and Carmel and Aphek! Why should he have been so reluctant all these years to accept this further premise, which every civilized people on earth except his own considered self-evident, that a human being had no value in himself?

He reached out his hand toward the crimson stain, attempted to touch it, but his fingers were turned to stone. Just so, on another morning long ago, he had let opportunity slip by while his hand remained frozen on a bowstring. No wonder Jezebel had all these years considered him a coward!

Suddenly she was on her knees beside him, the flame of her scorn diffused into pulsing warmth and energy. "Was I wrong, my husband? Should I have come to you in the garb of a maidservant? Shall I go from your presence again, loving—yet secretly despising? Or will you come with me now, wearing your crown and robes, and proudly ride out to take possession of that which is yours? The morning is still young, and outside the palace gates our litters are waiting."

Again Ahab reached out his hand, this time with a firm gesture, and laid his fingers on the crimson scepter.

3

She had won. At last she could look the country full in the face without apology, return its incredible insolence, stare for bold-eyed stare. She was fully queen at last, and, equally satisfying, priestess.

For it was her god Melkart, not the king, who was enjoying the greatest victory. In all except name the transformation of Yahweh, the desert god, into Melkart, King of the City, was near fulfillment. The issue had been decided, or would be today, and not in a contest of strength between two rival gods on a sacred mountain called Carmel, but in a contest of strength between two ways of life in the vineyard of a peasant named Naboth.

Yet she sat behind the grilled carving in the cedar panels, swaying with the litter's jerky motion and fuming helplessly. This was no journey of triumph. The swarthy, bearded faces beside the road looked even more darkly sullen than usual, eyes more truculently bold. One burly Israelite straddled his bare feet defiantly not a spear's length from her litter and made a lewd gesture. Another spat vigorously. If a new order was about to emerge in Israel, these Israelites themselves seemed unaware of it.

However, once the royal cortege had descended the ramp and entered the road below, Jezebel's mood of triumph returned. Here the wayfarers and laborers were all peasants, and there was proper servility, even a hint of panic. The haste with which they scuttled to the roadside or laid down spade or sickle to bend themselves double was proof that they had learned their lesson. The stubbornness of Naboth would not be repeated.

No, nor would his peasant daughter again flaunt her triumph in the king's palace. Whether or not her bastard son had died during those hours of unbridled passion—and Jezebel had reason to believe he had—the woman called Rachel would never again surrender herself or her child to the man whose royal seal had impressed her father's death warrant. Both were as surely lost to Ahab as if their bodies, like Naboth's, had been abandoned to the vultures.

The vineyard of Naboth lay just beyond the royal vegetable gardens, a ridiculous bit of soil for a man to cherish with such stubbornness. Yet, small though it was, it exuded an indisputable air of importance. Its stout hedge-topped wall bristled like a mother animal protecting its young, and its tiny watchtower looked for all the world like an indignant hen squatting on her nest of eggs. So perfectly did they reflect Naboth's stubborn defiance that Jezebel had to smile.

But she was not smiling when she passed inside the tight little gate and the bearers set down her litter. Where were the peasant hirelings who were to greet the king with songs and garlands? Where were the female dancers who had been instructed to accompany his entrance with music of *kinnors* and tambourines? Emerging with furious haste, she discovered with anger and consternation that Ahab's litter, ahead of hers, was completely hidden behind a tight knot of people whose bare legs and brown muscular bodies draped only in loincloths proclaimed them to be peasants. Her anger mounted to fury.

"Miserable wretches!" she cried sharply. "Why do you stand there like wooden posts, making no sound? Don't you know it's your king who has just come into your presence? It's your queen speaking, do you hear? Did I not tell you to greet him with songs and garlands and with dances of the harvest? Does this silence mean you want your tongues plucked out?"

But, though her shrill voice must have carried to the farthest limits of the vineyard, the brown backs and stolid legs remained as impervious to its sound as the vines' twisted trunks which, though clustered in greater dignity and aloofness, seemed but an extension of the tight knot of intent peasants.

She considered pushing her way through them, but the thought of her hands coming in contact with the bare brown flesh, moist and glistening with sweat, was unbearable. Turning to one side, she plunged into a network of dark green leaves and twisting vines. The tendrils clutched at her hair and coiled about her limbs. But she pushed on stubbornly and finally came through to the other side, where she could see Ahab standing alone beside his litter.

His eyes were staring straight ahead, all the life of his other features drained into their fiery intensity. She knew suddenly that, except for his eyes, that was the way he would look in death, and, though her clothes and loosened hair were clinging hotly to her flesh, she shivered. It was a long time before she could bring herself to turn her eyes in the direction of his gaze, but when she did she realized that she had known from the beginning whom she would see.

Her first emotion was one of hot anger. Always since her coming to Israel, she sensed suddenly, this stark figure in its odorous sheepskin had been blocking her path. Even in the last decade, though never visible in body, his specter had been present, thrusting its ramrod straightness into the stubborn figures lining each dirty street or plodding along each stony road. But the anger was followed by swift triumph. Here, he was in their power at last. Ahab had only to speak the word, and the burly *gibborim,* ranged in a half circle behind him, would spring into action. There was no other exit from the vineyard than the one behind the king and his bodyguard. This time the Man of Yahweh was trapped. Oh, she had been blind these past years! Instead of making sure of his exile she should have hunted him down, hung his body up there on the walls of Jezreel for all of Israel to see! But it was not too late. It could be done today. She was about to open her lips, to urge Ahab to act swiftly, when the king's voice broke on her ears.

"Have you found me, O my enemy?"

She caught her breath sharply. For the love of Melkart, was he going to display weakness at the very moment when he so desperately needed strength! And there was nothing on earth she could do to save him. With that meek and mournful look on his face no warning cry of hers would force him to issue sharp orders to the *gibborim*. She must stand here imprisoned within tentacles of vines, grinding her teeth or biting her lips, nails pressed savagely into her palms—and listen.

"I have found you, because you have sold yourself to do what is evil in the sight of Yahweh."

It was not the clear voice as she remembered it, with its cutting edge of steel. So small and thin was it that she had to lean forward in order not to lose a syllable of its gusty accents. *He's grown old,* she thought, with satisfaction which momentarily tempered her fury, and weak. *No one will listen to what he says.*

But as she leaned forward, holding her breath, to her mounting dismay the voice did not give the impression of weakness. Like the whisper of a footstep in an empty house, it inspired a more startled awareness than an army of marching feet.

"This is what Yahweh says to you, Ahab, king of Israel. *Because you have done what is evil in my sight, behold, you will be utterly swept away, you and your sons, and your servants, and your slaves. And your house shall be like the house of Jeroboam, and like the house of Baasha, because of the anger to which you have provoked me, and because you have caused Israel to sin.*"

Jezebel's senses reeled. A small thin voice, had she said? The words pounded against her temples with the strength of iron hammers. Her lips, crushed beneath her small white teeth, tasted the sharp tang of blood. Desperately she struggled to extricate herself from the vine's clinging tentacles.

"Ahab!" she cried. "Quick! Tell the *gibborim* to surround him! For the love of Melkart, don't let him get away!"

Then she stared at him aghast, for he had not even heard her voice. Even as she watched, horrified, he put both hands to his throat, seized the yoke of his rich embroidered overgarment of blue silk, and with a great wrenching of his fingers tore it from top to girdle.

"Yes, my father," he cried out in a fervor which seemed more ecstasy than grief. "All that you say is true. I have sinned, against Yahweh and against my people. I have broken the law of Mishpat. I have betrayed the rights of a man of Israel. Let all these things be done to me even as you have said!"

316

The hot barbs of the mounting sun pounded against the frail canopy of the litter in tempo with her throbbing pulses. Ahab... Elijah... Yahweh... Which was most to blame for this fury of frustration which now possessed her? Or were all three woven into a maddening tangle? Should she try to pick the knotted skeins apart, or, as she had been doing for the last ghastly hour, keep wadding them furiously into a greater and greater snarl?

Yahweh... Had she underestimated the strength of this strange desert god of the Hebrews? And if so, in what unique qualities did his strength lie? In those very elements which she had accounted his greatest weaknesses? Surely only a little god would concern himself with the life of a little man like Naboth! Indeed, no other god, little or big, would have done so. Why should this Yahweh be different from every other? Or—was he? She had almost succeeded in compressing him into the bronze mold of Melkart—would have, had it not been for the Man of Yahweh!

Elijah... It was not Yahweh, then, but Elijah on whom she should vent her fury. That was no hardship. The very thought of the lean, towering, ugly figure shot the rich purple of her curtained litter through and through with angry crimson.

Just what was the curse which the Man of Yahweh had pronounced? She could still see his bony, leveled finger, hear the thin voice, but the words escaped her. Had he called her a dog, or had he said she was fit only for dogs to eat? She could remember well enough the words he had spoken about Ahab!

"Anyone belonging to Ahab who dies in the city, the dogs shall eat; and anyone of him who dies in the open country, the birds of the air shall eat."

She shivered. The worst curse which could be pronounced, that a man should be given no decent burial! Although, after Ahab's shameful exhibition of penitence, the Man of Yahweh had relented a bit and promised that the curse should not take effect in his lifetime but in that of his sons! Relented! He should have been made to swallow the words at the point of a spear—would have if Ahab...

Ahab... Relentlessly, stubbornly, she dug at the last tangled strand. Yes, she might as well face it. It was Ahab with whom she was most furious. He had had the troublemaker within his grasp, and he had let him escape. One word to the *gibborim*, a single gesture... But instead he had stood foolishly gaping, the slave of the situation, not its master. And, as a crowning absurdity of weakness, he had seemed

317

proud in his own humility, exultant in his very acknowledgment of guilt!

The litter jolted to a stop, and Jezebel saw to her dismay that they had arrived in the palace courtyard. Eshmun, in obedience to her orders, had arranged a fitting climax to the day of triumph. Ahab's litter, arriving just ahead of hers, was already surrounded by a bevy of dancing *kedeshoth* from the nearby Temple of Ashtart, and her own now became the object of similar assault by a band of *kedeshim*. Small clay images of Ashtart were thrust, head or feet first, as far as their voluptuous breasts, through its fine-meshed grillwork. Flowers pelted on its roof. The air was filled with shouts of greeting.

"Hail, Jezebel, fairest of queens, second only to Ashtart!"

"May the fruit of your belly be as the sweet herbs that shall sprout to your lord's delight in the vineyard of Naboth!"

"May joy surround you as the crown of gold encircles your head!"

Hastily Jezebel composed her features into a wooden smile, pulled furiously at the puckers in her robe, lifted swift fingers to check the damage done by the vines to her coiffure—and uttered a gasp of dismay. The clutching tendrils had done more than pull and tear her garments, disarrange her hair. They had robbed her of the circlet of gold and sapphires which had been her crown.

4

It was a leper, scavenging about the stoning place in the half-light of dawn, who first made the discovery. In spite of his rotting flesh, his eyes were still keen and his memory long, and what he saw sent him hobbling with wild, hoarse cries to the gate.

"Unclean!" For all his excitement he managed, from long habit, to wail his constant warning of proximity. "It's the king, I tell you... Unclean!... If you don't believe, come and see... Unclean, unclean!"

One of the two guards flung an oath and a spear, turning the excited babbling into shrill vituperation. A peasant upset his basket of melons, and in the resulting melee—screaming peasant, scrambling beggars and lepers, swearing mule drivers—the cause of the undue excitement was forgotten. Only the second guard, meticulous for detail, took time to saunter across the esplanade for a cursory inspection. He was not sauntering when he returned.

"It's true! Yahweh strike me dead if I didn't see—"

By the time the rams' horns sounded the mounting of the sun above the crests of Gilead, there was scarcely a soul in Jezreel but knew that the king was sitting alone and silent in the place of stoning, clothed in sackcloth and ashes.

Slowly the silence in which he sat spread like the rippling circles of a pool into which a stone has been dropped. Footsteps became muted. The bargaining in the market place was hushed to whispers and finally ceased altogether. Artisans put away their looms and wheels and mallets. Even the children tiptoed about with scared faces.

Ahab was conscious neither of the silence nor of the remote waves of curious, anxious faces. All day the heat of the sun burned down upon him, searing his face, scorching his bared head, turning his coarse goat's-hair garment into a steaming, stinging compress. But if he was sensible of discomfort, it was only to welcome it as part of the desired agony of penance.

"I have sinned!" his spirit cried out again and again, while his lips moved soundlessly. "I have broken the law of Mishpat. I have sinned against you and your law, O Yahweh. I have done that which is evil in your sight. Let my punishment be according to my sin and upon my own head. Let not my people suffer."

Yet mingled with his guilt and anguish was a fierce exultation, a sense of discovery which, like the sun's blazing core, he dared not look full in the face. But it was enough for the present—this one luminous ray which shone through his darkness. *Yahweh had cared what happened to a peasant named Naboth.* No other god of any people would have done so. Not Melkart, nor Chemosh, nor Dagon, nor Hadad, nor any of the deities of the Egyptians. They were concerned, every one, only with how men treated them, not with how men treated each other. But *Yahweh cared...*

"The day is spent, my lord the king. Surely it is not necessary for you to remain here longer. We are concerned, my lord, for the health of the anointed one."

Vaguely Ahab recognized the unctuous voice, was dimly conscious of a florid face framed by grizzled locks.

"I have sinned..." His lips continued to move soundlessly.

"We know why you are here, my lord the king," the voice of Shemuel persisted. "We know that you are grieving over the sin and death of Naboth and the death of Naboth's sons. But we beg our lord the king—"

"Did you say—*the death of Naboth's sons?*"

The question burst from the king's lips like fire from a stone. Shemuel gasped. The florid serenity of his features dissolved into confused pallor. "Why—surely the king knows— The—the town went mad... We elders couldn't stop them..."

Elhanan, pushing past Shemuel, calmly faced the burning interrogation in the king's eyes. "It was only in their zeal for Yahweh and their king that the people acted. The greatest sin of all had been committed: blasphemy. By the king's own written order the sin was exposed. And did not Yahweh himself say to our father Moses, 'I am a jealous god, visiting the sin of the fathers upon the children even to the third and fourth generation'? Blame not the people of Jezreel, my lord, for their eagerness to avenge their king and their God. Commend them."

Ahab struggled to his feet, awareness stabbing his senses like the pricking pain which flowed through his limbs. He became suddenly conscious of darkness and, vaguely luminous in the torchlight, a tight circle of staring, anxious faces. To clear his vision, he passed the sleeve of his sackcloth garment over his eyes, and the film of ashes drifting down from his hair penetrated the lids. The faces swam, distorted, in an angry mist of flame.

"*You*—men of Jezreel!" he shouted. "*Murderers!*"

Stooping, he groped on the ground for a stone, and flung it with all his might...stooped again and found others...smiled grimly as he heard screams of pain and terror, the rushing of panic-stricken feet.

5

The woman's face showed no surprise, no animosity. It was completely without expression. Silently she opened the door and stood aside for him to enter.

"Obadiah?" It was as if he were compelled to relive in every detail his last visit to this house on that other night of death.

"Gone," replied Deborah, tonelessly. Even the little lamp she held gave no sign of flickering. "Gone since—that day, when he took Rachel away with him."

"Then"—Ahab wet his lips—"Rachel is—safe?"

"I'm not sure. How can one be sure of anything these days, when one's neighbors turn into beasts and one's king—" She took pity on what she saw in his eyes. "Yes. I have reason to believe that she is safe."

"Jeshua?" The word hung in the air between them, tenuous and bodiless as the flame of the lamp, while Ahab held his breath.

This time she showed no pity. "They said it was the will of Yahweh that a man's sons must also suffer for his sins—and his sons' sons."

Ahab's breath returned with a great wrenching. *A man's sons.* Jeshua also had been his son. He had put a curse on him, too, as on Eliah. The same curse? *At the cost of his first-born shall he lay its foundation, and at the cost of his youngest son shall he set up its gates.* Yahweh a God who cared? Cared enough to remember and fulfill a curse doubly after four hundred years!

"All dead?" he demanded harshly.

No, not all. The house was full of hiding places, as he must remember, and many of her grandsons were small. The blood lust of Jezreel had been short-lived. That night she had found it possible to help the wives of her sons and most of her grandsons to escape.

"But not Jeshua?" Ahab questioned desperately.

She returned his gaze steadily. "No, not Jeshua."

He followed her into the room beyond the courtyard, tenantless tonight, the fire pit an empty eye socket in the floor's blank face. From old habit he sat down beside it, stretching his fingers toward the charred sticks. Deborah squatted, facing him, work-worn hands tied idly together by the knots of their huge knuckles. It was the first time he had ever seen her without a child in her arms.

Then a stooped, misshapen figure shuffled from the shadows, and he started, staring. The ghost of old Abner? Then as it came steadily toward him, the blurred face materialized into half-strange, half-familiar features. "Dan!" he cried.

But it was only a caricature of the Dan he had known—round face distorted and battered, laughing lips twisted into a grimace. One arm hung stiff and useless, swollen to twice its size. In the other hand, raised high above his head, some object caught the reflection of the lamp's flame and glittered.

"Dan!" Ahab cried out again in an agony of remorse. "What have they done to you!"

"They! It was *you* who did it. If we were all dead, you thought, you could take our vineyard and enjoy it in peace! But I fooled you. Listen, son of Omri, laugh with me over Dan's last big joke! I was dead when they left me. Their stones had ground me to a pulp. But I outwitted them! Crawled out of the stoning place and took shelter

with the lepers. And here I am. Look at me, Ahab, my old friend, for it was you who did it."

"Yes, yes, I have sinned," mourned Ahab, beating his breast. "Yahweh help me, I know I have sinned. I have broken his law of Mishpat."

"There's a law older than Mishpat." Daniel's eyes were glittering now, like the bronze blade of the pruning knife in his hand. "Lamech knew it. I am going to obey that law now, Ahab, that oldest of all laws—blood revenge!"

Ahab lifted his eyes toward the gleaming blade. With sudden exultation he parted the folds of his sackcloth garment and flung back his head, laying bare his neck. Die? Yes, gladly would he die. Thanks be to Yahweh and to this old friend of his boyhood for making his penance so swift and easy! Let the blade be merciless. Let the blood flow red in the winepress of divine judgment! Closing his eyes, he awaited the moment of exquisite torture.

The knife clattered against the stone lining of the fire pit. "I—can't do it," groaned Daniel. "All I can think of is the time you—saved my life—up there on the mountain." He uttered a terrible cry. "Get out of my sight, for Yahweh's sake, lest I again be tempted to lift my hand against the Lord's anointed!"

Silently Ahab rose and let himself out into the street.

CHAPTER 8

1

Jezebel watched Ahab's intense program of expiation with amazement and contempt, saw him withdraw each day to the stoning place to mourn in sackcloth and ashes; observed his rigid fasting until his flesh fell away, and his eyes, glowing with fanatic brilliance, seemed to have absorbed all the vigor of his once energetic body.

The torture she experienced during these days was not of repentance but of uncertainty. Had she set herself an impossible task? Could this weakling deity, who could not endure the sight of suffering even in a peasant, ever be fitted into the stern mold of Melkart? He must be, she knew that now, or more than the future of Israel would be at stake. Suppose slaves got the idea that they were as good as their masters!...or peasants that they were as much entitled to the land they tilled as the landlords who had foreclosed their mortgages!...or magistrates that the function of law was to serve the welfare of the people rather than the interests of their rulers! Couldn't Ahab see that by lending ear to such heresies he was digging the foundations from beneath every throne in the world?

She was frustrated at every turn. After Ahab's self-prescribed days of mourning passed and he plunged with almost suicidal energy into the tasks of administration, he continued to treat her, not with condemnation, but with polite and complete aloofness.

I do not blame you, his manner tacitly proclaimed. *You were acting in accordance with your customs as a Phoenician. But I am an Israelite, and I have no excuse. I shall pay the full penalty for my sin and make expiation as I see fit.*

Decisions of importance were being made, she knew, without consulting her. The alliance with Syria was being negotiated. The absence of Obadiah and his wife and son was small compensation; Ahab, on the few occasions when court etiquette demanded his appearance beside her, greeted her with the perfunctory courtesy of a stranger. Nor did her frustration stem wholly from her impotence as queen.

It was Jael who brought her the strange object wrapped in a bit of faded blue linen which she recognized as a scrap from one of her own worn-out garments. The nurse's face was grim with malice and some more subtle emotion resembling terror.

"There! By Anath and her snakes, this will show you! If you don't believe now that chit is up to no good—!"

Jezebel stared at the unwrapped object. She thought at first it was a crude clay image of Ashtart. But no, all elements of seductiveness were lacking. It had by deliberate intent been rendered hideous. And it was not a clay image at all, but a crude figure of some pliable material, such as beeswax, fashioned roughly in the shape of a woman.

"What—who—" Jezebel frowned her perplexity.

"You mean you don't see what it's intended to be, with that hair piled in coils on top of its head and that round thing that could be nothing but a crown?"

Jezebel gasped, her cheeks flaming. "You mean—"

"It isn't what I mean that counts. It's what *she* means! Can't you see—!"

Jezebel saw. She saw the deep gash just below the left breast of the image where some sharp instrument appeared to have gouged, not once, but many times. She saw the marks of mutilation on the hideously grinning face, and the deep lines scored all around the long thin neck and scrawny wrists. And she saw lurid bursts of crimson.

"Send Tanath to me," she ordered harshly.

The maid seemed more exultant than frightened. During her mistress' bitter tirade she stood proud and unbending, lips curled in a slow, scornful smile. Yes, she admitted, she had made the image, and, yes, she had hacked it with a knife, again and again and again, exactly in the place where its heart should be, and nothing her mistress could do to her would change things now, because the magic spell was complete. It might not take effect for a long time, maybe not for years, but always from now on the queen would know her fate. She could punish Tanath any way she wished, even kill her, but it would do no good.

Jezebel regarded the maid intently, anger for the moment consumed in curiosity.

"Why do you hate me so?" she asked her for the second time.

This time she got her answer. Tanath had once been in love with Eshmun. Yes, and the eunuch, then one of the palace servants, had returned her passion, she was sure of it, or at least would have, had he not suddenly conceived this hopeless infatuation for Jezebel. But that wasn't the reason he had hidden himself in the royal apartment. He had done that merely because the other servants had dared him to, wagering two wineskins to his one that he would not be able to visit Jezebel's boudoir and bring back something to prove that he had been there. She, Tanath, willing in spite of her jealousy to do anything to win his favor, had helped him, hiding him behind a curtain in the royal bath. And—the queen knew the rest. Surely she could see...

Yes. Jezebel could see. A more ironical punishment than she could possibly have foreseen both for Eshmun and the girl—depriving him of his manhood and causing Tanath to suffer the continuous taunt not only of his impotence but of his subservience to the object of her jealousy! Jezebel could not help laughing aloud. Then she remembered the wax image with its gouged breast and deeply scored wrists and neck.

"I'm not afraid of your magic," she said furiously. "If the beloved of Ashtart is not protected from such evil, my lord Melkart will keep me safe from all harm. If I seemed for the moment uncertain, it was only inadequacy in devising a punishment of fit proportions for this preposterous offense you have committed."

The bright eyes glinted back at her, bold and unblinking. "Has my mistress considered the possibility of murder? Even as she murdered her own son that day, long ago, upon the housetop?"

Jezebel was still trembling when, much later, she stood by the lattice window in her bedroom, the wax image clutched in her hand. Oh, how stupid she had been to let her curiosity get the better of her prudence after that day on the housetop! She should have sent the maid at once to Tyre or even farther, seen to it that she was rendered as inarticulate as the luckless Almah. Now it was too late. She dared not risk sending her away. *Beat me if you want to, cut off my hands, gouge out my eyes, even kill me, but don't send me away where I won't be able to see him! If you do, I swear I'll find some way to tell the king!...*

Acting on a swift impulse, she opened the lattice and flung the wax image from her hand, then leaned out and watched, fascinated, while it fell to the stone-paved roadway below and was broken into pieces. There was a snarling rush as a half-dozen lank, wolflike shapes shot from the thin patch of shade close to the wall, sniffed at the fragments, gave them a few half-hearted licks, then slunk away. A naked child poked curiously at one of the pieces, picked it up, and, after chewing it tentatively, spat it out. A leper woman crawled from the shade not far from where the dogs had been lying, parted her matted hair to peer down at one of the fragments, then kicked it indolently with her stump of a foot.

Jezebel shivered.

2

The storm which Ahab had been long expecting broke. Shalmaneser and his hordes of Assyrians poured like an unleashed torrent into Syria. The panic spread abroad before their coming was like that of wild things fleeing before a hurricane. Even behind the secure battlements of Samaria men spoke of the terror in hushed voices and with blanched faces.

"Tall shields they have, high as a man's head, and all made of metal!"

"Swifter than leopards are their horses, and fiercer than wolves!"

"Engines of war they have, with the swift wheels of a chariot for feet and the hard, butting head of a ram! A wall of thickest limestone they can pound to pebbles!"

Ahab welcomed the necessity for action as a blinded beast welcomes release from the treadmill. No more the eternal and futile seeking to solve the riddle of Yahweh! It was Yahweh the Lord of Hosts who demanded his allegiance, and serving him was a simple matter. No more the pursuit of useless clues to discover the hiding place of Elijah, that he might ascertain the penance acceptable to Yahweh the Lord of Mishpat. He could forget for the moment that he had betrayed his best friend, slain the father of his beloved, set a double curse unto death on the son of his flesh and the son of his spirit.

Swallowing the memory of his bitter humiliation at the hand and tongue of Jehu, he summoned his former captain from the headquarters of the temple guild.

"I am willing to forget the unfortunate incident after the battle of Aphek, if you are," he said bluntly but without rancor. "The welfare of Israel should be of more importance to both of us than personal enmity."

Though the dark features remained wary and sullen, the slender fingers curled with involuntary eagerness. "What—would my lord want his—his servant to do?"

"Take off that haircloth garment. Put on a new uniform, not that of a captain of fifty, or of a hundred, or even of a thousand, but—" Ahab paused, eyes narrowing on the scowling features. "Put on the gold shield and scarlet cloak of the commander in chief of the horses and chariots of Israel."

The scowl merely deepened. The only token of Jehu's excitement was the darkening of the small blue veins lacing the shaven scalp. "Did—did my lord say—commander in chief?"

"Yes, of the two thousand chariots and their accompanying horses which are to be Israel's share in this combined defensive."

"Two thousand! But—my lord must be jesting—"

"You think there aren't that many chariots in Israel. There weren't, a few months ago. Even Damascus will be able to assemble no more than twelve hundred. You see how necessary it is that our commander be the most able strategist in Israel."

A bright flush crept up the scowling forehead and absorbed the network of blue veins. But the eyes beneath the knitted brows remained noncommittal. "I—am a servant of Yahweh."

"Listen, grandson of Nimshi! Have you heard what these Assyrians do to their conquered foes? They burn their prisoners to death, or bury them alive. Of some, they cut off the hands and arms; of others, the noses and ears; and of many, they gouge out the eyes. Would you run the risk of these barbarians overpowering Israel?"

"At least," said Jehu pointedly, "they obey the commands of their god. If he bids them destroy, they will spare no one."

"As we may soon discover," retorted Ahab, keeping his temper with great difficulty. "It is less likely, however, than if Ben-hadad had been slain. What do you say, grandson of Nimshi? Will you go back to your prophet guild and poison my chances of success with your antagonism, or will you come with me as commander in chief of the horses and chariots?"

Jehu hesitated only an instant. "I'll come with you," he said tersely.

Jehu was dispatched by swift horse to Megiddo, and the two thousand chariots of Israel were on their way to Damascus before

327

nightfall. For two days already Israel's ten thousand infantrymen had been on the march. Ready to leave Samaria in his own chariot at dawn, Ahab cast himself down on his couch fully dressed save for his armor. Only when he wakened at the trumpeting of the third watch did he remember with dismay that he had not asked the counsel of priests or prophets. He started up in panic. Elicit an oracle from Melkiah in the short time remaining? It would take the high priest until cockcrow to get fastened into his ephod and breastplate! Yet— dare he risk consulting the prophets who, since the return of Jehu from Aphek, had not been too friendly? He had no choice.

Members of the prophet guild were hastily summoned, and Ahab met them in the hall of audience. At sight of the slight, angular figure of Micaiah he knew an instant of uneasiness and irritation. Had the son of Imlah ever set the seal of divine approval on any act of his kingship? He was relieved when Micaiah withdrew from the group and took no part in the ecstatic singing and dancing. He was still further relieved when, after only the briefest of ecstatic trances, Zedekiah, the master of the guild, started to intone a favorable verdict.

"Listen, O Israel, to the word of Yahweh, King of the City, to his son who sits in the seat of the gods in Samaria. Thus says Yahweh: 'Even as is the heart of my son Ahab, so is my heart. Let him move against his enemy the Assyrians, and I shall go with him. In my arms of bronze will I lift up his enemies and cast them into the fire of my wrath. I, Yahweh, King of the City, have spoken it.' "

King of the City... His son who sits in the seat of the gods... Ahab stared at Zedekiah, bewildered. He was looking at a prophet of Yahweh. There was no mistaking the goatshair coat, the tonsure, the branded forehead. Yet he was listening to the words of a prophet of Melkart. Where—what... Before he could even formulate the questions, the voice of Micaiah, low, calm, yet penetrating, filled his ears.

"Listen to the word of Yahweh, God of Israel, to Ahab the king, who sits in the seat of a man, not of God, whose heart is not as the heart of God. You but deceive yourself if you think I promise you victory over the Assyrians. Go if you must, but not without counting the cost. It will be the peasants of Israel, remember, already chafed and bleeding from the bonds of your unholy alliance with Tyre, who will suffer the burdens and reap none of the benefits..."

Ahab did not let him finish. Wounded to the quick and determined that the fateful words, which might mean defeat for his crucial enterprise, should not be spoken, he ordered Micaiah removed from his presence and thrust into the palace dungeon. Then, for it was near dawn, he donned his armor and went immediately to his chariot.

3

The storm raged through Syria. The northern cities, Carchemish, Hattina, and Gurgum, capitulated without a struggle. Of the southern cities Barga, its tall, many-windowed buildings securely circled by high battlements, was the first to fall, the huge stones dropped from its bastions of no avail against the terrible Assyrian battering rams, its gallant defenders, feet and hands severed, impaled around its walls or dragged off with ropes around their necks.

The conquerors then moved up the Orontes toward Hamath, sweeping with them prisoners and booty like wreckage in the path of a relentless flood, and before them sped a vanguard of terrified refugees, each adding his score to the tally of horror.

"A great shield they raised before our walls which no arrow could penetrate, and behind the shield they built a huge mound which rose higher and higher and came closer and closer, until finally their ladders were set against our strongest towers!"

"Towers they have like mountains set on wheels, and archers in the midst of them!"

"Our maidens are despoiled and slain, our children lie trampled in the streets, the bones of our old men and women are ground beneath the wheels of their chariots!"

"Flee! For the love of Hadad, flee while there is yet time!"

But at Karkar, twenty miles north of Hamath, the fiercely flowing tide was suddenly stemmed. Here within a small fort set on a low mound but guarded by high battlemented towers, Irhuleni, the king of Hamath, and his allies boldly resisted the enemy's advance. And of the twelve kings who came to his aid, Ahab of Israel was by no means the least. Though several other members of the confederation equaled or exceeded his contribution of ten thousand infantry, none surpassed him in the number of chariots. And, though the great Shalmaneser recorded in his annals that with the help of his gods Asshur and Nergal he had effected the defeat of his enemies, boasting that he had "scattered their corpses, filled the surface of the wilderness with their many troops, and with weapons caused their blood to flow," he advanced no farther into Syria that year than Karkar on the river Orontes.

Ahab returned to Samaria plunged again in moodiness and despondency. The Assyrians had been halted, but only temporarily, and at a cost too great to calculate. Would he have done better to take Jezebel's advice and go caviling for favors like the Tyrians? Mattenbaal was sitting smugly now amid his profits. Or should he have listened to the voice of Micaiah and more soberly counted the cost? Who could say?

As he flung the reins to his groomsmen and watched the muddied, bloodstained chariot descend into the clear waters of the courtyard pool for its vigorous scrubbing, he wished it were as easy to wash from his memory the sight of mutilated bodies and wrecked chariots and plunging horses...of a river foaming red with the blood of the sons of Yahweh...of the hundreds of little fields that would remain unsown because the hands that should till them and the feet that should tread their plowed furrows were mingled with the dust outside the walls of Karkar.

CHAPTER 9

1

The writing tablet was of cheap, unpolished wood, its coating of wax barely thick enough to record a clear impression of the stylus. Even before Jezebel tried to decipher the words, her eyes were caught by the imprint of the seal at the bottom, an upreared horse with wings spreading from its shoulders, and she felt her cheeks flood with crimson.

I must see you alone. Without your help I am powerless to serve the king. Meet me tonight after the hour of feasting, on the roof of the small tower.

She was late in leaving the banquet hall that night. The embassy from Moab had just arrived in Samaria with its semiannual tribute, and as a matter of court etiquette she had been forced to put in an appearance. She was still wearing her robes of royal purple, together with the cap-shaped crown of meshed gold studded with emeralds, when she slipped through the lower rooms in the older part of the palace built by Omri, and mounted to the second story by a small, seldom used stairway leading to the small tower at the southwestern corner of the roof.

It was easy enough to mark her progress, even without a torch, for the moonlight falling through the long narrow slits in the eastern wall threw pale silver fingers across the stairs. Toward the top she moved more and more slowly, for the rendezvous had already become distasteful. It was Ahab she should be coming here to meet. Remember the first time they had climbed these stairs together and she had been afraid to look down through the slits to the plunging depths below?

Silly little coward! You could scarcely get your arm through one of those slits. Come here close to me, my darling, with your hair full of moonbeams. I'll hold you.

The memory turned her sick with longing, and she almost turned and retraced her steps. Then slowly she rounded the last turn and mounted, still noiselessly, into the familiar eyrie of windswept, moonlit duskiness. He was standing by the farther parapet toward the east, a dark, bulky shadow etched on a silver canvas of moonlight. A slow smile curled her lips. "Jehu!" she called softly.

* * *

"So—" There was still more of amusement than outrage in her voice when, sometime later, she broke into the earnest flow of his discourse. "You wrote me a letter summoning me to meet you here, caused me to leave the banquet hall earlier than I had intended, put me in an unquestionably compromising position—just to ask me to use my influence with the king to promote one of your pet projects!"

"But surely the queen can understand the importance—"

"I understand everything you've told me. The king, you say, incurred the displeasure of his god Yahweh by sparing the life of Ben-hadad. Hence Yahweh is angry and must be appeased. I can understand that very well. Indeed, I find it most refreshing to hear that your Yahweh is acting again like a normal deity."

"Then the queen will endeavor to persuade her lord—"

"To correct his mistake by finding some pretext to fight again with the Syrians?"

"The matter of Ramoth-gilead is no pretext. Ben-hadad promised to return it to Israel along with the other cities he restored across the Jordan. He failed to keep his promise. How can a good son of Yahweh endure such an insult!"

From her stone seat just beneath the parapet, her back to the newly risen moon, Jezebel could see Jehu's features distinctly, even the two deep furrows between his brows. They revealed none of the dependence, the acknowledgment of weakness she had expected, only stubborn purpose and—complete indifference.

"I suppose," she said, "you think that if Israel went to war again, the present Ben-hadad would be killed and Ahab would redeem himself."

"There's scarcely a doubt of it. Damascus is weak now. Her losses were even greater than Israel's. Now is the time to get back Ramoth-gilead."

"And"—she watched him narrowly—"suppose Ahab instead of Ben-hadad is killed? What then?"

The shocked surprise in his voice was surely genuine. "Yahweh in heaven! Surely the queen does not think—"

"The queen thinks what she has always thought—and known," said Jezebel. "That the grandson of Nimshi will never be content to ride crouching in the bottom of a chariot while another holds the reins. Come, sit beside me, Jehu."

He seated himself with obvious reluctance, his features, his whole figure, turning into a shapeless blur. Only one hand stood out, each curled slender finger sharply outlined against the crimson of his officer's cloak.

"Why did you really ask me to come here tonight?" she asked softly. "Not to beg me to persuade my lord to fight the Syrians. You know very well he no longer listens to anything I say. Is it—could it possibly be because—you're afraid of me, Jehu?"

"Afraid—" He made a vague, uncertain motion, but his hand did not move.

"Or—is it yourself you're afraid of?"

"I—I don't know—what you mean—"

She reached out her hand and touched his lightly, as she had done in the stable at Megiddo. His fingers quivered, but this time they did not draw away.

"Could it be," she whispered, "because all this time you've never been able to forget that little statue I gave you?"

She was prepared for anything—except the violence with which he took her suddenly into his arms, straining her to him with such savage strength that she thought her bones would be broken, crushing his lips against hers with the fierce urgency of one attempting to assuage a lifetime of thirst in one single burning draught...then with equal suddenness flinging her from him so abruptly that she lost her balance and fell back on the stone seat in an undignified huddle.

"There! That's what you wanted, isn't it? What you've always wanted since that day in the stable, either for yourself or for Ashtart, I don't know which! Or—aren't you satisfied yet? Must you have still more?"

He approached her again, long fingers curled like talons, outstretched, demanding, and she pushed him away with both anger and loathing. "You—you beast, you upland peasant! How dare you lay your hands on the king's consort! If you come one step closer, I—I'll have you given forty strokes with the lash! I'll have you seared with red-hot irons, I—I'll have your tongue cut out!"

He laughed mirthlessly. "Yes. By all your despicable gods and goddesses, I believe you would do all those things!"

333

She heard his laughter, harsh and bitter, echoing back up the hollow well of the stairs. With a strange mingling of emotions she straightened her garments, adjusted her gold cap, and rose to her feet. An uncertain smile, which should have been one of triumph, twisted her lips. Had she not accomplished one of her long-cherished desires—forced him to bend the knee in obeisance to Ashtart? Why, then, this rankling suspicion that he had flung her from him exactly as he had flung the little clay image of Ashtart on the rough stone floor?

2

Just outside the high western gate of Samaria was a huge, flat, outcropping of limestone which had once been an ancient threshing floor. Here, on a stone platform, flanked by the solid masonry of the gate tower in two splendid chairs of cedar overlaid with gold, Ahab sat with his vassal ally and relative by marriage, Jehoshaphat, the king of Judah. Both were arrayed in regal attire, Ahab, as was befitting, the more sumptuously. His voluminous robes with their gold-tasseled overgarment were of the finest Tyrian weaves and artistry. The bracelets on his slender wrists, symbols of his kingship and thick as a slave's collar, were of pure gold from Ophir, and his scepter, gem-studded and curved like a shepherd's crook, glittered between his knees like an upreared snake's head.

Ahab's magnificence was equaled only by his impatience. Already he and Jehoshaphat had been sitting here since the hour of morning sacrifice, and still the band of prophets seemed no nearer the climax of ecstasy than when he had propounded the question: Is it the will of Yahweh that Israel should march against Ramoth-gilead?

Jehu, he noticed with some satisfaction, sitting among the officers at his right, was as impatient as himself. A trickle of sweat kept making its way under the bowl of his helmet, disappearing into the deep cleft of his scowl. It was Jehu who had involved him in this whole distasteful proceeding—or—was it not? Had he been persuaded by the importunate pleas, all kindled, he was sure, by sparks from the young officer's blazing torch of patriotism? Or had the determining pressure been not one of heat but of coldness—one sharp penetrating thrust from an icy blade? *What's the matter? Is my husband afraid his Yahweh isn't equal to the task of reclaiming his own cities for his sons?*

Eyes narrowing, he studied the figure in the thronelike chair at his side. Jehoshaphat was lukewarm about the enterprise. The gain or loss of a little northern city was of small concern to Judah. He remembered very well the day, three months before, when he had broached the question—scarcely an hour after he had magnanimously lowered the southern kingdom's annual tribute.

"Are you aware that Ramoth-gilead belongs by right to us, and yet we do nothing to assert our ownership and take it from the king of Syria?"

The king of Judah had looked startled and, Ahab recalled, just a little sick. No need to prolong his suspense! "Will you go with me to battle at Ramoth-gilead?" he had posed abruptly.

Jehoshaphat had swallowed once, a little painfully, then risen nobly to the occasion. There had been no necessity to remind him of the time when Israel had come to his aid against the Moabites, or of the close marital alliance between them. The reduced tribute had already spoken with sufficient eloquence. "I am as you are," the king of Judah had responded gallantly; "my people are as your people, my horses are as your horses." Now both "horses and people" were making good their promise. The army of Judah was encamped beside his own in the broad valley just south of Samaria.

Jehoshaphat, Ahab suspected, was hoping for an unfavorable verdict from Yahweh. His gaze on the struggling, perspiring devotees was unswervingly attentive. As for Ahab, he did not want to look at them, so vivid was the contrast between their pampered bodies, now enervated from exertion, and the lean, gaunt, tireless shapes which still whirled with impassioned zeal through his boyhood memories.

Carefully he looked over the prophets' heads, fixed his gaze on the upper courses of the great wall above the gate. Here, at least, was something permanent and reassuring. Higher and more strongly buttressed than any other wall in Israel except Megiddo's, and bedded six feet deep in the solid rock! Yes, and beautiful too. He remembered with what awe he had watched the Phoenician stonecutters and masons take the great hoisting blocks, one stretcher to each two headers, cut their straight margins and match them with hairline accuracy, dress their tops to form a perfectly level bed for the next course, finally chipping the roughly bossed outer edges to the smoothness of pottery.

Yet even as his eyes rested upon it, the great wall seemed visibly to disintegrate. He saw the hill of Shamer lying bare and desolate, tenanted only by the wind and a stray flock of sheep. He saw the stones of his citadel and palace buried deep in rubble or strewn like whitened bones on a wasteland, his precious ivories broken to bits and sown like sterile seed in barren furrows. Horrified, he turned his eyes from the wall back to the whirling figures on the esplanade.

The dismay on Jehoshaphat's face was ludicrous. But Ahab did not smile. Knowing well the influence of Jehu, he could have told in advance exactly what the verdict would be. Suddenly he gripped the arms of his chair. *If it was Jehu's will which the prophets were interpreting, then how could one be sure that it was the will of Yahweh?* How could one ever be sure...

"Go up to Ramoth-gilead," chanted the four hundred prophets again and again in concert. "Let the king go up and triumph, for Yahweh will deliver the city into his hands. Go up to Ramoth-gilead..."

Whether Yahweh's will or not, there was power in the very utterance of a blessing or a curse. There was power in the act of Zedekiah, who had made for himself great horns of iron and fastened them to his head—no less power, certainly, because he looked so ridiculous charging, head lowered, about the esplanade.

"Thus says Yahweh," panted the leader of the prophets. " ' With horns like these you shall push the Syrians until they are destroyed.' Thus says Yahweh..."

Gradually the fervor waned and the noise subsided. It became possible for the kings to make themselves heard above the tumult.

"Well?" Ahab leaned toward his companion. "Is my brother the king satisfied?"

Jehoshaphat merely grunted. "Is there not some other prophet of Yahweh of whom we might inquire?" he suggested doubtfully.

Ahab laughed, a little harshly. "You mean four hundred aren't enough?" Following a sudden impulse, he said, more with amusement than seriousness, "Well—yes, there is one other person by whom we might inquire of Yahweh—Micaiah, the son of Imlah. But I can't say I'm too fond of him, for he is less likely to prophesy good of me than evil."

The king of Judah did not return his smile. "Let not the king say so," he responded earnestly. "Whether the will of Yahweh be good or evil, surely we want to discover the truth. Let us hear what this man has to say."

Ahab bit his tongue. What demon had entered into him! He had committed himself to the conquest of Ramoth-gilead, and Yahweh had approved the act. Why, then—? Suddenly his eyes encountered the furious gaze of Jehu, and his decision was made. He beckoned to one of his eunuchs. "Go to my son in the palace," he ordered in a loud voice, "and order Micaiah brought from the dungeon."

Once the words had passed his lips, Ahab was glad he had made the decision. Why shouldn't Micaiah have the right to speak his mind? This was Samaria, not Tyre. And what, in the name of all the fathers, was a free man of Israel doing in a dungeon? What had he, the king of Israel, been thinking of to put him there?

As news spread of the summoning of Micaiah, the tension of the crowd mounted. A buzz of angry murmuring swept through the ranks of prophets. Among the officers grouped about Jehu and their flanking army cohorts there was an ominous bristling of spears, followed by an uneasy stirring of metal scales. But when the two *gibborim* shouldered and speared their way through the dense masses swarming the gate, the excitement subsided to swift silence. All eyes stared fascinated at the wasted, stumbling figure being half dragged across the esplanade.

Ahab also stared. This withered husk, this shell—Micaiah? Why, it wasn't a man at all. It had the shape and face of a man, yes, but its limbs were spidery projections, its bones already skeletonlike beneath skin which seemed but the tenuous fabric of cobwebs. Ahab's own flesh quivered.

"The messenger who came to summon me," said Micaiah, "advised me to let my word be like the word of the other prophets, and to speak favorably. But I said to him, 'As Yahweh lives, what he says to me, that will I speak.' "

The voice was like the blast of a ram's horn issuing from a thin reed.

Ahab leaned forward. "Shall we march up to attack Ramoth-gilead," he demanded, "or shall we relinquish to the Syrians that which rightfully belongs to Israel?"

"Oh, march up and take it, by all means," replied the prophet quickly. "Surely Yahweh will give it into your hands!"

"Hear, hear!" There was a burst of applause, followed by a lusty chanting. "Go up to Ramoth-gilead! Surely the Lord will give it into your hands!"

Ahab fixed his gaze intently on the two burning eyes. Had he imagined that undertone of sarcasm? "Tell me the truth," he adjured earnestly. "You never have deceived me. Don't begin now. Tell me the truth or nothing."

Micaiah returned the king's gaze steadily. "Very well," he said. "I saw all Israel scattered over the hills, as sheep that have no shepherd, and Yahweh said, 'These have no master. Let each return to his home in peace.' "

Ahab turned to Jehoshaphat. "Didn't I tell you"—there was a note of excitement in his voice—"that he would prophesy no good for me, only evil?"

"But that is not all I saw," continued Micaiah, his voice cleaving the suddenly hostile silence like a sword thrust: "I saw the Lord Yahweh sitting on his throne and all the host of heaven standing beside him on his right hand and on his left. And the Lord said, 'Who will entice Ahab, that he may go up and fall at Ramoth-gilead?' And one said one thing, and another said another. Then a spirit came forward and stood before the Lord, saying, 'I will entice him.' And the Lord said to him, 'By what means?' And he said, 'I will go forth and will be a lying spirit in the mouth of all his prophets.' And he said, 'You are to entice him, and you will succeed. Go forth and do so.' So you see, O king, if your prophets are inspired by Yahweh and if they have promised you success, it must be because a lying spirit has entered into them. The spirit which spoke to me revealed nothing but evil concerning this venture."

Relief surged through Ahab's veins. He had no more taste than Jehoshaphat for this siege of Ramoth-gilead. He had agreed to it only because he had believed it to be his patriotic duty and the desire of Yahweh. But with the oracles uncertain, even Jehu and his henchmen must admit the wisdom of curbing their zeal. He signaled to an attendant, and was about to order that Micaiah be taken to the palace, fed, and clothed in decent garments, then released; but before he could open his lips Zedekiah had stepped forward and struck the prophet across the face, a hard blow which sent the frail figure reeling.

"Just tell me if you can," Zedekiah shouted harshly, the horns still bobbing above his flabby cheeks, "how the spirit of Yahweh went from me to speak through you!"

Regaining his balance, Micaiah regarded his former leader steadily and without rancor. "You'll find that out," he returned calmly, "on the day when you have to go into an inner chamber to hide yourself."

The angry muttering of the prophets swelled to shrill invective.

"Down with the traitor!" shouted a harsh voice which might have been Jehu's.

"Enemy of Israel! The dungeon is too good for him!"

"Syria-lover, is he? Then let him go there!"

"Ah, ay, but first rub that meddlesome nose in asses' dung!"

Ahab stared, dismayed, as they fell on Micaiah with the ferocity of wild beasts, shouting epithets, tearing off his garments, flinging dust in his face. Jehu had done his work well among both prophets and soldiers. They were ready to believe any dissenter a false prophet and a traitor—even their king. Yahweh's will or no, Ahab was powerless now to change his plans. Only by a sheer miracle could he keep this crazed mob from tearing Micaiah to pieces.

"Stop!" he cried. "You are men of Israel, not beasts! Listen to your king!"

But he might have been adjuring a plague of swarming locusts. The prophet, frail and naked, body already wasted by confinement, was as defenseless as a tender vine before their hungry assault. A stone spun through the air, hitting him in the shoulder. Another turned the deep brand on his forehead into a crimson gash. Just so, outside another city gate, a man named Naboth...

Ahab plunged down the steps of the platform. His heavy robes twined about his limbs, causing him to stumble, but somehow he managed to reach the naked figure, to cover it with the loose folds of his long, fringed coat. Gasping, the crowd fell back; then, aghast at the sight of the high-crowned cap knocked awry, at the trickle of blood staining the royal cheek, they subsided into horrified silence.

"Is it the province of a lawless mob," demanded Ahab in a loud voice, "to render judgment in the presence of the king of Israel?" He gestured to the two *gibborim* who had brought the prophet from the dungeon. "Seize Micaiah," he ordered abruptly, "and take him back to Amon, the governor of the city, and say, This is what the king says: Put this fellow in prison, and feed him with scant rations of bread and water until—" He hesitated only long enough to cast a swift glance over the hostile faces, then finished grimly: "Until I return victorious from Ramoth-gilead."

"If you return victorious," retorted Micaiah, his voice bold and clear, "then Yahweh has not spoken through me!"

The brimming excitement spilled over again as the thin figure was dragged across the esplanade, but no one made a move to touch him. Ahab returned to his chair and, hands clenched, stood watching. Not until Micaiah had disappeared in safety through the gate did he lower himself slowly into his chair.

3

It was settled at last. The two armies were to begin their march toward Ramoth-gilead in the morning. After a long argument Ahab had succeeded in convincing Jehoshaphat that the power for victory in the words of four hundred devotees of Yahweh would surely cancel the power for defeat in those of one. It had taken more than argument, however. Other inducements had been necessary. Now, Ahab told himself grimly as he paced the narrow confines of his tent in the valley below Samaria, all that remained was to convince himself. Somehow he must change the image of defeat created in his own spirit by Micaiah's words for one of victory.

Jezebel could have restored his flagging confidence. "Four hundred for and only one against? And still you are afraid?" But it would have been the touch of her lips, not their derisive scorn, which would have dispelled his doubts. Sometimes, as now, even though he knew his love was dead, his desire for her was overwhelming, frightening. His nerves tingled to the deep-piled rug beneath his feet as to the soft meshes of her hair, and so reminiscent of her smooth flesh was the touch of his linen sheet that each time he flung himself down upon it he was soon tossing aside the crimson coverlet and was up again to resume his restless pacing.

Suddenly he stood staring at the thick carpet, the couch so soft that it still bore the impress of his body. What was a soldier of Israel doing here in this—this perfumed jewel box? It had not been so in the old days, when in the zeal of youth he had gone out to fight battles for Yahweh. There had been hard, stony ground beneath his feet, and he had lain down to rest with a cloak of rough homespun about his shoulders and, like his ancestor Jacob, a stone for a pillow.

He knew suddenly that he must escape the soft, confining web, feel rough earth beneath his bare feet. But as he moved abruptly toward the curtained vestibule of his tent, one of the drawn flaps was lifted and an attendant stepped timidly inside.

"Well?" Ahab's voice was sharp with impatience.

Appalled by his audacity, the man was only half-coherent. Let the king slay him if he wished, he knew it was taking his life in his hands to break in on the king's privacy at this hour, but the woman had been so insistent—

"What woman?" demanded Ahab, his pulses pounding.

Aie! That was the trouble. The attendant did not know. She had refused to give her name or to remove her heavy veil. But, Yahweh strike him dead if he spoke an untruth, for some reason he had been sure she came from the palace, and,...

"Bring her here to me," ordered the king with harsh abruptness.

So she had sensed his need and come to him! Why? To rekindle the flickering lamp of his courage with the flame of her zeal? To tempt him to break his soldier's vow of chastity? It did not matter. Nothing had ever mattered, he knew that now—neither his kingdom nor his people, no, nor his God—as had this woman for whose coming he now waited in an agony of expectation, the very thought of whom had the power to set his pulses pounding and his flesh aching with desire.

But the woman who entered his tent and slowly drew back her veil was not Jezebel.

4

She was wakened by the sound of ram's horn trumpets. Slipping from her couch, she hastened across the room to a window.

The two armies were on the march, the vanguard of their swelling stream already foaming toward the pass between Mount Ebal and Mount Gerizim. The smoke of their morning sacrifice to Yahweh enshrouded the empty tents in a thin gray pall. Not too good an omen, noted Jezebel with a worried frown. Even though it might signify no displeasure on Yahweh's part, Ahab was likely to so interpret it. She wished now she had yielded to the mad impulse which, in a moment of sharp waking in the middle of the night, had almost led her to rise from her couch and go to him. But she had been afraid he would exact certain promises from her—promises which might have interfered with her plans for this day's important business.

Immediately she set them in motion. Summoning Eshmun, she plied him with terse questions, all of which he answered to her satisfaction. Yes, the caravan on its way from Egypt to Babylon had been easily persuaded—*cheaply* might be the better word—to postpone its departure until after the armies marched, and was now ready to leave, panniers laden, from the khan closest to the Damascus quarter. And, yes, the transfer of merchandise had been arranged to conform with the queen's desire.

Jezebel's sharp gaze probed the imperturbable features for some sign of emotion, but Eshmun might have been discussing the sale of a piece of common blue Samaritan pottery. Good. Apparently he was as devoid of sentiment toward the object of their discussion as—she frowned suddenly—as toward herself.

"Send Tanath to me," she ordered abruptly.

Now, at least, she was certain of arousing emotion. "I have arranged," she said without prelude, when the maidservant had been brought from the chamber where she was kept under constant surveillance, "to sell you to a company of merchants on their way to Babylon. You are to go at once."

The woman's sullen features might have been carved from stone. "I am a slave," she said simply. "The slave's owner may dispose of her property as she wishes."

Jezebel stared. She had expected tears, pleadings, ravings, and she felt oddly cheated. "You—you don't care? Before, when I threatened to send you away—"

"I know. I told my mistress that if she tried to do so I would find some way to tell the king something she would prefer he did not know."

"Well?" It was hard, flaunting her triumph in the face of this composure. "My lord the king is no longer in the city. By the time he returns you will be so far away you could shout your secret with a thousand tongues and never reach his ears. Tell it now if you wish. No one will believe you. They will think you are only seeking revenge for my having sold you into slavery. I suppose it did not occur to you that another more clever than yourself could play your game of wits."

The maid's gaze dropped discreetly. "It is as the queen says. We have played a game of wits, and one of us has lost. From this

moment my threats are as powerless to do my mistress harm as"—
the downcast eyes lifted suddenly—"as the little image of wax which
fell from the window and lay broken to bits."

The second and more important business required greater
preparation. She made sure first of all that the Tyrian artisans were
engaged at their task—they had been commissioned to enclose the
small sunken pool in the courtyard, just outside the winter palace.
Long ago she had conceived the idea of making the pool into a small
private bathhouse, but the arrival of the artisans just in time to
implement her plan was almost too perfect a—coincidence? Perhaps,
rather, it had been the sight of them working so close to the two little
chambers, piling one stone upon another with such perfect precision
and sealing them so tightly...

She dressed carefully, covering her robe with a coarse linen
mantle, and took with her, besides Eshmun, only two of her own
slaves, burly, oxlike eunuchs of large muscle and small intelligence.
The hour chosen was close to noon, and the stone masons were, as
she had expected, taking advantage of the period of siesta to dally at
their tasks. Two were taking turns drinking from a battered wineskin.
A third and fourth were mixing more ribaldry than lime in the mortar
they were negligently stirring, and a fifth, apron tipped back over his
head, was audibly snoring. She spoke sharply but in a low voice to the
foreman.

"So this is the way the master craftsmen of Tyre train their
apprentices these days! Israel would do better to import her builders
from Assyria."

The foreman's belated recognition and subsequent horror were
gratifying. She was not likely to be recognized by any attendants who
might be prowling in the courtyard, and—the workmen would be
available where and when she needed them.

The two additional slaves were waiting, as directed, with torches,
inside the first small chamber. Except for the absence of Obadiah,
thought Jezebel as she moved unerringly toward the low doorway in
the left-hand corner, she might be reliving her first visit to this place.
Even the brass studs marking the heavy wooden door glimmered in
the torchlight with the same bright watchfulness.

"Open it," she commanded tersely.

This time there were no *gibborim's* spears to prod the heels of the
timorous torchbearers. They seemed barely to crawl down the narrow
sloping tunnel. The chill of the stone floor penetrated her thin

sandals, and the walls felt like a snake's scales beneath her fingers. But it was not physical discomfort alone which caused her senses to sharpen into an agony of awareness. Was she too late? The stench of death seemed already mingled with the fetid breath which assailed her nostrils. But yesterday at this time he had been alive. She herself had seen him from the palace roof, being dragged across the great courtyard...

"Look out!" she cried sharply, then, startled by the resounding distortion which was her own voice, let it sink to a sepulchral whisper. "There's a sheer drop ahead. Hang your feet over the edge and slip down... Fools! Let yourselves drop!"

Finally she had to push one of them, then the other, running the risk of their falling and extinguishing their torches. Then she was down on the stones herself, lowering her feet, dropping unhesitatingly into the void. Snatching the torch from one of the slaves, she swept its flaring blaze about the cavern. But at first it blinded her so that she could see nothing but its trailing reflection.

"Where are you, Micaiah, son of Imlah?" she cried in vexation. "You needn't try to hide, because I know you're there, you little Man of Yahweh!"

His voice sounded promptly, calmly, and so close that she drew back startled, stumbling against the already unsteady body of a descending eunuch.

"I am here, daughter of Melkart. The queen doubly honors me, both with her presence and with her manner of address. She dignifies me beyond my deserts in calling me 'Man of Yahweh,' even though a little one."

Jezebel struggled to regain her balance, then lowered the torch so that its circle of light fell upon the patiently squatting figure, the tranquil features. "Hold it there," she ordered one of the slaves, "so it shines full on his face."

She had pictured him cowering in one end of the cavern, herself towering scornfully at the other end, between them the lurid glow of a torch which would signify a pit of fire. She would throw aside her cloak to reveal a robe of metallic cloth encasing her body like a coating of bronze. She would be the living embodiment of Melkart-Ashtart, towering triumphantly over this dying embodiment of a weak and subjugated Yahweh, this man who, even more than Elijah, had thwarted her plans at every turn. But his planting himself brazenly in the very center of the chamber and welcoming her like an honored guest placed her oddly at a disadvantage.

"You may feel less honored," she retorted furiously, "when you find out why I have come."

"I think not." The steadiness of his eyes was unmarred by the flickering lights and shadows. "What greater honor could be paid a man than to let him bear witness to the truth as it comes to him from the Eternal? I am certain the daughter of Melkart is here to give me just this privilege."

"You—call it a privilege to *die?*"

"Why not? Does it matter what happens to me, as long as the truth shall live?"

Jezebel's lips curled into a slow smile. "Ah, my little Man of Yahweh, but how long do you think your precious 'truth' will live after your lips are silenced? Who will go prating it about the country then? Elijah, sitting up there in his cave in the mountains of Gilead, without you to goad him? Zedekiah and his prophets? You know as well as I that they're more Melkart's than Yahweh's. My lord Ahab? He's no more certain what sort of god he worships than a child groping in the dark. As soon as his remorse over that affair of Naboth has worn a little thinner, he'll come back to me quickly enough—yes, and bending the knee to Melkart, even though he may call him by the name of Yahweh!"

As the prophet remained silent, her confidence mounted. "So you see, little Man of Yahweh, I shall win, after all. Whatever name he bears, Melkart shall be supreme in Israel. It's you, Micaiah, from whom I have always had most to fear, you and your insolent voice and your preposterous ideas about one man being as good in the sight of Yahweh as another. But you'll never stand in my way again. You may shout as loud as you want to, but no one will hear you."

"There will be other voices," returned the prophet calmly. "If the things I have said are true, there will be those to say them."

"Then I will destroy them, just as I am going to destroy you!"

The squatting figure moved, had the unspeakable insolence to shrug its shoulders. "Have your way. Destroy me. Destroy all of us. You'll not be the first, nor the last, to delude yourself that you can kill the dream by murdering the dreamer. So does the wind boast that, by its violence, it has destroyed the tree, root and branch, when all it has done is to scatter its seeds to the far corners of the earth."

In sudden fury Jezebel tore at the fastenings of her long cloak and flung it back. The sheath of metallic cloth caught and absorbed the uncertain torchlight, dispelled it again in a thousand tiny barbs of flame. "Look at me, little Man of Yahweh," she commanded, "you who dare to question my power, and tell me—*do you know who I am?*"

"Yes," came the quiet answer. "You are one who believes herself cast in the image of Melkart, as I believe myself created in the image of Yahweh, the Eternal. You are wind and earthquake and fire, and I am only a very little voice proclaiming what small truth has been given me. Yet after the wind and the earthquake and the fire have passed, there shall be heard the still small voice of the Eternal."

She was still quivering with fury when, a few hours later, taking only Eshmun with her, she went back to see what progress had been made by the workmen. The essential part of her command, she was told, had already been fulfilled.

Leaving Eshmun to guard the entrance to the outer chamber, she entered the second cubicle and, passing into the tunnel, traversed it again to its end, this time in the company of the foreman and a single torch-bearing slave, but remaining only long enough to satisfy herself that the door into the rock-cut chamber had been completely sealed with stone blocks laid in courses with mortar. The workmen had not relished the task and had wished to complete it as soon as possible, so the stones were roughly squared, the mortar streaked and messy. But she had told them to hurry, and they had obeyed. Was the man Micaiah still squatting in the center of the chamber, she wondered briefly, and would the look of tranquility remain upon his features until...

Uttering a little cry, she quickly retraced her steps, not waiting for the torch; she dropped to her knees and crawled up the steep incline, groping with her hands along the chill stone wall. She had forgotten how long the passage was. After crawling for what seemed an eternity, she fumbled for the wooden frame which should outline the open doorway; then, finding it, discovered that there was no opening. The door had somehow swung shut. She pushed hard against it, annoyance changing swiftly to fury and the fury to panic. Impossible that it should have bolted itself! Stupid, incredibly stupid of Eshmun not to notice! But of course he was standing, as bidden, outside the outer chamber.

She beat on the door with her fists, screaming the eunuch's name, but both the pounding and the words seemed to possess no sound. It was as if she were enclosed in a void, where time and action, even being, were utterly suspended.

Then suddenly, as abruptly as the turning of a key in a wooden bolt, the spell was broken. Light flickered on the limestone walls. The door swung slowly open, and the pale orbit of the torch moved forward to embrace the tall figure of Eshmun.

"May the queen of women forgive her stupid slave! Only now did he notice that the door had swung shut within its socket."

Jezebel sharply scrutinized the impassive features. "You—mean you didn't hear me pounding on the door and calling?"

"The door is of heavy cypress," the eunuch apologetically reminded her, "and the hands of the fairest of all women, even though they hold men's—and women's—destinies within their palms, are still but weak things of flesh."

Gratefully Jezebel yielded herself to the support of the strong hands, permitted them to guide her over the threshold into the outer chamber. With curt brevity she issued further directions to the foreman. The door between the first and second small chambers was also to be sealed, but the stones concealing it were to be expertly squared and matched to the masonry on either side. It should be built to deceive the years—perhaps the centuries. All that it contained should vanish as if it had never been.

The pattern of the day's work—like the coverlet of loosely woven woolen strands which the eunuch, noticing that she was still nervous and shivering, placed solicitously about her shoulders—was now complete, its threads neatly clipped. Only one small raveled end—or perhaps two—remained.

"Eshmun?"

"Yes, my lady?"

"You are sure you bribed the slave who takes food to the chamber beneath the inner court? He will not go near the place or spread the news?"

"Very sure, my lady."

"And—the little matter of the transfer of merchandise to the caravan bound for Babylon? It was completed without incident?"

"Yes, my lady."

"Did the—object of transfer betray any unwillingness—?"

"None, my lady."

"Very well, Eshmun. You have been, as usual, a loyal servant. You may go."

"Ah, but—may the mistress of men's destinies forgive my stupidity! These wretched lips were to be the bearers of a message from the—object of transfer to the ears of the queen."

"What message?"

" ' Say to my mistress,' she instructed me, 'The game of wits is not always won by the one who makes the last move. Say to her also—' "

"Yes?" prompted Jezebel sharply, her long nails plucking at a loose strand of the coverlet.

" ' Say to her also— It is no farther from Babylon to Samaria than from a slave's pallet to the tent of a king.' "

Left alone, Jezebel sat for some moments motionless, then began pulling idly at the loose raveling...pulled and pulled with a furious, savage intensity, until finally the whole pattern was a knotted snarl and the strands lay in a tangled mass all about her.

CHAPTER 10

1

If the woman Tanath spoke the truth, his son need not have died.

All day the words had bombarded Ahab's senses, blaring with the trumpets, whirling with the chariot wheels, burning with the sun's glare, pounding to the rhythm of the horses' hoofs and his own fevered pulses. Now that the day of march was over and the camp had been pitched on the edge of the Jordan valley a few miles below Bezek, he could evade the issue no longer. He must take the Thing the woman had told him out of his consciousness, handle it boldly, let its jagged broken edges probe as they would into his flesh. Carefully now, sitting quietly before his tent, he took the missing pieces buried deep within his memory, fitted them cleanly into the jagged edges of the story... Her first declaration of her vow: *Is there anything so strange in that? Do not your people also make sacrifice of their first fruits to Yahweh?*... Words muttered in delirium: *Look out! Don't jump or you'll fall! For the love of Melkart! For the love of*... Sharp, tense watchfulness in waking eyes: I don't seem to remember. *Did—did I say anything strange?*... And, most damning fact of all, *the sealing of the child's body within the foundation stones of the temple of Melkart.*

The woman Tanath had spoken the truth. And his son need not have died.

Strangely enough, the knowledge brought a feeling of release, as of a long-numbed body suddenly come alive. His senses quickened. So clear and still was the air that beyond the fertile plain and the dead, gray wilderness he could almost distinguish each separate thorn and bush of the dark green jungle which formed the glistening scales of the winding river-serpent. Snakelike, too, was the column of smoke rising from the evening sacrifice at Beth-shan a few miles to the north, thick and dark when it left the temple altars, but as it mounted upward and caught the last rays of the sun turning into twisted, tawny coils.

Yesterday, thought Ahab with curious detachment, *I would have noticed only that it was gold like her hair. All these years I have walked through life blinded, as by the blowing of her hair before my eyes. Now, for the first time since that day in Tyre, I see clearly.*

He continued to gaze, frowning, at the twisting coils of smoke, remembering how, as a small boy, he had gone with Grandfather Joseph to Beth-shan.

"Look, Grandfather, see the big temple high on the hill, all made of black stone! Why don't we go up and give some of our fine fresh grapes to Yahweh?"

"Because that is not a temple of Yahweh, my son. It is a temple of Mekal."

"And who is Mekal, Grandfather?"

"Mekal is the Baal of Beth-shan. See, there he is now, being carried through the streets, held high on the shoulders of his priests."

"You—you mean Mekal is the god of Beth-shan, the way Yahweh is of Jezreel."

"Yahweh is the God of Israel, son, not just of Jezreel"

"But—isn't Beth-shan a part of Israel? And isn't Baasha king here, too?"

"Yes, son, that is so."

"Then why—" He remembered how he had stamped his bare foot against the hard black stones. "Why does Baasha let them? Why doesn't he tear down their old black temple and build another white one? If I were king of Israel..."

In those days it had seemed as simple as that, this struggle between the God of his people and the baals of the land they had conquered. Yahweh too had seemed simple and easy to find—in the wisdom on his grandfather's lips, in the beauty of a white dove's-dung blossom, in the splendid strength of a man's golden limbs. It was in that moment when his hand had been stayed on the bow that he had first encountered this complex, confusing Yahweh who condemned as cowardice a reverence for his own creation, whose willingness to bless depended on the whim of the moment, but who remembered and fulfilled a curse...

Suddenly Ahab sprang to his feet, uttering such a sharp exclamation that Joel, his armor-bearer, rushed anxiously to his side.

"My lord, is anything the matter? Is the anointed one displeased? Are his gazelle steaks not cooked to his liking? But—my lord has not tasted—"

"It's all right, Joel." Ahab placed a reassuring hand on the narrow, bony shoulder. "Nothing is the matter. And I am not displeased. I just made a discovery, that's all. Look! That city, there across the valley, built on the two hills—isn't that Jabesh-gilead?"

The armor-bearer, acutely conscious of the unaccustomed touch, was so overcome with emotion that he could scarcely speak. "I—I believe it is, my l-lord."

"And isn't Elijah, the Man of Yahweh, called the Jabeshite?" His hand still resting on the armor-bearer's shoulder, Ahab turned briskly toward his tent. "I need your help, Joel. You must listen carefully."

Swiftly he outlined his plan. It was to be announced that the king had undertaken a three days' fast for the sake of Israel's victory over Ramoth-gilead. During that time no one except Joel was to enter his tent, or to know that, although fasting, the king was not to be found within the encampment of Israel. Did Joel understand, and would he keep the secret?

"With my life," promised the armor-bearer solemnly.

Ahab's fingers gently probed the hollows of the bony shoulders. "You eat the gazelle steaks, Joel," he ordered brusquely.

Entering the tent, he swiftly made his preparations, substituting for his uniform the plain garments of dark homespun which he stubbornly insisted on carrying with him on every expedition. Now, carefully adjusting the long folds, he knew the reason for his stubbornness; not sentiment, not the urge for penance, but prescience of this very hour, when he should cease to accept the word of other men as truth and set out to find it for himself.

For that moment of sharp exclamation had been one of discovery. It was Hiel who had remembered and fulfilled the curse spoken long ago at Jericho, *not Yahweh!*

2

Three days and nights to penetrate three centuries? If he could find Elijah, it might not be too difficult. But Ahab's keenest spies had been seeking him for months. They must have sifted Jabesh and its deep river gash with a fine-meshed sieve. He was doubtless a fool to think he could succeed where they had failed. And if he could not find Elijah, what then?

There was no ford across the river at Jabesh, so he must travel all the way to Beth-shan. Fortunately the moon was near its full, so the road descending northward unfolded like a silver ribbon. Long before he reached the green plateau into which spilled the widening valley of Jezreel, the tropical heat had become oppressive. His garments clung to his body. Sweat blinded his eyes so that he could not see the ground. After he left the main road beyond Beth-shan and turned eastward toward the ford, the path became obscure, and he spent hours crossing the green plateau and benches of gray marl, which descended in long steps to the deep cleft where the river lay hidden. Stubbornly he plunged into the dense undergrowth, groping his way through tangled vines and thickets of cane and oleander and twisted tamarisks, tearing his hands on thorns, but grimly heedless of obstacles and dangers. When finally he stepped into the swirling muddy river swollen by the winter rains, it took all his strength to keep from being swept away. He was drenched to the shoulders when he emerged, exhausted, to fling himself down in a tangle of clinging vines. But there was no time to rest.

He saw the sky pale behind the towering fortress of Jabesh-gilead, crowning the higher of the city's two hills. Finding a small stream flowing into the Jabesh, he washed his bruised limbs and face, his mud-caked garments; then, spreading his clothes on a rock to dry, he caught a few minutes' sleep before forcing himself to go on. The damp folds of homespun were soothing against his aching body. He lifted his stiffened arms and stretched them wide.

Within the deep, dark void of the wadi an embryo of silver mist was stirring. Ahab watched, scarcely breathing, as the pale hands of dawn reached into the void, outlined rocks and trees out of the mists, tossed up the dark bulks of mountains, gathered up the tattered silver remnants and spun them into the shining fabric of a river. His heart leaped in exultation at the sight.

The earth was without form and void, and darkness was upon the face of the deep; and the spirit of Yahweh was moving...

Perhaps he did not need to find Elijah. If he followed the canyon to its end... But no, once before he had thought he saw Yahweh in the dawn of creation, and been mistaken. Reluctantly he made his way up the hill toward Jabesh-gilead.

3

"Who's that, stranger? Man of Yahweh, you say? Never heard of him."

The old potter's words were too glib, the thrust of his left foot against the edge of the whirling wheel too jerky, and the graceful, slim-necked water jar taking shape beneath his skillful fingers assumed sudden surprising contours.

"What! A man of Jabesh has never heard of Elijah? I don't believe you."

"Then go back and tell the king the men of Jabesh are stupid dolts. It requires all their wits to keep an accounting of his taxes."

"I am not a messenger of the king," returned Ahab quickly.

The potter's eye gleamed. "Did you ever see a pack donkey in a golden harness, or a peasant with a fine jewel on his finger?"

Ahab remembered, too late, the ring with the gleaming ruby which he had forgotten to remove. "No, but I have seen a nobleman masquerade as a peasant, for a good purpose." He leaned closer, blending his voice into the gentle purring of the wheel. "Tell me, old father, would you like to see a new king in Israel?"

The wheel whirled spitefully. "Would I like— These stones have better ears than mine. I didn't hear you, stranger."

"Don't be afraid. Tell me. *Would you like to see a new king in Israel?*"

The gleam kindled into a blazing core of long-stifled resentment. "Would the slave like to see his chains broken, the starving man fill his stomach?"

"Then tell me..." Ahab watched the wheel spin crazily, then topple, the graceful jug reduced again to a shapeless lump of wet clay. "Tell me, for Yahweh's sake and Israel's, where I can find Elijah."

He had his answer. He was to go up the valley of the Jabesh nearly to its end, until he came to a certain wadi branching off to the left, at the entrance of which he would see a thorny acacia...

He walked unseeing through the market place of Jabesh on his way to the gate.

"Wool! Fine wool, bleached white as the snow on Mount Hermon!"

"Dates fresh from the palms of Jericho, sweeter than honey!"

"Fat cows from Bashan! See, udders plump as ripe melons..."

"This way, men of Jabesh, buy a slave! Strong as an ox! Not one of these imported dandies from Philistia, but a real son of Israel!"

Ahab stopped suddenly, his gaze focusing first on the swarthy slave merchant, then on the prize he was exhibiting, a boy of not more than fourteen years, his half-naked body as absurdly thin as it was defiant. Puny fists clenched and slats of ribs distended almost to bursting, he stood squarely in the center of the slave block, scowling with a giant's ferocity at the fast-gathering crowd. Even his hollow cheeks flared belligerently.

Bids were slow in coming. Finally a well-dressed landowner strolled up to the block, jabbed a blunt index finger between the protruding ribs, slapped the flesh of the bony thigh as if it were a horse's flank, and spat negligently.

"Five silver shekels," he offered with indifference.

The merchant's face purpled. "Five shekels for an able-bodied slave! Thief! Swindler! He was put in bonds because his father owed the landlord twice that much!"

"Then the landlord was a fool," retorted the prospective buyer with a shrug.

"Five shekels for a male slave! You'd bid more for an ass or an ox!"

"Right. An ass can carry its weight in burdens, and an ox can at least pull a plow. Besides," the landowner said as he moved away, "he's burning up with fever."

"Liar!" the merchant screamed. "You think he's no good because he's thin, but he's tough as a palm tree. If you don't believe it, watch this!" Unfastening a whip of leather thongs from his girdle, he curled it with resounding impact about the unbending back and sturdily planted legs. "And *this!*"

While the boy remained straight and unflinching, with each stroke of the lash Ahab felt his own body quiver. Then, unconscious of having moved a muscle, he found himself towering over the fat merchant, the lash in his hand.

"You—traitor to the faith of our fathers—selling a son of Israel for a handful of silver!" His words leaped like whip strokes. "Have you never heard of Mishpat? That's a *man* standing there, not an ass or an ox—a man, made in the image of Yahweh! What right have you or any other man to make a slave of him—yes, or lay a whip across his back?"

The merchant quailed, then gaped; finally, measuring the humble status of his accuser, drew off and, fat arms akimbo, laughed uproariously. "Ho! And who do you think you are, peasant? The king of Israel?"

Ahab dropped the lash. "I—I'll buy the slave from you," he offered the merchant hastily. "I'll give you thirty—" He stopped, aghast, remembering that he had forgotten to put even a copper ring in the pocket of his girdle. Exploring its flat folds, his fingers encountered a small hard object—the ruby ring which he had put away after his encounter with the potter. Slowly he drew it out. "I'll give you—this."

The merchant's eyes bulged, turned frightened, then crafty. "What! You're asking me to take a trinket—a bauble you've probably stolen!" But his plump fingers had already grasped the drop of gleaming crimson. "He's yours," he muttered, for Ahab's benefit alone. "Though where a peasant like you could have found such a jewel—or why you should want such a stubborn young colt... Robber!" he screamed, as Ahab stooped to unbind the rope from the boy's ankles. "For this my children shall go to bed hungry!"

4

One moment the air above the Jabesh valley was intensely clear and still as a drawn breath. The next it was hot and restless with the beating of wings. Leaves scuttled uneasily among the rocks. The drowsing earth tensed its roots, stirred to the frightened scurrying of small animals. Even the lazy river assumed an agitated pace. And, his face turned resolutely toward the eastern desert, Ahab felt a smarting in his eyes and a hot stinging in his cheeks.

"It's the *sherkiyeh,*" he grimly told the slave.

Though the boy must know as well as he what the coming of the dread east wind portended, his tight forbidding features gave no sign. Since the brief interchange of information soon after leaving Jabesh, no words had passed his lips.

"Your name, boy?" Ahab had asked him.

"Reuel."

"Reuel, the son of—?"

"I have no father. He died the night before they took me away to be sold."

"But—he must have had a name."

"He did. A good, honored name in Israel." The pinched nostrils had quivered. "Do you think I'd bring disgrace upon it by bestowing it on a—*slave?*"

"But—you're not a slave any longer, son. That's why I bought you, to give you your freedom. You're at liberty to go home."

There had been no gratitude in the defiant eyes, "I have no home. It's gone."

"What do you mean—gone?"

"The landlord from the city took it. He took the barley plot too, and the vineyard. He'd loaned us grain to pay the king's taxes, and everything went wrong. My father was sick, my brothers had to go and work in the king's labor levy, and a blight came and killed the barley. The landlord let us stay as tenants, but we had to pay him more grain than we could grow. Then he had us sold as slaves, all but my father. The landlord was angry. He said my father cheated him by dying."

Ahab had flushed darkly. "I'll find them—your brothers—set them free. I—I'll tell the king—"

"Tell the king! Ha! You make me laugh. Didn't you hear what happened to Naboth? You think anybody who would murder to get a poor man's land—"

"Then may Yahweh punish such injustice," Ahab had interrupted harshly, "even if it be committed by the king himself!"

"Yahweh? Who is he? The bull of gold in Bethel that makes a man pay the first fruits while his children go hungry?"

The boy had spoken not another word, only trudged doggedly at Ahab's heels, stiff limbs and swollen ankles so retarding their progress that now, with the blurred sun more than halfway to setting, they had traveled no farther up the winding canyon than a stout pair of legs could cover in an hour. Muscles strained to the crawling pace, ears rasping to the sound of the boy's labored breathing, Ahab cursed himself again and again for his stupidity in not leaving the slave behind in Jabesh. His real stupidity had been in playing the role of heroic defender of this young ingrate. His pilgrimage was the important thing. Unless he found the one man who could tell him the truth about Yahweh, discover what he should do to expiate his sin, his kingdom might be lost. Not merely to the Syrians at Ramoth-gilead. To Baal Melkart in Samaria. What, he asked himself grimly, was the freedom of a slave beside the salvation of Israel?

And now the *sherkiyeh!* "We must hurry," he gasped, his teeth already gritting fine particles. "He's coming fast, faster than I've ever seen him. Keep close to me. We'll keep on as long as we can and then find shelter."

The path left the canyon bottom, zigzagged up a sheer ascent to the plateau of rock far above. Intent on battling the wind and keeping his balance on the narrow ledge, Ahab had almost reached the top when his ears missed that sound of rasping, painful breathing from his companion. Hastily he looked back, saw through the haze of sand that what remained visible of the path was empty. Reluctantly he began the descent, despising himself for the relief he felt on reflecting that, if the slave had fallen, his fate had already been sealed in the narrow torrent below. But the boy had not fallen from the cliff. He was lying on his face just around the first turn of the path. As Ahab turned him over, his fingers recoiled, and he exclaimed in dismay. The slave's flesh was on fire. There was no recognition in the glazed eyes; the dry lips were muttering gibberish. He was already far gone with fever. There was not one chance in ten he would recover without medication. It would be easy—But only for an instant did Ahab toy with the thought of leaving him. Kneeling, he gently wiped away the sand from the parted lips, and, dipping an end of his headdress in his water skin, moistened the burning forehead and eyelids. Then, making a buffer of his own body against the rasping wind, he took off his coat...

At first he carried the boy in his arms, groping for the path with his feet, stumbling and falling over and over again when he missed it; then he lifted him to his back, draping him over one shoulder like a goatskin sack. This was better. It brought the path closer to his eyes and on he went, bending his head to the fury of the wind. Soon the dust became so thick that he could see no more than a few steps ahead. It stung and blinded his eyes, clogged his nostrils, and, since he was forced to open his lips to breathe, gritted in his teeth and scored his throat and tongue. His breath came and went in long, choking gasps. He dared not close his eyes, knowing how near the path ran to the precipice, and they streamed liquid fire. After every dozen steps he turned about, lifted his face, and cried out in a loud voice.

"*Ay-ee-ee-ee! Ay-ee-ee-ay! Ay-ee-ee-a-yah!*"

It was the old signal cry which he had used as a boy on the slopes of Gilboa, and now in his desperation it came to his lips as naturally as if he had used it only yesterday. Surely there must be a village or a shepherd's hut somewhere on these bare stony terraces!

Sherkiyeh! Terrible avenger from the eastern deserts! Was it the spirit of Yahweh himself come to meet him? He was seeking penance. Here was a scourge laid to his face, his limbs, his vitals.

"Yahweh!" he groaned, silently, to conserve the little strength he had left. "If you be Yahweh, have mercy! Deliver me—no, help me to bear this punishment."

357

Alone, it would have been easy to battle the spirit. He could have wrapped himself in his cloak, flung himself down in the shelter of a rock, like his forebears in Egypt, and waited for the vengeance to pass over. But there was the burden on his back. His mind, like his feet, kept stumbling from the path. Who was it he was carrying? Grandfather Joseph? Naboth? It did not matter. Enough to know that it was the burden of his sin.

Ay-ee-ee-ee! Ay-ee-ee-ay! Ay-ee-ee-a-yah!" The wind took the sounds and tossed them back, clogged with sand, into his throat. They sounded no louder than a whisper.

Was it his own unsteadiness which caused the earth to quake and sway and gape? Once, a long fissure yawned at his feet and he drew back just in time, shivering. After he had inched his way, crouching, down one side of the sheer incline and crawled up the other, he lay for a long time panting and trembling, the weight of his burden grinding his body into the loose stones.

Later, the wind turned to fire, striking barbs of flame into his skin, pouring through his veins. He would have thrown down the burden then if it had been in his power, but he could not. It had become bone of his bone and flesh of his flesh. He was the king of Israel, and this boy on his back was a slave. Yet he could no more separate himself from their mutual oneness than—the knowledge came slowly, as one painful step succeeded another—*than Yahweh could divest himself of the smallest creature of his creation.*

There came a time when he turned his back to the scourge and opened his lips to shout, but no sound came.

"Ay-ee-ee-ee!"

He was sure he had heard it, a small, barely audible voice, scarcely more than a whisper. He made another desperate effort. "Ay-ee—"

"Ay-ee-ee-ee!" Closer now, the other voice caught up his feeble attempt at utterance and finished it, even to the tiny trill which distinguished the last syllable. *"Ay-ee-ee-ay! Ay-ee-ee-a-yah!"*

Ahab trembled. There was only one man now living who knew the old signal cry—one man and perhaps one woman. Dropping to his knees, he crouched and waited, the fury of the wind beating against him.

5

The fire was still about him, but it no longer bombarded his flesh. It laved him with hot waves, submerged him, bore him gently to the surface where for brief intervals he lay, free of pain and half-conscious, seeing shapes and hearing sounds, yet unable to distinguish dream from reality.

In one of these intervals he awoke to find himself lying on his mat in his grandfather's house. That is, it looked like his grandfather's house. There were the same wooden roof beams, with bits of straw protruding, the same stone walls blackened by smoke from the fire pit and gaping with cracks where the mud mortar had dried and shrunk, although the cracks were not as he remembered them. Two men squatted by the fire pit, one with his back to the mat. Grandfather Joseph? No, the shoulders were too broad, the neck too straight. The other had a long beard, yellowish white, like whorls of raw wool. Elijah? It looked like him, yet never before had Ahab seen his craggy features so calm and in such repose.

"But—he came seeking you, my father. Surely you will not go before—"

"It was Yahweh you said he came seeking."

"Yes, but he needs you to help him. He said so. Those were his first words when I found him—'Came to find Elijah—Yahweh—' "

"He who seeks the Eternal with his whole heart will surely find him."

"But—surely you will wait until after the storm!"

"I am not afraid of storms. Did I ever tell you about that night on the mountain, my son, after I had run away?"

"No, my father."

"It was a windstorm like this, a *sherkiyeh*, straight from Yahweh's desert. I was sitting in a cave, trembling for fear, and I heard a voice say, 'Go forth and stand out upon the mountain before Yahweh.' So I rose to my feet and went out and stood in the entrance of the cave, and the wind came, so strong that it tore trees from their roots and broke the rocks in pieces. And I trembled for fear of the wrath of Yahweh which was in the wind. But the wind passed, and I knew that Yahweh was not in it. And the earth quaked beneath my feet, and the breath of the storm turned to fire, but Yahweh was neither in the quaking of the earth nor in the fire. And after the fire—"

"Yes, my father? After the fire?"
"There came a small voice, no louder than a whisper..."

Again he woke—or dreamed he woke—to the touch of a cool hand on his forehead. The room was dim, but he knew it must be her chamber, because she was sitting beside him, between him and the lamp, so that he could see nothing of her features, only the outline of slender fingers and of the bone comb she was pushing through the strands of her hair. Strange—he had never before seen her comb it herself. Always it had been Jael. Presently she would lean forward a little, and the flame of the lamp would catch its tawny filaments, spin them into a net of vibrant fire, but he would feel no emotion. As long as he lived, the net would never again draw him into its meshes.

The comb catching in a snarl, she leaned forward, and the flame of the lamp caught the fine filaments, spun them into a tangled web as dusky as Tyrian purple. Ahab trembled. No emotion? It swept over him in a great flood, not of fire, but of blessed healing coolness. The fevered nightmare was over. Life was as it should be, the two of them together, climbing the hill above Jezreel, feeling the wind on their faces; then, while they sat like this, side by side, on the warm grass among the spring flowers, his hand reaching out—like this—to pull a thistle from her tangled hair...

"Ahab! You are awake. I'd better call Obadiah—"
He remembered then, seeing her face turned toward him, mature, lines of suffering graven deep by the shadows of the lamp, and the healing flood turned ice-cold. "No, no—don't call him—not yet—"

Her hand lay soothing again on his forehead. "Don't try to talk. The sandstorm gave you fever. But it's all over now, and the storm has passed."

"The—boy—"

"He's still very sick, but we think he's going to live. Obadiah is with him in the next room. I'd better go—"

"No!" The panic in his voice reached out and held her. "Bring the lamp," he whispered hoarsely. "Hold it so I can see your face."

She obeyed, cupping the small clay saucer in her hands and moving with such flowing ease that the flame scarcely flickered. Then, quietly, she knelt beside him. Her eyes had never been evasive.

They were not now. As far as the lamp shone into their clear black depths, there was nothing but compassion.

"You don't—hate me," he said wonderingly.

"Where there is so much love," she replied, "how could there be room for hate?"

"You—forgive me?" he whispered.

Setting the lamp down on the floor, she gathered his head into her arms and rocked it against her breast, her tears falling with cleansing coolness on his face. After a moment Ahab lifted his hands, moved his fingers over the small pointed chin, probed gently into the hollows of the cheeks and up over the high ridges of cheekbones, the narrow, pulsing temples; then, reverently, as a priest might step into a holy place, his finger tips entered the soft familiar intimacy of her hair. Lingeringly he let them wander through the vibrant strands, caressing each finely molded bone and sculptured hollow with a tender but fierce urgency, knowing that it was all they would ever sense of her body's sweet mystery. Finally, fingers clasped and palms enfolding her head, he drew her face down and their lips clung together. It was a kiss bitter with the salt of tears yet more rewarding in its fulfillment than any mingling of flesh he had ever known.

"Beloved," she whispered. "Always my beloved."

Rachel, Rachel! Oh, my darling, my heart's love, why have I been so blind! Why have I spent a lifetime pursuing storm and fire, when all I ever really wanted was a soft whisper...

Gently but firmly she drew herself from his arms. "You must rest now, beloved."

Reluctantly his fingers threaded the strands of vibrant duskiness, tangled in a silken thicket. He laughed softly. She was not wholly lost to him. No one—not Jezebel nor Obadiah nor the dead sons of Naboth, nor even the king of Israel himself—could destroy or separate the children they had once been.

"Still getting burdocks in your hair," he chided, his fingers plucking at the snarl with the old brutal tenderness. "Hold still, my little mountain goat."

6

It was morning of the third day, and Ahab stood with Obadiah outside the village of Abel-meholah looking down on the empty desolation which had once been the lovely Vale of Dancing. The *sherkiyeh,* he noted, was not responsible for all its ruin; though leaves had been stripped from trees and grain bent flat and hedges torn and toppled, the furrows on most of the terraced slopes were long unturned, the vines unpruned, the hedges and watchtowers mere tumbled heaps.

"I can take you to find the Man of Yahweh," said Obadiah. "He is up the valley in the tents of the Rechabites. We can reach him in a few hours."

"No," replied Ahab.

For he knew suddenly that he no longer needed to find Elijah. His pilgrimage was finished. It had been finished hours ago when he had struggled against the fury of the storm with the infinitely precious burden of a slave on his back. He had not found Yahweh, but Yahweh had found him, had come to him, not in the wind and earthquake and fire, but in the voice no louder than a whisper.

"No!" he repeated with triumphant certainty. "I have more important work to do. First I must take food to strengthen me, for my fast is over. Then I must get back to camp by sundown, so that we can start for Ramoth-gilead early in the morning." His brows knit. "I wish I weren't committed to the expedition. I'd like to get on to Samaria at once." Turning, he gripped the square shoulders hard with both hands. "It isn't too late, Obadiah. I'm not an old man. I can still build a kingdom for Yahweh where Mishpat will be the law of the land. There will be no more injustice in Israel. No man shall have the right to take away another's freedom, even though he be the king himself."

The slate-gray eyes softened, darkened, but failed to kindle from the other's fire. "It sounds like Eden," returned Obadiah soberly.

"It shall be Eden. No more poverty, no more fear, no back bent beneath a slave's burden or a master's lash. Every man able to lift his head proudly, knowing himself to be a son of the Eternal."

"There was a woman in Eden," Obadiah bluntly reminded him. "What about Jezebel?"

Ahab's eyes fell abruptly. Far down in the valley he saw a peasant boy making his way up the hill by the steep path which zigzagged along the edges of the terraced vineyards. The boy was having a hard time, for the path was overgrown with weeds and choked with rocks and tangled thorn branches from the ruined hedges. But he was not skirting the obstacles. Each step of the way he took time to move stones, push stubbornly through the thicket, then, turning, securely fasten the untangled ends so that the path would remain clear behind him.

Jezebel. Ahab's lips tightened grimly. *His soft sons, Ahaziah and Joram, who would some day be kings in his stead. Zedekiah, who called himself a prophet. Melkiah, with his pudgy, fumbling fingers. Stones and thorns, all of them.*

"It won't be easy," he admitted, his gaze clinging moodily to the steadily climbing figure. "I shall need help." The word mocked even as it left his lips. Help? From whom? Elijah? The Man of Yahweh was a destroyer, not a builder. Rechab? He would want Israel to tear down her cities and return to tents. Jehu? His watchword had been always death for Yahweh's enemies, not life for his sons. Micaiah? His mood of depression lifted. Yes, there was Micaiah. And there was—

"You'll help me, Obadiah?"

"Yes." The reply came promptly. "I'll help you."

"You mean," Ahab's voice was eager, "you'll go back with me to Samaria?"

"No. I mean I shall stay here and help the people of Abel-meholah mend their broken hedges and repair their ruined watchtowers. I shall plant grain and prune vines and harvest grapes, so that when that young slave Reuel gets well enough to realize he is free he may have home and friends and a plot of land to call his own, and when the young men return from building the king's cities and fighting the king's wars they may find the vale of mourning has again become the Vale of Dancing."

"But—" Again Ahab felt thwarted and alone, like the stubborn little figure working its way up the zigzag path. The boy was closer now. He could see sweat glistening on the bare shoulders, the flexing of muscles in the reedy arms. There was a veritable thicket of thorns now ahead of him. Ahab's detached curiosity became all at once intense involvement. Just so, long ago, he had stood motionless, hand frozen on his bow, and watched another figure, golden in the morning sunlight. Only this time it was not man's creation he was witnessing. It was his long, persistent struggle upward out of bondage into freedom.

The boy burrowed his way through the tangle, emerged with arms and shoulders crisscrossed with long crimson scratches. Even at this distance Ahab could see them, could see also the sturdy familiar curve of chin and the crisp ringlets of black, curling hair as the boy tossed back his head. And Ahab began to tremble.

"And," continued Obadiah, "I shall teach my son to know and keep Mishpat, prepare him to be a good citizen of this kingdom of God you are going to build."

My son...

Ahab's lips moved, but he could not speak. The brightness of the sun pounded like drums against his temples. The boy looked up and waved his hand.

"Uncle Ahab!" he shouted joyfully. "Wait there. I'm coming, Uncle Ahab!"

CHAPTER 11

1

The new confidence of Ahab was more inspiriting to his soldiers than the blazoning of trumpets and the triumphant unfurling of Yahweh's crimson bull. That night they camped deep in the valley across the ford, and even the heat, sulfurous as a malignant monster's breath, failed to quench their optimism.

As the road left the steaming cleft of the Jordan and climbed into the cool uplands along the wadi, the spirits of the men mounted with it. This was the "Land of Giants," and they were going up again to conquer it even as had their fathers, in the fabulous days of Joshua. They marched that second day to the stirring rhythm of ancient tunes and words, first uttered by lips long turned to dust.

> "Yahweh is great
> and greatly to be praised!
> Our Yahweh is above all gods!
> He smote many nations
> and slew many kings,
> Sihon, king of the Amorites,
> and Og, king of Bashan..."

But on the third day they found the hosts of Syria waiting to give them battle before they had even come in sight of the walls of Ramoth-gilead. Instead of the swift, vigorous offensive they had planned, Ahab and Jehoshaphat were forced, during the first bitter clash of the two armies, to employ only defensive tactics, so that at the end of the day, though they had managed to maintain their positions, they were as far from attaining their objective as at the beginning—farther, for tonight in the camp of Israel there was no fervent repetition of hero tales about the flaming pillars of small glowing campfires...only darkness and grim silence.

As he often did when under the stress of emotion, Ahab walked through the camp that night alone and in the guise of a common soldier. He had already taken counsel with his staff and with

Jehoshaphat, and together they had decided on a plan of action. With the coming of dawn there would be no more defensive maneuvers. The most powerful of their archers should be sent forward to open the attack, protected by solid ranks of spearmen in wedge formation, to prepare the way for the horsemen and chariots. Even now, as he moved from one group to another in the hastily assembled camp, he noted signs of preparation: bowstrings being tested by nervous fingers, spear shafts glimmering in the moonlight, the faint whinnying of horses being fitted into harness.

Ahab's confidence was unshaken. He knew that he had only himself to blame for the day's reverses, not the ill favor of Yahweh. So engrossed had he been in his pilgrimage that he had neglected the simplest of military precautions—the sending of spies to ascertain the enemy's position. He deserved to be taken by surprise, as the face of Jehu, furious, accusing, openly contemptuous, had apprised him. Yet in spite of his self-reproach, so exultant was his mood that he knew he could not sleep. Jeshua was alive! And Yahweh was justice and mercy! And a new day for Israel would soon be dawning! He walked with a prodigal disregard of energy or time, and when finally he turned toward his tent, the sky above the black basalt piles was already beginning to pale. By the light of the hooded lantern outside the royal enclosure he saw a guard with a frightened prisoner in tow.

"Sir," greeted the guard respectfully, mistaking Ahab for a subordinate officer, "I found this man skulking near the chariots. From what I could understand of his wretched Hebrew, he said if I would spare his life he had some information which might turn the tide of battle."

"He can give it to me," replied Ahab. "I will see that it reaches the king."

The prisoner flung himself on his knees, releasing a torrent of gibberish which the guard abruptly stemmed. "Fool! Talk sense or I'll run you through!"

"Let him speak," said Ahab.

The man finally made himself understood. His master, Benhadad, was planning a new strategy. There was to be a massing of chariots, followed by a concerted attack, aimed not at the chariot strength of Israel, as might be expected, but at the person of Ahab himself. Once the king of Israel was killed, his opponent shrewdly anticipated, Ahab's armies would be thrown into confusion and routed.

"Take him away," ordered Ahab with such imperial authority that the guard's eyes bulged and his mouth fell open. "Hold him prisoner until such time as we may determine if he speaks the truth."

"Y-yes, my lord. Shall I—"

"I said, take him away!"

So shaken was Ahab that he did not lie down on his couch but paced the ground beneath the striped awning until his head seemed to burst with every step. So this was how his fine new dreams for the saving of Israel were likely to end—in a pool of blood on a wretched battlefield! No! He would find some excuse to remain out of the battle, even withdraw his troops without attacking. Better to make Israel and her king objects of contempt than betray his vow to Yahweh! But—no, he could pursue neither of these courses. In their present mood of uncertainty his men would need their king's presence, not behind the line but at the very heart of the conflict. And—his lips tightened—only a coward would deliberately bring dishonor to his country to save his own life, no matter how noble his true motive. There must be some other way. Yahweh help him, he must find it—and quickly! The dawn of a day that might well be his last on earth was just beginning to break.

Emerging from his tent a little later, he went straight to the quarters of his ally, Jehoshaphat. The king of Judah, substantial figure already encased in armor, with crimson cape and distinguishing crowned helmet, greeted his appearance with startled, unrecognizing disapproval. "What's this! A common soldier entering a king's tent? By Yahweh, I shall report this to— *You!*"

"Peace to you, son of Yahweh," greeted Ahab. "And may this day bring victory!"

"But—it's time for the attack, and— What are you doing in that uniform of a common chariot fighter?"

"I have decided to go into battle in disguise," explained Ahab briefly. "You shall give the signals for advance. You will be wearing your royal armor."

"But—your men don't know the battle cries of Judah."

"They'll soon learn them. Instructions have already been issued to my captains."

"But—I don't understand. Why—" Jehoshaphat's eyes narrowed shrewdly. "You were nervous about the evil prophecy of that Micaiah, weren't you, in spite of all your protestations! You think you can dispel whatever image of defeat he may have created about you by wearing a disguise. Well—that's not such a bad idea. I'll confess it relieves my own fears also. We shall see what happens."

Ahab was silent. Since he could never have explained to his colleague his real reason for withdrawal from impending danger, it was as well to let his action be attributed to caution as to cowardice!

2

Only once during the ensuing hours of bitter conflict did he regret his decision, when he saw from a distance the formidable array of Ben-hadad's chariots converging about the figure of Jehoshaphat.

They mistake him for me! he thought with sudden horror. Of course, if the chariot units of Ben-hadad had been ordered to direct their sharpest thrusts at the person of the king of Israel, they would be drawn inevitably to the only royal figure in sight. Stupidity of all stupidities, that he had not thought of it! But the danger was averted with almost equal swiftness. Startled by his peril, Jehoshaphat opened his mouth and bellowed forth a great shout, which the keen archers of Ben-hadad recognized immediately as the battle cry, not of Israel, but of Judah. Hastily they called off their assault.

But if Ahab remained unrecognized among the sons of Hadad, he was soon known among the sons of Yahweh. The news spread with the vigor of a ram's horn trumpet.

"The king, the anointed one! He's fighting like a common soldier!"

"No gold on his shield, no diadem about his helmet!"

"Not even the crimson coat and bronze breastplate of a captain!"

"With our king among us, what foe shall we fear?"

"Forward, men of Israel! For Ahab and for Yahweh!"

But loyalty to king, even assurance of the presence of Yahweh, was not enough. Ahab's three-day delay had given Ben-hadad, warned by his spies, opportunity to entrench himself solidly both in and around Ramoth-gilead. The high embossed towers were manned solidly with archers. Spears bristled around the foot of the city wall like a sunburst. And the valley leading to the ramp was massed with chariots.

Again and again the infantrymen of Israel and Judah charged forward, an impenetrable wedge of outthrust spear blades, in the sheltered hollow behind them a skilled company of archers shooting powerful volleys high over the protecting wall of interlocking shields. Again and again the tight wedge was broken, the bristling orderliness turned to confusion, the wall of stout bull's hide perforated, the bowmen routed. Rushing into the breach, Jehu's chariots encountered an equally formidable massed array of chariots, and as the sun mounted it bleared through a jaundiced haze of dust on a welter of flashing spears, spinning wheels, and plunging hoofs.

At least, thought Ahab, careful even while lending all possible encouragement to keep his chariot out of the dangerous forefront of the battle, his armies were conducting themselves honorably. Even though they might not attain their goal, they would return to Samaria without the ignominy of actual defeat. And he would still be alive to fulfill his vows. In the days to come he would restore to Israel lost treasures far more precious than this little border city.

In the heat of noon the fierceness of the struggle waned. Like two weary, battling lions, both armies by mutual consent crawled away in tacit truce to lick their wounds, take refreshment, even to indulge in uneasy siesta. Ahab dared not return to his tent, but managed to snatch a few moments of repose against the pole and curved railing of his chariot.

Dead tired, he fell asleep almost instantly, to dream that the battle was over and he had returned to Samaria—no, to Jezreel, for he was sitting on the stone bench in the little kiosk on the garden slope. Jezebel was there also. She must be, for he could smell her fragrance of roses and cinnamon and delphinium, and he could hear her voice, startlingly near, yet faint, as if it came from another world,

"I've been waiting...since I knew she had told you...couldn't rest until I knew...if only you could understand and forgive...

His body tensed, his pulses thundered in his ears.

"Yes. I forgive you. Who am I to judge you for the sin of being too loyal to your god, I who have failed so wretchedly in loyalty to mine?"

"My lord, then you have come back to me? It shall be between us as it used to be?"

She was closer now. Her fragrance was like a warm, sweet breath upon his flesh. A radiance that was like the fire of her hair danced before him. Deliberately he closed his eyes. He knew the truth now. She had no more power to enslave him.

"You don't understand. I have made a vow before Yahweh. There is to be no more of Baal in Israel, do you hear? Yahweh is to be the one God—"

"But I do understand, my lord. Of course Yahweh must be the god of Israel, the only god. And I shall help make him so. You and I together, my lord—"

"No, no!" He cried out in horror. Tearing himself from the bench, he attempted to flee, but his limbs locked and tangled in thick meshes which burned like fire and yet were soft as silk. Somehow he struggled through them. And just when he had made his escape, he felt her touch, possessive, confident, upon his shoulder.

"My lord, the battle cry has sounded!"

During the hours of bitter conflict which followed, the dream possessed more of substance than reality. He issued orders to his charioteer, drew arrows from the leather quiver fastened to the chariot pole and fitted them to his bow and sped them, was vaguely conscious of wave upon wave of wedged spearmen surging forward on either side, tumbling into disorder, or becoming absorbed in the heaps of tossed wreckage which had gone before them. He heard trumpet blares and battle cries, shrieks of pain and curses, the rumble of wheels and the twanging of bows, the shrill, agonized neighing of wounded horses...all muted and confused as if coming from another world. The sweat which blinded his eyes and gathered beneath the heavy scales of his armor was caused by fear—but fear of himself, not of the enemy.

Was the dream a portent? Would he go back, having seen the truth and made his vow, only to become again malleable clay in her soft hands? Clay she had been, too, but clay molded always in the image of Ashtart and shaped long before his hands had touched it. *Yahweh forbid that there be any meaning in his dream! Yahweh, who had revealed himself in the small voice proceeding out of the storm, let him become stone—no, fire and wind and earthquake, instead of clay!*

A chariot careened past, its horses lathered with mud and sweat; it wheeled about, its tires screaming, and drew alongside his own. Through the haze the scowling face of Jehu, dark with fury and scorn, confronted him.

"Did the days of fasting sap my lord Ahab's courage as well as his strength? Israel's armies might have won today had they had a king to lead them."

Ahab was jolted harshly to awareness. The battlefield sprang into focus. Horrified, as if finding war new and strange, his eyes burned with searing images—a wild horse tangled with a dead mate and an empty chariot...a screaming swordsman skewered on a spear through back and belly...the severed head of one of his trusted captains staring up at him from the ground. He tasted the salt of sweat, the hot tang of blood, and felt a spear twisting in his vitals. Jehu was right. In the name of all the fathers, what was Israel's king doing here in the backwash of the fighting! These were his people, his children. Even for the sake of his vow, he could not remain here in cowardly safety while his men were dying!

"Move forward!" he ordered his charioteer abruptly. "Wasn't our unit commanded to follow close on the heels of that last wedge of spearmen and archers?"

"But—the spearmen and archers were driven back, my lord!"

"Then we must go forward without them."

"B-but—for the sake of his people, the anointed one must not take so great a chance! Let others go, I pray you, my lord and my king!"

"Give me the reins!"

Seizing them from the reluctant hands, Ahab issued a sharp command, thankful that, though he had left behind his chariot with the gilded wheels, he had run the risk of detection by retaining his own horses, Midnight and Stormcloud. He could feel their quivering energy sweep through his finger tips as they leaped forward. Almost without guidance they charged through a yawning gap in Israel's disordered array of chariots, straight toward the spot where the latest unsuccessful wedge of spearmen, unable to protect their archers by maintaining a solid front against the furious barrage of Syrian arrows, were retreating in ignominious confusion.

Opening his lips, Ahab sounded a great battle cry. "Forward, I command you, in the name of Yahweh! See, it's your king who leads you! If the spearmen can't make a path for us, then let us go without them! Forward, follow your king!"

Recognizing him, they followed with a hoarse burst of cheers, chariot after chariot, the confusion of the first few moments of unbridled enthusiasm curbed swiftly into a disciplined but no less tumultuous advance. Emboldened by the sudden revelation of strength at their rear, the retreating bowmen and spearmen rallied and began functioning, defensively at first, then, as haphazard volleys

371

showed signs of hitting the mark, shaping themselves solidly into the familiar wedge formations and thrusting forward toward the enemy.

The tide turned. Driving relentlessly into the sector where the chariots of Israel seemed to be enduring the heaviest bombardment, Ahab felt the courage of his men mounting, surging, behind him. He had wanted only the opportunity to suffer with them. Now, it seemed, he was to be permitted also to triumph with them. Within the next hour they drove deep into the Syrian lines, their progress slowing as the way became choked with fallen men and horses and tangled chariots, yet for the most part unopposed until suddenly the dusty haze above their heads became charged with the shrill whirring of arrows. The charioteer pulled sharply on the reins and wheeled about. "We're in range of the archers on the wall!" he gasped.

At the same moment Jehu again drove close, his dark face flushed with triumph. "The city is almost in our grasp. We must devise new tactics, send up the battering rams. For Yahweh's sake and Israel's, let the king withdraw himself from danger!"

They would have been out of range of the arrows in a few swift seconds if Ahab had not seen the boy. His eyes registered a brief image of dark, tumbled curls matted with blood and dirt, a deep chest gash swarming with flies, a pair of terrified eyes, and pleading lips. "Wait!"

Seizing the reins and pulling on them with such vigor that the horses reared upright to the harsh screaming of wheels, he turned them about and drove back to the recumbent figure. Leaping to the ground, he knelt beside it, moistened the cracked, swollen lips from his water skin and gently sponged the wound clean.

"It's all right," he answered the terror in the pleading eyes, though the boy, being Syrian, probably understood none of his words. "The pain won't last much longer. The wound is deep. You fought bravely, my son. There is nothing more to fear."

"Hadad—"

But as he lifted the dark young head, the boy's prayer of gratitude ended in a choking burst of blood. A few moments later Ahab had pillowed the head on a mound of earth, gently closed the glazing eyes, and covered the still figure with his own cape.

As he rose, he scarcely felt the arrow which pierced his side in the vulnerable flesh between lower armor and breastplate, but when he sprang into the chariot, so sudden and swift was the pain that he stumbled and clutched at the rail. Alarmed, the charioteer looked down, saw the projecting arrow shaft, and blanched with terror.

"My lord—"

Ahab pulled himself from the agonizing blackness and regained his feet. "Turn about," he commanded tersely, "and carry me out of the battle, for I am wounded."

But even as the words left his lips he knew he could not permit himself the luxury of withdrawal. Even in dying, a king did not belong to himself. Once they were beyond the reach of the enemy's barrage, he ordered the charioteer to stop and, shielded from view behind the meshes of leather thongs which reinforced the rail, he plucked the arrow from his side and stanched the flow of blood with his companion's coat bound tight beneath his girdle.

"Now"—he spoke between clenched teeth—"drive me to that knoll—over there—and call to me—my captains of a thousand—"

The captains assembled, received their orders, couched in terms so terse that no officer was left in doubt of his duty or his ability to execute it. All viewed with awed respect, almost with reverence, the straight, commanding figure of their king, never more regal than at this moment, and wondered at the trembling and pallid mien of his charioteer.

"And I—your king—will be here watching—for Israel—and Yahweh—"

After they had gone, cheering, Ahab stood clutching the rail and struggling for breath, until the agonized young charioteer loosened his breastplate and removed his helmet, so that he could breathe more easily.

"Now—prop me—against the railing—of the chariot," he gasped, his features twisting with pain, "facing the—Syrians. There's a—long time—yet—"

The young man obeyed, and all through the rest of that afternoon he remained thus, shoulders high, black curly hair crowned with a nimbus from the lowering sun. And the armies of Israel, seeing him, fought bravely, with greater skill and valor than they would have dreamed possible, seeing only his upright, smiling figure, not knowing that the smile was locked in place over clenched teeth, or that the straightness was sheer indomitable will holding up a tortured body.

But when the sun, blood-red as the congealing pool on the chariot floor, drained finally into the fissures of the western hills, the life of Israel's king drained with it. "Tell Ahaziah—" he gasped.

"Yes, my lord, yes!" The arms of the young charioteer were strong and gentle. "What shall I tell Prince Ahaziah?"

"Tell him—" Ahab groaned. Yahweh help him, what should he tell him! What could one tell a miserable devotee of Baal-zebub, into whose soft, incompetent hands one must entrust the saving of one's people! Panic possessed him, engulfing him in wave upon wave of darkness. Suppose that because he, Ahab, had failed, the years passed—the centuries—with Naboths being stoned and cities reared on the crushed bodies of old men and children—*and no voice ever crying out again in protest that the Eternal was a God who cared!*

"Can you hear me, Ahab?" Words, harsh and bitter, stirred the dark waters into turmoil. "I saw you, stopping to give succor to that dog of a Syrian. It's your fault if Yahweh doesn't give us victory. You spared the life of Ben-hadad, his foe, and now you anger him again. Perhaps now at last you'll understand the true nature of Yahweh!"

Ahab struggled upward through the clear, still depths. Understand? Yes. Better than the fiery Jehu ever could. For Yahweh was not in the fury of destruction. He was in the still, small voice which had stayed a hand on a bow, and spared Ben-hadad, and carried a slave through a storm, and turned a king back in his chariot to bend over his dying enemy. And—as long as there were hatred and injustice in the hearts of men, *there would always be that voice, no louder than a whisper.*

He looked up smiling into the troubled face of the young charioteer.

It was about sunset that a cry went through the army of Israel, a cry neither of victory nor of defeat, but of such anguish and bewilderment as might spring from the tight throats of sheep who have lost their shepherd.

Every man to his city, and every man to his country! Return to your homes in peace, O Israel! For you have no master except Yahweh. Your king is dead.

3

Jezebel was watching, dry-eyed, from the terraced roof when the chariot was driven through the gate. She saw the charioteer step down, slowly; saw strong brown hands and knotted shoulders push the chariot across the floor stones to the pool in the northeast corner, lower it by the incline of heavy slabs into the waters to its wheel hubs, proceed systematically to wash it: first, the leather tires and six wheel spokes, next, the high curved cedar railing, and finally—this took the most scrubbing of all—the stout floor of plaited leather.

Only once did she reveal emotion—when the charioteer, moving slowly across the courtyard and passing almost beneath the spot where she stood, paused for an instant, believing himself unobserved, and, lifting a begrimed hand, drew the back of it across his eyes. Her sudden jealousy was more bitter than she had ever felt toward any woman. For this man had fresher memories of the beloved than had any other living person. He had held the king in his arms, perhaps pillowed the dark curls against the metal scales of his waistcoat, listened to his last words...

Hastily she summoned a slave, and presently the young charioteer stood before her. His features remained a blur. All she really saw of him was a dark, clotted stain on the skirt of his tunic—and the grime of his hands.

Yes, he had been with the king during his last hours. Always he would be proud to remember that it had been his privilege to serve such a master. Never had he or any other man in Israel beheld such courage. Never did they expect to again.

"Did—did the king speak any words that you can remember—leave any message or"—Jezebel held her breath—"or mention any name?"

Yes, at the very last the king had mentioned a name, had seemed to consider it most urgent that this person be given a message. But he had expressed himself with difficulty, not only because of failing strength but because—well, because he had seemed unsure of just what he wished to say.

Jezebel's pulses leaped. The torment of uncertainty, then, was to be satisfied. She would know what effect Tanath's perfidy had had upon him, if he had understood and forgiven her. Had he lived, she was certain, she could have canceled all ill effects of the disclosure. She had even planned her technique: removing herself to Jezreel, putting herself in voluntary exile until some time, at the right moment, and in the right place—perhaps in the little kiosk on the garden slope...

"What—what did he—?" The words choked in her throat.

"The king," said the young charioteer, "gave this person a certain commission."

Something he had wanted her to do? Blessed Ashtart, of course! Whatever he had asked of her, she would do it! In the fulfilling of his desire she would be brought close to him again.

"Did—did he mention my name?" The words came at last, tumbling in their eagerness. "Tell me quickly, what did he say? Don't keep me waiting!"

"I—am sorry." Had she looked above the stained tunic and grimy hands, she would have seen that the dark eyes in the sensitive face were grave and pitying. "It was to his son Ahaziah that he sent his message."

The disappointment fell like a leaden weight, then lifted. She could still, perhaps, fulfill his request, feel herself for a few moments at one with his purposes!

"What—did he say?"

"He said," replied the young man simply, " ' Tell him to release Micaiah.' "

4

The coarse white garments felt strange, yet she welcomed their roughness, their rigidity, as a long-numbed body welcomes the discomfort of returning life.

With at least an hour to dawn, the palace as yet showed few signs of wakening. In the courtyards through which she passed, the lamps, fitful in an uneasy wind, were burning low. But once she reached the great courtyard, her feet moved swiftly toward their objective, the temple of Melkart just beyond the palace wall.

The gatekeeper of the temple grumbled sleepily, but, mistaking her in her long enveloping cape for one of the *kedeshoth* whose observance of the rites of fertility had led her too far and too late afield, grudgingly produced a wide enough aperture to admit her slender figure. Hurriedly she passed through the big forecourt, open to the sky, and into the first of the inner chambers. Here she moved more cautiously, for the little rooms lining the walls beyond the two rows of carved stone pillars were occupied by priests, and Meribaal, at least, was a light sleeper. She wanted no witnesses to this tryst between herself and Melkart—this bridal commitment, after long years of conflict, to the lordship of one master.

The air was heavy with smoke and oil and incense, and in the fevered glow of the innumerable little lamps the carved bulls and lions and cherubim looked like bulks of hot, uneasy flesh. Stopping only to take a small oil lamp from one of the stands, she moved hastily toward the richly embroidered curtain at the far end of the chamber. A lifting of the curtain disclosed a door of carved cedar inlaid with gold, beyond which lay the cella—the small, dark, dwelling niche of the god.

For the second time in her life she was entering Melkart's presence, but not as a terrified child. Now she had nothing to fear. She had fulfilled her vow. She had put him above her only other love, and from even that lesser loyalty she was now free. Before him only she had humbled her will, made of herself a living Ashtart, a fit consort, moving always toward the consummation of this moment.

The door swung noiselessly and, lamp held high, in her face the exaltation of a virgin entering a bridal chamber, she moved into the small, dark cella where the towering bronze figure would stand waiting.

Meribaal alone heard her scream, for the walls were stone and the door was of heavy cedar; and after following her inside, he had closed the door behind him.

"So—you have come, my daughter. I have been expecting you."

The lamp's flame was a puny thing beside the conflagration in her eyes.

"Where is he? What have you done with Melkart?"

So old and shrunken was the priest that his body seemed lost in its mummy wrappings, his face a pale residue of ash in which two live coals were still glowing.

"Our lord was not in the image of bronze, my child. Better that it be made into tools and pots and pans, which are instruments of life instead of death."

Jezebel stared at him unbelievingly. "You—" So violently did she tremble that words at first refused to come. "You dared—destroy—"

"Not destroy. The Eternal cannot be destroyed. He is not made with hands. He is the creator of all things, of all men, and the peasant as well as the king is created in his image. You, yourself, my daughter, are no better than the meanest slave."

"Traitor!" Jezebel uttered the word through clenched teeth. "It is Yahweh of whom you speak, not Melkart."

"Some call him Yahweh," returned the priest steadily. "It was you who taught me that the name is unimportant. It is what God is that matters."

The fury within her was like the boiling pressure of a volcano, but she feigned amusement. "So—you actually swallowed all that nonsense in those odorous writings!"

The coals glowed brighter. "And it was you, my daughter, who helped these eyes discover a little of the truth at last. My one sorrow is that I did not find it sooner, so that your son—"

"Yes?" Her voice was dangerously quiet. "What about my son?"

"I was wrong, my child. The Eternal does not want the sacrifice of his children. I would give this right hand—these eyes—I would gladly die—"

Her palm closed so tightly on the clay lamp that she felt an edge of it crush within her fingers. "No! Dying is too quick, too easy. By Melkart, you *shall* lose those eyes! They'll never discover any more of truth."

With all her strength she flung the flaming lamp straight into his face. He did not cry out. The shattering of clay on the stone floor made more sound than the gentle falling of his body. In the darkness and silence which followed she dropped to her knees, groped frantically until she found him, then fumbled in an agony of suspense until her fingers closed about his wrist. The skin felt dry as ashes, the bones light as bits of charred wood. There was no pulse.

His body has been dead a long time, she thought with bitter comfort. I didn't *really kill him.*

Dry-eyed, she let her fingers explore the familiar details of his bruised features—high, bony forehead, gentle lips, deep crevices where the light of discovery would never glow again. Only when she gathered him in her arms did the core of ice within her break. Then, weeping, swaying, she rocked him against her breast.

When she emerged from the temple, dawn was breaking. But, though she gazed and gazed, opening her eyes wide until they felt ready to burst from their sockets, they encountered no blazing radiance at which a numbed spirit might be awakened into warmth, of pain if not of ecstasy. The rising sun was a pale, weak thing drifting on the dying wind from a pit of burned-out ashes

.

CHAPTER 12

1

After half a century, Jezebel's eyes were as keen as when, a child of six, she had been first to spy the tip of a blue sail heralding the return of a Phoenician fleet from far-off treasure lands. Long before the watchman on the palace tower sounded the signal of an approaching company, she was studying the train of black dots on the road winding up to Jezreel from Beth-shan, so engrossed that the luscious green-white grape in her fingers was poised halfway to her mouth.

"What's the matter, Mother?" called King Joram lazily. "What could this dirty little town offer of sufficient interest to tempt you from this glorious Hebron vintage?" He made a languid gesture toward Ahaziah, his sister Athaliah's son, the king of Judah. "If my nephew Ahaziah had only visited us earlier with his succulent offerings, I might possibly have recovered from my wounds and been back fighting with my troops at Ramoth-gilead." He cast an avid glance toward his newest concubine, the dusky, full-bosomed daughter of an Arab sheik who had rendered favors in a recent struggle against Moab. *"Possibly."*

Jezebel was too preoccupied to comment. Moreover, she had no words to express her contempt for this son who, during a full decade of kingship, had through careless siring contributed more to Israel's population than to her prosperity or glory. His brother Ahaziah, who after reigning two short years, had died as the result of an unfortunate accident—he had fallen from one of the latticed windows in his bedchamber in Samaria—could not possibly have done any worse. Even the one triumph of his reign, the raising of a prolonged siege of Samaria by the armies of Syria—was the result, not of Joram's statesmanship, but of a mere piece of luck, the Syrians having been forced to return home to prepare for invasion by the Assyrians! And of course it was not Joram, but Jehu, who conceived the idea of utilizing this involvement of the Syrians by making another attempt to recapture Ramoth-gilead—Jehu, who was now in full authority over the forces of Israel while their king lolled on a couch under a silk canopy, devouring grapes and ogling a stupid female!

"Has it ever occurred to my uncle the king," suggested Ahaziah with the slow caution of a timid yearling in the presence of a veteran, "that there might be danger in leaving all the armed strength of Israel in the command of a strong general?"

Jezebel crushed the succulent grape between her teeth. What were these apologies for men which she and Athaliah had conceived and borne and bred? A coward and a sluggard! She waited scornfully for Joram's answer.

"Pah! Jehu! That blundering thundercloud? For the last dozen years he has had no thought in his head except annexing that dirty little border town of Ramoth-gilead. Now that he's occupying it, all but the citadel, nothing could turn him from his purpose. He's finding Hazael an even more formidable enemy than Ben-hadad."

Ahaziah cleared his throat timidly. "Has—has my uncle the king heard the rumor that—that the prophet Elisha was in Damascus at the time Hazael was made king?"

The king spat seeds. "Suppose he was. What of it?"

"It's being whispered in Jerusalem, my uncle, that Ben-hadad, being sick, sent Hazael to inquire of the prophet Elisha as to whether he would recover, and that—*that Hazael went straight from the house of Elisha and murdered Ben-hadad.*

"And you think Elisha put him up to it?" Joram laughed tolerantly. "How gullible, my dear nephew, can you be? Elisha is a man of Israel. What possible interest would he have in manipulating politics in Syria?"

"None, surely none, my uncle," Ahaziah agreed hastily, "unless... Hazael is a great warrior. Could—could his kingship imperil the dynasty of Omri?"

"You—you mean Elisha might wish to rid Israel—" The faint alarm in Joram's voice dissolved into swift amusement. "But—that's absurd, my dear nephew. Elijah, perhaps—yes. He was always a venomous old scarecrow. But Elijah has been dead these many years—walked off a mountain into the clouds, some say, others that he was swept up into heaven in a blazing chariot, fools' tales, all of them—but Elisha! Quite a different sort of person, suave, genial, even a bit of a fop. Flew into a high dudgeon because some urchins down Bethel way called him 'Old Baldy'! Why in Anath's name should he desire evil to fall on the house of Ahab?"

Why, indeed? Jezebel smiled grimly. The ground pulp of the grape tasted suddenly bitter on her tongue, and, leaning over the parapet, she spat it from her mouth. The black dots were climbing higher now, taking shape clearly into toy chariots, the one in the lead slowly gaining in distance from the others, like—like an eagle rising steadily above a flock of pigeons. Suddenly the very stones seemed to spring into life beneath her feet. Emotion coursed through her such as she had not known since that morning on the steps of the temple of Melkart. Exultation? Terror? No matter. Enough simply to be alive again. Unobserved by the group beneath the awning, she moved quickly across the housetop and down the stairs.

2

"I see a company approaching." The watchman's clarion voice carried clearly to the royal ears beneath the awning.

"My lord the king," relayed one of the *gibborim* with mechanical precision, "the watchman on the tower reports the approach of a company."

"So I hear," commented Joram without changing his posture. "He has a voice like a bull of Bashan." Noting Ahaziah's expression, he chuckled softly. "What's the matter, son of my strong-minded and stubborn sister? Are caravans so few in your little province that the mere thought causes your cheeks to pale?"

"My lord the king," announced the second *gibbor,* who had been at the far parapet conferring in loud exchange with the watchman. "The company is not a caravan. It seems to be made up of chariots moving swiftly up the valley from Beth-shan."

"Chariots?" Joram frowned. "That's strange. Are they chariots of Israel?"

"I do not know, my lord."

Joram reluctantly hoisted himself. "Can't see a thing, but I'll take the watchman's word that they're there. Send a horseman to meet them," he commanded the *gibbor* negligently. "Let him find out if they come in peace."

"You don't think—!" Ahaziah started up, hands tense on the arms of his chair.

"Exactly, my dear nephew. I don't think—unless I have to." Joram returned to his couch. "Whether the chariots are our own or another's, we'll soon know. Meanwhile I'll enjoy one of these luscious

Hebron grapes—or, rather, two. They go in pairs, like many delightful things. I swear they're as round and smooth to one's lips as a woman's breasts. Or—are they? Come here, my little Arabian dove!"

The girl crept shyly into his embrace, and Joram, pulling down her bodice, shamelessly fondled her soft flesh and covered it with kisses. With a stifled exclamation Ahaziah rose and, turning his back, moved to the parapet.

"My lord the king," the *gibbor* interrupted sometime later, "the horseman you sent to meet the approaching company has reached them, but he is not coming back."

Joram looked irritated. "Weil—why bother me about it? Can't you see I'm busy? If he doesn't come back—why, then, in Yahweh's name, send another!"

"I can see them plainly now, my uncle," muttered Ahaziah worriedly, "and they are a large company. There's one chariot in the lead. I—I do wish you'd look."

"It would do no good," Joram assured him cheerfully. "I'm so nearsighted I couldn't tell if they were chariots or camels." Again a period of time elapsed, short for the pleasantly occupied Joram, interminable for the nervous Ahaziah.

"I—I know I'm foolish, my uncle," he blurted out at last. "It's no doubt just a routine visit of some officer or foreign emissary. But—In heaven's name how can you lie there and eat grapes and—and make love to a woman when—"

Putting the girl from him regretfully, lingeringly, the king rose to his feet. "So you're still worried about that caravan."

"It's not a caravan. Didn't you hear the *gibbor* say—"

"That's right. So I did. Chariots. And I sent a messenger—"

"Not one messenger, my uncle. Two."

"Two?" The king looked genuinely startled. He gestured to the nearer *gibbor*. "Find out what happened to that second messenger and be quick about it!"

The watchman's reply resounded through the whole palace area,

"He reached them, but he is not coming back. He has fallen in behind the leading chariot. And the driving of it is like the driving of Jehu, the grandson of Nimshi, for he drives furiously."

Joram dropped his indolence like a cloak. "Make ready our chariots," he ordered tersely.

3

"And about time, blessed be Ashtart! Years it's been that I've waited to see you give some sign that you cared how you looked, you stupid little daughter—"

"Hurry, Jael. Don't spend precious time in words. Just—just make me look like a queen again. But do it quickly. We have only minutes!"

"Who did you say is coming? That scowling thundercloud of a Jehu? It won't hurt him to wait for an audience with the most beautiful queen in the world. Yes, keep your mouth shut, I know what you're going to say. You're not a queen any more. But if you think I'm going to call any one of those brazen chits of Joram's—!"

"Jael!"

"I'm hurrying. The rouge is already on your lips and cheeks, the turquoise under your eyes, and the kohl as sleek on your brows and lashes as a raven's wing. That Jehu always had an eye for you, Anath strike me dead if he didn't! I wonder—"

"Jael! If you ever loved me—"

"Tsk! Tsk!... There now, my work is finished. And more beautiful a queen never walked the face of this earth. Go now, wherever it is you must go, my lovely jewel, my sweetest lotus blossom, and may the blessed Anath go with you, whose heart was overcome with grief like the heart of the wild cow for her calf, like the heart of a ewe for her lamb!"

The two pairs of women's eyes exchanged a long look of complete and naked understanding, the black swimming in tears, the copper-brown bright and steady as two highly polished agates. Then Jezebel, stooping, touched her crimsoned lips lightly to the old nurse's seamed brown forehead.

4

As she opened wide the lattice, she heard the clatter of hoofs and, looking down, saw, far below, the two chariots of Joram and Ahaziah spin through the gate, swerve at abrupt right angles across the esplanade, and rattle toward the ramp along the road of paving stones which hugged both the city and the palace wall.

Startled by the dizzying height, she clutched at the sill, then closed one of the half windows and fastened it securely. Since her final return to Jezreel nearly ten years ago, distaste for these lattices in her apartment had become almost an obsession. Her son Ahaziah's accident, no doubt—or was it the memory of that little image of wax, falling—falling—? She shivered, waiting until the room had stopped spinning before she looked again.

The whole landscape seemed to be holding its breath, waiting for the coming together of the three chariots, the two going down from Jezreel, the one—alone now, having outstripped all the others—coming up from Beth-shan. And beside the splendid motion of the one, the two seemed cumbersome and earth-bound, their means of impetus but wooden replicas of its wings of fire.

She could see it clearly now: the two jet-black horses (Were they issues of Midnight or Stormcloud, and did one of them have a white star on his forehead?), the gilded wheels forming fiery disks in the sunlight, the straight figure in tall helmet and crimson cloak, hands firm on the reins, head thrown back and eyes lifted (They must be lifted!) to the battlements of Jezreel. In response her own muscles tensed, her pulses quickened. Unconsciously she flung back her head, as if lifting her face to a driving wind.

I shall drive them. And when I do, when I'm standing in the chariot with the reins in my hands, there'll be nothing on earth can stop me. I'll be like—

"I know," she had said "You'll be like the lord Melkart—" *No. If I'm going to be like any god, I'll be like Yahweh.* Well, he was fulfilling his promise. For whatever reason he was riding now to Jezreel, his coming could mean only defeat for Melkart, for herself. Defeat? What else had been her lot since the day she had stood down there in the vineyard of Naboth...

The vineyard of Naboth. Incredible that, of all the thousands of spots on the road, this tiny strip bordered by a hedge-topped wall should be chosen by destiny as the meeting place of the three chariots! Fascinated, scarcely breathing, she watched the steady narrowing of the space between them...felt an inexplicable relief when Joram's chariot swept by the vineyard gate, past the boundaries...then saw the uprearing of the two blacks, the swerving of Joram's two grays, followed by a sudden arresting of all motion.

So quiet was it then that she could have sworn she heard Joram's familiar voice, not languidly drawling for once, but sharply crisp and staccato.

"Is it peace, Jehu?"

Peace! Of course it was not peace. She knew it even though she could hear nothing of Jehu's answer, knew it before she saw Joram's powerful grays rear, his chariot wheel about and dash back in swift flight along the stony road which led past Naboth's vineyard...swift, but not nearly as swift as a bow lifted and drawn with a practiced warrior's speed and strength...straight, but not nearly as straight as an arrow flying unerringly to its goal.

"Treachery, O Ahaziah! Treachery!"

She saw Joram lift his arms in a wild groping, his terrified horses and reeling chariot barely miss the stones of Naboth's wall as they plunged back up the road toward Jezreel. But Ahaziah had not waited for the warning. By the time Jehu's chariot had reached the fallen figure, the king of Judah was already fleeing at a headlong pace, not by the left-hand road leading to the ramp, but to the right, toward the main thoroughfare which crossed the great plain southward toward Jerusalem.

Jezebel's fingers clutched the wooden sill so hard that her knuckles turned white, yet she felt nothing. She saw men running below, knew from their distorted faces and upraised arms that they were shouting, but she was conscious of no sound. And yet, seeing, she both heard and felt with a poignancy transcending the senses...heard Jehu's sharp command to his captain, Bidkar, when the latter's chariot overtook his own beside the fallen king: *Take him up, and cast him on the plot of ground belonging to Naboth the Jezreelite. For did not the Man of Yahweh promise in this very place that the house of Ahab would be swept away? Then follow Ahaziah!*...

He felt the tautness of leather beneath the fleeing king's constricted fingers, the coldness of the sweat pouring from his limbs as he heard the thundering hoofs behind him, waited for the shrill whine of an arrow. . .

So vivid were the sounds, the sensations, that they seemed more real than the voice in her ear, the touch on her shoulder.

"Quick! Come with me! I know a secret passage leading from the palace under the city wall. I can take you to safety."

Jezebel turned slowly. She had difficulty focusing her eyes. "You—"

"Rachel, the daughter of Naboth. Don't you remember?"

"Rachel." Strange how she could repeat the name, look into the tranquil, still unlined face, and feel no jealousy! "The woman he loved."

"He loved you too. That's why I want to save you. Come, there's not a moment to lose."

Jezebel's lips twisted. "Save me? Have you forgotten it was I who had your father and your brothers killed—and your son?"

"Not my son," returned the other quietly. "Jeshua still lives."

"Then it's he you had better think of saving," retorted Jezebel harshly. "If I know Jehu, the sons of Ahab are as safe this moment as flies in a spider's web."

The woman's eyes widened, turned gravely pitying. "Did you think that? I'm sorry, for it must have caused you pain. Jeshua is Obadiah's son, not Ahab's. The king loved him because he was born on the night his own son died."

Strangely, Jezebel was more angered than comforted by the knowledge. She wanted to hide her face, but less from shame than from knowledge that beneath its garish crimson it was old and wrinkled as a crumpled rag of silk, while this woman's was still smooth and freshly glowing. Instead she lifted her head high.

"I—don't need pity—or forgiveness."

"Then let me give you life and safety."

Jezebel trembled. Life? That sweet-bitter cup already drained to the dregs? Safety? Purchased by skulking and crawling through the dark? No! Melkart forbid! Better one last swift motion, with the wind in your face!

"Come! For the sake of him you loved, please come—and quickly!"

For Ahab's sake! Yes, after all these years there was still one thing she could do for him—keep from endangering the lives of these two he had loved. Life was kind, after all. She smiled suddenly and reached for the woman's hands.

"No. For the sake of him we *both* loved—no. You go. Flee from this palace as if it were a lepers' lair, and go to your son. And—may peace go with you!"

5

I shall drive them. Someday I shall drive them straight up to the king's palace...and when I do...there'll be no power on earth can stop me!

She watched him come, up the stony road from Naboth's vineyard, paying no heed to anything human or animal which lay in his way...even when a child screamed, neither delaying his progress by so much as an involuntary tightening of the reins nor bothering to look back. Why should he? What was one more tiny scrap of human flesh among the seventy or more small offshoots of Ahab doomed to fall by his hand? She should understand well enough what he was feeling, she—*a good daughter of Melkart!*

And suddenly she knew. This was no son of Yahweh, this man riding triumphant to lay the foundation stones of his kingdom in Yahweh's name. This was one like herself, a worshiper of Melkart and all his kind. She had known only one true son of Yahweh, a little man of not much strength or stature, whose lips were now sealed as tightly as the small dark chamber which had become his tomb. And this man, Jehu, had no kinship with Micaiah. He was the storm and the fire and the earthquake, as she herself had been, caring not what human life lay bruised or destroyed in their wake.

Her tensed lips curled into a slow smile. *So she had won, after all.* She could leave it to men like Jehu to complete the task she had begun. Call him by whatever name they would, Melkart, god of power through violence, would be supreme in Israel and—yes, in all other nations. Unless...

There will be other voices, Micaiah had said calmly. *If the things I have said are true, there will be those to say them.*

"Then Jehu will destroy them," she cried out silently in answer, this time, strangely enough, in despair rather than in triumph. "He will destroy them, do you hear, you little Man of Yahweh, just as I destroyed you!"

As he came thundering up the ramp and along the road of paved stones beneath the palace windows, she flung wide the other half of the lattice and, leaning out, called to him sharply. Reining his horses so swiftly that they reared up and nearly overturned the chariot, he came to a jolting stop and stood looking up at her.

"How are you, Jehu?" she taunted. *"You Zimri, murderer of your master!"*

It was the worst insult she could have paid him, and, far though he was below her, she could see the infuriated flushing of his dark features.

"You slaves up there!" he cried loudly. "Who among you is on my side?"

There was the rasping creak of another opening lattice, followed by a chorus of voices which Jezebel recognized as belonging to some of her own eunuchs.

"We are, master!" "Your will is ours!" "Command us, and we will obey!"

"Then throw her down!" cried Jehu harshly.

Jezebel caught her breath. The room reeled, then turned slowly black. No, no! Anything that men or gods could possibly devise but—*that!* To fall like a little wax image...like a small figure swaying on a parapet...to scream... Melkart have mercy—no, not Melkart, Yahweh! It was Yahweh who showed mercy, who cared what happened to people!

The darkness cleared, and the room steadied. She saw the green valley dropping, the sky clear and blue and fathomless above the high hill which sprang from the deep cleft to meet it, and knew them to be good. They too had known storm and fire and earthquake, had seen their violence pass. And afterward—afterward...

"My lady."

So transformed was his face by hate and bitter triumph that at first she did not recognize it. "Eshmun!" she gasped.

But it was the sight of his hands, outstretched and slightly curved, which told her more even than his distorted features could convey. She stared at him in sudden horrified comprehension. "So— it was you—at the foot of the stairs—you who locked the door in the little chamber! You—you've always hated me!"

The black coals blazed at last. "Yes, *mistress of men's destinies.* You thought you could take a man and treat him like a beast, and have him grovel on the soft carpets at your feet. But you couldn't. When you thought I was eating from your hand, licking your fingers, I was really spitting on them. When you thought I was loving, I was hating. And I could have killed you—a hundred times, had I wished. You left me the strength of a man, if not my manhood, and I saw to it that even your sweet oils and soft women's garments didn't take that away. But I was waiting for this moment. Always I have known it would come—the perfect consummation of these years of hatred. To see you devoured by the very beasts you've tried to make of men!"

She began to laugh harshly, then remembered that laughter was close to both hysteria and tears, and, the gods help her, she would neither scream nor weep! But when he moved toward her, great muscles flexing, a sudden panic seized her.

"No—not yet, Eshmun! I—I don't blame you for hating, and I don't ask you to forgive, but—if you ever loved me, give me just one minute more—while I try to remember... For Melkart's sake, wait!"

He waited, for, after all, he had loved her once. She closed her eyes.

"You—call it a privilege to die?" she had mocked Micaiah.

Why not? Does it matter what happens to me...as long as the truth still lives?

When she opened her eyes again her features were composed. She lifted her hands to see if her diadem of pearls and emeralds was in place, then moved toward the window with the calm dignity of a proud queen about to step down from her throne.

"It's all right, Eshmun. I'm ready now. I remember all his words I need."

You are the wind and the earthquake and the fire...

She did not scream. Indeed, when the moment came, there was a certain exultation in its fulfillment. Far better this than a dark inner room of a shrine filled with emptiness and death! A fitting, final irony for one whose life had been but a rushing of wind, a cleaving of earth, a blaze of fire!

For after the wind and the earthquake and the fire have passed, there shall be heard the still small voice of the Eternal.

ABOUT THE AUTHOR

Dorothy Clarke Wilson (1904-2003) was an amazingly prolific American author and playwright, who published more than 25 books and over 70 plays, as well as writing numerous essays, poems, and other literary works. Dorothy was a biblical scholar and social activist specializing primarily in biographies and religious subjects with themes running to faith, altruism, and fortitude.

Her historical fiction focused on the lives of Jesus, Moses, and other biblical figures. *Prince of Egypt*, perhaps her best-known novel depicted the early life of Moses, was published in 1952, and won a prize for the best religious novel of the year. More than 500,000 copies were sold and it became the primary source for Cecil B. DeMille's famous 1956 film, *The Ten Commandments*, starring Charlton Heston and Yul Brynner.

Ms. Wilson's biographies were mostly about women who overcame the prejudices of their time to make a difference in the world. Martha Washington, Dolley Madison, and Alice and Edith Roosevelt, as well as groundbreaking doctors and reformers such as Elizabeth Blackwell, Mary Verghese, Clara Swain, and Dorothea Dix were all topics.

Other works tackled ordinary people living under extraordinary circumstances such as Hilary Pole, a British woman with a rare, degenerative disorder. She also put pen to paper about life in rural Maine. Books on India and its people included a travelogue and a novel whose subjects were missionaries and doctors treating the "untouchables."

Dorothy Wright Clarke was born in Gardiner, Maine in 1904, the daughter of a Baptist minister and his wife. She excelled throughout school, was valedictorian of her high school graduating class and began attending Bates College at seventeen. In her senior year at Bates, Dorothy won an essay contest for "Arbitration Instead of War." This experience began her lifelong interest in activism for peace and social justice.

After graduating Phi Beta Kappa in 1925, Dorothy married a college classmate, Elwin Leander Wilson, who went on to attend Princeton Theological Seminary and the School of Theology at Boston University. After Elwin completed his graduate studies, he and Dorothy returned to Westbrook, Maine where he became a minister and she began her long and distinguished literary career.

She traveled extensively (Palestine, India, Egypt, Mexico, and England) always conducting thorough research in order to capture the authenticity of her subjects and settings. Over her lifetime, Dorothy Clarke Wilson presented over one thousand illustrated lectures, and received numerous honors—including Doctor of Letters from Bates College (1948) and the University of Maine (1984). She was the recipient of the Maryann Hartman Award from the University of Maine in 1988 and the Deborah Morton Award from Westbrook College in Portland in 1989. Other honors include the New England United Methodist Award for Excellence in Social Justice Ministry (1975); the Woman of Distinction Award of Alpha Delta Kappa (1971); the Award for Distinguished Achievement from the University of Maine at Augusta (1977); and the Achievement Award from the American Association of University Women, Maine Division (1988).

Today, deserving students attending Orono High School and the University of Maine are presented with the Dorothy Clarke Wilson Peace Award. The Maine Christian Association Board named one of its buildings, The Wilson Center, honoring her support of their organization.

Dorothy Clarke Wilson's papers (including many unpublished works) can be found in the Edmund S. Muskie Archives and in the Special Collections Library at Bates College. Ms. Wilson's work has been translated into dozens of languages and condensed into guides and digests for readers worldwide. Collectively, she is the author of 213 works in 473 publications in 17 languages with 16,154 library holdings.

Elwin, her husband, died in 1992; and her only son, Harold, died in 1977. Dorothy's own death occurred in 2003 in Orono, Maine after a brief illness.

www.ingramcontent.com/pod-product-compliance
Lightning Source LLC
Chambersburg PA
CBHW071156250626
47159CB00001B/120